A SURGEON FOR THE SINGLE MUM

CHARLOTTE HAWKES

FROM DOCTOR TO DADDY

BECKY WICKS

MILLS & BOON

First Published in Great Britain 2019
by Mills & Boon, an imprint of HarperCollins*Publishers*
1 London Bridge Street, London, SE1 9GF

A Surgeon for the Single Mum © 2019 by Charlotte Hawkes

From Doctor to Daddy © 2019 by Becky Wicks

ISBN: 978-0-263-26970-3

MIX
Paper from
responsible sources
FSC® C007454

This book is produced from independently certified FSC™ paper
to ensure responsible forest management.
For more information visit www.harpercollins.co.uk/green.

Printed and bound in Spain
by CPI, Barcelona

A SURGEON FOR THE SINGLE MUM

CHARLOTTE HAWKES

MILLS & BOON

To Monty & Bart.

How I enjoyed seeing my two little men
walk all the way to the stone bridge on our section of
the Canal du Midi for the very first time. xxx

CHAPTER ONE

'REALLY? *THIS* IS what you dragged me down here for?' Talank Basu pressed his shoulder against the doorjamb of the hospital's resus department and rolled his eyes at his kid sister. 'I expected some medical emergency, not a schoolyard blind date request.'

'Oh, relax,' Hetti snorted, in a way that no one else talking to him would ever have dared. 'I'm not asking you to marry the woman—just take her to the hospital ball as your plus one.'

'No.'

'Please, Tak? Effie's new to the air ambulance job, and new to the area, and what's more she's really nice. But she has already fended off advances by at least four single doctors and two nurses that I know about, so going alone to the gala would be like painting a bullseye on her back. She could use a bit of support.'

He grinned, unable to resist his habitual teasing of her. 'Ah, *now* I understand. She's another one of your waifs and strays, is she, Hetti?'

'Stop it.' She swatted him good-naturedly. 'You're as bad as Mama. You know *she* wouldn't know compassion if it walked and swamped her in a massive cuddle.'

'Don't disrespect her, Hetti.' Tak frowned automatically.

But instead of backing down, his sister held her ground, narrowing her gaze. 'Why does she always get a free pass with you, Tak? *Still?* We're not kids any more, so you don't have to protect us from who she really is. You sacrificed your entire childhood practically raising Sasha and Rafi and me, being Mama and Papa all rolled into one just to shield us from our parents' inadequacies. Papa was off having his never-ending affairs, and Mama… Well, you know. And that was *before* Baby Saaj.'

Tak didn't bother answering. It wasn't worth the argument. Their parents weren't worth the argument.

Over Hetti's shoulder he could see people milling about, waiting for the next trauma victim to come in. A rare calm before the proverbial storm. The helicopter was only a few minutes out now, and Hetti had got her team together and all the equipment she thought they might need. Now it was just a matter of waiting, and soon the place would be a flurry of activity again.

'Anyway…' Hetti shook her head as though dislodging the argument. 'Effie isn't one of my *"waifs and strays"*, as you so indelicately put it. She was an A&E doctor with me back when I was at Allport Infirmary last year. Turns out Effie has landed herself a plum role on the air ambulance across this way, too.'

'Air ambulance? She must be particularly good.'

'Oh, she is.' Hetti nodded. 'Effie was always exceptional. Noticed things other doctors missed…knew stuff even senior consultants might not know. It was no wonder the air ambulance snapped her up. Even *you* might be impressed.'

'If you're that taken with her then why don't you make her *your* plus one?'

For a moment it looked as though Hetti might want to say more, but then she sucked in a deep breath and grinned back at him in that disarming way of hers that he recognised from when she was a toddler.

'Well, I would, but I'm on call that night,' she shot back instantly, making Tak smile. 'And, no, before you say anything, I *don't* want you to get that changed for me, because then it will mean some other poor sucker who hasn't got a medical god for a brother will end up missing out on the ball instead.'

'Your choice.' Tak shrugged. 'But I told you—I'm going to the ball stag. Although right now I'm going home.'

He should have gone ten minutes ago—well, technically he should have gone three hours ago. However, he'd wanted to stay with his last patient a little longer, and his neurology emergency department had been busier than usual for the time of night.

And now he was here. Because Hetti had asked him to be and because, doctor in her own right or not, she was always going to be his baby sister.

If he'd known Hetti's call wasn't about a patient but about dating he wouldn't have bothered. Especially when she was giving him grief. Like right now.

'Wow, the rumour mill will *love* that. Eligible bachelor Tak Basu attends one of the highest profile events of the year alone? Congratulations. I don't think you could have come up with a better way to stir up the already feverish interest in your love-life, whilst simultaneously encouraging Mama to push you towards an arranged marriage of her preference.'

'It's precisely *because* of those reasons that I'm going alone,' Tak growled—not that it had much effect on his unperturbed sibling. 'I've had enough of being potentially married off to every woman I speak to, let alone date.'

'Only because you'd rather be married to your career. The King of Awake Craniotomies—determined to be better than all the rest of us who want such humble things as relationships, and love, and someone to share their life with.'

'You're enjoying this, aren't you? I never said I was better than anyone,' Tak pulled a face.

'No, but I know you think it. Still, as someone who is *actually* allowed to love you and want the best for you, I have to warn you that if you attend the gala alone then, despite your intentions, it will look like an advertisement for the fact that you're shockingly single right now.'

'Well, it isn't.'

'*I* know that. But every woman within a hundred-mile radius who fancies her chances is going to be beating down your door. And that's a conservative estimate. Pretty stupid for an intelligent guy.'

He laughed despite himself. 'So, let me get this straight. *Now* you're saying you want me to take some new trauma doctor to the ball for *my* benefit?'

Hetti wrinkled her nose. 'I'm saying you and Effie could be the perfect foil for each other. Neither of you wants a relationship, but you both need someone to keep would-be suitors at bay. And to buy you some time with Mama and the various so-called aunts who have a whole host of potential brides for you all lined up.'

'Yes, this Effie woman might *say* she doesn't want a relationship, but she will. They always do.'

'Geez, big-headed, much? Watch you don't get stuck in the doorway on your way out, won't you?'

Hetti thumped him hard in the arm. Or at least she tried to.

She shook her hand and grimaced. 'My God, they're right. You really *do* have the body of a PT instructor rather than a doctor. No wonder you're so ridiculously arrogant.'

'Not arrogance,' Tak hunched his shoulders. 'At least not intentionally. It's just fact. No matter how clear I try to be at the start that I'm not in it for a relationship which is going to lead to marriage down the line.'

'Well, not this time. I've met her, and I've seen what she's like with every guy who has tried to flirt with, bar none. She totally shoots them down. Nicely but firmly, no hesitation. Trust me—she is definitely not going to change her mind about wanting a relationship any time in the next lifetime or so.'

'I don't have to trust you.' Eyeing the clock, Tak began to make his move. 'I'm not doing it. Even for you, Little Hemavati.'

She swatted him, laughing. 'Only Mama calls me Hemavati. Just like she calls you Talank. It's her twisted way of trying to show she's in control. But at least wait and see Effie. You never know. You might actually like her. She's focussed and driven—just like you. And she's also pretty stunning.'

'I'm going now.'

Tak slung his bag onto his back and prepared to head out into the corridor just as the double doors on the other side of Resus banged open and the air ambulance crew burst through with their patient. The new doctor with them had to be this Effie person.

Suddenly he realised he'd seen her once before. A couple of months ago when she'd brought in a forty-eight-year-old head injury patient—Douglas Jacobs, who had taken a tumble down a rocky hillside.

'This is Danny, a male cyclist in his twenties,' the young woman announced clearly, expediently, her eyes moving quickly across the resus team, taking in the faces and commanding them with ease. 'About one hour ago he was travelling at approximately twenty-five miles per hour when a car pulled out of a side road in front of him. Danny tried to swerve but hit the car and was seen to be thrown about three metres into the air before striking the ground with some force.'

Tak lowered his bag again, his attention focussed on the new doctor. He couldn't have said what made him stay. Or perhaps he just didn't want to acknowledge it.

Hetti had been right—although neither of them had realised it. Dr Effie Robinson had indeed impressed him. Along with Douglas Jacobs their patient.

'He was wearing a crash helmet but it shattered on impact. Witnesses say he was unconscious for possibly ten seconds. On arrival GCS was nine.'

There was nothing unusual in any of this. Not the patient, not the injuries, not the doctor. So why was he so transfixed? Watching her command the team in her bright orange flight suit, with her glossy hair—a rich, deep red colour—scraped back so severely and twisted so tightly into a bun that it made his eyes water just looking at it?

Last time he'd seen her but hadn't paid attention. He'd been too focussed on his patient. But this time it wasn't *his* patient. And his attention was all on her.

Why? Because she had red hair and blue eyes? Unusual, but hardly unique. So…what?

There was nothing to soften her appearance—not even a hint of make-up. Yet there was no doubt that she was beautiful. And something else—something he couldn't pinpoint, something innate that spilled out from those icy blue eyes. Despite himself, Tak found he was staring, caught up by her and helpless to do anything other than stop and listen.

She barely needed to pause and check her notes. Words flowed smoothly whilst her control of the situation was flawless. He had seen plenty of efficient, skilled air ambulance doctors but she stood out—just as she had a few weeks ago.

There was no reason he should be edging closer, as though he was a latecomer to the team. Her gaze took in the team again, and then she lifted her eyes and connected with his.

Everything stopped. Any thoughts in his head evaporated, leaving…nothing. It was like nothing that he'd ever experienced before.

So this was Effie.

He stared, unable to look away, and then, incredibly, she blinked once and moved on to the rest of the team. Her voice as steady, and as clear, as even as before. Whilst *he* felt, by contrast, as though his chest had just been belted by the downdraft from a set of helicopter rotor blades. It was an unfamiliar experience.

'He has been intubated and has a right thoracotomy with a flailed segment. Top-to-toe injuries: closed head injury, a six-centimetre right temporal laceration, right clavicular fracture, suspected dislocated shoulder, suspected multiple rib fractures, right thoracotomy and a pelvic splint was applied. He's had morphine and midazolam for sedation and was stable during transfer. Immediate needs are further assessment and imaging to check for internal organ damage.'

She wrapped things up neatly, her gaze steady.

'Okay, we're going to need a whole-body CT, but he isn't stable enough yet to take for imaging.' Hetti stepped in smoothly. 'Allison, what's his BP and heart-rate?'

Effie stepped back to allow the team to take over, nonetheless still on hand to answer any further questions. It was testament to both teams that the handover was seamless, and Effie was soon completing her final paperwork.

Whilst he still stood there. Still watching her. His brain still struggling to get back into gear.

The only thoughts rattling around his head now were echoes of Hetti's words to him. Her ludicrous suggestion which wouldn't have been out of place in a school playground.

And yet here he was, unable to get it out of his head. As though, fittingly, he was nothing but a schoolboy. Yet he'd never been a schoolboy—at least not in that sense of the term.

Even as a teenager he'd been the man of the house. Hetti was right—he *had* practically raised Hetti and Rafi and Sasha. Sometimes alongside their mother—or Mama as Hetti called her—but oftentimes in lieu of her. Especially after Baby Saaj had been born. Ill from the start, his two years on this earth had been a fight every second of every day.

For years Tak had shielded his younger siblings from his father's absences as much as possible. Listening to their mother offer up one convincing excuse after another, praising his father's work as a doctor so they wouldn't realise what a derelict father and cruel husband he was.

The kind of man Tak never wanted to be like.

Hetti might think it was because he was more interested in his career than in having a family, but she'd be wrong. At least she would only be partly right. Forging a career as the kind of neurosurgeon capable of performing a vast array of brain surgeries on awake patients automatically made him the worst kind of unreliable boyfriend. And he was happy with that.

Even so, his career wasn't the whole of it. The whole of it was that he feared being the kind of man whose selfish, self-centred actions hurt any wife, any child, the way his father had hurt them. Time and again. And the truth was that he *would* be that kind of man. However much he abhorred the thought, it was unavoidable. Inexorable. It was in his blood.

Just as it was in Rafi's blood.

Much as he loved his younger brother, Tak wasn't blind to the fact that Rafi was their father all over again. And Tak hated that. Yet here he was. Staring at this doctor as though he'd never seen anyone, any*thing* quite like her before.

It made no sense.

There was something about her which snagged his attention and made him think she possessed a unique quality, even if he couldn't put his finger on what that was. He told himself that he certainly wasn't following the long, impossibly elegant line of her neck, or wondering what that glorious hair might look like free of its rigid net cage, or imagining what lay beneath that less than flattering orange suit.

Still he didn't move.

Once Effie was done with her notes she'd be back to the heli and to her base, ready for the next shout. Which was a good thing. A great thing. It meant he could get past this crazy moment and back to real life.

A life that didn't include his baby sister interfering in his life and picking out potential dates for him, he reminded himself firmly. Least of all dates with a woman like Effie.

Except hadn't Hetti told him that it wouldn't *be* a date? Not in any real sense of the word, anyway. What had she called them...*the perfect foil for each other*? Each of them using the other to keep the world off their back?

It should sound ludicrous. It *did* sound ludicrous. But in between women taking his single status as evidence that of *course* he must be yearning for the perfect wife, and his mother becoming relentless in her desire to see all of her children settled down, even against their will, ludicrous might just work.

It wasn't as though he could simply turn around and tell Mama to stay out of his personal life, much as he might want to. She would always be too fragile, too weak to handle it—their father had made sure of that. And she might not have been the perfect mother, but at least she'd always been *there*.

Hetti was right. He needed a foil. A distraction. *Effie.*

Tak turned back to eye the new air ambulance doctor again just as she was finishing up her notes.

As if it was meant to be. Effie. *Dr Effie Robinson.* He remembered her name now, from Douglas Jacobs's notes. He narrowed his eyes for a moment.

'Dr Robinson, I wonder if we could have a word? In private.'

CHAPTER TWO

'LET ME GET this straight—you're asking me out on a date?'

Effie was infinitely proud of the way she'd kept any shake out of her quiet voice. The same could not be said for her stentorian heart.

'No. I'm asking you out on a *fake* date.'

'I don't know whether to be amused or insulted.' Her eyebrows felt as if they were somewhere up in the vicinity of her hairline. 'Is this some kind of practical joke? Hazing the new member of staff? Because I can tell you right now—'

He made no attempt to conceal his irritation as he cut her off. 'It isn't. I don't have time for stupid pranks, and I hardly think this would be a particularly funny one even if I did. I need a date for the ball and you fit the bill.'

'There are probably a hundred women in this hospital alone who would jump at your *oh-so-romantic* offer.' Effie felt she'd injected just the right amount of sarcasm into her tone. 'But I am not one of them.'

She wasn't some green doctor, about to go giddy because the gorgeous Tak Basu was talking to her. She'd refused to do that six weeks ago, when one of her first ever air ambulance cases had thrown her a hillside rescue and a man, Douglas Jacobs, suffering from expressive aphasia.

Tak had been the neurological consultant on call. He'd threatened to steal her breath away on sight. But she'd been determined not to let him.

Tall, with archetypal brooding dark looks, he wasn't exactly a playboy, but rumour had it that he had dated some high-profile stunning women in his time.

Well, good for him. But good-looking, arrogant males held little interest for her. Hadn't she been there, done that, and ended up at just turned eighteen years old, heading to Oxford University with a newborn infant in tow?

For the past thirteen years Nell had been her life. She hadn't wanted anything—even her longed-for medical career—as much as she'd wanted to take care of her daughter. But something about this man sent her body's warning system into motion, into an internal flurry, like ants who had just had dirt knocked into their nest.

'I don't think you are remotely *one of them*. Which is precisely why I'm asking you. No jokes, no hazing—just a mutually beneficial arrangement.'

She opened her mouth to reply but no words came.

A fake date, indeed. It should sound insane. Nonsensical. Yet his rich, even tone and neutral expression made it sound utterly plausible. Normal, even. As if a fake date was a completely run-of-the-mill daily event.

Perhaps it was in his world.

Tak Basu—one of the hospital's brightest stars. Talk about an eligible bachelor. His reputation for medical excellence preceded him only slightly more than his brooding good looks and an immorally stunning Adonis physique that would make even the most pious woman ache to sin.

Yet now she realised that not even the most fevered description could accurately convey just how devastating he was in the flesh, or just how paralysing his sheer magnetism truly was.

Every hair on her body felt as though it was standing to attention. Ready to do his bidding—eager, even. It was like nothing she'd ever experienced in the whole of her life.

Then there were the smaller things. Like his big hands, strong forearms, the way he stood as though he owned the world. Or the shock of thick black hair, longer on top than she might have expected, which only added to his already six foot three height. It looked soft and inviting, and it took Effie a moment to realise that her fingers were actually aching with the urge to test it out.

And so she perched there on her stool, pretending she was still working so that she didn't have to turn to him and withstand the full weight of her inconvenient attraction. The fact that he didn't seem to date much only enhanced his appeal—and his mystique.

Finally—mercifully—she found her tongue again. 'What on earth makes you think I want a fake date?' She flushed. 'Or indeed *any* kind of date.'

She studiously ignored the little voice in her head taunting her for engaging with him. Telling her that had it been anyone else she would already have declined politely before walking away.

'Isn't that rather the point?' His mouth curved slightly in what could only be described as a sinful smile. 'If it's a fake date, then it *isn't* really any kind of date.'

'Semantics.' She pursed her lips. 'Or riddles. In any case, I've never really cared for either. Just as I really don't need a date—fake or otherwise.'

Still she didn't make herself walk away. Why *was* that?

'I don't understand how I…how a *fake date*…concerns me.'

And she wanted to understand. Perhaps a little bit too much. Even if he *was* eyeing her as though to him she rated as about as intelligent as the average sponge in the animal kingdom. She could take offense, but that really wasn't her style. Who had time in a job like her?

'Hetti suggested otherwise.'

'Hetti?'

'Yes, Hetti. The other Dr Basu.' He jerked his head towards where his sister and her team were focussed on the cyclist. 'Hemavati.'

Something clicked. How had she missed it before? Probably something to do with the stress of moving house, moving town, moving halfway across the country. And at every step fighting with her thirteen-going-on-thirty-year-old daughter, who hadn't wanted to leave everything she knew.

'*Hetti?* Yes, I know who Hetti is. I just don't understand why she would have mentioned me to you.'

She and Hetti had worked together for a couple of years back at Allport Infirmary's A&E. They'd even been friends. Well, as close to being friends as two rather guarded individuals could be. Probably that was one of their shared traits, which had drawn them to each other.

'She mentioned that you were caught on the horns of a dilemma—not wanting a date for the charity gala on one side and risking being hit on all night if you're without a date on the other. Apparently you've swiftly shut down any man who has asked you.'

Nothing about Nell, then. That was good. The last thing she wanted was people gossiping about her having been a teenage mum, or privately questioning whether she was *really* up to the job of being an air ambulance doctor. It was such a demanding, limited environment, and lives literally depended on her and her two paramedics.

No one else. Just the three of them. Not like in the A&E, where she'd been a doctor up until now, where she could call on a colleague for a consult if she needed to.

So she was still new to the air ambulance team—still in her probationary period. Her employers might have liked her CV and her references, and the way she'd come across in her many interviews, but they didn't know the first thing about her. Mainly because she kept her private life just that. Utterly private.

If they'd known the truth about her would they still have

hired her? Would she have been good enough for them? Or even *enough*?

A jolt of something that felt altogether too much like insecurity bolted through Effie before she could stop it. Before she could shove it back into the distant shadows of her brain where it belonged.

The only person who had never made her feel she had something to prove was Eleanor. The one woman who had seen through Effie's tough, angry exterior to the frightened, lonely kid beneath. The woman who had loved her so much that she'd been willing to fight Effie's sorry excuse for a mum and to adopt her. The woman who had seen Effie's potential and encouraged her to really *do* something with her life—starting by going to university. And not just any university, either.

But Eleanor had been gone from her life for so many years now that it was getting harder and harder for Effie to remember how it had felt to have someone to lean on.

It would hardly have been surprising if her bosses and colleagues had panicked about hiring a single mum with a young daughter. If Nell was ill she couldn't just call in sick herself, like other parents. There was no one to cover her. Her team depended on her being there every single time she was supposed to be. On never being distracted.

Including right now.

Effie jutted out her chin and met his gaze. 'And so you stepped up to save me from myself? How chivalrous.'

Her tone was a little tighter, a little sharper than she might have preferred, but that was better than giving in to this absurd heat trapped low in her belly. The kind which threatened to melt a girl from the inside out.

Surely she was past all that nonsense? Hadn't having a baby at eighteen taught her that much, at least?

'You could call it chivalrous. Or you could call it selfish. I'd prefer the term *mutually beneficial*.'

'Really?' Even as she asked, she knew it was a bad sign that it made a difference to her. Made her a little bit too eager for an excuse to break her usual no dating code. 'So what do I gain from it?'

'Hetti mentioned you were too career-focussed to have time to date, and that your move here has invited attention. Fresh blood and all that. We both know that attending this function alone would be tantamount to inviting people to hit on you all night. Going with me should make anyone else leave you alone.'

She could point out that it sounded arrogant for him to say that other men would naturally back away if Tak was her date. The problem was she could imagine that was exactly what would happen.

'Fine. So what about you? Is this your way of ensuring no-strings sex for the night? Because I have to say it's a pretty pathetic way of—'

'No sex,' he cut in definitively.

'Sorry?'

'If I want sex I can get sex. The point is that I don't.'

'A single man in his thirties who doesn't want sex?' Incredibly she found herself raising an eyebrow at him as though she was actually...*flirting*?

'I don't want sex with *you*,' he corrected.

How was it possible to feel suddenly deflated when she didn't want complications herself?

'Oh. Right.' She sounded so stiff, so wooden. 'Well, good. Glad that's cleared up.'

He raked his hand through his hair and she found the unexpectedly boyish gesture all the more disarming.

'I didn't mean it to sound that way.' Clearly this was as close as she was going to get to an apology. 'My point is that I want a date as a buffer. I don't want complications from it. My extended family have it in their collective heads that if I'm not going to find a wife for myself then they need to find one for me. A date will buy me some time.'

There was no reason for her chest to constrict the way it did at that moment. No reason at all.

'Couldn't you just tell them *no*?'

'I could…' He shrugged, as though it didn't matter to him one way or another. 'I have. Many times. But that doesn't stop them from trying and pushing. I was just about to offend every single one of them by making it unequivocally clear that I'm not interested. However, it's been pointed out to me that there is another way to handle it. A softer way.'

'By Hetti, by chance?'

'Indeed.' Tak flashed another of those wicked smiles which seemed to liquefy her insides within seconds. 'She also pointed out that if I do that they'll turn their focus on her. And no doubt redouble their efforts in revenge.'

Curious.

Hetti had alluded to the fact that her big brother was always looking out for her but, given Tak's formidable reputation, Effie hadn't really bought it.

'And so you're trying to project a softer Tak Basu? Now, *there's* a curious notion.'

The words were out before she could swallow them. Revealing far more than she might have wanted him to know. Effie could have kicked herself.

'Is it, indeed?'

His eyebrows lifted, his incorrigible expression stealing her breath from her lungs. God, he was magnificent. It should be illegal.

She forced herself to straighten her spine, make her tone just that bit choppier. 'Although conning your extended family is one thing, but conning your mother rather than simply telling her the truth—'

'You don't know what you're talking about.' His low,

deep voice, every word uttered with a razor-sharp edge, cut her instantly. 'Consequently, I suggest you don't even try.'

Despite the words he'd used, it would clearly be a mistake to actually believe it had been merely a suggestion.

Effie swallowed. Hard.

Silence enveloped them, and she found herself unable to move. Awkward in her own skin.

His expression softened. 'I shouldn't have spoken to you that way,' he said, and abruptly Effie realised this was Tak apologising to her. 'I'm just…a little protective of my family.'

It was such a familiar pain that it shouldn't hurt her as much as it did. Her throat felt too tight, but somehow she managed to reply. 'That's…admirable.'

What would she have given, growing up, to have had a family who were protective of each other. Even one of her foster families. But instead…

She shuddered at the memories. An endless merry-go-round of girls' homes and foster families, all of whom had either looked at her as though she should be grateful to them for even knowing her name, or else had resented the fact that she wasn't an adorable baby they could cuddle. Or worse. But she didn't like to remember the nights she'd spent sleeping rough on park benches because it had been safer than any given foster home.

There had been a couple of nice families. She could remember both of them with such clarity. They had wanted to adopt her and she'd prayed that they would, even though she'd long since had any sense of faith knocked out of her. But on both occasions her biological mother had somehow—shockingly—managed to convince the authorities that she had gone clean, and they had been compelled to return Effie to her.

Of course it had never lasted.

'I suppose you might call it admirable…' Tak's voice

mercifully broke into her thoughts. 'Either way, it seems we both have our reasons for wanting a buffer.'

'I can handle myself.' She narrowed her eyes at him, irked to concede that he might actually have a point.

'I'm suggesting that you don't *have* to. That our attending the ball together could make it a smoother night all around.'

'Right...' she conceded slowly, without knowing why.

'So, do we have a deal?'

There were a hundred reasons why she should say no. Thirteen of them even had the same four letters. Nell. But suddenly all Effie could think of were all the reasons—as flimsy and as spurious as she knew them to be—why she might say yes.

'My car is in the garage right now, so it would save me having to drive myself...'

She couldn't believe she'd said it aloud. It didn't even sound believable. What on earth had made her think it was better to say that than admit her car was such a clapped-out old mess she didn't want people seeing her in it in case they asked too many questions?

It had been bad enough convincing her new colleagues that she kept it because it had sentimental value, rather than tell the truth about the fact that she'd been going to change it, but Nell's new school had offered a last-minute place on a ski trip they'd been planning for twelve months and, given the lateness, she'd needed to make full payment of a sum which had made her eyes water.

She knew what people's expectation of a doctor's salary was—and why they couldn't equate her career with her always-tight finances. Even those who know about her daughter.

However much the news made an issue of student debt, and the tens of thousands that medical students especially could incur, it was easy for outsiders to forget that such debt incurred heavy interest every year. Even many of her colleagues had had family to support them financially, at least to some degree.

But none of them had also been raising a daughter at the same time.

Effie still shuddered when she thought of how she'd had to beg and plead—and sometimes gloss a little over the truth—in order to secure every available student and bank loan out there. She could have chosen a different career, of course, but she'd had something to prove. Both to herself and in memory of the one woman who had ever believed in her.

Even when she'd qualified, every penny of her salary had been swallowed up, not just by basic living costs, but by the additional costs that a child had incurred. Food, children's clothes which never seemed to fit for more than a year, but especially the crippling childcare costs, Especially for a junior doctor working long shifts, night shifts, and even sometimes ninety-plus hour weeks.

True, nowadays her career was more established and she was a lot more financially stable, but even now she couldn't break the habit of putting her daughter first. Maybe it was because she needed to give Nell the opportunities she herself had never had, or perhaps it was guilt at having had to work so hard for all those years.

Either way, it was why her clever, beautiful, funny daughter was at the most prestigious private school in the area, to the tune of several tens of thousands a year—even without the additional ski trips, French exchanges, and Summer Activities program—whilst she herself kept her old car for just one year longer.

Not that she would ever confess to someone a single word of any of that to someone like Tak.

Still, his expression flickered slightly and Effie couldn't be sure what he was thinking. She had a feeling he was laughing at her and she gave herself a mental kick. And then she kicked herself again for even caring what he thought about her.

Good job she was immune to cocky, arrogant, too-handsome-for-their-own-good playboys.

Although the way her traitorous heart was reacting to him was galling. This never happened to her. *Never.* She had never gossiped with colleagues about the latest developments in an eligible guy's sex-life. Or lusted after men around the water cooler. Or gone out to clubs and picked up guys.

That didn't mean she hadn't lusted after the odd guy on TV, or in a magazine. Though never in person—not like this. At least not since Nell's father, as gargantuan a mistake as *he* had been. Not that she would ever give Nell up for a second. But he had been an idiot boy whom she'd lusted after but never loved. Had barely even known—not really. He'd had no hopes, no dreams. He'd relied on his good looks and he certainly hadn't wanted to *achieve* anything. He'd laughed at her dreams of going to university to study medicine. Told her to get real. That places like that didn't take kids like them.

They'd dated—if it could even be called that—for a handful of months. And even that had been because a lethal cocktail of grief and lust, had given her the desire to get one thing to make her forget the other, if only for one night.

Eleanor's shocking death had rocked her more than all those awful years in and out of foster homes, or care homes when her mother had been deemed 'too unfit' to care for her. The fact that something as ugly and banal as a drunk driver could have snuffed out such a warm, glorious light, in the blink of an eye, made it that much worse.

In a matter of hours Effie had gone from being on the brink of being adopted, and finally having a loving family in the form of Eleanor, to having absolutely no one. No one but him. And she'd let herself believe that he could ease her loneliness.

But when she told him she'd fallen pregnant he'd wanted nothing to do with her, and she'd never felt more abandoned. That had been the moment she'd vowed she would never again let anyone into her personal life, never let a guy know she was attracted to them.

Immune, she reminded herself now, crossly.

Tearing her eyes away from the approaching figure, Effie checked her watch. 'I have to get back to the heli.'

'No one's stopping you.' Tak twisted his mouth into something which was too amused to be a smile. 'You're the one who has prolonged things, preferring this verbal sparring to answering a simple question.'

It was as though he could read her thoughts. As though he knew that a part of her was aching to say *yes*.

Effie drew herself up as tall as she could. 'Is that right?' she managed primly. 'Then allow me to be clear. My answer, Dr Basu, is *no*. No, I do *not* want to accompany you to the hospital charity ball as your date. Fake or otherwise.'

So why was every fibre of her screaming at her that this was the wrong answer?

'I see.' His lips twitched. 'Thank you for letting me know.'

Before she could ruin the moment, Effie filed away her notes and marched out through the Resus doors. It took her a moment to realise that she wasn't alone.

Spinning around, she confronted him. 'Why are you following me?'

'Apologies if it's spoiling the dramatic effect of your exit.' Tak didn't look remotely apologetic. 'I'm heading home. My car is in the car park next to the helipad.'

He had to be kidding?

She hesitated, unsure what to do next. It was a two-hundred-metre stretch from here to there. If she marched

off ahead of him he might think she was employing one of
those flirtatious tactics of making him look at her backside. But the alternative was walking together in an awkward silence.

There was no reason for that to hold the slightest amount
of appeal, she berated herself silently. Perhaps it would be
easier if she pretended she'd forgotten something inside
the hospital and headed back inside for a moment? Yes,
that might be best.

Turning around, Effie took a step towards the hospital
doors just as one of her more dogged suitors—who had so
far asked her out three times and showed no signs of getting the message—walked out.

A smarmy smile slid over his features and she panicked.
A little bit of pursuit might be considered flattering, but the
problem with this particular guy was that he truly deemed
himself too good a catch for any woman in their right mind
to reject him. It seemed the more she turned him down,
the more he took it as a challenge that she wanted to be
pursued harder.

She could report him, of course, but she needed the
money and not the hassle.

Her brain spun on its wheels. For the second time in as
many moments she turned to Tak, ignoring the little voice
inside her head which was doing the most inappropriate
celebratory jig all on its own.

'So, what time did you say you'd collect me for the hospital ball?'

She could see it instantly. His eyes flicking from her to
her would-be admirer, then back again. Sizing up the situation in an instant. Then there was that wicked gleam in
his eye which had her heart beating faster as she wondered
whether or not he was about to land her in it.

For a long moment, they stared at each other. Amusement

danced across his rich brown eyes, whilst she could only imagine the desperate plea in her own. Finally, Tak spoke.

'Shall we say seven-thirty?'

'Seven-thirty.' She bobbed her head—a little too much like the nodding dog in the back of one of her foster family's cars for her own liking. 'I'm looking forward to it.'

She should hate it that a traitorous part of her actually was.

CHAPTER THREE

'YOU DIDN'T HAVE to wait down here.'

Tak frowned as he sauntered into her lobby like some kind of Hollywood action hero. Sleek and burnished and sheer masculine magnificence—a stark contrast to the shabby, grubby, in-need-of-repair surroundings.

Effie felt her heartbeat actually hang for a moment, before galloping wildly back into life as an unexpected, unwanted tingle coursed over her skin. It was a momentary reprieve from the anxiety which had flushed her body ever since her daughter had dropped the mother of all bombshells on her, barely a few minutes ago. Just as she'd been about to walk out of the door.

If it hadn't been for the knowledge that Tak would come up to the flat if she wasn't in the lobby to stop him, she might have dropped everything and spent the entire night talking to—or rather yelling at—her daughter about her monumentally stupid lapse in judgement.

In some ways this night with Tak was a silver lining. It would give her space and a chance to calm down. If she blurted out to her daughter all the things that were racing around her head at this moment in time, then she might easily ruin their relationship for a long, long time to come.

Still, Effie told herself darkly that her reaction to Tak was simply due to the rush of cold night air accompanying his entrance.

She knew it wasn't true.

So much for her efforts these past couple of days in telling herself that she had a handle on the situation. That her initial reaction to Tak had simply been a result of being caught off-guard. That now she'd had exposure to him she would be able to build up her resistance.

How on earth had she ever agreed to this?

'I would have come to your door,' he continued pointedly.

Effie thought of Nell, several storeys above them, and was pretty sure her daughter could sense her fury from all the way up there in the flat. And that was without the additional consideration of old Mrs Appleby from next door, who was babysitting Nell and never let the fact that she was practically deaf prevent her from sniffing out even a whiff of gossip. Seeing Tak Basu would be her scoop of the year. Of the decade, even.

'It's fine.' She shook her head and forced a smile. 'It isn't a proper date, remember?'

For the next few hours she would welcome the distraction. It would do her and Nell good to have the evening apart. Time to think.

'I'm glad to see that *you* do.' His voice sounded different from how she remembered. As if he was distracted. 'Although I should say you look stunning.'

Heat flooded her cheeks—and something else that she didn't care to identify. She pretended it was merely concern that people might recognise her dress for the cheap, off-the-sale-rack, several-seasons-old gown that it was.

'Thank you.'

It didn't seem to matter how many times she told herself that he didn't mean anything by it, that it was just something any date would say—fake or otherwise. Her body didn't seem in the least bit interested in listening to such reason.

'Your hair is…stunning.'

She didn't know how she managed to stop her hands

from lifting automatically to touch her head. It had taken her hours to get her hair like this—she would say she was hopelessly out of practice, but she wasn't sure she'd ever been *in* practice—and she was pleased with the results. Thick, glossy, soft curls. It was the most glamorous she'd felt in a long time.

It was only fitting that she should spoil it all by saying something ridiculously prosaic and work-related. 'Did you know there's a study showing that natural redheads often need around twenty percent more anaesthetic than people with other hair colours to reach the same levels of sedation?'

'There have been several studies,' he confirmed gravely, but she couldn't shake the impression that he was concealing his amusement. 'They appear to confirm redheads as a distinct phenotype linked to anaesthetic requirement.'

Of course he knew. He was a neurosurgeon, after all. Well, that was her bank of small talk exhausted. Not that it seemed to matter when her brain froze as he stepped up to her and offered his arm.

For one brief moment the sight of Tak—so mouth-wateringly handsome in a bespoke tuxedo, the cut of which somehow achieved the impossible by allowing his already well-built body to look all the more powerful and dangerous—made her wonder what it would be like to go on a *real* date with someone like him.

She might have said made her *yearn*, had she not already known that was impossible. She hadn't yearned in over thirteen years. She'd learned that bitter lesson—although she would never change her precious daughter for anything in the world.

Effie clicked her tongue impatiently—more at herself than the man standing in front of her. 'Right, shall we go and get this over with?'

'A woman after my own heart,' he said, and his mouth

twisted into something which looked more like the baring of teeth than an actual smile.

And then he stepped closer, his hand to the small of her back to guide her, and it was all Effie could do not to shiver at the delicious contact. She could put it down to nerves, and the fact that this was the first time she'd been out in two years—ever since the last hospital gala she'd been compelled to attend and had hated every moment— but she suspected that wasn't the true root of it.

'There's no reason to feel nervous—' He stopped abruptly. 'Did you know we'd met before when we talked the other day?'

She twisted her head to look at him, surprised that he remembered her. 'Yes, actually. I brought one of the first casualties I ever attended with the air ambulance to your hospital. You were the neurology consultant. Left-sided temporal parietal hematoma.'

'Douglas Jacobs.'

'You remember his name? I'm impressed.'

'I remember,' Tak confirmed.

She couldn't have said what it was about his tone, but in that instant he made her believe that he remembered *all* his patients. That they weren't just bodies to him. They were people.

It took her aback. Worse. It made him all the more fascinating.

'You're the one who diagnosed the expressive aphasia?' Tak asked.

It had been in the notes, but she knew he was testing her. Because it mattered to him. It was a heady thought.

'I did.' It was all she could to sound casual. As though her body *wasn't* beginning to fizz deliriously at Tak's interest.

'He wasn't talking much and his vitals were stable. You did well to spot it. It was very subtle on presentation.'

His compliment *didn't* send a tingle rushing along her spine. Not at all.

'It worsened over time?' she asked.

'Very quickly, I'm afraid.' Tak nodded. 'CT revealed a depressed skull fracture and an underlying subdural bleed, so we took him straight into an OR. When he awoke the aphasia was still present, but reduced.'

'So he's in rehab?' She squeezed her eyes shut, remembering how sweet the guy had been, and how close he and his worried wife had seemed.

'He is,' Tak confirmed. 'He's doing well, and he has a good support network, so with any luck he should be fine.'

'That's good.' She smiled, more to herself than at Tak.

It occurred to her that he'd been distracting her. Telling her a story—a work-related story—which he'd known would make her feel less tense, more at ease.

She should be angry that he'd played her, but instead she just felt grateful to him.

Allowing Tak to guide her to a large, chauffeur-driven limousine, she slid inside, trying not to marvel at the bespoke rich plaid wool and leather seats. And then he was climbing in gracefully beside her, closing the door, and the entire back seat seemed to shrink until she was aware of nothing but how very close his body was to hers.

Now it was just the two of them together, in such a confined space, it was impossible for her to keep up the pretence. To keep telling herself that his voice *didn't* swirl inside her like a fog which refused to clear, that his eyes *didn't* look right into her soul as though they could read every last dark secret in there, that his touch *didn't* send electricity coursing through her veins only to conclude in a shower of sparks as breathtaking as the best fireworks display.

The realisation thrilled and terrorised her in equal measure.

'You shouldn't be embarrassed about where you live, you know.'

It took a moment for her to focus, and then another for shame and guilt to steal through her. 'I'm not,' she said, and lifted her chin a little higher.

'Then why did you insist on meeting me in the lobby instead of letting me pick you up from your apartment?'

'I just… It wasn't about being embarrassed.' Not entirely true, but close enough.

'Then what *was* it about?'

There was no justification at all for her wanting to tell him the truth. Effie had spent her whole life shutting people out—as soon as she'd learned it was either that or *be* shut out. It shouldn't be difficult to tell Tak to mind his own business.

Yet there was a quality about him which reminded her of the one woman who had cared for her, helped her so long ago. She couldn't explain it, nor shake it. It was bizarre. This wasn't even a proper date, and the fact that she kept finding that detail so difficult to remember was concerning in itself.

'It wasn't about where I live, although I know it's no penthouse. It was more about keeping the two parts of my life separate. My private life and my professional one.'

'Does it matter that much?'

Was she guarding her personal details because they were none of his business? The way she would keep any other one of her colleagues at bay? Or was there a part of her that wished she could be—just for one night—the kind of carefree single woman that a man like Tak might actually *want* to date? And not just pretend.

Ridiculous.

Guilt speared her. She *wasn't* that kind of woman. She had barely been that kind of girl. Her carefree single days had ended the moment she'd found out that she was going to become a teenage mum. And there had been absolutely no one in the world to support her.

For the last thirteen years it had been just her and Nell. Together. She was ashamed that a part of her should want to pretend otherwise, even for a few hours.

'Yes, it does matter.' She nodded. *It was now or never.* 'To me. And to my daughter.'

Silence dropped between them like the thick, heavy curtain on a stage, separating the players from the audience. Her from Tak. What on earth had possessed her to say anything? Was it simply because Tak reminded her of a woman who was long gone?

'You have a daughter?'

His voice was even, just as before. Perhaps the silence had only been in her own head.

'Nell. Short for Eleanor. She's thirteen.'

'Thirteen? You must have been...'

'Just turned eighteen.' She didn't mean to sound so snappy, but she couldn't stop herself. 'Yeah, you don't have to do the maths. I've lived it. Now you know why I don't date. Why I *won't* date.'

Whatever she'd been expecting him to say, it wasn't the words which came next. Or the soft, almost melancholy tone.

'Difficult age, thirteen. I imagine she hasn't taken kindly to the move?'

She floundered. 'Um...no. Not really.'

'She's acting out?'

It was less of a question, more of a statement. As though he knew. And there was something else, too. Effie couldn't quite pinpoint what it was, but if she'd had to hazard a guess she might have thought that he didn't *like* the fact that he knew. That he felt it was a connection between them which he didn't want to feel.

Hadn't Hetti once told her that Tak had spent much of

his childhood taking care of his younger siblings—not just the usual big-brother-as-playground-protector stuff, but all the tasks that a parent would ordinarily do? If that was true then it had to be hard for him to shake that responsibility, even now they were all grown up.

It was certainly hard for herself, trying to let go of the past. Trying not to let it cloud the way she dealt with Nell. Trying not to let her own life experiences turn her into an over-protective mother. But maybe she was just imagining it. Either way, it was all she could do not to nod in agreement and wonder...

'What makes you say that?' she asked.

'Because you were agitated when I met you in the lobby. Like you'd had a run-in with someone. I assumed it was the teenage lads I saw hanging around outside.'

'Those lads are fine. And the place isn't that bad. It's a desirable city-centre location. Besides, it's the closest thing I could find to Nell's new school on such short notice.'

'Desirable is a matter of opinion,' he disputed. 'So the run-in was with someone else? I'm thinking it was with your daughter. Nell. Want to talk about it?'

'Nope.' But she couldn't fault him for being astute. It was impressive, really.

'It might help.'

She opened her mouth, then snapped it shut again. Surely she shouldn't be discussing this with him, an almost stranger? Effie wanted to shut the conversation down, but found that she couldn't. There was something about Tak, about those broad shoulders, which suddenly made her think how nice it would be to get another perspective and some adult support.

She did, however, find herself tugging on a stray thread from her clutch bag. A habit she'd formed decades ago, when she was anxious and unhappy. Or feeling cornered.

'I don't see why I would talk about it,' she managed stiffly.

'Because everyone needs to talk sometimes.'

She might have believed him if she hadn't caught the flash of irritation in his expression. However fleeting it had been.

Being a foster kid had made her sensitive—some might argue *over*-sensitive—to when people were asking questions out of a sense of obligation rather than any actual desire to hear the answer.

What she didn't understand was why she wasn't consequently shutting the conversation down with her usual practised efficiency. Why any part of her was actually considering opening up to Tak Basu, of all people. It was madness.

'Who says I don't already have someone to talk to?' She twisted her mouth before catching herself. 'If I need to, that is.'

'Maybe you do.' He shrugged. 'But I think you're too pent-up…too defensive. As though you're trying to deal with too much all by yourself. A teenage girl comes complete with a wealth of complications. Trust me—I know.'

For a moment his eyes met hers, deep brown and filled with understanding, as if they were stealing her very soul. And it hurt simply to breathe.

Effie didn't understand what was happening. Not inside this car, and certainly not inside *her*. She had the oddest sense of…*connection*. As if something was binding them and she didn't understand what it was.

Then the vehicle stopped, and she realised they had arrived at the gala. Plastering a bright smile on her lips, she tore her gaze away and injected an upbeat note into her voice. 'We're here—shall we go in?'

He didn't answer straight away, and the moment stretched out tautly between them until he finally inclined his head. 'As you wish.'

And as the driver opened their doors to let them out Effie told herself that she was relieved.

CHAPTER FOUR

TAK WAS GRATEFUL to be released from that endless icy blue gaze of hers. The one which was flecked with shards of gold. The one which shot right through him to the deepest caverns of his chest, expanding and shattering all that it touched.

At least he told himself that he was grateful. He was pretty sure that what he actually felt was a damn sight closer to disappointed. Yet that made no sense at all.

Moving around the vehicle to walk Effie up the steps and into the imposing, architecturally spectacular old building, he couldn't help himself placing his hand at the small of her back, and the jolt of awareness at the contact both took him by surprise and, simultaneously, did not.

It was a long, long time since any woman had sneaked under his skin the way this woman had. If ever. It was rather extraordinary. It made a part of him want to whisk her away from here, from these people and the crowds, and take her somewhere quiet where he might actually be able to talk to her. One on one.

A preposterous notion.

The problem was that he'd been entirely floored by her the moment he'd walked into that grotty lobby and seen her standing there, so startlingly beautiful, so elegant, looking so wholly incongruous to her surroundings.

He'd wanted to pick her up and carry her out of there, if only so that her feet didn't have to tread a single step on that filthy stone floor. If there had been a puddle he might even have thrown down his cloak, or at least his jacket.

Then again, if he'd picked her up, taken her in his arms, he might have been in even more trouble than he was in now. Because if simply *looking* at that tantalising body was having such an effect on him, then what might touching it actually do?

That orange flight suit hadn't even hinted at the glorious figure now poured into a dress which looked as though it had been hand-crafted just for Effie. All soft, lush, feminine curves, deliciously naughty, which drew the eye and yet had the brain filling in the gaps for all the other senses.

God, how he wanted to see what that body was like beneath those clothes. Feel it pressed against his. Lick every last inch of it…

Tak came back to his senses with a rude crash. What was he thinking? This wasn't even a real date—it certainly wasn't going to end up like *that*. Wasn't that the whole point of them coming here together? To avoid such complications?

Whatever was going on here wasn't in the script. It hadn't been in the plan. The sooner he got tonight over with and took this bewitching woman back home, the better. In fact he should start by finding Hetti—after all, wasn't she the one who had asked him to bring Effie here?

So why, instead, did he find himself guiding her inside? Find his hand moving from a light touch on her back to something arguably more possessive in sliding around to her waist to draw her in closer as several male colleagues made no attempt to conceal their envy? And why did a sense of triumph pound through him when Effie seemed to lean in to him that little bit closer, as if seeking his protection?

Unexpectedly, a couple of women caught his arm on the way in, flirting with him without a single glance at the woman who had come in on his arm, and Effie disengaged herself lightly, discreetly, in order to step ahead.

His head was still stuck back in his earlier conversation with her, and he let her go. It hit him several seconds later, when it felt altogether too much like a loss. Suddenly Tak found himself quickening his pace just to catch up with her.

'What are you doing?'

She blinked, as though she wasn't quite sure of herself. 'Giving you space.'

Something moved through him. Something hot and frustrated. Like temper, only not quite. 'Do I need to remind you that the whole idea of us coming together was to be each other's buffer?'

'I know that.' She tried to sound indignant, but couldn't disguise the catch in her voice. 'But you didn't seem to want a buffer from those women.'

Was she jealous? He was unreasonably glad.

'I disagree. Giving me space rather defeats the purpose, wouldn't you say?'

She looked at him, and there was something too bright, too electric for comfort in her gaze.

'So we're really doing this?'

'Doing what?'

'Pretending to be a couple?' Her voice faltered. 'Not just arriving together but...*being* together?'

It hadn't been his original intention. *Had it?*

'That's exactly what we're going to do,' he said.

She swallowed, but he could read women well enough to know it wasn't out of any kind of sense of feeling intimidated. She was fighting this attraction just as he was. She *wanted* him.

The knowledge shot through to Tak's very core.

Another group of women appeared without warning. 'Show-time,' he muttered, too quietly for anyone else to hear. 'Let's make it a good one. Can you do that?'

She scowled at him, which did nothing at all to lessen her beauty, then tipped her chin upwards. 'Of course I can,' she declared. 'I can play any game just as well as you can.'

He stamped out the voice in his head telling him he wished it wasn't quite such a game and led her into the crowd.

It turned out that Effie could indeed play any game as well as he could, Tak was forced to acknowledge several hours later. Perhaps even better.

She had charmed everyone to whom he'd introduced her. More like the bold, confident doctor he'd watched in action than the nervous, self-conscious woman who had been standing in that apartment lobby tonight, shifting her weight awkwardly from one foot to the other.

All evening he'd watched her smile and chat and laugh, so skilful that she had befriended the women whilst simultaneously captivating the men. It was a completely different side to her from the professional, even standoffish, air ambulance doctor he had seen a few days ago. Who cared for her patients but who had no time whatsoever for the flirtations of her eager colleagues.

Now she was gracious and sweet, even coquettish, and as far as anyone was concerned very much *his*. She had leaned into him, her fingertips brushing his arm, her fringe skimming his chin, with that flirty little laugh floating around the two of them had almost bound them, despite the rest of the crowd in the room.

No wonder she had fooled the other guests perfectly, even better than he could have imagined she would. Because at times she had nearly fooled him. He, Tak Basu, had found himself caught up in the moment, caught up in *her*, scowling at any other man who might get a bit too close, whose hand might linger on Effie's that fraction too long.

As if he was feeling jealous. Possessive. When the entire world knew that wasn't him.

He should move away. Re-establish a few boundaries. Instead he found himself bending down until his mouth was by her ear, far closer than it had any need to be. 'There's still a few minutes on the silent auction,' he murmured, revelling in the way her skin instantly goosebumped. 'Shall we take a punt together?'

Obediently she moved with him in one single direction-change. 'I thought you'd already made your bids? Quite a few of them, if I recall correctly.'

'I did,' he returned smoothly. 'The Grand Master golf experience is for Rafi, the balloon ride for Hetti and the chocolatier master class for Sasha. Plus I always enjoy a race day. But I didn't bid on anything which might be considered remotely romantic. The Parisian weekend for two, for instance...'

He shouldn't celebrate the way her eyes dilated, nor the way her nostrils gave a tiny flare. And he certainly shouldn't exult in the resultant shallow, squally breaths.

'It's a fake date,' she managed.

'Indeed it is. But no one here knows that. It's been *quite* an impressive performance you've managed this evening...' His voice was far softer than he'd intended, and he watched as she struggled to compose herself.

'I could argue that your performance was even more outstanding.'

'I make a point of ensuring *all* my performances are outstanding.'

'We... I mean, I... That is...you...' Effie stumbled, a delectable crimson blush staining her cheeks.

This reversion to her more prim side was a welcome step away from her flirtatiousness. Why was it that he couldn't get enough of the overly demure, innocent side of Effie?

'I apologise.' He grinned and let her off the hook. 'That was uncalled-for. Now, what about that weekend for two?'

She cleared her throat delicately. Once. Twice. 'Say all of your bids turn out to be the highest?'

'Then I go home a very successful man.'

He couldn't have said what had changed in her expression but he noticed it. Just as he noticed the way she began absently pulling at a loose thread on her clutch.

'That's got to be an obscene amount of money.'

Tak balked at the edge in her voice. His tone when he answered was harsher than he had intended. 'When was the last time you and Nell went abroad?'

'Nell's going skiing in a few weeks.'

He didn't miss the dark shadows dulling her blue eyes, for a moment turning them almost grey.

'And you?'

'Does it matter?'

'Humour me.'

'No.'

'Have you *ever* been abroad?' He had no idea what made him ask the question. It wasn't as though he knew the first thing about this relative stranger.

She chewed on her lip, her discomfort undeniable.

'I was a junior doctor and a single mother with a young kid.'

His voice softened of its own volition. 'I'll take that as a *no.*'

She glowered at him, but still said nothing. And, as with all the little nuggets he'd been pretending he hadn't been filing away all evening, he slotted that new piece of information into his mental picture of Dr Effie Robinson.

The real Effie. Not the one she presented to the world.

'Listen, it's no big deal. It's just for charity.'

'Yes…still—' She stopped abruptly.

The slight tic in her jaw betrayed how tightly her teeth

were clenched. As though the more he dismissed it as nothing, the more it riled her.

'Just forget it, Tak.'

And he might have forgotten it. Or he might have defused the situation with his usual ease. But instead Tak found himself focussing on the hostility of her tone. More than that, *welcoming* it.

Because if she was being judgemental then here, finally, was something which knocked her off the virtual pedestal upon which he couldn't even remember putting her. He could shake off this inexplicable attraction which snaked constantly between them.

Tonight was about making other people wonder about him and Effie and if they were in a relationship. It wasn't about making *himself* wonder what it would be like to be in a relationship with the woman. It made no sense.

He barely contained a *harrumph* of displeasure. Even if a part of him *was* attracted to her, there was still no way he was going to go there. She had a daughter. Responsibilities. Something told him that she wasn't the kind of woman to be interested in a one-night stand. By contrast, he'd lost his entire childhood by taking responsibility for his siblings and it had put him off marriage and children for life. So the last thing he needed was to get involved with a woman who came complete with a ready-made family.

Which begged the question as to why he was intrigued by the woman standing so straight-backed in front of him at this instant. He used it to prod Effie and rile her all the more. 'You resent me doing it because the more obscene the amount of money I spend, the more it draws attention to us.'

'No, it isn't… Well, it doesn't…' She drew in a deep breath. 'Like I said, forget it.'

'Isn't that why you agreed to this charade? Because you knew dating…?'

'*Fake* dating,' she interjected.

Her teeth were gritted so tightly he was sure her jaw had to be in pain. So what made him flash his most wolfish smile?

'All right.' He inclined his head as if amused, though they both heard the sharp edge to his words. 'You knew that by fake dating someone as high-profile as me that word would get around the hospital faster than a superbug.'

'Yes, but—'

'No buts.' He cut her off. 'Part of my high-profile status is down to my wealth. But you already knew that—so why is it suddenly so distasteful to you?'

'It isn't.'

She pursed her lips and he didn't doubt that she was holding back, biting down the words she desperately wanted to say. He couldn't have said why that got to him the way that it did.

And then another thought struck him. One which he knew instantly wasn't true, even though he couldn't have said *how* he knew that. But he couldn't stop himself from voicing it all the same.

'Or perhaps that was what you *wanted* me to think?'

She stopped. Blinked at him. Leaving Tak with the oddest sensation that he was skating over the thinnest sliver of sparkling blue ice: ice that could crack at any second, letting him plunge into dark, fatal, sub-zero depths.

'Say that again?' Even her voice crackled icily.

'Is that what you *want* me to think, Effie? That my money repels you? You must know how many women are attracted to the lifestyle I could offer them. Just as you've probably heard how little women like that appeal to me. Did you think you could reel me in if you pretended to abhor the material side of things?'

'What? *No!*' She managed to look angry, insulted and hurt all at once. 'Is that what you truly believe?'

No. 'It's possible.'

'It's ludicrous.' She sniffed, somewhat inelegantly. 'Do I need to remind you that this whole thing was *your* idea. Not mine.'

'Hetti's.'

'Pardon?'

'It was Hetti's idea,' he repeated coolly, calmly, though he had no idea how he managed to be either. 'Maybe *you* just saw a way to get to my money.'

It wasn't supposed to be going this way. He wasn't meant to be this affected by Effie. He felt like the kind of floundering, out-of-his-depth adolescent he'd never actually been. It was ludicrous.

Effie, meanwhile, sucked in a breath, her face pinched and white. Yet, to her credit, she held herself straight and tall. The epitome of dignity.

'Whilst that may be true, I could also point out that you may be making your own money *now*, but much of what you have comes from having a famous gynaecologist for a father and the *in*famous Basu wealth.'

Anger bubbled through him, and even that, too, was welcoming in its own way. He'd learned to contain his emotions from such a young age, trying to keep his sisters and brother in check and getting along, that he found it hard to do anything else as he grew up, bottling things up too often.

What *was* it about Effie that got under his skin in a way that no one and nothing else had been able to do for so many years?

He opened his mouth to respond, but Effie beat him to it.

'And, for the record, I didn't want to do this but *you* pursued me.'

'I was under the illusion that you were shy, retiring and aloof—not some kind of siren capable of charming every man she meets,' he bit out.

Hell's teeth, what was that? He sounded almost...pos-sessive. Jealous.

He was only grateful that Effie was barrelling on, clearly oblivious.

'Well, then, may I say that *I* was equally duped. The man your sister described to me was a focussed genius doctor and a kind and dedicated brother. *You*, however, are act-ing like a spoilt brat.'

God, but she was truly stunning. Flame-haired and flame-tongued, her arctic blue gaze as lethal as a pick-axe stabbing shards of ice off a gloriously frozen waterfall.

'I'm sorry.'

The apology came out of nowhere. Apparently to both of them. But suddenly it actually mattered to him how this evening went.

She eyed him warily. 'You're sorry?'

'I was baiting you,' he conceded flatly. 'I'm sorry.'

'Why? Why were you baiting me, I mean?'

There was no reason at all for him to want to be honest with her. But... 'It was beginning to feel a little too much like a proper date.' He shrugged. 'I didn't want there to be...mixed signals. Ridiculous, I know.'

She hesitated before muttering a reply. 'Not entirely ri-diculous.'

He liked the flush which crept up her neck. Perhaps a little bit too much. And then, as though he couldn't help himself, he thought of the fact that she had been eighteen when she had a baby. That she had somehow put herself through medical school. It was impossible not to admire the woman.

'I also could have been a little more thoughtful with re-gard to money. A little more sensitive. It can't have been easy to raise your daughter alone, at that age, and still work towards becoming a doctor.'

He didn't remember moving towards her but suddenly

she was right there, and his hand was covering hers, stilling her movements and stopping her from worrying at that loose thread any further.

'Well,' she whispered softly, 'that's my issue to deal with, not yours. And not anyone else's.'

There was something so...*lost* in her expression that he didn't even think about it—didn't even consider how much of his own private past he might be giving away—he simply said the one thing that he wished someone had said to *him* when he'd been eighteen and trying to deal with a bullheaded thirteen-year-old Hetti. Despite everything else, Tak found himself reaching for that connection between them.

'You've done well, Effie. Give yourself a break.'

'I do,' she lied.

His gaze said everything. 'Not enough. I saw how agitated you were when I picked you up from your building. I... I have sisters. I know how hard it is to keep a wilful teenage girl from going off the rails, and I can only imagine what grief your daughter gave you tonight for coming out with me. But that's just part of growing up. And so what if you don't have a lot of money? You've obviously given your daughter love and guidance—and, frankly, one hell of a role model. She'll come back to you at some point.'

Then, because her eyes looked glassy and she seemed as though she was desperately fighting to hold it together, and he knew if he hugged her it might look too obvious that he was comforting her, Tak ushered her quickly back into the main hall and swung her out onto the dance floor before she had time to pull away.

'I don't dance,' she said, panicked.

'All you have to do is follow my lead. Come here.' He cut her off gruffly, drawing her to him and letting her body settle against his, feeling her stiffen, and resist, and then ultimately crumple slightly against him as she realised there would be no release.

He didn't want to analyse what it was that had made him do it. What compunction had caused him to pull her onto the dance floor just so that he could hold her body to his. Where he'd imagined her being all evening.

And, as she pressed her head so tightly against his chest that he wondered if she could hear his heart thumping, Tak couldn't help feeling that this fleeting lowering of her defences was something of a bittersweet victory.

CHAPTER FIVE

EFFIE WAS STARTLED, but then a sense of calm seemed to flow into her. She lifted her gaze to meet his. Those rich mahogany eyes saw so deeply into her she was half afraid he might be able to read her entire past.

First he'd baited her, then he'd argued. And she'd been only too happy to play along, because she'd felt, and resented, the connection that they had. The electric spark. He wasn't the only one to think it felt more like a real date than a fake one. Worse, she couldn't bring herself to lament the fact. As though she wanted something...*more* with him.

'How?' she whispered, barely even hearing her own voice. 'How would you know she'll come back to me?'

'Hetti wasn't the easiest thirteen-year-old. Or fourteen or fifteen-year-old, for that matter. I remember my grandmother used to say, *Oh, to love a child and yet simultaneously want to strangle them.*'

Effie shook her head, not wanting to read too much into this magical insight into the infamously private Tak Basu's life 'You have a whole family. It isn't the same.'

'My father was working...' Something flashed across his face too fast for her to identify it. 'Mama was...going through her own thing. So I stepped up.'

Why couldn't she shake the impression that there was more to it? Then again, did it matter? Maybe it was the wine making her feel tired, or maybe it was Tak's demeanour, so capable, so authoritative, so *there*, which made her want to stop having to be the strong one—if only for a night—and let someone else bear the weight.

'Nell shoplifted today,' she announced, before she could think better of it.

Because he had been right when he'd said he thought she had no one to talk to, and because he was offering to be that someone, and because it wasn't a real date so why not take him up on it? Not because there was something about him which made her feel some kind of bond. That would be nonsensical.

'You know this how...?'

'She told me. Just before I walked out to come and meet you.'

'Ah.'

'Maybe I should have stayed.' She lifted her shoulders, exhaling deeply. 'Another night I probably would have done. But I just felt so drained, and so angry I was afraid of losing my temper, and I figured the space might do us both good.'

'Wise choice,' he muttered, his gaze never leaving hers, his fingers stroking her hand. As if he might actually... *care.*

It was laughable, of course. He barely knew her, let alone cared about her. Yet it was the closest thing she'd had to caring in a long, long time and, as exhausted as she was, the idea of someone else sharing the burden—if only for a few hours—was altogether too tempting.

'But you know it's a good thing that she told you, don't you? She clearly isn't happy about it, and she knows it's wrong.'

'Of *course* she knows it's wrong,' Effie spluttered. 'I haven't brought her up to think it's acceptable.'

'Relax. No one is questioning your parenting skills. I'm just saying she wanted to tell you, so she wants your help. Even if she doesn't know how to ask for it directly.'

'She knows she can come to me any time.' Effie shook her head. 'With anything.'

'She always has in the past?'

Snapping her head up with a glower, Effie raked her gaze over his face, expecting sarcasm. But she didn't find it. Only empathy.

'Yes.' She couldn't eliminate that last trace of defiance. 'She always has in the past.'

'Because you're friends as well as mother and daughter? And because that was when she was twelve and now she's thirteen? And because that was before you dragged her to a new town and a new school and no doubt ruined her life?'

Despite herself, Effie couldn't help a wry smile. 'All of the above. How did you know?'

'I told you, Hetti wasn't always the super-doc you see now, with her sunny disposition.'

And then he laughed. And everything…*shifted*.

It poured through her like the warm heat of the sun on her skin, permeating right through to her very bones. Making her head spin. She held on tight as he kept dancing, just so that she could keep her balance. But that only pulled her closer to Tak, making things worse.

Or better.

Certainly not clearer. Though she wasn't sure she wanted it to be.

'What did she take?' he asked at length.

'A lipstick.'

'Just the one?'

'That isn't enough?' she breathed. Yet she couldn't help being taken aback by his understanding demeanour.

'You do see that your daughter is still coming to you now, don't you?' he murmured.

It took a moment for her to focus. '*After* the fact,' she managed.

'Which is better than not at all.'

'Not doing it in the first place would be best.'

His wry smile *did* things to her.

'Is this going to be a productive conversation or just one in which we list comparatives and superlatives?'

'I don't know—do you have any ideas of how to make it more productive?'

'Interesting that you have such a dry sense of humour. You use it to defuse your anxiety.'

She wasn't sure what galled her more: the fact that he could read her so easily, or the fact that she was like this in front of him. Usually she was too closed-off for strangers even to begin to understand her humour. And all this while he hadn't released her, hadn't slowed as they danced around the floor.

'Shall we just forget this conversation,' she asked cheerfully, 'and get on with the night?'

'Why? Am I getting too close for your liking?'

Yes. 'No.'

'I think I am,' he said softly.

She made herself raise her eyebrows at him, as though she was merely amused. As though her heart *wasn't* lodged somewhere in the vicinity of her throat. 'You think altogether too much.'

'And you deflect.'

'Tak…'

Without warning he spun them around, and all she could do was hold on, following his lead the way he'd instructed her to do, praying she didn't trip over her own feet and slowly realising that she was holding her own. Under Tak's unspoken guidance.

The last vestiges of her reticence seemed to melt away. And Tak gauged just the right moment to speak.

'Nell is acting out because she's a thirteen-year-old girl and that's what they do—to a greater or lesser degree. You've just moved home, area, left her friends, and she's

feeling like she has no control. The shoplifting was probably a result of peer pressure and bad influence, and she
went along with it—even though you've taught her better—because she's trying to exert some kind of dominance
but doesn't quite know how. I suspect you already know
all of this, because you're clearly a good mother who cares
about your daughter.'

'How do you know?'

'The way you've talked about her. The fact that I deal
with people day in and day out. I have to operate on them,
on their brains—often when they're awake. It pays to be
able to read people so you can try to alleviate their deepest fears.'

A myriad of thoughts raced through her head, every
one of them too fast for her to catch hold of. 'Yes, I suppose that *would* pay.'

He ignored her, though not unkindly. 'I also suspect you
know that what your daughter needs is for you to try talking to her rather than simply punishing her.'

'She can't just get away with it,' Effie objected, refusing
to acknowledge that she'd thought pretty much the same
thing.

'I didn't say that. Obviously you're going to want to show
her that there are consequences—I can see that's who you
are, and I don't disagree. I'm just saying don't second-guess
your instinct to talk *to* her rather than *at* her. Trust yourself. You're not being a weak mum.'

It was as if he could see right into her thoughts. 'And
these consequences?'

He fixed her with an unwavering look. 'That's down to
you. You might want to take her back to the shop and face
up to them. Pay for the goods.'

'I thought of that, but then I worried that they might
prosecute her.'

'It's a possibility, but in my experience they won't. First-time offence…and a teenager taking *one* lipstick? Most likely the staff will appreciate that she's taking responsibility for her mistake and accept her apology and the fact that she's willing to pay for the item.'

It sounded like the ideal solution. However, fear still gnawed at Effie. 'But you can't guarantee that?'

'No, I can't.'

She chewed her lip. 'It might be scary but it's the adult thing to do…'

'And she knows that, or else she wouldn't have told you,' Tak offered. 'She came to you because she isn't happy about it. She wants your help and she needs your understanding.'

'I know that.'

Yet hearing it from him somehow helped her to believe it. He made her feel stronger. This night was turning out to be so very different from anything she might have expected. *Tak* was so very different.

It was a very dangerous realisation indeed.

All he had to do was walk her to her apartment door, then see her inside, and finally leave.

Three steps. *Easy.*

So why had he felt the need to repeat them to himself the entire car journey? As though it was the only way to distract his mind? His body? The way he'd had to do all night.

The effect her proximity had on him had been impossible to ignore. Not least when he'd made the stupid mistake of luring her onto that dance floor in order to haul her into his arms.

Only it hadn't felt like a stupid mistake. It had felt like a fire raging so savagely that he hadn't thought it could ever be smothered. Like a hunger so desperate it had eaten its way through him. Like nothing he'd ever felt before in his entire life.

He'd wanted it never to end.

Tak would never know how he had managed to hold it together on that dance floor, conversing calmly with her whilst his body had been talking itself up into a veritable showdown. He barely remembered much about the rest of the night, save for the fact that Effie had been at his side. Stoking that internal blaze without even realising it.

If it had just been the physical reaction then he could have withstood it. *Couldn't he?* But it had been more than that. It had been that inexplicable emotional connection, too. It had called out to something deep inside him. Reminded him of things he'd once thought best forgotten.

Yet now, finally, the night was almost over and he would soon be released from this pretend date he had never wanted in the first place. However many times he told himself that was a *good* thing, his body seemed determined to protest, its fight only growing stronger.

When the car stopped, he hurried around to let her out himself, and then walked her into the lobby.

'Thank you.' She stopped abruptly. 'I'm fine from here.'

He eyed her obliquely. 'It's late at night. I'll walk you to your door.'

'Really, I'm fine.'

'This isn't up for debate, Effie,' he growled. 'Now, do you want to lead the way or should I carry you?'

She sniffed delicately. 'Don't be ridiculous.'

He didn't recall anyone ever calling him *ridiculous* before. Except perhaps his sister Hetti, and she certainly hadn't said it with the kind of undercurrent that was rippling between Effie and himself right at this moment.

It was intoxicating. And unexpected.

The whole night had been so unpredicted. So voltaic.

He didn't realise they'd reached her apartment until she stopped outside the door and turned to him, her hands playing with each other in that way of hers that he shouldn't already be able to recognise as showing anxiety.

'Well… This is me.' She screwed up her nose. 'Um… thanks for this evening. It was…'

He was too close, he realised belatedly. Too close and too intent. Wholly unable to tear his eyes from the rise and fall of her chest, which betrayed how shallow her breathing was, from her lips and the way her tongue flickered out to moisten them, as though her body knew what it was doing even if her head didn't intend it.

He knew exactly how that felt.

Before he could think twice Tak lowered his head, the fleeting sensation of her hot breath on his chin only charging his body all the more, and claimed her mouth with his own.

He knew he was in big trouble in an instant.

She tasted of lust and longing and pure sensation. All exploding inside him. As if he'd detonated a charge he'd known all along would send him skyrocketing.

He couldn't get enough.

And as her arms looped around his neck, without even the slightest hesitation, and the most delicious of sounds escaped from the back of her throat, he felt as though the whole evening had been building up to this one single moment.

Something rumbled through her, soft and low at first, but as he kissed her and caressed her, sampling her over and over, taking his time and allowing every millimetre of his mouth to become acquainted with every millimetre of hers, it grew louder and more insistent. Tasting, touching, teasing. Angling his head for a better fit and feeling Effie mould her body to his as though by extension. Driving him wild. Heaven and hell all rolled into one. Sweet and sinful, wistful and wild.

He certainly wasn't prepared for Effie to wrench herself away, pushing him back with her palms even as her fingers still gripped his lapels.

'I... That is... You...' She dragged her fingers over her temptingly raw lips incredulously. Her eyes were slightly wide, but still dark with desire. Without warning she swung around, fumbled with her key in the lock, opened the door and finally disappeared inside the flat.

He let her.

He had enough experience with women to know that her head and her body would be at odds with each other right now. If he'd wanted to sway her one way or the other, he could have. But he hadn't, because he wanted her to come to him herself. To beg him to take her. To be sure there was absolutely no doubt in her mind about what she wanted from him.

He pretended not to hear the voice in his head, telling him that this was far removed from what this evening had been *meant* to be about that it made a mockery of their 'buffer' plan. And he let her go even as the sweetness of her mouth still danced on his tongue.

For several long moments he stood, his eyes glued to the closed door, imagining her on the other side, leaning against the wood and struggling to regain her composure.

But before he had a chance to turn around and make his way down the corridor to the elevator, Effie's door abruptly swung open and she pushed straight past him, rushing to the adjacent flat, where she began to wildly hammer on the door.

'Nell? Mrs Appleby? Are you in there?' There was a distinctly frantic edge to her voice.

'Will you calm down? You're going to wake the whole building,' he said.

'They aren't in there.' She jerked her head maniacally, and he could only assume that she was indicating her own flat.

The blaring TV was a good sign. Still, Effie yelled

through the door, her voice higher-pitched than ever. 'Mrs Appleby? Is everything—?'

Effie practically toppled inside as the door swung open without warning, and Tak found himself lurching forward so as not to be shut out.

'You're lucky Mrs Appleby is so deaf that she doesn't realise you're trying to beat down her door,' Nell said, and scowled at her mother before catching sight of Tak. Her eyes narrowed curiously.

If he had any sense of self-preservation at all he would leave. Right now. This wasn't Hetti. Or Sasha. This wasn't his responsibility. This was Nell, and she was Effie's albatross. He prodded himself. Which was why he should already be halfway down the hall.

Instead, Tak folded his arms across his chest and met the kid's bold gaze.

Effie struggled to slow her hammering heart. Though whether it was her panic over the fact that Nell hadn't been where she should have been, or the fact that Tak had been glued to her side since the moment she'd started to freak out, she couldn't be sure.

She didn't think she wanted to analyse it too deeply, anyway.

'Why are you both here?' She turned her attention back to her daughter. 'You're supposed to be in our apartment. You should be in bed.'

'So you've been into the flat?' Nell didn't even attempt to drag her gaze from Tak.

He wouldn't be finding it easy to hold firm, Effie thought, sucking in a breath. 'Yes. And when you weren't there I got worried. You couldn't have left a note? Some indication that you were here and why?'

'The fact the place is freezing didn't give it away?' Nell retorted, finally dragging her focus back to her mother.

Her young voice held an edge of sarcasm that wouldn't have been there six months ago, but Effie wasn't ready to call her out on it in front of a stranger. Not *this* stranger, anyway.

Had the flat been cold? She hadn't noticed—had only registered the fact that the TV was off—unheard for old Mrs Appleby. Effie wrinkled her nose. In fact she'd been far too preoccupied with that kiss.

It was high time she put that momentary madness behind her. Except that even now her body heated at the memory of what had happened in the hallway with Tak.

Tak's low voice broke into her thoughts. 'Why is your home freezing?'

'The boiler has probably broken down.' Jerking her head up, Effie told herself that there was no need for her to feel ashamed. It was none of his business how they lived.

Her daughter, however, had no such qualms. She eyed Tak. 'It does that a lot.'

'Not a *lot*,' Effie said quickly.

'Oh, come on, Mum. It's all the time.'

'We've only been here three months.'

'And it's the fourth time it's gone.' Nell snorted unapologetically. 'The thing is ancient and you've said it yourself— the landlord is too penny-pinching to replace it.'

'You've called him tonight?' asked Tak suddenly.

'Of course.' Nell pulled a face. 'He said it's the weekend, so the earliest he can get someone out will be Monday, but Tuesday is more likely.'

'Okay—' began Effie, but Tak cut her off.

'Not okay. It's barely spring, it's been a sub-zero winter and there's another cold snap on its way. Repairing your faulty boiler is clearly his top responsibility.'

'As he said, it's the weekend, so that's a reasonable time frame.' At least it was if she didn't want to risk being seen

as a troublesome tenant and risk eviction. 'We don't *all* have
the kind of money which gets instant action.'

'I'm not challenging your financial circumstances,' he
commented unexpectedly. 'I'm neither blind nor stupid. I
do understand how putting yourself through medical school
at the same time as raising a child must have crippled you.'

'Oh.'

Of all people, she didn't expect Tak to understand so
readily. At all, even.

'And I realise you must still be sacrificing to send Nell
to that school.'

'It's worth it,' Effie cut in quickly, glowering at him.
'Besides, as soon as I have time to house hunt, I'll be able
to find somewhere much better now that I know the area.'

'Effie…'

'Can we just drop it? Please?'

Tak didn't look happy but, ultimately, he obliged.

'So you aren't going to call your landlord again?'

Not quite what she'd meant by 'drop it', but at least he
wasn't talking about the school any more. She didn't want
Nell uncomfortable at her new school.

'Nell just said she called him.'

'She's *thirteen*.'

'Nell's very responsible.' *If only she'd never mentioned
the shoplifting to Tak.*

Her daughter had had to be responsible—it had always
been just the two of them. As much as Effie had tried to
protect her daughter from growing up too fast, being a
single parent and a doctor had nonetheless played its part.

Still, she could be proud of herself that Nell didn't really
understand the kind of true ugliness out there that Effie
herself had dealt with for most of her childhood. She'd
used select parts of her past to teach her daughter how to
be strong, confident, and able to think for herself. Yet she'd
kept so much of it back—partly out of shame.

'I've no doubt she's extremely responsible…for a thirteen-year-old. Call your landlord.'

It was ridiculous that she found herself squaring her shoulders. 'No.'

There was no way that Tak would understand that calling him a second time would only cause him to push their boiler to the bottom of his list. And she didn't need him—*anyone*—telling her what to do. She would protect her own family the way she always had. She'd got this far on her own, hadn't she?

She threw off the niggling fact that for once—with Tak—she was almost tempted to let someone else in.

'We don't need you swooping in, playing some kind of unwanted superhero. We can sort out our own problems.'

For a long moment they glared at each other.

'Fine.' Tak turned to her daughter abruptly, as though—insultingly—he considered the thirteen-year-old to be the more reasonable of the two of them. 'Give me his number and I'll call him myself.'

'You can't!' Effie gasped.

There would be repercussions if he did. Their landlord wasn't exactly renowned for his understanding nature. And as much as she might be ready to look for a better home as soon as she had some free time, she didn't want them to be kicked out by an irate landlord before she had time to line up somewhere new.

'Wait here,' she instructed, in as firm a voice as she could manage. 'I'll pay Mrs Appleby and then you can argue with me.'

When she got to know the area, and had more than a couple of hours of downtime—hours which were usually spent washing, cleaning and doing the grocery run—then maybe she would have a moment to look for somewhere better.

She found herself shaking the dozing Mrs Appleby

awake as gently as possible and thrusting the babysitting payment into the old woman's hand before hurrying out of the flat to catch up with Nell and Tak. Predictably, they hadn't listened to a word of her instructions.

She stood back, chewing her lip, as Tak conducted what seemed like a remarkably one-sided conversation, during which he was doing most of the talking and her usually dominant landlord appeared to be doing an unusual amount of conceding.

'He'll have someone here first thing in the morning,' Tak said, ending the call with something approaching satisfaction. 'You can't spend the weekend with no heating. It's unacceptable.'

'It's called reasonable,' Effie countered. 'At least in *my* world.'

Tak didn't appear remotely swayed. 'I'll wager that if his own boiler broke down he'd have someone there within the hour.'

'Well, this isn't his flat. It's mine.'

They glared at each other for a long time before Effie finally broke contact, all too acutely aware of Nell's curious gaze.

'Pack a bag,' Tak commanded abruptly. 'You can't stay here.'

It was the crossing of the line in the sand that Effie needed. She rooted herself to the spot and lifted her steady gaze to his. This was *her* daughter, *her* little family, *her* problem. She would deal with it. Just as she always had done.

'Absolutely not.'

'This place is—'

'We're really grateful for you for talking to the landlord,' she said, cutting him off abruptly, 'but we're fine now.'

She didn't know what was galvanising her—she only knew that something was. Perhaps it was the fact that she had long since learned that ultimately people would let you down and she relied only on herself. No one else. Never anyone else.

Not even him.

It was a bit terrifying that the idea of leaning on Tak Basu—even just a little—was so damn tempting. What *was* it about this man that slid through her in a way that no one else ever had? *Ever.*

The next thing she knew she was standing with her hand on the open door. 'I said that we can take it from here.'

Tak scowled, and looked as though he was about to argue. And then, without warning, he gave a terse nod of his head and strode out. Once in the hallway, he paused long enough to instruct her to call him if she had any more problems and then he was gone.

She chanted over and over in her head, that she was glad.

But even as she closed the door with a flourish, knowing that she would inevitably get the third degree from a barely contained Nell, Effie took a moment to lean her forehead on the cold wood and wonder exactly what she had done.

CHAPTER SIX

'THAT'S IT! THAT'S it—stop!' Effie called to the paramedic to stop chest compressions before shouting to her patient above the noise of the helicopter as it raced through the air. 'Emma, are you with me, sweetheart? You're okay. You're in a helicopter, my love. I'm Effie—I'm a doctor. You're doing well. You're back with us.'

She exchanged a relieved glance with one of her paramedics. It was a hard enough job even without the additional complication of the cramped helicopter space. For several long minutes they continued tending to their patient, before Effie finally sat back on her heels.

'Okay—quick recap. We're back in normal sinus rhythm and she has a line in. We've carried out CPR and one shock, straight up. She's had oxygen, aspirin, no adrenalin.'

The pilot's voice came over the system. 'We're a couple of minutes out from the hospital.'

'Good,' Effie acknowledged, smiling brightly down to her patient, whose eyes were finally open. 'Okay, Emma, we're nearly at the hospital. You've done really well. Now, let's see if we can keep that heart-rate up, shall we?'

For the next half-hour Effie concentrated on the task in hand: keeping her patient comfortable and carrying out her observations before the helicopter finally landed. There wasn't time for her to think about whether or not Tak would be in the resus room when she rushed her patient in. But later—much later—she might acknowledge that deep down there was a tiny part of her which prayed that he wouldn't be there, just as there was another tiny part of her that always hoped he would.

The two parts had been sparring with each other for the last few days.

As they lifted her patient off the helicopter and onto a hospital gurney Effie kept chatting to Emma while the team navigated the long ramp to the hospital. It felt like a win when she finally handed over to the hospital team without Emma going into arrest a second time.

And then there were no distractions or excuses. She was here, in Tak's hospital, and every corner she turned, every corridor she walked, seemed to be a home for ghosts of him.

Had it really only been three days since that night at the gala? Since that kiss? Since he'd seen exactly how she lived? It felt like a lifetime, and if she never had to see him again she would be just fine with that.

She ignored the traitorous part of her which whispered that wasn't true. Just as she pretended that her eyes *weren't* scanning through every door, every window, wondering whether he was just on the other side.

'Are you looking for Tak?'

Effie jumped guiltily as she swung round to see his sister, Hetti. 'Of course not,' she lied brightly. 'I was looking for James, one of my paramedics.'

'Oh.'

She tried not to react to Hetti's all too knowing smile.

'How are you, anyway? How was the ball?'

Effie hesitated 'Good. Yes, fine.'

'You enjoyed it?' Hetti pressed.

'I...yes. Sure. What did Tak say?'

'Not a lot, really,' continued Hetti airily. 'You know Tak.'

But that was the issue, wasn't it? Effie *didn't* know Tak. Not at all, really. Yet she couldn't help thinking that Hetti was watching her a little too closely, as though hoping for a reaction.

'Sure,' she lied, her grin almost painful.

'Having said that,' Hetti added, a little too casually, 'I've never seen him so…shall we say *buoyant*?'

She would not react. She would not.

'Oh. Well. That's good,' she offered brightly. And then she spoiled it all by smoothing her flight suit down as though it was some designer gown. 'Well, I'd better find my paramedic and get back to the heli.'

Hetti practically leapt forward to grab her arm. 'Oh, but…not yet, Effie. There's something I want to ask you.'

'There is?'

'Yes.'

Effie waited patiently.

Hetti clapped her hands and clicked her tongue. 'Yes. There is.'

The moment was eked out until it was almost uncomfortable.

'Well… I really should get going…'

'The thing I want to ask you is…' Hetti shifted awkwardly. Then, as the doors banged at the other end of the corridor, she grinned, exhaled heavily and shook her head and began to hurry the other way. 'Never mind. It'll keep.'

Effie turned away, bemused. And slammed into a solid wall. A warm, *human* solid wall.

She didn't need to see his face to know who it was. A tremor ran through her body like the after-effects of an earthquake.

'Tak.'

'Effie.'

'I've…just been talking with Hetti.'

'So I saw.'

She pursed her lips. 'Did you ask her to stall me?'

If only she wasn't willing him to say yes. Instead he offered a wry smile, and that long, slow ache started up inside her all over again.

'I did not. But I did just receive a call from her saying that she needed me down on this floor.'

So Tak hadn't actually been looking for her. They'd merely been set up. Then again, Tak had come anyway. Was that a good thing or a bad one?

Effie was sure her stomach had no business vaulting and somersaulting the way it was.

'You didn't leave a patient?' she asked feebly.

He eyed her disdainfully. 'Of course not.'

'No,' she cut in hastily. 'Foolish question.'

They stood, the silence stretching uncomfortably between them, whilst Effie tried, and failed, to find something—anything—to say.

'What about the boiler?' He finally broke the silence. 'Did your landlord send someone round the next morning?'

She hesitated as a hundred different thoughts raced through her head. It was barely a beat but it seemed to hang between them for an age, and when she finally spoke her voice was strangled. 'It's in hand.'

'It isn't fixed?' he said sharply.

Another beat.

'It's being fixed.'

'Effie—'

'Actually...' she cut him off hastily '...since you're here, I do owe you a thank-you.'

For a moment, she thought he was going to argue.

'What for?' he ground out instead.

'For Nell. We went to the shop together this morning. You were right—they took one look at her white face, heard her shaky confession and apology, and were more than prepared to let her pay and let her off with a warning because it was her first—and only—time. But they were clear that if they see her in there again with those girls stealing then she won't get off so lightly.'

'And she understood that?'

'I made sure of it.'

She *had* made sure Nell understood. She'd spelled it out in no uncertain terms. But she'd also chatted to her daughter, just as Tak had suggested, and just as she'd known she needed to do all along. And she was confident in her own mind that it had been a stupid, ill-judged, one-time mistake. It wasn't the start of Nell going off the rails.

Not the way she herself had, anyway.

'Am I the first man you've ever taken home, Effie?'

The question came out of nowhere, pulling the proverbial rug out from under her.

'I… Sorry…what does that mean?'

'Exactly what it sounds like.' He sounded amused. 'Am I the first man you've ever taken home?'

'Does it matter?' Not an ideal way to buy herself some time, but it would have to do.

'Only your daughter seemed more curious about me than perturbed. I wondered if she thought you never dated at all.'

She didn't know whether to be impressed or irritated that he was so astute. 'I date,' she lied, pretending she couldn't hear the defensive note running through her tone.

Because he was right. From the moment she'd lifted her forehead from that cool wooden door that night, to see the sharp gleam in her daughter's eyes, Effie had known something was different. There had been a shift in their mother-daughter relationship, although she couldn't have articulated what that shift was.

Possibly she was hindered by the fact she was still finding it difficult enough trying to process that kiss with Tak—and the fact that even now her body seemed to be aching for it to continue—without dealing with a frowning thirteen-year-old to boot.

'Glad to hear it.'

His reply was so smooth that it took Effie a moment

to recall that they'd been talking about whether or not she dated.

'Well...' she declared. 'Um...good.'

It was getting more awkward, more painful by the moment. Yet she couldn't bring herself to move. Which made it all the more humiliating when Tak strode away with apparent ease, talking to her over his shoulder.

'Okay, then, if that's all you wanted me for I should get back to work.'

'I *didn't* want you. Hetti wanted you,' Effie managed at last.

But it was too late. He was already gone and she was left to make her way back to the helicopter, her head now full of memories of Nell's none too subtle interrogation the night of the ball.

'Who was the guy?' her daughter had demanded without preamble.

She might have known Nell wouldn't easily let it go. 'No one,' she'd ventured.

Her daughter had scoffed in the way that only teens could. 'Is he your boyfriend?'

Effie remembered opening her mouth to answer, but then catching herself. What kind of example was it to set for her thirteen-year-old daughter? She had been kissing someone who had, when it came down to it, been more of a ride to the gala than anything else. Or at least he was supposed to have been.

So she'd fibbed. 'He was my date but... I don't know if we'll be seeing each other again.'

For a long moment her daughter had eyed her without answering, whilst Effie had tried to pretend to herself that she didn't secretly wish it really *had* been a date. Her first one in years.

When Nell had finally spoken, it hadn't been at all what Effie had been expecting.

'Was it a bad date?' she'd asked, her voice softer than anything Effie had heard from her in a long while. Sympathetic. 'Did he flirt with another girl? I was on a date with Adam Furnisson, but all he did was flirt with Greta Matthews the whole time. It was…humiliating.'

A date? Nell? When the hell had that happened?

Effie had bitten her tongue so hard that she was sure, even now, she could still taste blood. But demanding the details would have only made her daughter shut her out again.

She'd never even heard those names before. How was it that an unexpected kiss with Tak—the kind that had probably meant nothing to him but which had shaken her so—had put her back into a position where her daughter suddenly wanted to confide in her again?

She'd had to choose her words carefully when she'd warned Nell that, 'If a boy treats you like that then he simply isn't worth it.'

Nell had twisted her mouth in a way which had suggested she knew that in her head but her innocent neo-teen heart was having some difficulty with the concept.

'I know…' She'd blown out a deep breath. 'But it's Adam *Furnisson*, Mum. He's, like…the hottest guy in school, and it's a big deal to even be part of his squad.'

Oh, to love a child and yet simultaneously want to strangle them.

Tak's words had come back to her unexpectedly and for a moment they had helped to take some of the heat out of Effie's instinctive response. What else had Tak said…? That maybe she should try talking to her daughter? Well, it was worth a try.

Hesitantly, she'd taken her daughter's hand and led her to the sofa, promising to make them a hot drink and have a chat. *Like grown-ups.*

Nell's eyes had begun to narrow suspiciously, but then

she'd offered a surprised, pleased, but wary nod, before following her mother across the room.

To Effie it had felt like the kind of victory she couldn't even have dreamed of a few hours before. Before Tak. Before his advice.

Yet with his words resounding in her head—his assurance that she was doing a good job and his instruction to give herself a break—she'd felt a renewed confidence to tackle Nell. And the rest of her conversation with her daughter, including about the shoplifting, had followed from there.

None of it had been ground-breaking. It had just been everything she should have known for herself. Probably *did* know, deep down. But somehow, somewhere along the line, she'd lost confidence in herself and begun second-guessing the way she was with her own daughter.

It made her wonder exactly how Tak had understood the situation so well.

And what was it that made Hetti so very protective and fiercely proud of her brother? Because it was more than just the fact that he was a renowned neurosurgeon.

Suddenly Effie was more than keen to find out.

It had taken Tak hours of ward rounds, surgery and ultimately hated paperwork for Tak to finally push Effie out of his head. Even when he was focussed on his job she still lurked there. Somewhere in the back of his subconscious.

He was sure she had been lying about the repair to the boiler in her flat being *in hand.*

Taking the stairs two at a time—always faster than waiting for the hospital elevators at this time of day—Tak thrust all thoughts from his head. It shouldn't matter to him. They weren't his business. Not Effie. Not her daughter. Not their boiler.

Effie had been a means to an end—as he had been for

her—a mutually convenient arrangement for one night only. There was absolutely no reason for him to think about her any more. No reason for him to tell himself he needed to find something to douse this *thing* that was simmering dangerously inside him.

It had almost been a relief when he'd managed to walk away back there in the hospital corridor. He'd managed to break the spell Effie had unknowingly woven around him.

Yet he couldn't shake the memory of the way she'd watched him. With a look approaching disappointment in her eyes. And something else, too. Something altogether too much like hurt.

Consequently, the last thing he expected was to get an emergency call from Resus, patching through a familiar, if crackly voice from the air ambulance.

'Effie?'

Had she called just to talk to him?

'Tak?'

The shocked tone was too palpable to miss. Clearly she hadn't asked for him by name.

And then she shook off her shock and plunged in. 'I'm with a casualty—forty-year-old female. Road traffic accident. GCS six. Pupils uneven with left pupil dilated and fixed. Infrascanner showed a subdural haematoma.'

'So get her in to me,' he barked.

'We can't,' she replied simply. 'We're not cleared to fly. There's been an explosion and there's thick, black smoke around us so we can't see to fly out and no one can see to get to us right now.'

He processed the scenario in moments. This patient needed surgery to alleviate the pressure on her brain. A delay of mere hours could result in permanent brain injury. Which meant someone needed to do it out in the field. *Now*.

A tiny part of him was relieved that it was Effie on the

other end of the phone rather than anyone else. But he could process that bit of information later. In his own time.

'You're going to need to perform an emergency burr hole evacuation.'

'Yes.'

That quiet, calm affirmation was like the final puzzle piece slotting in. Any residual doubts Tak had dissipated quietly.

'Okay—the patient is intubated?'

'Yes, and in a C-spine.'

'You're going to need a knife, a drill, swabs, a self-retainer... Saline should ideally be hypertonic...'

'Tak, we're not an emergency department or an operating room. We've got some kit on board, but the rest is mix and match and DIY stuff. I really need you to talk me through it.'

'Okay, give me your mobile number and I'll call you back on it. And I'll send you an image showing the standard position of burr holes, which you're going to need to modify depending on what the Infrascanner shows.'

He grabbed a pen and jotted down the number she gave him, replaced the department phone and headed for a quiet room as he sent her the image.

He called her back.

'Tak?'

She picked up on the first ring, her nerves controlled but nonetheless evident. He didn't blame her.

'You'll be fine.' He kept his tone as brisk as he could. 'I'll talk you through it as we go, but here's a summary. You're going to need to shave about a five-centimetre strip of hair. Then you'll mark a three-centimetre incision and clean the area, preferably with chlorhexidine. You'll make an incision right down to the bone, controlling any bleeding with direct pressure.'

'Understood.'

She had to be nervous but she was mastering it, which boded well for the casualty. His respect for Effie hitched up yet another notch.

'You're going to need to use either the knife or a swab to push the periosteum off the bone, and ideally this is when you'd insert the self-retaining retractor. Or whatever it is you've got.'

'Right,' she confirmed.

'Now comes the hard part. The drill *must* be perpendicular to the skull, and you're going to need one of your paramedics to hold the casualty's head and apply saline as you drill. Effie, you're going to have to push down hard, and once you've started drilling *keep* drilling until the drill bit stops spinning. If you stop too soon it's going to disengage the mechanism and make it that much harder to start again.'

'Understood,' she said again.

Her grim tone crackled over the connection, and he could imagine she had swallowed. Pretending she didn't feel sick with adrenalin as it coursed wildly around her veins. She needed it to. There was no way she was going to get through this unless she was fired up enough.

But still, as he outlined the rest of the procedure and then waited for her to ensure everything was in place before beginning to talk her through it step by step, it occurred to Tak that there was no other doctor he would rather have on the end of the line right now. No one else he would trust to perform such a procedure whilst they waited for either a road ambulance to get to them or for clearance to fly the heli out with the patient.

This was so much worse than just a physical attraction. It seemed he liked and admired Effie, too. When had anyone *ever* got to him like this? When had this constant awareness *ever* shot through him? It was an awareness which flared into something infinitely more palpable—more forceful— every time he saw her. Even spoke to her.

The woman's nature was as fiery and captivating as her glorious red hair.

Just like that, an image locked itself in his mind. So detailed that she might as well have been standing right in front of him. Her lilting voice, her delicate fragrance, the way her skin felt so soft and yet so electric beneath his fingers. And as for the way she'd tasted when his mouth had plundered hers...the way she had given herself up to him as though they had been the only two people to ever to kiss that way in the history of the world...

It made no sense.

Neither did the way his whole body combusted at the mere memory. As though he was the untried, untested boy of his youth rather than a man who had enjoyed his fair share of sexual encounters.

It was bizarre. But not altogether unpleasant.

Although it *was* inconvenient.

Which could mean only one thing. He really was in deep trouble.

CHAPTER SEVEN

'WHAT ARE YOU doing here?' she asked testily, thirteen hours later, as he found himself hammering on her apartment door.

His gaze swept down, taking in her multiple layers of jumpers, and the expression in his eyes hardened.

'The boiler hasn't been repaired at all. You lied to me.'

She bristled instantly. 'I did not lie.'

'You told me it was repaired.'

'No, I told you it was in hand. Which it is.'

'I hardly see how,' he remarked dryly. 'Unless you're trying to recreate the Arctic Tundra in there.'

Effie wasn't sure what took her aback the most. The fact that they were sparring about this, on her doorstep, or the fact that they were sparring at all. Surely it didn't matter to him one way or another whether one of his colleagues had heating in their home or not?

More than that, there was the fact that something had changed between them. So subtle that she couldn't exactly put her finger on what it was, but there seemed to be a deeper affinity there now.

Then again, he had very recently talked her through drilling a burr hole into a brain at the roadside. Surely that had to alter any relationship?

Still, she couldn't stop her eyes from flickering over his shoulder and along the corridor beyond. If Mrs Appleby saw him—again—the rumour mill would really start cranking up.

'If that's what you came for, perhaps you should now go.'

There was no justification for the way her mouth fought against her uttering the words. Or for the way her heart skipped so merrily when he didn't move. If anything, he seemed to root his feet to the cracked hallway floor all the more.

'It isn't what I came for.'

'Then what?'

It was almost indiscernible, his hesitation, as if he was trying to think quickly of something to say. But then he continued and Effie realised she must have imagined it.

'I thought you might like to know how your first brain surgery patient is.'

She was torn. A sense of self-preservation warred with the professional side of her, which ached to know that she hadn't caused any harm to her RTA casualty.

'She's okay? I did okay?'

His mouth curved softly at one corner. 'You did okay,' he confirmed. 'Better than okay. You saved her life.'

'Thanks to you, talking me through it so concisely.'

Pride whooshed through her, making her feel at least ten feet tall. She couldn't control the smile as it took her over her face, her eyes locking with Tak's. For a moment he looked as though he was about to say more, but then changed his mind.

'Obviously. Now, if you don't want the whole building buzzing about the strange man on your doorstep, perhaps you should let me in.'

She ought to refuse, stand her ground. Instead she found her fingers reaching for the bolt, her hand shaking a little too much with eagerness.

'Hurry up.' Agitation and excitement vied for supremacy in her tone. 'Before someone sees you.'

The temperature hit him the moment he entered.

'It's really is like the tundra in here.'

It sounded more like an accusation than a comment. It was all she could do to eye him with disapproval. No doubt he wouldn't be used to that. When was the last time anyone had eyed Tak Basu with anything other than approval? Admiration? *Lust?*

She pushed that thought out of her head in an instant. 'Why are you here, Tak?'

'Did the repair guy even turn up?'

'Tak—'

'Did he turn up?' he interrupted.

She glared at him. 'Yes.'

'But he didn't repair it?'

'Oh, he did.' She narrowed her eyes. 'But Nell and I don't use it because we *like* it this cold.'

'Why didn't he repair it?' Tak chose to ignore her sarcasm.

She tried to out-glare him, but when she saw that clearly wasn't going to work she finally relented with a sigh. 'It seems it's a little complicated.'

'How complicated?'

'The boiler is on its last legs. It needs to be replaced. But a new boiler won't connect to the old system. I'm not entirely sure, but I think it's something about microbore pipework. They need to run in a fresh central heating line.'

He nodded, as though he understood what she was saying. Which didn't really surprise her.

'And how long will that take?'

'A few weeks. Maybe.'

'A few *weeks*?' Tak was disparaging. 'It's a small flat, surely a week would suffice?'

'As I understand it, they think they will need to take down at least one ceiling from the building plant room above, access at least one wall void, and then certainly take up every floor covering, floor board and re-lay all new pipework. Without disturbing any of my neighbours in the building. Even a layperson like me can see that could take a while.'

'I see. And where does this landlord of yours expect you—and all your belongings, to live during this period?'

'Here,' she tried for a nonchalant shrug They can work in one or two rooms at a time so we can move around with them.'

'Then forget a few weeks! If they're stop-starting like that to work around you—and your furniture—then that could take a month. Longer, even.'

'I guess...' She shrugged. 'But that's just how it is. At least we still have somewhere to live.'

'And you just accepted that? For pity's sake, Effie, can't you see that your landlord is walking all over you?'

'Probably—but what can I do about it? There's nothing in my tenancy agreement stating that the landlord is legally obliged to find us alternative accommodation. If I shout and rage then he'll only take it out on us in an even worse way.'

She'd thought it would help, but her calmness only seemed to creep under his skin all the more. As if her acceptance made him feel as though he needed to shout louder, fight harder on her behalf.

Or maybe that was just because she wanted him to.

It made no sense. She'd long since given up expecting anyone else to fight her battles, or even stand beside her whilst she fought them herself. She'd wanted someone to do that for her, her whole life. But they hadn't. Except for that one time, but look how that had turned out.

'No, that's unacceptable.'

Effie blinked, barely recognising Tak's voice. It sounded odd, somehow. Tight. A little like her smile felt as she twisted her mouth into some semblance of one. Something was bugging him. She couldn't explain why that pleased her, but it did.

'It's unfortunate, I'll grant you, but it's just the way it is.'

'I won't accept it.'

His words were sharp, edgy. She could almost see them cutting the air. Something sloshed inside her.

'What are you going to do? Repair it yourself? After having conjured the obsolete spare parts out of thin air, of course. We all know you're a superhero surgeon, of course, but I didn't realise your expertise stretched to boilers and central heating as well.'

A hundred thoughts were racing through Tak's head at that moment. She could see them but she couldn't grasp a single one of them. And the way he was watching her... It made it impossible for her to explain this dark thing which fogged her head and swirled in eddies around her chest.

'You can't stay here.'

His voice was too thick. It *did* things to her. She could almost *feel* her smile. It was sharp, edgy, so un-Effie-like.

'And yet here I am.'

'What about your daughter?' he challenged, and her non-smile disappeared in a flash. 'It's like living inside a freezer.'

'You think I don't know that? But where else should I stay? I could stay at the hospital, but I can't take Nell, and I can't afford a hotel.'

'You'll stay with me.'

'No!' Effie exclaimed, a shrill note of panic echoing through her voice.

'Effie, what does it tell your daughter that you're putting up with this landlord messing you around? Taking advantage?'

He might not have intended it, but what he'd said played on every insecurity she had.

'I don't need someone to swoop in and save me,' she growled. 'I've been taking care of my daughter alone for thirteen years. I don't need a…a…stranger telling me he knows best.'

'For pity's sake, this isn't some test as to whether you're a good mother or not,' he countered. 'Are you trying to tell me that you *aren't* both absolutely freezing and miserable?'

She clenched and unclenched her fists at her sides. 'We can cope. We've put up with worse.'

'I don't doubt it—more's the pity!'

His voice was too even, too level, and somehow that got under her skin all the more. Her temper—which she'd kept hidden away for more years than she could remember—began to flare.

'We don't need you charging in thinking we need saving. Offering us your goodwill like we're some charity case. Suggesting we can't manage.'

'It wasn't an offer,' he replied grimly. 'Or a suggestion.'

'Really?' Effie could barely contain her incredulity. 'You're *that* high-handed you think you can just *order* me and my thirteen-year-old daughter to come and stay with you and I'll obey? As if that doesn't set a worse example to her than anything else?'

'Fine.' His jaw pulled taut. 'Then I'm at least calling the creep to find out exactly what's going on.'

She couldn't possibly have articulated what it was in his expression that rooted her to the spot. That made her whole body shiver so deliciously despite everything. And before she could analyse it further he'd turned from her, pulling out his mobile phone. It was only when he began speaking that she realised with whom he was having his rather commanding one-sided conversation.

Goodness, he must have saved the number when Nell had given him their landlord's contact details. She should react. Stop him. Grab the phone and take control. Awkwardly, stiffly, she reached her hand out, but abruptly his face darkened menacingly as he growled into the phone.

'Asbestos?'

Effie froze solid. She was watching and listening, but unable to move or to say a word. Her brain was apparently not even capable of understanding Tak's side of the conversation, save for the fact that she would be eternally grateful his barely contained rage wasn't remotely directed at her.

Finally, he terminated the call with a grim sound. All she could do was wait. Immobile. Barely even breathing.

'It seems your flat is located directly below the plant room,' he bit out at length. 'It seems that since the last conversation, he found asbestos in the lagging around the pipes. It's going to need to be cleared out immediately—which means taking your ceiling down to get to the pipes.'

She felt as though she was fighting to swim through treacle. 'Okay, but that won't take long, surely? It's a small flat. Pulling out a bit of insulation might take a day? Two?'

'They'll have to remove the ceilings from your entire flat, clear out the lot, re-insulate, board the ceilings, then plaster then. You're talking a minimum of a week. Then there's still the week or so to replace all the pipework in your flat.'

'Two weeks?' it would eat up all her savings, and then some.

'It isn't just that, Effie. Your landlord is going to need surveys, HSE approval, and then find a fully licensed contractor to remove the asbestos. You're talking a minimum of six weeks—and that's assuming he can find someone available to start straight away.'

The ramifications came at her almost in slow motion. 'Nell and I are going to have to move out?' Her voice didn't even sound like her own.

'Yes.'

'For six weeks?'

'At least.'

'*No!*' Effie exclaimed, unable to cover the note of panic in her tone. 'How dare you? You…you've no right.'

There was a note in her voice which threatened to betray the fact that it wasn't just her pride talking, but rather her flip-flopping traitorous heart. A note which gave away just how wickedly tempting his offer was.

'I didn't create this, Effie.' He sounded unperturbed. 'I didn't put the asbestos there.

'No right to meddle!' she cried. 'You called him. You pushed him.'

'Which meant he told the truth *now* instead of in a few days or weeks.'

'And it's just my flat?'

'No, it's all three flats on this floor.'

Her stomach somersaulted. 'Oh, no—Mrs Appleby!'

'Apparently, she's going to stay with her sister, a few hours' drive away. I don't know about the other flat's occupants.'

What did it say about her that she didn't even know their names?

'I have no idea where we can go,' she whispered, more to herself than anyone else.

'Like I said. You'll stay with me. Only this time I'm not offering.'

Effie didn't miss the edge to his voice, but her mind was too busy reeling for her to be able to take it on board fully.

'Anyway, my home is expansive enough that we could live in separate wings and not even see or hear each other.'

She hesitated. What other choice did she have? And why couldn't she shake the part of her which was secretly revelling in this horrible turn of events?

'Really?'

'Unless you *want* us to see each other, of course.'

It was an attempt at a joke, she was pretty sure, but they were both too tense to laugh. The air was so fraught she was almost suffocating. And then something lurched inside her chest that she pretended not to notice.

She tilted her head a fraction higher. 'You're funny,' she said, her voice cracked.

'Did you just chin-check me?'

He grinned suddenly. It was a stunning, heart-stopping sight. And incredibly, impossibly, everything simply *shifted*.

'Why are you being so nice, anyway?' Effie valiantly fought to eye his obscenely tantalising grin with something she hoped approached disdain. 'What's in it for you?'

'Would it make it easier for you if there was something?'

Would it? Probably.

She lifted her shoulders as casually as she dared. 'Maybe.'

He laughed. A warm, rich sound which seemed to seep through her very bones like the sun on a gorgeously hot day.

'Fine. Then what if I told you that my extended family have backed off on the whole arranged marriage idea since word got back to them about me being at the gala with you.'

She *didn't* feel a tingle ripple through her. *She didn't.*

'Is that so?'

'It is.'

She waited for him to elaborate but he didn't. He was deliberately waiting for her to probe him. To show her hand. She wanted to hold her nerve, but curiosity won out—as galling as that was.

'Go on, then. I'll bite. *Why* isn't your mother insisting on an arranged marriage any more?'

'I guess because her endgame is for me to provide her with grandchildren. Whether she sets me up or I meet a future wife on my own terms is really neither here nor there to her.'

She could feel his words all over her. Sliding over her skin and slinking through her veins. He hadn't meant it like that, but she couldn't stop hearing the words echoing in her head, over and over...

His future wife. As if it could be her. As if she *wanted* it to be her.

She'd spent her whole life certain that she would never want that. People let each other down and betrayed each other—that was just human nature. They only wanted to know another person if there was something in it for themselves.

Except, perhaps, a very rare few—like Eleanor Jarvis, the closest thing Effie had ever had to a loving maternal figure. And look what had happened to *her*.

'What about sex?' she asked abruptly.

'Are you offering?'

That sinful curve of his mouth was almost her undoing. *'No!'*

'Relax. I'm teasing. No sex.'

'And kissing?'

She hoped her cheeks didn't flush as she recalled the spine-tingling kiss they'd shared outside her apartment door that night.

'Not even a superficial air-kiss,' he answered solemnly.

She narrowed her eyes. It sounded suspiciously as if he was teasing her.

'Good,' she offered at last.

She didn't even sound as if she believed herself. But if Tak wanted to offer her and Nell a roof over their heads, as long as his gain wasn't their downfall surely she could live with that?

'*This* is where he lives?' Nell whispered beside her as they both stood outside the house, staring up in undisguised shock. Suddenly she sounded small and...thirteen.

Their argument during the drive over here had been momentarily forgotten and Effie was grateful. She wasn't sure she had the energy for dealing with living in Tak's home as well as for another full-scale debate on why she was refusing to let her daughter attend the birthday party of a girl Effie had never met before.

Fortunately, the sight of the former seemed to have rather knocked the latter into the dirt, and Nell kept on staring up, her hand moving to clutch her mother's arm.

Effie didn't blame her. The place was imposing. Unquestionably huge and unfeasibly stunning. And yet somehow it was also surprisingly inviting.

How it achieved that Effie couldn't quite be sure, but the arresting building seemed to ooze the personality of its owner through every substantial wall, every imposing sheet of glass and every single breathtaking view of the lush countryside.

'It's like…like a castle or something.'

It wasn't. For a start it was far too modern, too sleek. But Effie could understand what her daughter meant. To a girl who had been brought up with as few material goods as Effie had been able to give her this must seem like something out of a fairy tale.

Heck, if it hadn't been for the unwelcome memories flooding her brain even to *her* it would have felt like something unbelievably enchanting and idyllic. But instead her stomach heaved and churned.

She felt like a thirteen-year-old herself, although *her* reactions were a lot more emotionally charged than her daughter's. How many times had she stood in a stranger's hallway, a battered duffel bag—which she'd held onto because somehow it reminded her of where she'd come from, and how hard she'd struggled to get to where she was now—in her hand, staring around at another person's home and plastering a stiff smile on her lips in gratitude that they were deigning to let her into it.

'It can't *all* be his, Mum. I bet they're luxury apartments and he just has one of them.'

Effie didn't agree, but before she could say anything the front door swung open. A man stood on the doorstep, looking down on them. He was about fifty years old, perhaps sixty, in a dark, neat suit, his shoes polished to within an inch of their lives, and his face neutral. Some might say carefully so.

'Dr Robinson? And this must be Miss Robinson.'

It took Effie a moment to realise that she should step forward. 'Um…yes. That's right. You can call me Effie, and this is Nell. And you are Mr Havers?'

'Just Havers,' he stated crisply. 'Now, *Dr Robinson*, allow me to show you and Miss Robinson around—unless you'd prefer to go directly to your wing? Mr Basu hopes that you will be comfortable here.'

'Our *wing*?' Nell whispered at her side as Havers gestured to invite them in. 'It really is just one big house?'

'Leave your luggage over there. I'll see that it's taken upstairs.'

'Thank you.' Effie gritted her teeth, cringing inwardly—their bags were hardly the designer luggage she suspected most women visiting this place used—and headed inside.

The tour progressed in a blur of one incredible space after another, so vast that her head was already beginning to spin and she had the impression that they were barely halfway through. It was a blessing and a curse when she heard footsteps tapping up the wooden hallway behind her and knew, without even turning around, that it would be Tak.

No one else made her body…*prickle* quite the way that he did. Right then she determined that she wouldn't turn around.

'Ah, there you are, Havers. Is it all going well?'

'Mr Basu!'

The genuine warmth in the older man's smile caught Effie by surprise.

'I wasn't expecting you back so soon. I thought this was your evening with your brother?'

'I'm sure Rafi can manage without me for one week. Besides, I thought I could finish the tour myself—no doubt you have plenty of other work you'd rather be getting on with.'

'As you wish.' The older man nodded sagely and began to take a step away.

Was it panic or something else that made Effie spin around in an instant? Either way, it was calamitous the way her heart clashed with her head in that moment. She was grateful that her head won out. Just.

'We're fine with Mr...with Havers,' she retorted primly.

But at exactly the same time her daughter boldly accepted Tak's offer.

'Then let us continue.' Tak grinned at Nell as though Effie herself hadn't even spoken.

And then her thirteen-year-old daughter straightened her shoulders and looked her host in the eye, as though she wasn't remotely intimidated by him or the situation. As though her momentary lapse into awe had never happened.

'We're fine,' Effie echoed, a little hollowly. 'We've seen enough already. We don't need to intrude on the rest of your home.'

'We do if we don't want to get lost,' Nell objected.

'We won't get lost.'

Her daughter's snort wasn't the most ego-boosting of responses.

'Let's be fair, Mum, you're geographically backward. Don't you remember that estate we lived on a few years ago? It took you almost ten months to work out which way led to the supermarket and which way led to the motorway.'

'The roads all looked the same,' Effie muttered.

Tak chuckled loudly. There was no reason at all for that smooth sound to ripple over her as it did.

Nell continued, oblivious. 'And here the corridors all look the same.' She blew out a faintly triumphant breath. 'So all the more reason to learn the layout. You don't want to go wandering into Tak's bedroom thinking it's your own, do you?'

Fire rushed through her and Effie yanked her head up sharply, but her daughter's expression was wholly innocent. Either Nell had a better poker face at thirteen than Effie herself had ever possessed, or she genuinely hadn't intended to sound so inappropriate.

Effie chose to believe the latter. Still, she couldn't stop her gaze sliding to Tak. Wondering if he'd caught on. Hoping that somehow he hadn't.

'We certainly can't have that, can we?'

His amusement was palpable, as though he was reading her mind. And that voice, as rich and indulgent as ever, meant the undercurrents inside her only sloshed around her all the more turbulently.

She straightened her spine. 'No, we cannot.'

Too prim. Too uptight. But too late now.

'So you live here all alone? Just you?'

'My other sister Sasha and my brother Rafi used to live here before they each got married, which was nice...' Tak shrugged, but his voice held that soft note she'd heard once before at the ball. 'But now it's mainly just me and Hetti.'

And then the moment was gone and Tak was smiling down at Nell.

'Anyway, what do you want to see next?' Tak grinned down at Nell. 'The cinema room, the pool, or the games den?'

There was no mistaking Nell's expression of awe, even if it *was* smothered in as neutral an expression as a thirteen-year-old girl could muster.

'What's in the games den?' Nell demanded with a grin of her own.

'Pool table, football table, two-lane bowling alley, some arcade machines.'

Nell's attempt at teenage blasé acceptance crumbled in an instant.

'Of course there is! You could fit our flat into this place ten times over. At least. You're so lucky, having a games room that you don't have to share with anyone else. You must be, like, a gazillionaire!'

'*Nell!*'

Instantly her daughter mumbled an apology, but Tak merely laughed.

'It isn't about that. My life is being a doctor—a surgeon. I don't always get enough time off and when I do it might not be the most sociable hours. Sometimes it's nice to have a place to come and wind down, even if it's four in the morning.'

'Chillax.' Nell nodded sagely. 'Mum could do with more of that.'

'*Mum* doesn't always have time for that,' Effie interjected pointedly, wishing they would stop talking about her as though she wasn't even there.

Not that it made much difference as she traipsed politely down a sweeping metal staircase and into a basement area. Tak swung open the door and both Nell and Effie were helpless to contain their shock.

It was like something out of those 'millionaires' cribs' shows her daughter was addicted to watching. All coloured LED strip-lighting, white stone floors and lots and lots of man-toys.

Table games dominated one zone: a pool table and table football, air hockey and table tennis. Arcade machines dominated another, with racing motorbikes and basketball hoops. A two-lane bowling alley ran the length of one side, and a full-size snooker table stood proudly in a section of its own.

Nell turned abruptly to eye Effie. 'I guess this is what you could have had if you'd just concentrated on your career and hadn't had to raise a baby all by yourself.'

'Not at all,' Effie choked, emotions rushing at her so violently that it was all she could do not to take a step back, as though that might somehow ward them off.

'The way she talks about you I can't imagine that your mother would trade you for any of...*this*.' Tak waved his hand around dismissively. 'You're the most important thing in her life—anyone can see that. And you must know that the only reason she's come here is because she's thinking about what's best for you. She would have suffered that igloo you call home indefinitely if it had just been her!'

There was a beat, then Nell scuffed her canvas shoe against the pristine stone floor. But all Effie could do was stare at the back of the head of this man—this relative stranger—who she was pretty sure she'd just heard defending her.

She told herself it meant nothing.

Inside her chest a heavy drum tattoo suggested otherwise.

'I know,' Nell muttered eventually. 'She's always put me first.'

Tak's smile was surprisingly soft. 'She's also your fiercest advocate.'

'Yeah, I know that too. Even if she can be a bit of a walkover in other areas.'

'I am *not* a walk-over,' Effie spluttered.

The pair ignored her, as though they were banding together to disprove her point without either of them saying a word.

It was the oddest sensation in the word. Nell and Tak, clicking together as if they'd known each other for years, not merely met on two brief occasions. Something swept through Effie and it took her a moment to realise it was regret tinged with perhaps a hint of guilt.

In trying to protect the two of them all these years— trying to do her best for her daughter—was it possible she had been wrong to deprive Nell of any male presence in her life? A role model if not a father figure?

Not Tak, of course, that would be bonkers—true bats in the belfry, as Eleanor would have said. But someone. There had been enough date offers over the years, even from men who had known she had a child.

Had she been selfish in not even trying? Claiming to be protecting her daughter from people dropping in and out of her life when actually she'd been protecting herself?

Effie shook her head almost imperceptibly and pulled her shoulders back. *No, she hadn't been selfish.* The simple truth was that no man had ever appealed to her enough for her to *want* to risk opening her life up for them. They hadn't been enough.

'Right.'

Tak's voice broke into her reverie.

'You've seen your wing and the main areas of the house. I'll leave you to settle in at your own pace. Havers is around if you need anything.'

And then he was gone, and Effie was staring at the doorway as though it might bring him back. It seemed all she had to do now was ignore the needling voice in her head pointing out to her that none of those men had been Tak Basu.

'You aren't going.' Effie was determined to remain steadfast, however torn she felt internally. 'It's a school night.'

It had been two days since Tak had left them to settle in. True to his word, their paths hadn't crossed since then, although between Havers and the rest of the staff she and Nell hadn't ever felt alone in the vast house.

But still, it was hard not to feel that their every move was being witnessed by someone. Especially when they were arguing.

As if to prove Effie's point, Nell glowered at her in disbelief. 'But it's her *birthday*.'

'So you already said. Several times.'

'I thought you *wanted* me to make friends,' Nell threw out, making no attempt to hide her frustration. 'You're the one who upended our lives by dragging us here.'

She shouldn't bite back—she knew that—but whether her daughter realised it or not it was a low blow. Guilt scraped at her. She *had* uprooted her daughter, she *was* always telling Nell she had to make new friends, and yet she *did* stop her from going anywhere on school nights.

Despite herself, Effie vacillated—and that lent her voice a sarcastic note she would have preferred it not to have. 'Yes, I'm *sorry* that getting a new job that earns more money and gives us a few luxuries has interfered with your social life.'

Nell tipped her nose into the air with all the authority of a teenager who knows everything. 'It's not just about money, Mum.'

'Says the thirteen-year-old who has never understood the fear of receiving an eviction notice.'

'My God, you're being unreasonable.'

'Who's being unreasonable?' Tak asked, sauntering into the kitchen as though Effie and Nell's rather public argument didn't perturb him in the slightest.

'I'm sorry. I didn't realise you were back from the hospital. We'll leave you in peace.'

'*Mum's* being unreasonable,' Nell announced, ignoring her.

'I'm sorry, this really doesn't have anything to do with

you—' Effie began, but she was drowned out by an indignant Nell.

'There's a girl at school and it's her birthday party tonight. A group of girls are going bowling at that big place just outside of town? You know—looks like your games suite downstairs, only bigger, and with a lot more people? Anyway, she's invited me, even though I'm new. It's a really big deal.'

Effie opened her mouth to respond, but Tak nudged her discreetly. She turned to him with a frown and then, although she couldn't explain why, decided to trust him.

'Are these the same girls you went shoplifting with?'

'You *told* him?' Nell swung around to her mother, her face on fire.

But once again Tak answered before Effie could say a word.

'Of course she did. She had to.' He shrugged calmly, as though it was obvious. 'Surely you know there are always consequences to your actions, Nell? I've opened up my home to you—it would have been wrong of her not to mention it.'

For several long seconds Nell continued to scowl at her. Then, to Effie's surprise and pride, she smoothed her face into an expression of acceptance and nodded. 'Yes, I know. And I am truly sorry for stealing. For what it's worth, I'll never make that mistake again.'

'That's good to hear,' Tak replied graciously. 'Nell, would you excuse your mother and I for a moment?'

Effie watched in shock as Nell nodded again, then obediently left the room. If it had been just herself and her daughter she knew Nell would have been like a dog with the proverbial bone.

CHAPTER EIGHT

'YOU'RE REALLY AGAINST her going?' Tak's low voice broke across Effie's thoughts as soon as the door clicked shut.

'I can guarantee I'm not the only mum who would be worried if she didn't know her daughter's new friends. In fact, I happen to know that a couple of the other mums are actually going. But I'm working. And I can't just change shifts at the air ambulance.'

Still, her conscience pricked her, as it seemed to be doing more and more these days. If this was what the next few years were going to be like with her daughter then she didn't think she could stand it.

'I'm just lucky that Havers is here and has generously promised to look after Nell the way Mrs Appleby does when she gets home from school.'

'So you aren't averse to Nell attending the party in general?' Tak asked suddenly.

'Of course not. Contrary to what you might have overheard before you walked in, I *do* actually want my daughter to make friends.'

'I know that,' he replied evenly.

Effie swallowed. She couldn't put her finger on what it was about the way he was looking at her, but in an instant the room seemed to fade away.

'This…this isn't about me,' she managed.

'I'll take that as confirmation.'

'Take it however you want,' she shot back, but even she could hear there was no heat in her tone. 'This is about

Nell and whether I'm deliberately stopping her from going to a party.'

'And you're adamantly trying to show that you aren't?'

'Of course I'm not,' Effie bristled. 'If I knew she was going to be safe that would be different. But I don't know any of these girls and I can't be there because of work.'

'In that case, what if *I* took Nell to the party?'

It was surreal. Effie stared at Tak, unsure what to say. Was he really offering to parent her child, reasoning with her as though it was the most natural thing in the world?

'I don't think it's a good idea,' she said slowly. 'I mean, people might get the wrong impression.'

'You mean, people might actually think there's something going on between you and I?' Tak rolled her eyes. 'As if the fact you're staying here doesn't already do that?'

There was no reason her heart should be slamming into the wall of her chest like this.

Effie sucked in a deep breath, not that it helped. 'We're only staying here until our central heating is fixed and the asbestos is removed.' But she floundered. Temptation was vying with common sense. 'It's... Well... Are you sure?'

'I offered,' he pointed out. 'I only have one condition.'

'Condition?'

He smiled, and that delicious curl of his mouth, which made her chest leap and burst like popcorn in a microwave, made Effie narrow her eyes.

She told herself it was nerves that she felt and not anticipation that coursed through her.

His mouth curled up even more sinfully. 'I need you to come on another date with me.'

Pins and needles scattered through her body. Heat and cold. Dark and light. Exhilaration and fear.

It didn't matter how long she might stay there, scanning his face and trying to analyse what was going on in his mind, he was too closed-off, too controlled.

'A date?'

'Yes. You know—two people getting together for a social activity where romance is a distinct possibility.'

She frowned. 'Or, in our case, the pretence of romance?'

He paused, and for one glorious moment she thought he was going to deny it.

'Of course,' he confirmed, and something darted over his features, too fast for Effie to work out what it was.

Probably relief. Which, she told himself, was just fine.

'I thought we might go to a restaurant frequented by some contacts of my parents. News of our date—and no doubt the odd phone photo—will have made its way across two continents before Chef Michel's world-renowned soufflé can even be served.'

'I thought that was what our gala date was supposed to have been about?'

'It was.'

He shrugged, as though he wasn't remotely affected by this conversation. And, of course, she reminded herself hastily, neither was she.

'But that was a work thing. This is a private date. It will consolidate the image of us as a proper couple.'

A proper couple. The notion affected her exactly the way it shouldn't have done. Yet somehow she managed a curt nod. As one might acknowledge a point of fact in the operating theatre. Or the boardroom.

And it *wasn't* disillusionment which rumbled through her. Of course it wasn't.

The restaurant was excruciatingly romantic.

Intimate tables for two were dotted under a starry sky in one of the most booked-out restaurants in the city. Exactly as he'd planned. A place to see and be seen, just as he wanted. A set-up guaranteeing that word would get back to anyone in his family who hoped they could use him in a marriage arranged only to further their own agendas.

And yet all Tak wanted to do was lift Effie out of her chair and get out of there. To somewhere far more discreetly intimate. Where it would be just the two of them.

He fought to tune out the loved-up diners around them and concentrate instead as Effie chatted to him conversationally. He hadn't brought her here tonight to seduce her, or to further any romantic entanglement, so why was it that all he could think was that he wanted to taste her lips again, the way he had the night of the hospital gala?

'So *that's* what brought Nell and I halfway across the country,' Effie concluded.

He let his eyes linger a little too long on her mouth, fighting the impulse to lean right across the table and scoop her up, settle her on his knee and lick every inch of that smooth, elegant neck with his tongue. To hell with all the people, all the camera phones around them.

'That's a fascinating but I fear highly diluted story of what brought you to the air ambulance.' He hadn't intended his voice to sound so raw, so raspy, but she had him on edge tonight. Even more than usual.

Effie flushed, sucking in her bottom lip in a way that shot right through his body.

'I don't know what you mean,' she said.

'I think you do. You haven't really told me a single thing about you.' He had no idea why it even mattered, and yet the words kept coming. 'My few questions about your childhood were met with a wave and a comment that it was just like everyone else's—fairly standard. When I enquired after your family you smiled prettily and pointed out that in a job like ours we're so busy we never get to see people as much as we would like.'

'I don't see what's wrong with that.' She leaned back in her chair defensively.

'They weren't particularly intrusive questions, Effie. Just the usual kind of questions when two people are getting to know each other on a date.'

'Well…' She shrugged awkwardly, as though looking for an excuse, babbled on as soon as she thought she'd found one. 'Well, this isn't a date, is it? You said it yourself—it's just shoring up the falsehood of our being in a relationship to distract your extended family from pushing the idea of an arranged marriage.'

Yes, he *had* said that, hadn't he? Tak clenched his fist, unseen. The problem was, even at the time he had known that wasn't true. Even in that moment when he'd asked her on a date a part of him had known that it was because he'd genuinely wanted to take her out.

Fooling his extended family was merely an added bonus, a justification. Though whether for Effie's benefit or for his own, he couldn't be sure.

And so all through the meal he'd felt his frustration growing as she fed him her all too practised response, telling him the carefully crafted version of her life that she wanted him to hear.

Nothing more, nothing less. Certainly not the truth. Nothing that would help him to understand the real Effie.

And he realised with a jolt that he *wanted* to know the real Effie. More than that, he *needed* to know the real Effie. Even if he couldn't understand why any more than he could understand why, as he'd listened to her prepared formulaic story, he'd let her soft, lilting voice distract him into imagining that mouth doing so many other things. Imagining her in his bed. As though he was some kind of hormone-ravaged teenager.

It was galling. He didn't *want* to want her, and yet since she'd swept into his life he'd felt as though everything he'd carefully built up around himself had been knocked down.

And the solid foundations he'd thought he'd put down were now shown up for little more than wet sand.

From the instant Hetti had thrown Effie into his path as his plus one he'd been entranced. He could dress it up any way he wanted, label it with any number of excuses, but the unavoidable truth was that Effie made him hard, and greedy, and savage. And he wanted her with an intensity that was almost suffocating.

All the things his father had claimed to feel about every one of his mistresses when he had rubbed them in the face of Tak's mother. The old man had never shown an ounce of respect for his wife or for his children. And he hadn't had a shred of self-control over his own vices. His father had been selfish right to his very core.

Fury and self-disgust flooded Tak's body. He'd spent his entire life trying not to be like his father—*ensuring* he wouldn't be like him by avoiding any kind of serious relationship. Which wasn't to say he hadn't enjoyed casual relationships...girlfriends lasting a few months...good sex.

But nothing had come even remotely close to this... *hunger* gnawing inside him ever since Effie Robinson had walked into his life. He wanted her. In the most primal way that a man could want a woman. He *wanted* her. *Only* her. And he couldn't pretend otherwise any longer.

'Why did you agree to accompany me to the hospital ball that night, Effie?' His voice was harsh, commanding, yet he still couldn't read the expression which flitted across her face.

'You know why. This is a new place for me...there are men who view my single status as a challenge, and I have a daughter who is the sole focus of my life. Fake dating you was the quickest way to make anyone else back off, and when we "break up" I get to pretend that I'm not dating because I'm not over you.'

'You have it all worked out, don't you?' He ran a finger

around the rim of his wine glass, if only to stop himself from reaching over the table and touching her.

'As much as you do,' Effie hedged, with that inscrutable darkness shadowing her eyes again.

'Except that you've made me curious about you. I want to know why you're so untrusting of people. Of men.'

'It isn't just about men,' she answered—too quickly, not realising she was giving herself away until it was too late.

There was no reason for it to feel like such a victory. And yet he leapt on it all the same. 'Everyone, then. Why?'

'That isn't what I meant.' She flushed crossly.

'It isn't what you meant to *say*, no. But it *is* what you meant. Deep down.'

'I thought tonight was about giving a convincing show?' she bit out. 'Not about delving into areas of each other's lives which are best left unexplored.'

It had been. Only he'd changed the rules. Unfairly, perhaps, but he hadn't been able to help himself. It seemed his usual sense of boundaries was slipping, sliding away from him. Certainly where Effie was concerned.

Why would he have offered to take Nell to that party if not because he wanted to make Effie happy? To show him she needed him?

Why?

The realisation hit him hard and low, and something gathered inside him, gaining momentum, and power, and a voice. So loud that it howled inside him with all the truths that it brought.

It was one thing to want Effie physically. Sexually. But it was quite another to sit here, in this restaurant, in the middle of this *performance*, and realise that he wanted more. That he wanted her on an emotional level, too.

He wanted to know about her life and her family, about what had happened to mould her and shape her, about every single event which had led up to her and her daughter living in that awful flat in that awful building.

He wanted to know her, *truly* know her, and to understand her. And he wanted to tell her all the things he'd never been able to tell anyone in his life before. Not even Hetti.

The urge was almost overwhelming. He even opened his mouth to speak. But nothing came out. An internal struggle was going on inside him and it was as though he was floating outside his own body, able only to watch. Never to intervene.

Somehow he managed to rein himself back in. Curb himself. Stifle this insane compulsion which had come out of nowhere.

But it cost him. He couldn't talk to Effie. Not about any of it. He would never be able to do that. Because if he did then it would mean he was putting his own selfish desires ahead of what he knew to be best for others. Just like his father had done.

He knew the pattern. He'd seen it so many times before, and each time he'd watched it rip out another little piece of his mother's soul.

Once this initial fervour wore off—and whether that was in a month, six months, a year, much as it felt impossible now, he knew it would happen, it was inexorable, just as his father had always said—he would end up letting Effie down. Hurting her. Betraying her.

Yes, he knew the pattern. He'd just never imagined he'd be the one copying it. It was madness and it had to stop.

He had to stop it. *Now*.

'Are you all right?'

Effie peered at Tak and tried to control her racing heart. The entire evening had been unsettling, from the fancy restaurant to Tak's too-close-to-home questions. In all her life she had never found it so hard to recite her practised lies. Never before had she felt such a desperate yearning to throw away her mask and finally let somebody see the real Effie.

But what if Tak hated that person? What if he hated the mess, the ugliness that was her past? And it was so very, *very* ugly. There was no dressing it up and passing it off as something palatable.

An ache pooled deep in her belly as she watched Tak through lowered lashes. He looked more incredible than ever tonight, in that sleek, smart-casual suit. A lesson in sheer male perfection—all hard lines and intriguing shadows. Solid and utterly, devastatingly imposing.

And he was all *hers*.

At least he was pretending to be.

And that was the irony of it, wasn't it? They were out in public so that they could fool other people, but the person most at risk of falling for the charade was herself.

'I'm quite well, thank you.'

His rich voice glided over her skin like silk.

'Did you imagine otherwise?'

'You seem…distracted,' she offered, before correcting herself. 'On edge.'

'On the contrary, I'm feeling very much at ease in your company.'

It wasn't so much the way he said it—in that throwaway style of his, as though it was an easy compliment but didn't mean very much at all. It was more the way his eyes darkened sinfully, possessively, almost as though against his will.

Her pulse beat out a thrilled tattoo. She could feel it thrumming in her neck. And she could feel it thrumming somewhere altogether more intimate.

Everywhere Tak went people turned their heads to watch him, to admire him. He inspired admiration and envy alike, and his renowned career made him a man to hold in the highest esteem.

But when he looked at her like that he made Effie feel as though she was the only thing in the world that he saw. The only woman he would ever want. And when he laughed it was as if he'd shot her through with a thousand bright volts. It was heady, and intoxicating, and utterly, completely dangerous.

Because it made her forget that this was all simply a game.

'So, what's the plan? We've been here an hour already. Do you think the news will have got back to your family, or do we need to do something more memorable?'

'More memorable?' he arched an eyebrow. 'What, exactly?'

'I don't know!' Effie chuckled, for no obvious reason but that he made her feel happy. 'Maybe… Well, perhaps… Hmm…

'Causing a scene about the food before sending it back?' he speculated, making Effie gasp.

'No. That would be horrible! The staff—goodness the chef!'

'Why doesn't that surprise me? I imagine you're the kind of person who smiles and says the meal is lovely even if it truly is ghastly.'

She knew she looked sheepish. She certainly felt sheepish. 'I suppose that is what I do,' she conceded. 'Not that I dine out often, that is.'

'Perhaps we should do something about that.' He laughed, and then, before she could ask him what he'd meant by that, he changed the subject. 'So, if not memorable that way, then how?'

It made no sense that her heart should be beating so hard. And this time when she smiled it didn't feel quite so easy. 'I don't know. Forget I said anything.'

'Do you suppose I should stand up and come around the table? Haul you into my arms before kissing you? Not a light peck, you understand, but a thorough, unmistakable kiss, designed to conquer rather than simply confide.'

'No!' she denied, even though every fibre of her was screaming that she was lying. 'Of course that isn't what I was saying.'

And then she swallowed. Hard. It was a fatal mistake.

Tak's eyes snapped to her throat, then locked onto her gaze, and it was as though she was laid bare and he could read every inch of her soul. Could appreciate every last one of her darkest desires.

All of which seemed to centre around him.

'You *do* want me to do that,' he declared, and she might have believed that he had not truly thought so before. That a part of him even welcomed the revelation.

But then his expression turned hard, cold. 'I was given to understand that you don't want a relationship with anyone. It was one of the reasons I agreed to take you to the ball as my plus one.'

She felt as if he had stamped his foot into her chest and crushed it down. Later, when she actually thought about it, she still wouldn't understand how she didn't crumple with shame right there in front of him.

'You *invited* me as your date to the ball because it was mutually convenient. We were each other's buffers and we played our roles to perfection.'

'Yet now here you are...wanting more.'

She could feel the heat spreading across her neck, her cheeks, but she lifted her head and refused to be intimidated. 'I have never suggested I want more. *You* are the one who insisted Nell and I couldn't stay in our flat. *You* are the one who was so quick to open your door to us. And *you* are the one who has been interrogating me about my past and my family all evening. Almost as though you're interested.

Perhaps I might suggest that this unexpected talk of kissing is more a reflection of *your* state of mind than mine.'

It had been a ruse. An attempt to bat the proverbial ball back into his court. Effie certainly hadn't expected her words to elicit any reaction—and certainly not one that suggested her words might not be as fantastical as she had thought them to be.

She watched, fascinated, as he scowled, and his eyes glittered almost black as he sat unnaturally still—rigid, even—in his seat. Her words had hit a target she hadn't even known existed.

'I'm right…' she breathed, almost in awe. 'You want me.'

His mouth flattened, and his glower was enough to intimidate even the boldest of women, but Effie stood her ground even as the blood roared in her ears.

And then, unexpectedly, the frown cleared and he eyed her in a way which was far more threatening—for it was pure desire and unrestrained hunger.

'You're right. I do want you,' he murmured at length. 'Just as you want me.'

She opened her mouth to deny it again, then snapped it shut. What was the point in lying? She didn't even know who she'd be lying to most. Tak or herself.

'Therefore why not embrace it? Use it to our advantage?'

'Use it?' she echoed, not following.

'Use this sexual attraction, this chemistry…'

His mouth curled into something so spectacularly sinful that she could feel the heat blooming through her very core.

'And fool everyone into thinking there is something really serious between us.'

'You mean, pretend…*more*?' she asked.

'I mean, pretend less,' he growled.

It took her a moment before the full implication of what Tak meant hit home.

Effie gasped. 'You mean, give in to this…this physical

thing between us?' Her voice sounded too raw, too naked. 'Indulge? Have…have sex, or whatever, and let the rest of the world draw their own conclusions?'

'I'm curious,' he said almost idly. 'What's the *whatever*?'

She shook her head, confused. 'Pardon?'

'You said, *"have…sex, or whatever"*. I want to know what the *whatever* is? It sounds deliciously naughty.'

His lips curved licentiously and he made no attempt to hide his amusement. Effie's entire body trembled—and not, she feared, with disgust.

'You're being deliberately provocative,' she accused shakily.

'Is that a problem?'

'It's…aggravating.'

'Is that so?' Tak demurred. 'Any time you think I have it wrong, be sure to let me know and I shall stop at once.'

And there it was. The way to put this entire evening back twenty-four hours, to make it clear that she wasn't interested in anything other than a pretend show. All she had to do was tell him he was wrong.

Instead, she deflected. 'This all started because I asked you if you needed a scene to ensure word of our date got back to your family.'

'I remember,' he agreed, a little too knowingly. 'And *I* asked if you meant me to kiss you.'

'I told you I didn't.'

'Which I believe we've already established was a lie. We appear to be going around in circles, *priya*.' Abruptly he stood up, dark and intent. 'Allow me to break the cycle.'

She knew what he was doing even before he moved around the table. She ought to say something. She had to stop him. Instead she raised her hands slightly to meet his as he drew her out of her seat.

And then she was pressed against his body. Soft heat against inflexible steel. White-hot explosions in her body competed with the thrilling fireworks in her head. She was like a coiled spring, held under tension, and it was all the more unbearable as Tak lowered his mouth to hers and held it there. Refusing to close that gap completely. The heat of his breath on her lips was driving her delirious with longing.

'Do you think they've had a good enough show?' he pondered.

'Hmm...?'

'The other diners. Will they have their phones out yet?'

She might have been insulted, but she heard the crack in his voice and knew he was only holding on by the skin of his teeth.

'Good point.' She stopped, as though to consider, although it nearly killed her. 'A little longer, I think.'

Her reward was a rumble of disapproval from Tak before he lowered his head to claim her lips.

The kiss was every bit as electrifying as their first one outside her apartment door. Had it only been ten days ago? It felt like a lifetime. Or a life sentence. Perhaps because she'd been waiting her entire life for a kiss like this. For a man like this.

She forgot completely where they were, or the game they had been playing. All she knew was Tak, and the way he was kissing her. She was drowning in him all over again, pouring herself into him as she moulded every inch of her body to his.

All that subtle flirting, all those heady glances, all that repressed desire was unleashed in this single moment. As though it would never end.

He plundered her mouth, demanding and devouring with every scandalous swipe of his tongue and every luscious graze of his teeth. And Effie was all too happy to lose herself in the lustiness of it all.

Right up until the moment he moved his hands to her shoulders and pushed her back.

'I cannot do this,' he ground out, his face twisted into something she didn't recognise.

'Tak...'

'I cannot do this,' he repeated quietly. Obdurately. 'With you, least of all.'

Effie was wholly unprepared for the pain as the words sliced through her. A lifetime of being told, directly or indirectly, that she wasn't good enough—that *she* wasn't enough—flooded through her. Hateful and merciless. She'd thought she'd buried her past a long, long time ago. Yet one utterance from Tak and instantly she felt like that pathetic, rejected girl she'd never really left behind.

Grief blinded her, but she knew the one thing she couldn't afford to do was let Tak see it.

With Herculean resolve, Effie turned slowly and forced herself to take her time picking up her clutch. She would not run out of here. She would not turn and flee with her tail between her legs like some unwanted, abandoned puppy.

'Well, then...' She cleared her throat, amazed at how collected she'd managed to sound. 'That settles that debate, doesn't it?'

And she turned and stalked off, head held high, out of the restaurant and into a parked taxi before Tak had even moved a muscle.

Her tears could wait until she was alone. The way they always had.

CHAPTER NINE

'THAT SOUNDS LIKE an emphatic crack,' Tak approved, as he carefully lifted out a section of his patient's skull and began to clear away the dura to expose her brain. 'Okay, we have good access to the temporal lobe now, and the tumour is hiding in there. Time to map her brain, so go ahead and wake her up.'

He waited as his co-pilot and the anaesthetist worked together to bring the patient to the level of awareness he would need her to have in order to carry out his language tests as he passed a series of electrical currents over her brain to map it.

The lull was unwelcome. It created a void in the operation and allowed his own brain the chance to reflect on things he would rather not have to mull over.

Like the way everything had changed when he'd touched Effie, held her, kissed her last night.

One minute they'd been playing some kind of game, and the next he had completely taken leave of his senses. Felt the same kind of madness taking hold of him that he had always despised in his selfish, ruthless father. The man who had taken such delight in telling his wife time and again that his latest mistress made him feel alive in a way that Tak's mother never could.

The same kind of selfishness that Rafi had shown, taking a mistress of his own and believing it was perfectly normal even though he'd seen how it had devastated their mother. Worse, Rafi had said contemptuously that Uma

Basu—he hadn't called her Mama since he'd turned fifteen—was foolish, emotional, even irrational. That her depressions and addictions were of her own making, and even that they excused their father for needing to find companionship elsewhere, rather than it being his father's actions causing Uma's devastation.

Tak couldn't say he thought his brother was entirely wrong—their mother *was* quite the master manipulator—though what had come first, her machinations or his father's cruelty, was a question he couldn't answer.

Either way, he'd spent his whole life avoiding being like either his father or his brother. He'd thought he'd succeeded. His relationships had always been fine. He had sated his physical and emotional desires without ever feeling as though he wasn't in control.

Until last night. Or, more accurately, until Effie.

He could no longer deny the attraction which had been evident between them since that first meeting. Or the fact that he'd been acting irrationally since the hospital gala—not least when he'd commanded her to pack her bags and move herself and her daughter into his home.

He could couch it in whatever terms he liked—Effie needing somewhere to live or him wanting to distract his mother from her obsession with arranging a marriage for him—but ultimately it all came down to the fact that he'd wanted an excuse to spend more time with Effie. To indulge this attraction which had slid so insidiously into his entire body.

'Madeleine, can you hear me?'

As the neurologist dropped down behind the sheets Tak switched quickly back to the task in hand.

'Can you open your eyes for me, Madeleine? Good. Now, can you stick out your tongue for me?'

Working quickly and efficiently, Tak moved the electric current over different areas of his patient's brain. As the tests went on, through actions and various language tests, he could work out which parts of Madeleine's brain were responsible for key activities and try to avoid these areas when he moved in to try to remove the tumour.

They were partway through the first series of exercises, the reciting of the alphabet, when the neurologist signalled to him to slow down.

'Okay, Tak.' Her voice carried low but clear. 'We have some problems in this area.'

'Understood.' Tak nodded to his colleague.

It seemed as though they were near a vital speech area of Madeleine's brain, from where he would be unable to remove the tumour. But they were only a short while into the operation and their patient was already becoming increasingly tired, finding it harder and harder to stay awake.

He had ideally anticipated three hours' brain-mapping for this size tumour, but they were barely ninety minutes in. If they didn't work quickly Tak risked missing out on the vital brain-mapping information that would enable him to remove the tumour without compromising their patient's brain function.

It was the kind of challenge which spurred him on—even more so today, when he didn't want to think about anything but his work.

If only everything in his life could be pigeonholed so damned easily.

For several almost blissful hours Tak concentrated on his surgery.

And the next. And the next.

Yet the minute he was out of the operating room, and his shift was over, his brain was flooded afresh with images of Effie. They had been becoming more and more insistent all week. Ever since he'd taken Effie on that disastrous date, since he'd taken Effie's daughter to that bowling alley.

He had no idea what it was about Effie—about wanting to make the woman happy—that had possessed him to volunteer to chaperone her kid at a party. Not that it had been a chore. The girl had chattered non-stop, even whilst climbing into his sleek, muscular super-car. Undisguised happiness had danced off her every word, and as far as she was concerned the evening had been a resounding success.

Just as undisguised happiness had danced around in *him* at the idea that he was doing something for Effie, making her life a little easier.

Nell had been happy. Which meant that Effie was happy. Because her happiness was intrinsically linked with that of her daughter. It was sweet.

When the hell had he ever cared about anything *sweet*? But it mattered to him. *She* mattered. Yet he had no explanation for why. He didn't even stop to consider it. Deliberately.

He didn't want to dig into his emotions or responses. He didn't wish to ask himself why he had practically jumped at the chance to insert himself deeper into Effie's family life. He hadn't allowed himself to ask any one of the hundreds of questions which charged around his head.

He told himself that the only reason he'd insisted they stayed with him was because it would have been inhumane to knowingly leave mother and daughter in that freezing flat. He refused to acknowledge that it had anything to do with the kick which had reverberated around his body that first time he'd seen her stride into Resus. Or the fire which had ripped through him when he'd walked into that lobby to see her standing there so regally. Not to mention the passion that had later flared between them on that restaurant date.

It made no sense. Perhaps it was because he knew that soon Effie would be gone and life would revert back to normal.

The knowledge should please him. Not make him feel as though a weight was pressing down inside his chest.

It was the familiarity of it all, he concluded eventually. It was simply that he was drawing parallels between Effie's life, caring for her only just teenage daughter, with *his* life growing up, when he had often had sole responsibility for his younger teenage siblings, Hetti and Sasha. And Rafi too, for that matter, although he'd barely been nine at that time.

He remembered those feelings of loneliness and being scared, especially when his mother had been going through one of her episodes.

But wasn't that part of the issue? He and Effie had agreed to be each other's buffers. Nothing more. She wasn't supposed to be making him take trips down memory lane. He certainly wasn't supposed to be playing at happy families and helping out with her daughter.

Was he somehow giving her the impression that there was something between them? Playing with Effie's emotions in much the same way that his father had always so cruelly toyed with his mother's feelings? Surely it was a case of *like father like son.* Rafi had definitely suggested that was the case with his own wife.'

'I'm not our father,' Tak growled to himself, but the accusation pounded through him, making the blood heat in his veins.

Abruptly he realised he was outside the hospital and at his car, with no memory of how he'd even got there. He hit the ignition button, revved the engine, and pulled neatly out of the parking bay and onto the road beyond. He'd go for a drive. A long, fast drive in his prized car—the kind of vehicle which wasn't at all conducive to a man with a wife and kids. It would clear his head and remind him of exactly what he wanted his life to look like.

And it wasn't settling down. Because what if he was wrong? What if he *was* like his father, much as it might gall him? If there was any chance he was like that man, then

Tak knew he would inevitably hurt his family, exactly the way his own father had hurt his.

Which was why he couldn't go home. Not with Effie and Nell there. Reminding him of the family he could never have. That life wasn't for him, and the sooner he remembered that, the better.

It was the early hours of the morning when Tak returned home, his head finally clear. Or at least as clear as it was going to get.

He still hadn't solved the puzzle that was Dr Effie Robinson, or why she so intrigued him. But he *had* convinced himself that he didn't have time for riddles and games.

Their original agreement—to play each other's buffer at the hospital gala—had worked perfectly. The rest of it was unnecessary complications which they should have avoided. That date at the restaurant should have been avoided. The kisses certainly should have been avoided.

But the beauty of it was that as soon as the central heating was fixed in Effie's flat and the asbestos was gone, *she* would be gone. And he could pretend all this had never happened.

In the meantime, sleep was certainly going to elude him.

Tak wandered down to the games suite.

The last person he'd expected to see there was Effie. And he certainly hadn't expected to see her, cue in hand, making the perfect pool game break, as though she was some kind of hustler.

He stopped, ridiculously enchanted all over again. Just like that.

It was only when he watched her pot the final black that he realised he'd watched her play an entire game. Lurking in the shadows like some kind of admirer from afar. Like some kind of adolescent kid.

'I didn't know you played,' he said, stepping out into the room.

She jumped, as if he'd caught her red-handed.

He made a mental note to get the lighting in the room changed. It had been designed to be ambient, but right now he didn't like the way the soft glow bounced off the walls, making the place feel so cosy, so…intimate. Yet ironically making him feel just that little bit too exposed.

He could put it down to the time of night—*bewitched at the witching hour*. But that suggested a ridiculous fancifulness with which he wasn't commonly associated.

'I don't play nowadays, but that doesn't mean I can't play.'

'So I've just witnessed. Misspent youth?' He quirked an eyebrow.

'You could say that.'

Her tone was casual. Perhaps too casual.

'Sounds intriguing.'

'It isn't,' she bit out, and he hated it that there was such a divide between them now. Especially when he knew he was the one who had created it, with that kiss the other night.

He should walk away. But not for the first time he stayed still instead. 'I owe you an apology.'

She grimaced.

'I should not have kissed you the other night. Perhaps I shouldn't have even taken you there.'

It was as if a hurricane was raging around them, but in the eye of it there was simply stillness. A hush.

'You didn't force my hand,' she said at length, gritting her teeth. 'And at least I now know where we stand. What you really think of me.'

'What I really think of you?' He frowned, but she merely turned away.

Clearly Effie didn't want to elaborate, and he tried to convince himself that he didn't care. This was exactly what he'd spent the last few hours repeating to himself. *It…she…*

wasn't his business. When it came to Effie there *wasn't* something clawing inside him, desperate to find its way out.

But, despite everything he'd thought during that exhilarating drive, nothing compared to this unexpected wallop of insatiable need. This urge to learn more about this surprisingly enigmatic woman, even as a part of him knew she would never tell him.

'Effie, I shouldn't have kissed you because of *my* reasons. Nothing to do with you. Not really.'

'Is this the old *it's not me, it's you*?' She turned on him instantly, her voice a little too bright, too high, too tight. 'Only I've heard that a hundred times before.'

He wasn't prepared for the jealousy which sliced through him.

'Is that why you reacted the way you did? And why you don't date? Because some idiot bloke—Nell's father, maybe—once used that cliché and hurt you?'

'You think this is about some *guy*?' She shook her head incredulously. 'That I would carry around something so banal and frankly inconsequential for thirteen years?'

'Then *what*?'

She stared at him, and then suddenly she wasn't seeing him any more—she was staring right through him.

'What is it that I don't understand about you, Effie?' he asked softly. 'You're intelligent and driven and beautiful. You're career-minded and you have Nell—I know that—but why are you so insistent on doing everything alone? On making sure no one ever gets close? You get more than your fair share of male attention but you shut every bit of it down before you can even think about giving it a chance.'

She flattened her lips together, clearly not about to answer him. He knew if he pushed her she would only shut down all the faster.

'I'll leave you to your game,' he managed softly, turning around to leave. Pretending that, for all the difficult things he'd had to do in his life, walking away from Effie wasn't one of the hardest.

Whether it was the hour, or the quiet, or the windowless nature of the games den which made it feel as if they were totally disconnected from the rest of the world, he couldn't be sure. But he heard her as she carefully placed the pool cue down on the table.

'Tak, wait.'

He turned and came back down a couple of steps. Effie was staring at the rich burgundy baize and it took Herculean strength for him not to speak. He couldn't remember the last time he'd wanted to know something about a woman so badly. So desperately. But she had to open up to him voluntarily. If he pushed her then she was likely to shut down again.

For long moments the quiet swirled around them, like the soft artificial smoke rising on the stage in one of the shows he'd taken his mother to see during her visits.

Tak had a feeling they were the only times Mama had got to do something *she* liked for a change. Even now his father would never deign to give her an hour of his time for something he termed so *terminally dull.*

'I'm sorry.' Effie seemed to brace herself. 'It's more about my childhood than some stupid lad—it wasn't exactly conventional. Anyway, it was wrong of me to take it out on you.'

She was trying to relegate her outburst to the past. But he wasn't about to let her. It was the closest he'd come to seeing the real Effie.

'What was so different about it?'

'Please, can we just leave it at that?'

'Is this why you don't talk about your family?'

'I don't *have* a family,' she burst out before checking herself.

Pursing her lips, she inhaled and exhaled heavily through her nose. And still he held himself still. Silent.

'I had a mother—some of the time—but I spent a lot of time in and out of children's homes and foster families.'

'You were a foster kid?'

'On and off. Not enough to be given a family of my own, but enough that I spent most of my childhood shunted in and out of other people's homes. I grew up resenting everything. Not least the fact that my mother couldn't get herself together enough to keep me safe whilst other kids were complaining that their mums had given them cheese sandwiches for lunch again when they'd wanted ham.'

If she'd punched him in the guts he couldn't have felt any more winded. Effie had been a foster kid? She was so not what he might have expected of one. Although now he thought about it he had no idea what that might have been.

He was only grateful that she continued.

'You know one of the worst things about it? You always feel like you're nothing and no one. And the older you get, the fewer families want you. Because they think you're going to give them attitude. And maybe it's true. But that's only because you're always made to feel like you should show more gratitude.'

'Gratitude?'

'Yes. And I *was* grateful—inside. But I also hated the fact that this was my life, so it was hard to be grateful when you saw what other kids—normal kids—got. So many foster families acted as though I should be doing cartwheels up and down the street in gratitude for a safe place to sleep, a warm bed, food on the table. It just reminded me of how different I was, because those were things that normal kids wouldn't even think twice about.'

'Is that why you were so resistant to take up my offer to come here?' he asked quietly, unable to help himself. 'Why you balked at my spending all that money at the silent auction?'

As her jaw set, her eyes going a steely grey as though

she was shutting down, he mentally kicked himself for allowing the words to come out of his mouth. She was going to pull even further away from him now. The knowledge saddened him far more than it had any right to do.

CHAPTER TEN

Tak was about to leave again when Effie suddenly hunched her shoulders lightly and—incredibly—answered him. Even if it sounded as though her mouth was struggling to form every single syllable.

'I guess. Yes.'

He waited a little longer, not about to make the same mistake again by pushing her.

Still, it felt like an eternity before she rewarded him by elaborating, 'It was the way you didn't think twice about what would happen if you won all those lots. You could just…*pay*. I spent so many years worrying where my next meal came from even before Nell came along.'

'You've done an incredible job,' he pointed out.

'I guess…'

Effie dipped her head slightly, and he was gratified that the words didn't sound quite as stiff and awkward now. Almost as if she was beginning to trust him.

'My flat might not be anything compared to this, but it's mine. At least I pay the rent. I keep a roof over my kid's head. I keep her warm and fed and happy, and I give her the things she needs. I suppose I felt as though coming here was an admission that I wasn't a good enough mother.'

'That boiler breaking down and your crappy landlord are no reflection on your ability as a mother.'

'But they *are*.' She lifted her head finally to meet his gaze and Tak stepped down the last couple of steps. 'At least they feel as though they are. If I could afford somewhere better, a house of our own, I wouldn't have to rely on some landlord. Or even if I could afford a better apartment closer to the helicopter base. Or even a car I could rely on if I lived further out.'

'Effie, you've raised a child from the age of eighteen and managed to get through medical school—and not just at *any* university, but one of the top places in the world— as well as forge a career as a trauma doctor. You've proved yourself a good mother over and over again.'

'And yet you've just walked in and seen me playing pool and I feel like a teenage kid caught red-handed again.'

Red-handed? Tak frowned. 'You weren't allowed to go to youth club and shoot pool when you were a kid?'

'It wasn't a youth club.'

A red stain crept over her skin and yet she kept talking to him. It suddenly occurred to him that this was Effie trusting him.

'It was an adult snooker hall. When things were bad at home, or a foster home, it was sometimes better to be elsewhere. It was safer—and warmer—than a park bench.'

'You slept on a park bench?'

'A few times,' she shrugged, and he wondered what that meant.

Once? Five times? Twenty?

'One night I realised I could sneak into the club and hang out in the warmth until at least two in the morning when it closed.'

'How old were you?'

'At that time? I guess about thirteen. The same age that Nell is now.'

Tak's fists clenched, and it was all he could do not to identify the emotion which charged through him in that moment. 'And no one noticed you?'

'The owner did.'

She shrugged, as though it was no big deal. As though

she didn't feel any of the anger which constricted his chest, choking off his ability to breathe with ease. He couldn't have spoken if he'd wanted to. All he could do was listen and wonder why it rattled him so much. Why *this woman's* past got under his skin as it did.

'But she turned a blind eye at first—except for warning some of the guys that if they went near me she'd kill them. Then, when my mum started going through her bad spells, and they became more frequent than not, she put a couch in a back office with what she called "leftovers". She said it was hers, but that I could use it if she wasn't in there.'

'Let me guess—she only put it there for you to use?' His smile was bittersweet.

The woman's kindness was touching, but the fact that Effie's childhood had necessitated it was saddening. But for the circumstance of money they had both suffered because of weak mothers. How easily could this have been *his* life or his life been Effie's?

'Right.' Effie lifted her head a little, as if she was making a point of not letting her memories pull her back under. 'We both knew what she was doing, but neither of us ever said it aloud.'

'So she was the one person who didn't make you feel like you had to do cartwheels?'

'Pretty much.'

Her voice sounded thicker. Clogged. He wanted to know more but he didn't want to put her through it.

'How long did that go on for?'

'Every time my mother went through a bad patch I would go there, and Eleanor would see to it that I had food, clean clothes, a warm bed. Then, as the years went on, we began to talk—until eventually she gave me a key to her house and I could sneak in whenever things got bad at home.'

'She wasn't a foster parent, though?'

'No, but she was the closest thing to a mother I've ever

had. She was the one who saw I was bright but that I'd slipped behind because of my circumstances. She worked with me—even got on to one of the snooker players whose day job was a teacher to come and give me some private tuition. She paid him by giving him a year's annual pass.'

'She got you to believe in yourself?' Tak realised.

'Yes. I'd always dreamed of being a doctor—God knows where *that* came from—but she was the one who convinced me I could get into Oxford.'

'So what happened?' The need to understand burned so impossibly hot inside him. 'Did she get mad about you getting pregnant with Nell?'

He felt something shifted in an instant. He couldn't shake the fear that Effie was about to shut down again. Thrust him away. But slowly, eventually, she lifted her gaze to his.

'She never knew about Nell, Tak. Eleanor died two days after she'd received confirmation that she could officially adopt me. I went off the rails for a few months. I mean I *really* went all out. Which is when I fell pregnant.'

The cruelty of it slammed into him with a truly brutal force. He opened his mouth to speak but nothing came out. What words existed?

'Eleanor was the first person who'd ever made me feel wanted. Cared for. Loved.'

She shrugged. as though it was no big deal. and all of a sudden Tak appreciated the enormity of the weight Effie had been carrying around with her all these years. He understood why she didn't want anyone in her life. Why she felt as though she had to protect herself from any more heartbreak or rejection.

He wasn't even aware of closing the gap between them but suddenly there she was, in his arms, looking at him with a curious expression. He tried to make himself let go but it was impossible. Her inexplicable hold over him wouldn't allow it.

Effie watched, so still he didn't think she was even breathing. Her eyes locked with his, as though she was searching for answers he didn't want to give her, and he tried to block her out, stop her from seeing the truth. Stop her from realising just how desperately he wanted her.

He made to move away from her just as she twisted towards him. The contact rocketed through them both.

As her eyes widened with understanding Tak froze, very much afraid he was about lose his infamous control all over again. And that couldn't happen. Whatever the attraction between the two of them, he certainly couldn't give her what she needed. Hell, he would only detonate every rejection and insecurity she had ever had.

He dropped his arms, though it cost him dearly to do so. 'I'm sorry,' he said again, but this time he injected it with every ounce of the regret and empathy he felt after hearing her story. As though he thought an apology for his own actions could somehow make it up to her for all the people in her life who should have apologised to her but hadn't.

'Why are you sorry?'

The sweet, soft smile which curled her lips might as well have plunged into his heart and twisted it into a knot.

'My past isn't your problem.'

'Then I'm sorry for those kisses.'

'Sorry you kissed me?' she challenged. 'Or sorry you stopped?'

'Don't do this, Effie,' he bit out.

His body felt supercharged, and he was all too aware that if he weakened, if he kissed her again, this time he might never stop.

'You actually meant it when you said it was more about you than about me.' It was a statement more than a question. A recognition.

'Effie…' It was a whisper carried on his hot breath.

She didn't heed the warning. Instead she smiled, and it wrecked him like nothing he could ever have imagined. Then she closed the gap and lifted her mouth to his, and as the blood roared in his head like a waterfall, or a drumbeat deep in his veins, pumping around his body, he gave himself up to the intensity of the kiss.

It was madness, but he couldn't bring himself to care…

There was no escaping it.

Not the kiss so much as the emotions which coursed through her as a result of it. And a heat so scorching it was almost white. Searing her from within and making her feel as if a thousand fires were all blazing inside her at once.

Everywhere.

Like nothing she'd ever known before.

And then Tak used one hand to cup her cheek almost tenderly, skimming the other hand down her body, his fingertips igniting every inch of her as it moved. She forgot every superfluous thought and merely revelled in the sublimity of his touch, his kiss, the way his eyes glittered with undisguised hunger.

He kissed her over and over, his tongue partnering hers in a sensual dance of their own, his teeth grazing her lips with just the perfect amount of pressure. He tilted his head for a better fit, a slicker fit. First one way and then the other, as if he needed to taste her thoroughly. Completely.

Effie had never felt so desired. Not that she knew how to show it, and she was all too aware of her inexperience, expecting Tak to be put off at any moment. But he wasn't. He just kept kissing her, holding her, helping her to relax with every delicious glide of his tongue. And all Effie could do was grip his shoulders—his strong, muscled shoulders, which only played even more havoc with her spinning, somersaulting insides—and hang on for the ride.

Abruptly Tak lifted her up, carrying her easily back to the snooker table and perching her on it. She wasn't sure what instinct made her wrap her legs around him, but there he was. The hardest part of him nestled against the softest part of her.

'Better...'

His thick-voiced murmur only sent her insides skittering all over again. She wasn't sure how she found a way to respond. 'Glad you approve.'

'Oh, you have no idea.'

His voice was like a hum, low and demanding, seeping through her flesh and reverberating around her body. And then he was slipping his T-shirt over his head, with hers following, and she could only savour the moment as he dipped his head and traced the line of her neck with his impossibly carnal tongue.

'Tak...' she breathed, scarcely recognising her own voice.

He didn't answer, instead dropping hot, sensual kisses behind her ear and into the oh-so-sensitive hollow by her throat.

Effie gave herself up to it. To every single, incredible sensation screaming through her body, telling her that this—*this*—was what she'd been missing all these years. The way her entire body seemed to melt against his, moulding itself to him as though it had been handcrafted just for Tak.

It felt like an age before he slid the thin strap of her bra down, his kisses blazing a trail over the creamy swell of her breast but stopping short and leaving her actually *aching* for more. She arched her back in silent objection and he actually managed a throaty chuckle. As if he liked teasing her this way.

If she was honest, she liked him teasing her this way, too. Especially when he unhooked her bra with a deft flick of his wrist and drew it from her, lowering his mouth to take its place, closing over her tight nipple with something approaching reverence.

Effie had no idea how long he stayed there, kissing and licking, his tongue swirling in intricate patterns, eliciting from her sounds which she'd never heard from herself before. He took his time, moving from one breast to the other and back again, unhurried and deliberate. An eternity of bliss.

She couldn't have moved or stopped him even if she'd tried. Even if she'd wanted to.

At some point she arched into him, pressing closer against his length. Hot and steely. Unmistakable. *For her.* A tantalising shiver racked her body.

And then he was stepping back, away from her.

Effie's eyes flew open. For a ghastly minute she thought he was leaving and her heart actually paused, like a trapeze artist flying through the air in that second before the audience knew whether she was going to be caught on the other side.

Before she could think, however, Tak lifted her up and carried her over to the couch. He laid her down with a sort of gentleness, before reaching for her jeans to unhook them and slide them off in a single, smooth movement.

The last scrap of lace followed and then she was naked. She might have expected to feel awkward or flustered, but Tak's hooded expression stopped her from throwing her arms across her chest and instead lent her an air of unanticipated confidence.

'Stunning,' he breathed, his eyes raking over her body just as effectively as if they were his hands.

'Now it's your turn,' she said, and there was a hoarse pitch to her voice.

He stepped towards her, then stopped himself. 'Are you on the pill?'

'Sorry?' The question jarred her.

'The pill?' he pressed, his urgency offering her a crumb of relief.

She bit her lip, offering a curt shake of her head. How had that not even entered her head? 'No. I haven't needed it.'

'You haven't needed protection?' he frowned.

Her cheeks burned. 'No. Yes. It's just… I haven't… Not since Nell was conceived…'

If he was surprised, he hid it well. Closing the space between them again, he let his hands cradle either side of her face, dropping a long, deep kiss on her lips.

'Then we're just going to have to find a different way,' he murmured, setting tiny kisses at the corners of her mouth and back down her neckline.

As his hands moved over her body, slightly callused thumbs flickering expertly over the straining pink buds of her nipples, all other thoughts slid out of her head. And then his hand traced down her body from her long throat, over her breasts to her stomach, and finally to her aching core. He nestled his head between her thighs.

Effie froze. She wasn't completely naïve. She knew what he was about to do. But a part of her brain still couldn't process it. No one had ever done this to her before. Sex with Nell's father had been fumbled, missionary. Two kids who'd had no real idea what they were doing. Not like this. Not like *him*.

'Tak.' Her voice was tense even to her ears.

'Relax,' he soothed, kissing his way up the inside of one thigh. 'I've been dreaming about tasting you since the first moment I saw you.'

'Yes, but…'

'Relax,' he murmured again as he moved over to the other thigh. His grin was nothing short of devilish.

'Tak, listen…'

And then he licked his way into her and a thousand fireworks went off in her head all at once. Long, slow strokes of his tongue were followed by darting little licks which had her lips moving entirely of their own volition, her hands reaching down to his hair. She slid her fingers into the thick depths, urging him on as if she couldn't help herself.

Frankly, she couldn't.

She wanted Tak so badly that it almost scared her.

And for his part he seemed to read her mind, knowing what she needed from him even before she knew it herself. His tongue was like a weapon, conquering her and inflaming her all at once, whipping her up until she felt she couldn't take any more. And then he eased back long enough for her to catch her breath before stoking her up all over again.

Effie was powerless to stop him. Not that she really wanted to. Beneath his mouth her hips rocked and lifted, as if she couldn't get enough of him—and perhaps she couldn't. Perhaps she never wanted this to end. But then he was driving her on, driving her upwards to where it was dazzling and spinning, and she knew there was no coming back from it this time.

And she broke apart. His mouth was still on her as she shattered around him, scarcely recognising the sounds coming from herself, only knowing that nothing would ever be the same again.

What the hell was he doing?

It took Tak a superhuman effort to stand up, away from Effie, but if he didn't then he wasn't sure he was going to be able to stop himself from claiming her as his—right there and then, protection be damned.

She was like no woman he'd ever been with before. Her taste was still in his mouth, her exquisite scent too, and all he could think was that he wanted more. He was greedy for her, *aching* for her. He wanted her completely.

But he couldn't let that happen. Sex was one thing. Emotions were something quite different. Yet, as impossible as it seemed, where Effie was concerned the two seemed wholly intertwined.

Incredibly, his legs were actually shaking as he made himself move away.

'Where are you going?'

Her low whisper halted him instantly. Evidence of her climax lingered in her tone, rushing straight to his sex as surely as if she'd taken hold of him.

'This was a…' he paused, unable to bring himself to say the word *mistake* '…an error of judgement.'

'Oh.'

A bright red stain covered her cheeks and neck, but he pretended not to notice as he located her clothes and passed them to her. He wanted to take it back. To tell Effie that she was the most incredible creature. He would never know how he held his tongue. He only knew that if he gave her any indication of how close he was to losing control—if she tested him in any way—he would fail. He wouldn't be able to resist her.

Such was her power over him. And the worst thing about it was that there was a part of him which silently urged Effie to do just that. Because failing to resist her would, at the end of the day, be a win.

Where was his damned T-shirt?

'We won't speak of this again,' he ground out, trying not to notice how she still sat on the couch, gloriously naked and making no attempt to conceal the soft curves which seemed to call every last inch of his body.

And then she shifted—stiffly, awkwardly, yanking her T-shirt on and concealing herself from him. Tak feared his resolve might crumble there and then. His only saving grace was that she clearly had no idea of the inexplicable hold she had over him.

To hell with his T-shirt. He needed to get out of there.

CHAPTER ELEVEN

WALKING INTO THE hospital to check on old Mrs Kemp—a woman she'd brought in on her last shift, who had no family—Effie was congratulating herself on having successfully avoided Tak for four days.

Yesterday's day off had been spent walking Nell to school, then spending the morning window shopping for things she couldn't afford. Anything to stay out of Tak's house. As huge as it was, it had felt small to her, knowing he was off too, that they could have spent the day together.

Today she'd come in to the hospital to see old Mrs Kemp and Tak was the last person she'd expected to see as she hurried on to the ward.

And he saw her instantly.

If only he'd been facing the other direction.

Unable to look away, or move, she simply stood there as he headed over, her throat dry. And Tak just walked closer and closer, until they were almost toe to toe. Not close enough to touch, but certainly enough that she could feel the warmth of his breath on her forehead. It was oddly intimate.

'You've been avoiding me.'

She could deny it. But he would know. And she didn't want to look even more pitiable than she already did. The shameful truth was that Tak's opinion of her had begun to matter. Which only made it all the more ludicrous that she should have opened herself up the other night, thereby confirming just how much of a charity case she really was.

'What were you doing, talking to Mrs Kemp?'

'And now you're changing the subject.'

His voice poured through her, altogether too liquid. 'I was merely asking a question,' she replied dryly, impressing even herself.

She might have known it wouldn't fool Tak.

'You were asking an *obvious* question,' he corrected. 'But, to answer, I'm here doing the same thing I imagine *you* are intending to do. Providing a bit of companionship to a lonely, frightened old woman.'

Something shouldered its way into her chest and lodged there. As hard as she tried, Effie couldn't ignore it. Was it sentiment at his show of compassion?

'And you came down here just for that?'

'*You* did,' he pointed out. 'She's asleep, by the way. Best not to disturb her.'

'You didn't really come to see her.' Effie was sceptical. 'How do you even *know* her?'

'You're the one who brought her in. How do you think?'

'They called you for a consult,' Effie acknowledged grudgingly. 'She told me she hadn't hit her head when she'd fallen but I suspected otherwise. She's okay?'

'Fine. But I'm also checking over a couple of other patients.' He quirked an all too astute eyebrow. 'Is that a more plausible reason for you? Or perhaps you were hoping that I was using Mrs Kemp as some sort of excuse to see if I could bump into you?'

Her cheeks were burning. She could feel the heat. Because the humiliating truth was that a small part of her possibly *did* wish there was an element of the latter to his visit. How pathetic did that make her?

Not for the first time, she wished she was the kind of person to whom witty retorts came easily. Instead she found her fuzzy brain scrambling for *anything* to say whilst it seemed more interested in the electrifying sensations that darted all over her body when Tak was near. Just as they had the other night.

She remembered barely getting to her room and slamming the door behind her before her legs had given out and she'd collapsed to the floor. She'd had no idea what had just happened. Or, more to the point, she'd known *what* had happened, she just hadn't understood how she'd let it happen. And with Tak Basu.

Forget the sex, she'd instructed herself as the familiar flush had soared through her. She would be able to over-analyse that particular turn of events later, and she certainly hadn't been ready to deal with that yet. What of the things she'd told Tak? Things she hadn't told a soul in almost fifteen years.

Eleanor Jarvis.

She'd hugged the name to herself like a favourite comforter. The woman after whom Effie's daughter had been named.

Eleanor. The woman who had seen her potential and convinced her to try for Oxford University, even though the kids in school had called her *thick* or *stinky* or a heck of a lot worse because she might not have been able to get home to have a shower for days. Even the teachers had let their distaste for her outward appearance blind them to the clever child she'd been underneath.

Eleanor. The woman who had been about to adopt her. To finally make Effie a part of something good. Something loving. Something special. Before a car crash had stolen Eleanor's life away. Hit by a drunk driver on her way home from the snooker hall one night.

And with that the driver had stolen away the last lifeline at which Effie had been grasping. Gone. Snuffed out. In a single instant. Even now Effie still relived the pain, the loneliness, the suffocating blackness, whenever she thought about that night.

Which was why, the day after her daughter's birth, she'd made a point to banish those memories from her mind. Never to let herself go back. Only to look forward.

That she should remember Eleanor at that moment, after Tak had…*done* things to her, had been bad enough, but that she should have unravelled so instantly at the memories had been so much worse. Yet none of that had compared to the confused storm raging inside at the idea that, of all people, Tak Basu, her colleague, should have been the one to rake up all these memories.

She'd glanced at the clock. Six-thirty. Little point in trying to go to sleep. Even though her tiredness had gone bone-deep, she'd known sleep would still elude her when her head was on that pillow. Her head had been too full. Her brain too feverish.

In the end she'd sneaked down to Tak's home gym for a run, relieved to have the place to herself.

Unlike right now, when she couldn't seem to get any privacy from him if her life depended on it.

'You're very welcome to join me if you want,' he offered.

As if he somehow knew that her life, aside from Nell, was her career. Nothing more existed. It hadn't for over a decade.

'Sorry.' She forced herself to sound jovial. 'I have things to do. With Nell.'

'Yeah? Like what?'

Effie balked. *Think fast. Faster.*

She glanced up at the TV by the nearest bed. Some baking show. Perfect.

'We're making a cake,' she announced, before her brain had even had chance to get into gear.

'A cake?'

'Sure.' *Hell, why not?* 'Is there a problem with that?'

'Only that in all the time you've been staying at my

home I haven't seen you cook once. I thought you didn't know how.'

'There's a huge difference between cooking and baking, you know,' Effie managed loftily.

'Indeed?'

Why did she get the impression that he was deliberately setting her up.

'What's that then?'

'Well…' She floundered. 'It's obvious, isn't it? Anyway, I have to go. Things to buy and all that.'

Before the shops closed and preferably before Nell decided to go out for the evening with a couple of friends. And if she could grab someone who actually knew the first thing about baking, then she would do that, too.

'Mum, you can't be serious! We're *not* spending a Saturday night baking fairy cakes together. I'm thirteen, not seven!'

Effie took it as a win that for all Nell's exclamations her daughter was still hovering at the door to the vast high-tech kitchen, as though a part of her wanted to come in.

'The flat will be ready soon, and then we'll be back home. I just wanted to do a personal thank-you to Hetti and Tak.'

'But a *cake*, Mum? You're not exactly the world's best baker.'

Which they both knew was an understatement. It was something Eleanor had promised to teach her. Before she'd died.

'What *else* are you going to do, Nell?'

It wasn't easy to make herself sound blasé. Not when a part of her was so desperate to find things to do—any time she found herself at a loose end—which were so family-orientated it would ensure she wasn't alone with Tak for the rest of their stay here.

Because he was right that what had happened between

them the other night should never have transpired. Worse, since it *had* happened she hadn't been able to stop replaying it in her head. And even worse again was the fact that in her re-runs the fantasy went far beyond what had happened in reality.

She was wrecked. Bedevilled by a man who wanted nothing more to do with her. And the pain which scraped inside her was inexpressible.

She could pretend it was because of the echoes it had of the one other man with whom she had been intimate—the boy who had fathered Nell. But she knew it was more than that. *Tak* was more than that. In her whole life she had never imagined meeting anyone who made her body dance and resonate and exalt the way he had succeeded in doing.

So if she could just get through the next few days without having to see him, or at least without having to be alone with him… It was the only antidote she could think of.

'I thought maybe you might like to have a girls' weekend with me,' Effie said, and laughed brightly.

'Why?' Her daughter frowned, unconvinced.

'Why not?'

Nell twisted her mouth from side to side as if weighing up the options. 'Where did you even *get* that stuff, anyway? I can't see Dr Lover-man having a ready supply of fairy cake cases and all that.'

'I went shopping this morning. I also bought popcorn we can throw into the microwave as we gorge on fun chickflicks on that enormous cinema screen downstairs.'

'What is going *on* with you?' Nell cried. 'You don't even *like* baking.'

'I do,' Effie objected. 'I just like eating what's at the end of the process far more than the actual process. Now, can you just show me how to crack these eggs into the flour without getting shell in it?'

They were halfway through a mess when Tak walked in.

'How's the cake-baking?'

'Fine!' Effie declared a touch maniacally.

'Awful.' This from Nell.

He advanced into the kitchen with a grin and Effie was suddenly hit by an incredible urge to throw the electric mixer at him. If he was lucky she might actually turn it off first.

'What seems to be the trouble?'

'Nothing.' Effie tried again. 'No trouble.'

Nell eyed her impatiently. 'Mum has no idea how many eggs, or how much butter, flour and sugar to use. She also thinks any kind of flavouring is a luxury, rather than a pre-requisite—including vanilla.'

'I see.'

'I'm fine,' Effie repeated, in a way that suggested that if she told herself enough times she might actually make it so.

'You're really *not*, Mum.'

'Effie, come on. Let me help.' he said. 'I've made a fair few cakes in my time—including birthday cakes.'

Nell, it seemed, had heard all she needed to.

'Fab. Here.' She had untied her apron and whipped it off in an instant. 'You take over. If I spend any more time in here with Mum one of us isn't going to make it out alive. And I'm afraid it might not actually be me.'

'Sorted.' Tak nodded, taking over as though there was nothing else he'd rather be doing on a Saturday evening. 'Okay, Effie, what do you want me to do?'

He really did look delectably divine, standing there.

'You can cream the eggs and sugar,' Effie managed at last, and she knew he'd heard the catch in her voice when a tiny frown creased his forehead.

She reminded herself that he couldn't read her thoughts. That only she knew the delicious secret she was holding inside at this moment.

* * *

'You've really made cakes?' Effie asked, after they'd been working together for a while.

'I have. Growing up, I found that baking cakes with Hetti and Sasha was a good way to get them to talk about any problems that they were having in school.'

'Is that how you knew the best way I should handle Nell?' The words tumbled out clumsily, as if she knew that if she didn't just *say* it she might lose her nerve. 'That night at the ball when we were talking about the shoplifting? Do you remember?'

'I remember.'

He should shut her down. Tell her it was none of his business. He would have done with anyone else. But Effie was different—even if he couldn't explain what made her so. A part of him wanted to tell her, and therein lay the dilemma. Because if he told her then he knew—just *knew*—that it would change things.

She would change things.

She would change *him*.

'Don't forget I have sisters,' he offered at last. 'Both of whom were teenagers in every sense of the word. I remember what it was like.'

'But it's more than that, isn't it?' she asked softly. 'You don't just remember things in the abstract, the way an older brother might recall. You *understand*. The way a parent who has really been through it might.'

Something dark and cutting and raw scraped within his chest, making even breathing become difficult. 'I have never been a parent. And I never intend to be one.'

'Which is what makes it all the more curious,' Effie whispered. 'The way you knew what to say that night. The way you couldn't stop yourself from checking that we were okay. The way you've taken charge of us now and brought us to your home.'

'It's simply looking out for a colleague.'

Any other person might have heeded the warning note in his voice. But not Effie. 'I don't think so.'

'Perhaps you want to think carefully about antagonising the person who has provided a roof over your head.'

It was a jagged threat couched in the silkiest of tones. He hated himself for playing the game.

But instead of acknowledging the danger and stepping back Effie stepped closer. Metaphorically and physically. Her voice slid under his skin.

'Or you'll do what? Throw me out on my ear? I don't think so; your sense of responsibility wouldn't allow it.'

How was it that he could barely breathe? His lungs were too constricted?

'You'd be foolish to mistake my professional attitude for my personal one. Where my job is concerned I take my responsibilities exceedingly seriously. But you must know that where my private life is concerned I dodge responsibility at every turn.'

'The trouble is I don't believe that.'

'I can't make you.'

He made himself lift his shoulders. In all his life no one aside from his siblings had ever made him want to reveal his true self before. No woman had ever got to him like this. What was it that made Effie so different? Like a law unto herself.

He could see something was whirling inside her, even if he couldn't be sure what that something was.

'Do you ever slow down?' he asked abruptly.

'Not if I can help it.'

It was possibly the most honest answer she could have given him.

'Why not?'

Effie bit her lip and Tak perched on a tall bar stool, prepared to wait it out.

'Why not, Effie?'

'Because if I slow down then I give myself a chance to stop, to think. And there's a part of me which doesn't want to do that.'

'Because then you'll end up thinking about where you are in your life and wondering if you'd made different choices where you might have been?'

'It drives me insane,' she frowned.

'It's allowed to.

'Not when it sometimes throws up more questions than answers. It ends up confusing everything.'

'It doesn't have to.'

'I suppose,' Effie conceded after a moment. 'But I wish it wasn't like that.'

'You're not alone.'

She stopped abruptly, waiting, wondering, and Tak suddenly found himself speaking—filling the silence—even though he'd had no intention of doing so.

'I had another brother, you know. Saaj. He was eight months old when he was diagnosed with a neurodegenerative disease. To this day we still don't know the cause, but my suspicion is that it was immunopathic.'

'I'm so sorry.'

Her tone was so sincere, so gentle, that he could feel the emotion balling in his throat. He waved her aside with his hand.

'Saaj spent most of the next fourteen months in hospital unconscious, or if he was conscious then he was usually in pain. And as a baby he couldn't articulate it. He was simply inconsolable, but unlike a normal baby there was nothing my mother could do to help him. She was there with him every day, but she couldn't talk to him, or comfort him, or even cuddle him, because as the illness progressed even that caused him too much pain.'

'Tak…'

She uttered his name softly. Neither a plea nor a statement, just a reassurance that she was there, and he realised that at some point she'd taken his hands, as though lending him support. He'd never thought he'd needed it. Until now.

'She was in hell—unable to comfort him and equally unable to take his pain away.'

He couldn't bring himself to tell her the truth about his mother. The way Saaj had been her excuse to abandon the rest of her children when they too had needed her. The way she'd already been doing before Saaj had been born. But with Saaj she'd had a clear-cut reason which no one—especially not his ten-year-old self—had been able to argue with.

And so he'd taken on the responsibility of caring for his siblings—from changing nappies to washing clothes and finding them something to eat every day. He'd hated his mother for not caring for them enough. And he'd hated his philandering father for caring for himself too much.

But what if Effie didn't believe him? Worse, what if she took his mother's side and decided he was being callous, lacking any empathy?

'What about your father?'

'He wasn't around.'

That was all Tak was willing to offer. What else was there to say? That his father had been so busy with his whores that he hadn't cared about anyone else?

'I was a kid. I took care of my siblings.' He wrapped it up neatly. 'That's why I don't want that life now. I don't want a family. I feel like I've already been there and had that. I love being a surgeon.'

'Baby Saaj is why you became a surgeon, though, isn't he?' she asked abruptly.

Her quiet but clear words cut through the air. Through him. Incredibly, Tak found he couldn't answer her. His tongue simply wouldn't work.

'And not just any surgeon.' Her eyes might as well be pinning him to the spot. 'But a neurosurgeon.'

She could read him in a way that no one else ever had. It should unnerve him more.

'If I wanted you to psychoanalyse me I'd get on a couch and give you a clipboard,' he managed to bite out eventually. 'The point is that I don't need any distractions. I don't need a wife or a family at home, reminding me that I've let them down or abandoned them because I've got caught up with some case, some patient.'

It was intended as a conclusion, but she looked as though she was about to say more. He needed something to distract her. Words pressed urgently against his tongue, as if they were desperate to get out, whatever logic his brain might be using to restrain them.

'Come with me to the neurology conference in Paris,' he said. It certainly wasn't what he'd expected to say.

'No.' She shook her head at once.

'Why not?'

She eyed him apprehensively, as though trying to work it out. How he'd gone from shutting her out to inviting her to go away with him.

He was still trying to work it out himself.

'Nell's going on her ski trip at the same time,' he said. 'And you told me yourself that you've never been abroad but you've always wanted to. Here's your chance.'

She bit her lip and he had to fight the oddest impulse to draw it into his mouth and kiss her thoroughly, just as he had before. More.

'Where would I stay?'

It was as though she could read his every salacious thought where she was concerned.

'I'll get you a separate room.'

'Won't everything be booked up with the conference?'

Not if he flashed his credit card and offered them extortionate sums to solve the problem.

'I can ask…' He shrugged.

'But you won't think I…? You won't expect…?'

She flushed and he knew exactly what she was trying not to say.

'Effie, I can assure you there will be no expectations on my part. We got it out of our systems the other night. Now we can go back to how it was before.'

'You think so?'

'I do,' he asserted, wishing he felt half as sure as he sounded.

'Well, okay, then.'

She smiled. A gentle half-smile which blew him away.

'If you're sure?'

'Sure.' He nodded.

Only he wasn't sure. Not at all. Where Effie was concerned he couldn't seem to control himself.

But this time he had no choice.

CHAPTER TWELVE

EFFIE STRODE THROUGH the hotel lobby, through the doors and practically skipped down the steps and away from the stuffy, windowless, airless conference room.

She stopped abruptly and tipped her head up. The sun was glorious in a cloudless blue sky. Like every stunning glossy magazine photo she'd ever seen all rolled into one.

Only better.

Not just because she was actually here, rather than merely standing holding a holiday brochure and imagining she was, but also because of the man who had brought her here.

For the best part of a week she'd been nodding courteously to Tak when she'd seen him at the hospital, smiling politely at him when he'd passed by whatever room she and Nell had been in at his home, and chatting amicably to him whenever actually meeting him had been unavoidable.

She absolutely, definitely, categorically had *not* been imagining him kissing and licking her, turning her inside out and making her cry out with unabashed abandon as she climaxed over and over again.

Shaking her head—her hair was wild and free, as it so often seemed to be these days—Effie tried to eject the memories from her head. She was here, in Paris, without a single other person to think about. She could do whatever she wanted, whenever she wanted to.

So, where to go first? Effie wondered, picking one cobbled street at random. Would she find herself in a square full of artists, all gathered together to share their creativity, or perhaps the famous cabaret house of the Moulin Rouge, or perhaps she'd even stumble upon Montmartre Cemetery, the last resting place of literary greats like Zola or Dumas?

She wound through the streets, scarcely able to believe she was here—*abroad*. It felt so different from anything she might have anticipated and yet simultaneously exactly as thrilling, from the sights and sounds to the language itself.

Effie had no idea how long she'd wandered, taking in a museum here or a sculpture there, wandering in the footsteps of Picasso and Van Gogh, when suddenly she rounded on a tiny *crêperie*, squashed between bigger, sturdier, architecturally more attractive buildings, and the mouthwatering smells lured her inside.

By the time she exited, sugary crumbs from her glorious hot treat still coating her lips, she felt like a kid again, practically skipping up the steps she saw opposite her. Steps and steps and yet more steps.

And suddenly there she was, with the white dome of the Sacré-Coeur, Montmartre's sacred basilica, right in front of her. Like a perfect dollop of whipped cream in the dazzling sunlight. People were spread out everywhere—on the steps, in the grassy areas, even on walls and benches—laughing and happy and making her feel like a part of something without even saying a word to her.

Which made it all the more curious that Tak should once again sneak into her thoughts. That she should wonder what it might be like to visit a place like this as a couple. *With him.*

It didn't matter how much she pushed that night into a box and tried to turn the key on it, reminders always found their way out. Into her head and her chest, until she ached for him all over again.

Stalking away, as if she could somehow outpace it, Effie's eyes alighted on a caricaturist impressively capturing the fun, carefree young girl who was willingly posing for him. Her friends were jostling to be next as they gasped and admired the image.

It was a symbol of all the things Effie had never, ever been able to be, let alone when she was their age. She'd spent her entire life just trying to stay safe and under the radar. Watching other people have fun but never being able to enjoy it for herself.

She even held herself back with Tak—with the exception of the other night—and suddenly Effie couldn't help but wonder what she thought she was achieving by it. Was she protecting herself, as her head would argue, or was she in fact depriving herself of even a few snatched moments of something good for herself?

These few days in Paris with Tak were *her* time. And if she didn't seize the moment then who knew when it would present itself again?

'You look breathtaking,' Tak murmured as she met him that evening in the hotel bar, as per her own instructions.

She inclined her head to one side and just about kept her smile of delight from taking over her entire face. 'Thank you.'

She should hope so. An afternoon at a spa, and swimming, and even an indulgent visit to the hotel's hair salon had taken every bit of spare money she'd had. But it had been worth it to pamper herself for once. To feel as though she was being spoiled.

Carefully she took Tak's proffered arm and walked with him into the dining room, where the maître d' accompanied them to their table with economical gestures and an expansive smile and the sommelier fluttered around them as they made their wine selections.

The meal passed by pleasantly enough. Tak asked about her day, and in between her tantalising starter and succulent main course she told him about Abbesses, the Bateau-Lavoir, the Sacré-Coeur. She kept to herself the lingerie boutique she'd visited on her way back from Montmartre. And after the cheese course was done and her dessert had arrived she enjoyed surprising him by telling him that she had eventually plucked up the courage to sit for a caricature.

Tak looked impressed. 'You'll have to let me see it.'

'Only if you promise not to laugh,' she warned him.

'Isn't that the point of a caricature? To amuse?'

'Yes,' she conceded, savouring her *crème brûlée*. 'But pleasantly.'

'Then I assure you I shall not laugh.' He managed to look solemn. 'And what about tomorrow?'

'Tomorrow I'm taking the Métro, and I'm going to visit the Eiffel Tower and walk along the Seine.'

'You could always come and join our team for a day. You could provide a different perspective for one of our talks—the first-on-the-scene account.'

'No, thanks!' Effie laughed. 'I'm here to play, not to work.'

'You haven't really ever had time to play, have you?' asked Tak, without warning. 'Time to yourself.'

'Have *you*?' she threw back softly. 'I mean, *really*? You have your games suite, and you see your brothers and sisters, but isn't it all really still your way of taking care of your siblings? You didn't buy that house for yourself, did you? You bought it for your sisters and your brother to live in with you until they had their own families. And you always meet up with Rafi because you want to check on him—although I'm not sure why.'

Something shimmered in the air between them. All around them was the hum of chatter, the clinking of glass and the scrape of cutlery against china.

It felt like an eternity, but then at last Tak answered her. 'You really want to know?'

'I do.'

He took a long drink of wine, quite unlike his usual carefulness. Effie stayed still. Patient.

'I told you about Saaj, and how I had to hold things together for my other siblings whilst my mother was with him,' he said. 'But I didn't tell you that he was a deliberate mistake. That my mother had him late in life as a way of trying to win my father back.'

'I don't understand...'

'My parents had an arranged marriage. She was a good match for my father and she was determined to be a good wife. But my father was handsome, a doctor, and to some a meal ticket. He had women throwing themselves at him and he was weak and greedy and he wanted it all. A very proper wife back home, having his children and raising his family, and a naughty young mistress who would do all the dirty things with him he felt a wife should not do.'

Every word cut into her. Tak's mother might have suffered a different fate from herself, but ultimately it was still rejection, betrayal. She couldn't imagine what Tak's mother must have gone through.

A thought occurred to her. 'Did your mother know?'

'Oh, she knew. She made excuses for him. Told us all that he was a clever, powerful man and that it was his entitlement—even though it killed her so much she used to self-medicate.'

'Tak, that must have been awful for her. For all of you.'

She wasn't prepared for the fury he directed at her.

'Don't make excuses for her! Everyone makes excuses for her. Including me. For years. But we were *there*—Hetti and Sasha, Rafi and I. We *lived* it. And what she did to us is inexcusable. I've finally started to accept that fact.'

For a moment she felt as if he'd shouted the words, hurling them at her with all the rawness and the pain he'd bottled inside for far too long. But one look around the oblivious diners at the restaurant told her that he had barely hissed them loudly enough for her to hear.

It didn't lessen their impact one iota.

'Tak, she must have felt so isolated…so alone—'

He cut her off before she could say any more.

'You have empathy because you're kind and you're caring. That's who you are, Effie. But in this case you're wrong. She didn't have to make excuses for him, or stay with him. She didn't have to put us, her children, through years of suffering because of their twisted relationship. But she did—because she was selfish.'

'Tak—' She stopped abruptly as the waiter arrived to clear their plates and bring them coffee.

All she wanted to do was send him away, so that she could talk to the man sitting stiffly, wretchedly, opposite her. Not that anyone else could see it but her. And what did that say about their relationship—or lack of one?

'No, Effie,' he snarled as they were finally left alone again. 'You feel for her because you think you see a parallel, but the two of you are nothing like each other. You went through far, far worse than my mother and yet look what you did. You put your daughter first from the instant she was born. You put her needs ahead of yours. You struggled alone through university, with a baby, because you knew that was your responsibility.'

'It isn't that simple,' Effie offered slowly. 'Not everyone is the same.'

'She could have left him. She had family—quite a lot of family—who would have supported her leaving with her children rather than staying with him. They knew he was cruel, and that he deliberately rubbed his affairs in her face. He even told me, *his son*, that he was more compatible in bed with any one of his whores than he was with my mother. Despite the fact they'd had four children together.'

Effie hesitated. With Saaj, that was five children, which meant it had been going on long before Saaj had been born.

'*Now* you're getting it.' Tak laughed, but it was a hollow, grating sound. 'Yes, he was throwing those insults about, sleeping with his tarts, and my mother was still weak enough to let him into her bed. Still stupid enough to believe that if she fell pregnant one more time he would finally come to his senses and realise that he wanted to be a family man, after all.'

'She always hoped he would change,' Effie whispered sadly. 'But he was never going to.'

'Of *course* he was never going to,' Tak scorned. 'Which was why she spent fifteen years medicating herself into oblivion and leaving *me* to raise *her* children when I was still a child myself. I was ten when I first took over responsibility for them. When really I needed her just as much.'

'Is that why you're so adamant about never marrying? Never letting anyone close? Because you've already practically raised a family and now you want to reclaim the childhood you lost?'

Somehow that didn't fit the Tak she knew.

'I don't want a family because I don't want to do to anyone what my father did to my mother.'

He bit the words out, stunning her into silence. For a moment Effie couldn't move. And then she sucked a breath in. 'Why would you even think you would do that? That isn't you at all.'

'I'm more like my father than you know,' Tak countered darkly. 'My mother said so often enough when I was growing up.'

And all of a sudden it was desperately, painfully clear to Effie. In her despair and devastation and depression, his mother had taken all her fears out on her oldest son. Perhaps it had been her way of venting, or perhaps it had been her way of ensuring her son wouldn't turn on her, but

Effie could imagine it in crystal-clear detail. A half-out-of-it mother screaming at her ten-year-old son that he was just like his father. She'd seen it often enough. Hell, she'd even lived it herself.

No doubt whenever Tak had voiced anything about doing something for himself—from playing a game of football with his friends, or going to a friend's house—anything which had meant he might not be there to care for his younger siblings, his mother would have thrown that accusation at him. Saying the one thing she knew would get the reaction he needed, likening him to the one person who disgusted him the most.

In spite of all that Tak had told her, and the empathy she had for his mother's situation, for that part of it Effie couldn't forgive her. A mother was supposed to look out for her children, love them, protect them. Tak's mother had made Tak responsible for his father's shortcomings, and she'd used his father against him every time he'd looked as if he was going to step out of line. She had damaged him emotionally. It had been cruel and it had been entirely avoidable.

And now all Effie could think was that she wanted to be the one to help Tak see the truth. To heal him. She didn't know if she could. She didn't know if anyone could. But she'd be damned if she didn't at least try.

'You aren't your father, Tak,' she offered softly.

'I know that,' he growled. 'But I'm his son. It's there somewhere. I have his genes.'

'You and I both know the nature versus nurture debate. You're a completely different person to your father. To both your parents, for that matter. Look at Hetti and the rest of your siblings.'

'Rafi is like him,' Tak ground out.

'Sorry?'

'Rafi. He lived through the same childhood I did. He

knew exactly how that man destroyed everything. He hated him every bit as much as I did. And then, six months after he got married, I discovered he was having an affair. That he'd had a mistress on the side before he even got engaged.'

It took her a moment, but she finally thrust her shock aside. 'That still doesn't make *you* like him, Tak. It isn't what you stand for.'

'You can't know that for certain.'

'I can. Because that isn't who you are.'

But it was pointless. The conversation was over and Tak had shut her out. Again.

They sipped their coffee in silence, with Tak clearly marking time until he deemed it polite to leave. And then they were in the lift, the silence almost suffocating her as she stood next to him. He was only inches away and yet it might as well have been a whole continent. His fury and resentment were coming off him in waves.

He didn't so much walk her to her room door as stalk there, barely waiting for her key card reader to flash green before marching to his own door.

'Goodnight,' she ventured as she stood just inside her room.

But he was already gone.

For several protracted minutes Effie paced up and down in her sitting area. It was hell knowing he was only on the other side of that wall but that he was shutting her out. Torturing himself with accusations that should never have been hurled at him. Believing himself to be the kind of man who would do something which so disgusted him.

And what kind of willpower did it take to hold himself back from people—girlfriends—the way he must have done all his life?

Much the same as the willpower you've shown, a small voice whispered in the back of her head. *And was it really so difficult to stand back before Tak walked into your life?*

The thought lent her strength. What if *she* was to Tak what *he* had been to her? The one person to break through those barriers? She felt as though her day alone in Paris had unleashed something in her which hadn't been there for almost two decades. She felt wild, reckless and free. Maybe now it was time to put it to the test.

She didn't give herself time to think, lest she talked herself out of her. Talked herself back down to being the woman she always was—never seizing what she really wanted. And she wanted Tak.

Effie marched to the connecting door and slid the bolt, pretending she didn't see her hand shaking before she lifted her chin and strode through into Tak's room.

It was empty.

For a moment Effie hesitated. Did she turn back? Wait? Where *was* he, even?

And then she heard a door open around the corner and Tak walked in, with a damp sheen on his body, wet hair, and a small towel around his waist. He stopped, stared, and Effie didn't miss the tiny flare of his nostrils or the way his eyes widened a fraction.

It restored her waning courage and she propelled herself forward, towards him, stopping inches from his face. 'Pleasant shower?'

She couldn't resist lifting her hands, allowing them to skim over the glorious pectoral muscles of his well-honed chest. Her insides turned to mush just at this mere contact. Her only comfort was that she could feel coolness coming off his skin. A cold shower? Surely that had to be a good sign? As was the slightly hoarse edge to his voice when he spoke.

'What are you doing, Effie? I didn't bring you here for this.'

'No, I know. But still, I wanted to come and thank you for bringing me to Paris.'

He blinked, clearly surprised. She didn't blame him. She sounded bold, sensual—so unlike herself.

'You've already thanked me.'

'Well, I wanted to thank you properly.'

Before he could say anything else she tipped her head forward and pressed a kiss to the hollow at his throat, her hands tracing the rigid contours of his torso, her fingertips deliberately grazing his nipples.

And he let her. Not even moving as she dropped a trail of kisses from his neck downwards. His lack of reaction might have concerned her, but his breathing was too harsh, too shallow, and it betrayed him.

She inched closer, felt the unmistakable evidence of his growing arousal pressing instantly against her hip just as she heard the catch of breath in his throat. He hadn't been rejecting her at the door before—he'd been trying to respect her. But there was no doubt that he wanted her—*really* wanted her—as much as she wanted him.

It made her feel powerful, suddenly. In absolute control. Before he could stop her she hooked her fingers around the towel, unsecured it and then dropped to her knees in front of him. Finally a side of herself which she'd always wished she had was making itself known.

And it was all because of Tak Basu.

Her head was spinning with desire. With exultation. With the way Tak was completely at her mercy and apparently more than happy to be so. He was male—so utterly, gloriously, solidly male—and yet he was letting her do whatever she wanted to do to him.

It felt intoxicating to be entrusted with such power, such control. And, whatever happened next, she was determined that she would have this one perfect night with him.

CHAPTER THIRTEEN

HE SHOULD STOP HER.

Dimly the thought moved around Tak's head. But he couldn't. Not when she was kissing him, licking him, *torturing* him the way she was right now. An exquisite kind of torture which he thought might be the perfect death of him.

And then she took him in her hand, tilting her head up to him, her eyes clear and wanton, her lips curled up mischievously, and he felt a kick, low and hard, in his abdomen.

But that was nothing compared to the blow that hit him when she opened her mouth and took him deep inside her mouth. A blow which almost felled him.

He couldn't even breathe.

Effie. *His* Effie.

He couldn't say it. He had no right even thinking it. But she undermined his walls with every conversation and every revelation. And now with every wicked flick of her tongue. She was so incredibly perfect, and all he could do was thrust his hands into her hair in some kind of attempt to root himself to the ground, to keep himself from exploding there and then.

Slow and lazy at first, her mouth and her tongue were playing, teasing, toying with him. Every flick of her tongue sent rivers of need cascading through his entire body, drowning out every other thought in his head. Carefully, she built up the pace. Taking her time as though she was enjoying every second of the lethal control she had over him.

And she *did* have control over him, Tak realised with

a jolt, and not just because she had her mouth wrapped around him in this moment. She'd been gaining dominance over him every day since that first night at the hospital gala. Making him wish he really was a different man from the one he'd always feared he might be. He hadn't done a damn thing to stop it, and now he feared he never could.

She was under his skin, in his veins. Her touch, her scent, her voice. And he never wanted to let her go.

Her teeth grazed gently over his tip and with a start Tak realised he was embarrassingly close to losing himself.

'Stop,' he bit out. 'Not this way.'

It took everything he had to brace his fingers against her and pull back, hoisting her up into his arms as he did. His fingers were reaching for her zipper and releasing her from her dress until she was standing there in just her underwear. Not that it helped.

The black lace bra and brief set with its tiny red bows would have been enough—feminine yet seductive, transparent enough for him to see everything. But then his eyes dropped to the matching suspender belt, the sheer stockings which only seemed to emphasise those impossibly long, sexy legs, and the heels which enhanced already shapely calves.

It was a devastating collection. Heady in the extreme. And Tak couldn't contain himself any longer.

In one move he scooped her into his arms, carrying her to the bed and lowering her as softly as his throbbing, aching body would allow before nestling between her legs and pressing his mouth to her where she needed him the most.

She was feverishly hot, magnificently wet, honey-sweet. She gasped instantly, bucking her hips, making him feel more turned on than he thought he'd ever been in his life. More desperate for her than he'd known possible.

'Tak…'

'Call it payback,' he growled, sliding his hands beneath

her rounded peachy bottom and lifting her to him again. Wrapping those incredible legs around his shoulders. 'And I intend to exact every last bit. With interest.'

Then he hooked the fabric of her briefs to one side and simply licked into her. Over and over as she moved against his mouth and on his tongue.

The guttural sounds ripped from her throat were becoming more urgent and more needy by the second. And he didn't think he would ever be able to get enough of her. Of this. He traced whorls around her core with his tongue and his fingers, slipping them inside her, revelling in her gasps and the way she opened herself up to him as if she couldn't help herself. All the while maintaining a steady flick over the tiny bud at her core and stoking the fire which burned so brightly inside her.

And then he felt her changing, beginning to pull away. He heard a weak protestation on her lips, something about wanting to do this together, and Tak couldn't help himself. He held her in place and sucked deep and hard at her core, refusing to let her go.

Instantly her body trembled, and stiffened, and finally shattered all around him. She was exploding as though he'd driven her beyond all control, crying out his name as though she knew it too.

'I didn't want it this way,' she whispered regretfully when she finally came back to herself.

'Then you gave a rather good performance that you were enjoying it,' Tak murmured, standing above her, his desire still painfully obvious.

Effie struggled to lift herself on to her elbows. 'I don't mean I didn't enjoy it.' She blushed prettily. 'I think it's obvious that I did. More than enjoy it. I just meant I wanted both of us to...'

'We don't have protection,' he ground out, wishing his body wasn't urging him to ignore such a substantial obstacle. 'I didn't bring anything. I told you—I didn't bring you to Paris for this.'

And he had no intention of sleeping with anyone else whilst he felt this way about Effie. What did that say about their non-relationship?

'But *I* came prepared.' She offered a wry smile, fishing something out of her bra.

It took him a moment to recognise it for what it was. Then something slammed into his chest. Hard.

'Then it's a good job I'm not finished.'

Her eyes flew to his and she twisted her mouth nervously. For the first time it occurred to Tak that but for that one time in her youth—a one-off fumble which had resulted in Nell—Effie had no idea what she was doing.

For some reason that knowledge ignited some primal sense inside himself. She was rare, unique, otherwise untouched. She'd kept herself that way out of her own choice. She truly was *his*.

With a groan, he took the small packet from her fingers, lowering himself on the bed and moving over her body, his arms either side of her bearing his weight. Every inch of him was alive to every touch. Revelling in the way her hands roamed his body constantly, as though she couldn't get enough either.

She skimmed her hands over his chest, then his shoulders, and down over his back, tracing his braced shoulder muscles and the way his body tapered to his waist.

For his part, he feasted on her mouth, taking his time, giving her the chance to come down from her orgasm and beginning the process of building her up to another. He rained kisses on her face, on the bridge of her nose, over her eyebrows and to her temples. He pressed his lips to the sensitive spots below her ear and at her throat until her nails dug into his shoulders and she whispered for more.

Tak was only too happy to oblige.

He bent his head, pulling down one bra cup to expose her breast, which he kissed and licked and finally sucked, and then turned his attentions to the other. Back and forth, he ignored the throb of his desire, the way he ached to plunge himself so deep inside her that neither of them would know where he ended and she began.

The rawness, the need with which he wanted Effie, was like nothing he'd ever experienced before. Not least when she shifted and he nudged against her wetness. He feared he might be lost there and then.

It took him moments to open the wrapper and deftly slide on the condom, but it felt like an age, and then he settled back between her legs and eased himself close to her, his hand reaching down to stroke her silken folds and ensure she was ready.

He wasn't prepared for her to wrap herself around him and draw him quickly inside, her muscles stretching around him as though she'd been made exclusively for him, clenching over him, her heat making him sear.

'Easy, Effie...' He barely managed to get the warning out.

'I can't.' She lifted her hips, as though a slave to the rhythm they were setting on their own, completely independent of her. 'I want this. I've wanted this for so long.'

As her hands moved down his back to clutch his backside, as if she must drive him even deeper inside her, Tak couldn't stand it any longer. He slammed into her hard, again and again, and her cries urged him on as she rode out every wave with him. He moved his hand between them, stroking her, never letting up, and when he felt a shiver ripple through her body he pressed down hard and felt her orgasm take over.

For a while, he made himself hold on. Throwing her off the edge all by herself and watching her plummet, then soar. Waiting as she came back down to him. But before she could land he gave himself up to the moment, climaxing into her with a primitive sound which didn't even sound like himself.

This time when she took flight he soared with her.

And he never wanted to come back to the ground.

'It really must be something to be the King of Awake Craniotomies,' Effie pondered at some point in the early hours, after he'd reached for her several times more, sating her, exhausting her, and then doing it all over again.

'Hmm…?'

'All those people at the conference today. They all came to hear you speak.'

'There were lots of speakers there.'

'But it was you who packed the room. It was your speech which had the applause practically raising the roof off this hotel.'

'I've always thought, in many ways, that I'm lucky,' he replied eventually. 'People come to me when there's already a fair suspicion that there's a brain or spinal issue. But you, out there in the field, you never know what you're going to get. You have to be ready for anything, thinking of everything, catering to all possibilities.'

'It's…frightening sometimes,' she admitted. 'But it's also rewarding. Especially when a patient and his family make a trip to the air ambulance base months later to thank you for what you did. But you must get that, too.'

'Yes. Still, I'd love to see it from your perspective.'

'So come along.'

Effie shrugged, as if they were in a real relationship. As if considering the future wasn't strange. As if meeting up in a month or so, when she was back in her flat and any non-relationship she'd ever had with Tak wouldn't be awkward.

'We do ride-alongs for press and medical professionals sometimes. You could join us for a day. Because of your expertise you could probably even take the place of one of my paramedics for the shift.'

And he nodded, and kissed her thigh, and told her he would arrange it as soon as they got back. Then he reached for her again, already hard, already wanting her. Just as he would for the rest of the weekend.

And Effie—as foolish as she knew it was, she couldn't stop—wished it never had to be over.

CHAPTER FOURTEEN

'GEORGE IS SEVENTEEN years old. Half an hour ago he was with a group of friends climbing on Thor's Rock when he missed his footing and fell approximately eight feet onto a raised ledge.'

The paramedic from the land ambulance met Effie, Tak and the rest of the air ambulance crew at the base of the rock.

'He landed on his backside around thirteen feet up from here, on a raised ledge, and there's suspected spinal compression. He was apparently unconscious for approximately fifteen seconds.'

Effie nodded as she calculated the easiest way up the sandstone structure.

'He has severe pain in his lower back, and a pins and needles sensation in his legs. We've administered ten milligrams of morphine. Marco, the other paramedic, is up there holding the lad's head and spine straight so that he doesn't move. We were in the area—we were one of a couple of crews heading out to another incident—and they diverted us here instead.'

She nodded again, then turned to James, her own paramedic, and to Tak, who had chosen today to accompany them, just as they'd talked about in Paris.

It was impossible to pretend to herself that it didn't feel significant. It was an unspoken acknowledgement that their relationship wasn't just about sex—which they'd enjoyed night after night since their trip together—but about connecting in the real world as well.

Slowly, bit by bit, she was beginning to shake the fear that it could never last. That this shred of happiness was bound to be ripped from her the way that everything else bar Nell had been.

'It should be simple enough for us to get to the patient.' She spoke quietly. 'There are quite a few people already milling around up there, including George's friends, so clearly there's plenty of room on the ledge. However, getting him down—likely on a spinal board—will be a very different matter.'

'We have Mountain Rescue on hand to help,' James pointed out. 'I can start sorting that out.'

'Good. Okay—Tak, you come with me. We'll get up there and see what's going on,' She located her first hand-and foot-holds and began making her way up, reaching the ledge more quickly than she'd anticipated, with Tak right alongside her.

'Hi, George—I'm Effie, the air ambulance doctor. How are you feeling?'

Within minutes Effie had completed her first round of checks. The lad was clearly in a bad way, and getting him down was going to be tricky for both the crews and George himself.

'He can't straighten his legs, so we can't get him onto the board and therefore we can't get him down.'

'Quite a severe mechanism of injury,' Tak murmured. 'I suspect a broken pelvis and spinal damage.'

'Yep—and time is ticking by. I'm going to administer ketamine, just so that we can get him onto a board. We're really going to have to be careful getting him down. The last thing I want is for anyone to slip on the rocks trying to lower him. It could end up causing him even more damage.'

'Understood. Do you want to put him in a pelvic brace?'

'Yes.' Effie bobbed her head.

Tak was every bit as proactive as she would have expected. And the way they worked together was so easy, so harmonious. It was a constant battle not to keep reading too much into it. Or into the fact that, even though they'd returned from Paris a week ago, her relationship with Tak didn't seem to have slowed for even a heartbeat. Even the level of discretion needed to keep Nell from realising the truth only seemed to have added a delicious air of adventure to it.

'You'll need to cut his joggers off,' she instructed, shaking the thoughts from her head.

But when Tak showed the scissors already in his hand and grinned, clearly on the same page, her stomach still flip-flopped deliciously.

'Good. Tak, I'm going to need you to help organise the Mountain Rescue teams onto staggered ledges, as equal in strength and height as you can, so that moving him out of here is as smooth as possible.'

'Sure.'

'Okay.' She nodded, plastering a smile on her lips and heading back to her patient. 'Right, George, what do think? Fancy a ride in a helicopter today?'

Effie tried not to skip downstairs the following morning, clad only in one of Tak's pristine bespoke shirts.

It was ridiculous that she felt so happy. Ridiculous, and amazing. A few days ago she could never have imagined herself sneaking down to a man's kitchen in order to prepare the two of them breakfast—or in her case something which might resemble breakfast. Least of all imagine sneaking into a man's kitchen after having made a superhuman effort to resist joining him whilst he stood in his huge walk-in shower. Never mind 'two-person'—an entire coachload could fit in it.

She was still smiling to herself as she practically danced along the hallway and through the wide archway—only to come to a sharp halt.

If she could have backed up, cartoon-like, then she would have. For there could be no doubt that the older woman who was sitting elegantly at the counter, sipping coffee from a bone china cup and saucer, was anyone other than Tak's mother.

Effie tugged ineffectively at the hem of Tak's shirt—the wearing of which now seemed like the stupidest idea she'd ever had. The woman's head turned slowly to meet her, her lips pulling instantly into a tight, disapproving line.

'Ms Robinson, I take it?'

A statement, not a question. And a less than enamoured one at that. It was worse than any cold reception she'd ever encountered as a kid, and something seemed to snap inside Effie.

She made herself drop the hem, stand a fraction taller and meet her critic's gaze head-on. 'It's Miss, actually.' Polite but firm. Not a trace of that shake which rocked her from the inside.

'I beg your pardon?'

Clearly Tak's mother wasn't accustomed to being challenged.

'Miss—not Ms.' Effie even forced herself to smile. 'For the sake of clarity.'

The woman's eyes narrowed. Then, if we are being so… *clear*, I should point out that my son's shirt barely covers the fact that you aren't wearing any underwear.'

Effie felt physically ill. But she cranked her smile up a notch. The censure and disapproval meant nothing to her, she reminded herself over her thumping heartbeat. She didn't need validation from other people—she wasn't that young kid any more.

'I don't believe Tak knew you were intending to visit,

or I'm sure he would have made sure he was here to welcome you.'

'He didn't. Hemavati gave me a key. I imagine she was concerned. I let myself in.'

Effie chose to ignore that. 'Then will you excuse me whilst I go and find him?'

It wasn't really a question, but the woman darted her hand out to snatch Effie's arm, her grip decidedly painful.

'You mean *warn* him,' she replied evenly. 'No, I don't think so. My daughter told me you are staying because your flat is uninhabitable?'

'The boiler broke down and asbestos was found. The ceilings needed to be repaired and the central heating needed to be re-plumbed throughout.' It was all Effie could do not to cringe as the words came out. How easily it could sound like an excuse.

'I see. And Talank offered you his home?'

'He did.' Effie wrinkled her nose, imagining how that must sound.

'And, tell me, how long do you expect it to take? This repair?'

Effie felt too hot, then too cold.

'Actually, it was all done last Friday.'

'So…let me see…four days ago?'

Effie loathed the way the older woman made such a dramatic show of counting back the days. She smiled cheerfully and made herself sound as breezy as she could.

'Must be, yes. Anyway, I should leave you to enjoy your morning drink in peace.'

Tak's mother smiled, though it was too sharp, too edgy to be sincere. And still it locked Effie in place.

'I wouldn't dream of it. Sit down—tell me about yourself and how you met my son. I understand that you're a doctor, too?'

She could still go. Ignore the woman's instructions, turn

around and leave. Tak's mother was intimidating enough, without the fact that Effie was hardly even dressed. But if she went it would feel like a retreat, or that she had something to be ashamed of. And Effie couldn't explain it, but she didn't want to feel ashamed of anything that had happened between her and Tak.

And so she stayed, quietly moving around the kitchen to make herself a coffee and then discreetly pulling the shirt as low as possible and sliding into the seat across the table from Mrs Basu.

Only then did she finally speak.

'I'm a trauma doctor with the air ambulance,' Effie confirmed neutrally. 'I take patients to several hospitals in the area, including the Royal Infirmary.'

'Quite an impressive career. You don't look much older than Hemavati.'

Effie recognised the test. She offered a light laugh, as if she hadn't noticed. 'Hetti's barely twenty-six. It's many years since I was that young.'

'I see.' The other woman sipped her coffee carefully. 'So, then, are you all about your career, like Talank, or do you imagine yourself having a family?'

'You don't need to answer that, Effie.'

Effie jumped at the sound of Tak's voice over her head.

'That's an incredibly personal question, Mama.'

'Talank.'

The older woman's eyes narrowed as she tilted her cheek up for her son to kiss. Tak obliged, albeit stiffly, formally. It was a duty and a mark of respect, but not a sign of love. More than she would manage with her own mother, though.

For a moment Effie's stomach knotted into a tight ball. What must it be like to have a mother look at you differently? Feel differently about her child? Tak hadn't had it and neither had she. Did Nell know how much *she* was loved? Effie panicked. Had she succeeded in ensuring her daughter felt it every day of her young life?

Before she could stop herself, Effie opened her mouth. 'Actually, I already have a family, Mrs Basu. I have a daughter. Eleanor. Although I usually call her Nell.'

'You have a baby?' The woman's gaze slammed into her like a hard, stinging slap.

It was all Effie could do not to raise her hand to her cheek, to check that the older woman hadn't, in fact, made contact. She took a moment to breathe, but to her surprise, Tak stepped in seamlessly.

'Nell is thirteen. She's a warm, friendly young girl, and a credit to Effie.'

'Is she here?'

'Effie and Nell were here whilst the repairs to their home were being dealt with.' He inclined his head, his tone firm, smooth. 'They moved back last week. Not that it's any of your concern.'

Tak's mother's eyes narrowed, as if in triumph. 'So you've left a thirteen-year-old girl alone in an apartment whilst you and her mother *frolic* here?'

It was bait, and even though everything in her screamed at her not to rise to it Effie felt her face heat with anger. 'Nell's at a friend's house,' she snapped. 'It's her friend's birthday and she's having a sleepover. And I am not *frolicking.*'

'Do you have a reason for coming here, Mama?' Tak demanded, his tone clipped.

Effie felt him cover her hand with his soothing touch.

'Or are you simply at a loose end because Father has dragged you over to the UK for some conference or other?'

It might have been phrased as a question but Effie knew an accusation when she heard one. And Tak's voice invited no further challenge.

'Are you comfortable?'

He turned to Effie with a wry smile. It was a shared moment which probably meant nothing to him yet it made something in her chest mushroom with happiness.

'Or would you prefer to leave?'

'I have a busy day.' Effie moved carefully out of her seat, grateful to Tak for providing her with the opportunity to leave. 'I might go and get ready now.'

'You're going to leave...*her* to roam around your home unsupervised?'

The implication was clear—*watch the family silver*—and Effie felt a tight band constrict around her chest. It was an accusation she'd heard enough times before, as she went into different foster homes. She hadn't felt that dirt-poor and pathetic in years. It was testament to just how manipulative this woman was that she'd located Effie's vulnerability within barely a five-minute conversation.

'Effie,' Tak corrected. 'Not *her*. And, yes, she knows the layout of the house well enough not to need a guide—but it's very thoughtful of you to be concerned in case Effie becomes lost.'

Effie flinched on his mother's behalf. She recognised that tone, and it wasn't as neutral as it seemed. The undercurrent and the subtle put-down made her skin bump. His mother had pursed her lips, as though she knew it, too.

For a moment silence descended on the room as the woman clearly burned with curiosity and Tak merely busied himself with breakfast. Completely at ease, the King of the Castle. Just as he was king everywhere he went.

She should go. Escape the tension. Instead Effie hovered in the doorway, unable to bear the thought of herself being the cause of disharmony between mother and son. And still his mother stared at the deliberately laid-back Tak, as if her eyes boring into him could somehow reveal all the answers which she was clearly so desperate to know.

An age dragged past, though it was probably less than a minute, and finally Effie excused herself.

She had no idea whether the words which followed her down the corridor came because his mother thought she was out of earshot, or because the older woman intended her words to be overheard.

'You're using her, Talank. *I* can see it, but does *she* know it?'

There was the briefest of pauses and Effie couldn't help it. She slowed her pace, wishing fervently that she could see Tak's face.

'I will concede that when Effie and I first got together it was something of a mutual arrangement. A buffer, shall we say?'

As much as she knew it was the truth, Effie wasn't prepared for the shard of regret which stabbed through her.

'A buffer?' his mother replied coldly.

'Why not? Clearly you already know this, Mama. You wouldn't be here if Hetti hadn't already spoken to you. She *did* explain it all, didn't she?'

'You sister mentioned some mutual agreement, I suppose. Something about you and that woman both being single...'

'You are my mother, and as such I try to respect you. But if you wish me to continue this conversation,' Tak interjected, his voice quietly dangerous, 'then you will refer to Effie by her name. Am I making myself clear?'

'You don't respect me, Talank. You never have. Have you?'

He ignored the question. 'Am I making myself clear?'

'Effie, then,' his mother bit out coldly.

Clearly she didn't like it. It was surely testament to Tak's authority that she nevertheless obeyed.

'There, now, was that so difficult?'

Still immobile in the corridor, Effie realised she didn't

want to linger there, eavesdropping. She didn't want to hear any more. She was genuinely afraid of what might be said. Tak's voice was barely recognisable. It held a tone she'd never heard before. A tone she never wanted to hear directed at *her*.

She tried to force her legs to move, but they felt rooted to the spot. As though they might fold if she attempted to force them.

'According to Hemavati, you and… *Effie*—' Effie could practically hear the gritted teeth '—were only together for show. To redirect attention for an evening.'

'Originally, yes.'

'Your sister also believes that you only invited *Effie* here—and now I discover her daughter as well—because she had nowhere else to go.'

'Is this conversation going somewhere relevant? I was under the impression that I could do whatever I chose, given that it is my *own* home. Or would you rather I'd seen them out on the streets?'

'I would rather hear that you had told *Effie* that it wasn't an action made out of the goodness of your heart so much as you making her and her daughter pawns in your quarrel against me. And against your father.'

'You talk about him as though you're a *team*,' Tak spat out instantly.

Something in his tone had Effie spinning around, as though she could hurry back down the corridor. As though she could somehow soothe his pain.

'He's never been a team player. Not for you. Not for anyone.'

'He loves me in his own way,' his mother hissed furiously. 'If it hadn't been for my becoming a mother—if it hadn't been for *you*—then he would have wanted me for a lot longer.'

'He *never* loved you—can you really not see that?' Tak

roared. 'He is selfish and cruel and he only loves himself. He has only ever loved himself.'

'And you are just like him,'

The accusation hung in the air like a knife thrown at a spinning board just as time was frozen. Effie couldn't move. If she did then she might race back down to that kitchen, take that virtual knife and stab that woman right in the heart with it. The way *she* had been stabbing at Tak all these years, trying to beat him into submission with her cruelty, her callousness.

How he had become such a decent, compassionate man in the face of it all was a miracle.

'If you think that, Mama,' Tak managed icily, 'then why push me for an arranged marriage? If I'm so like him, how could you want to put some innocent bride through everything you went through?'

'Because, contrary to what *I* know of you, people think you're a catch, Talank. And your father will benefit from a lot of contacts if we make the right match. You owe us that much. You can keep this tramp of yours on the side, if you really need to.'

Effie could feel Tak's fury even from where she stood. His mother's words might have cut into her, but every time Tak defended her it felt like the most soothing of balms.

'Effie is not a tramp. And if I were to marry anyone I would marry *her*. I would have no mistress. She would be enough.'

'But you *aren't* going to marry her, are you, Talank?' his mother continued victoriously. 'And for all this noble talk of yours, you and I both know the truth, don't we? You didn't just choose Effie as this *mutual buffer* you claim. You chose her deliberately.'

There was no reason for Effie's blood to chill and slow in her veins, she told herself anxiously. No reason at all.

'Careful…' Tak warned.

But his mother had clearly smelled blood and now she was going in for the kill. Whether it was Tak or Effie, she didn't care. In any case, one equated to the other.

'You *chose* to align yourself with a woman who would sully your reputation by association.'

'That's enough.' Tak's voice was icy.

'She is unmarried with a child. Damaged goods. Even *you* couldn't carry that kind of toxic baggage and still be useful to your father and me.'

The truth slammed into Effie like a knee to the chest. Powerful enough to cause internal bleeding and even cardiac arrest. It catapulted her back to a time when she hadn't been good enough. When people had done everything they could to disassociate themselves from her and she had been wholly ashamed of who she was and where she'd come from.

But this time she had no one to blame but herself. From the start Tak had warned her that he would hurt her and she hadn't believed him.

More fool her.

'I warned you—that's enough!' he bellowed.

It was enough for Effie. The silence stretched out, straining, twisting, pulling taut. And with it came a tugging on her heart, until she felt as though it might tear in two.

She couldn't bear it any longer.

With her hand over her mouth to stifle any sound, she finally found her strength and raced up the corridor to her room. All she had to do was find her clothes and she would be out of there within minutes.

And she would never come back.

CHAPTER FIFTEEN

TAK EYED HIS MOTHER, feeling an odd, unexpected kind of fury building inside him. He ignored her question and the fact that he didn't—couldn't—answer her. He was only glad that Effie had left long enough ago that she wouldn't have heard that. It would have hurt her more than he could have borne.

'You will not repeat that to Effie. Ever,' he said with deliberate calm. 'Do you hear me? I don't know what you think you're doing here, but the time for me to pretend that you are any kind of mother is long gone. I made excuses for you because of Saaj, but you were never a mother in the truest sense of the word. Not to me, and not to the others. The only reason you mourned Saaj was because you had some twisted idea in your head that he was the key to winning my father back.'

Instead of paling and slumping in her seat, as he might have feared, his mother narrowed her eyes, drawing her face into an ugly, cruel expression. 'Is this *her* influence? Damaged, toxic, and now she causes you to speak to your *mama* that way?'

In one terrible instant the scales fell from Tak's eyes. He would never be able to reason with this person and he would never be able to save her. She'd thrown her lot in with his father a long time ago and the man was like a wild, savage sea, with no respect for life or safety. Uma would drown because his father fed off her struggles. He sucked her under time and again, and she refused to right herself or grab hold of anything that could rescue her.

There was nothing Tak could do. Nothing anybody could do. She was anchored to him and she loved it.

But he wasn't going to let some sense of filial duty or honour tie him up any longer. He couldn't throw his mother out—that would be a step too far. But Effie had told him that he wasn't like his father and he was choosing to believe *her*. He was choosing *her*.

Turning his back on his ranting mother, he called Havers. 'Tell Effie we're leaving. We'll return as soon as my mother has left this house. And as soon as she is gone change the locks.'

'Effie has gone, Mr Basu.'

In all the time Tak had known the old man, he'd never seen him upset.

Time seemed to slow. 'What is it, Havers?'

'She looked rather *distressed*, sir.'

The room closed around Tak. Everything felt too tight, too constricting. Even his skin seemed to compress on his bones.

She had overheard. There could be no other explanation.

He turned to face his mother. The gleam of delight in her eyes was unmistakable.

'And so the mighty fall,' she proclaimed. 'All this disgust and disdain you show for your father, and all along I've warned you that you're just like him. That you will hurt any woman who doesn't know what she's getting herself into with you. All those names you've called him and all that hatred you have for him. How does it feel, Talank, to know that you *are* him?'

Tak didn't answer. He couldn't. It was as if a storm was closing in on him. It had come out of nowhere, so fast that he hadn't even known it existed before. But he was getting caught up in it now, and he didn't know which direction to even begin to turn.

How had he let himself believe he could be a better person? A man worthy of a woman like Effie? He should have gone with his gut—pushed her away the minute he knew something was happening between them.

But he'd known even from that first moment in Resus that there was something unique, something incredible about Effie. It had lured him in and it had seduced him. And he, in turn, had seduced her. Into his life and then into his bed. He'd taken advantage of her, and what was more he'd justified it by telling himself the attraction was mutual.

'You could go after her, Mr Basu,' Havers said suddenly. 'She would probably appreciate that.'

For a perfect instant Tak nearly obeyed. Then reality set in. He couldn't go to her now. That would only be rubbing salt into an already very raw wound. Calculating and insensitive. The best thing he could do now would be to stay away from Effie. To let her get back to her life and some semblance of normality.

Swinging around, Tak dismissed Havers and faced his mother. It took everything he had not to react to that cruel triumph radiating from her eyes.

'You may have won this round,' he told her, as evenly and as calmly as he could manage. 'But you won't win any more. Get out of my home and out of my life. I'm not my father and I never will be, and you'll need to find a new punch-bag. And if you go anywhere near Hetti or Sasha or Rafi I will make sure you regret it for the rest of your life.'

He didn't even wait for her to answer. He simply walked away. Out of the room. Out of the house. Into his car.

He didn't care if he drove all night or all week. As long as he stayed away from Effie—didn't hurt her any more than he already had—that was all that mattered.

* * *

'This is Maggie, thirty-four...' Effie briefed the team, relief pounding along her veins as she noted that Tak wasn't the neurological surgeon assigned to the case. 'At around six forty-five she was on a ladder, painting the first-floor window frames on her house, when she fell approximately four metres to the ground and landed on her back on a concrete path.'

In truth, she had no idea whether or not Tak was even in the hospital today. And she'd spent her entire shift—the entire past thirty-six hours, in fact—telling herself that she would never think about him again.

But it was like outlining a specific image and then telling someone not to instantly picture it in their head. Impossible.

'When we arrived GCS was thirteen, transmitted upper airway sounds equal air entry bilaterally, blood pressure was low and she was complaining of lower lumbar pain and looked very pale. Suspected internal bleeding. From top to bottom, she has a deep three-inch laceration to the head, lower back and pelvic pain, suspected spinal fractures. We administered one-fifty milligrams of ketamine for the pain.'

It might almost have been possible to lose herself in her cases, with shout after shout ever since she'd arrived at the air ambulance base at six o'clock that morning—if it hadn't been for the leaden ball filling her chest every single second.

She was grateful when the rest of the hand-over passed off without a hitch and she could get out of there. As soon as she got back to the base she would be done for the day. Maybe another night's sleep would finally begin to shake Tak from out of her head.

She snorted to herself. Well, she could live in hope.

'Effie.'

He caught her as she was exiting the building.

She wouldn't have stopped, but her legs refused to work

and she didn't want to risk humiliating herself any further by forcing them to move only to collapse right there on the ground. Worse, have him pick her up in his arms.

She heard him jog up behind her and then move around to face her.

'I have to get back to base,' she managed. 'They're waiting for me on the heli.' But there was no concealing the quiver in her voice and she knew he heard it, too.

'No, they aren't. They've left. Your pilot was close to his maximum flying hours and he had to get back to base. You were still in the middle of the hand-over in Resus, and technically your shift finished an hour ago, anyway.'

'Oh.' She swallowed. 'Well, then, I need to get back to my paramedics so we can head back together.'

'They've left too. I said I'd give you a lift back to your base and your car.'

Of course he had. A sliver of irrational anger cut through her. *Taking charge as if he had every right to do so.*

And then he opened his mouth and with two simple words took the heat out of everything.

'I'm sorry.'

She let the apology linger between them for a moment.

'What for?' she asked eventually, her voice soft. 'The fact that I'm damaged goods or the fact that you didn't tell me that was why you were using me?'

'She's gone, Effie,' he said quietly.

If she hadn't known better she'd have thought he was ashamed. But that was impossible, because Tak was *never* ashamed.

'She's out of our lives.'

The anger rushed back, flooding her. 'There is no *our lives*,' Effie exploded before she could check herself. 'You *used* me.'

'We used each other at the beginning,' he reminded her. 'That was the deal.'

It hurt. Too much.

'No, the deal was that we would be each other's buffer. The deal was never that because I was so damaged and toxic you would become tainted by association. I suffered enough of that growing up, because of my mother and where I was from. I will *not* accept it as a proud, hardworking single mother of a beautiful daughter.'

She wasn't prepared for him to reach out and snag her chin, forcing her to tip her head up, making her meet his eye.

'Nor *should* you accept it. Ever. But those were *her* words—they were never mine.'

'They might as well have been,' Effie argued, wrenching her head away, feeling the hurt blistering inside her like a chemical burn she couldn't get to. 'You gave her the weapon and you gave her the ammunition. You even marked me out as the target and you never even warned me. All she had to do was point and shoot.'

'I didn't even know you had a daughter when I asked you to that gala. Neither did Hetti. How could I have possibly chosen you on the basis she accused me of doing?'

He sounded rational, yet urgent all at once, and Effie realised there was some comfort to be taken from that. She felt her shoulders slump slightly, and there wasn't a thing she could do about it.

'You might not have intended it. At least not initially,' she conceded. 'But once you knew about Nell—once I told you that night at the gala—you must have known people would find out. You must have known this would be your family's reaction.'

He didn't deny it, although he looked as though he would give anything to, and there was some small comfort to be taken from that, too.

But then a horrid thought stole into her mind. 'Is that why you kissed me? After you'd assured me that everything would be platonic between us?'

'No!' he refuted instantly, a little too loudly for comfort. 'No. That isn't what happened. I kissed you because I wanted to. More than that, I couldn't stop myself. But I didn't intend to. I didn't plan it.'

'And that's where the problem lies, isn't it?' Effie smiled, but it was a weak, bitter smile. 'Because I don't believe you. I *can't* believe you. You could have told me at any time that Nell's existence had changed me from being your "buffer" to being your dirty little mistress, but you never did.'

He blanched at her words. Of course he did. Because she'd chosen them deliberately to really hit her point home. To hurt him. Anywhere near the amount he'd hurt her.

'*You're* the one who said I wasn't like him,' Tak said darkly. Thickly.

She wanted to stop but she found she couldn't. She had to ram the knife in a little bit deeper. 'That was when I thought I knew you. Now I know better.'

For the longest time he stood and stared at her. And she wished she had even an inkling of what he was thinking.

'You were right,' he said hoarsely. 'I am nothing like him. I never was. It was just something my mother said to keep a desperate ten-year-old in line. But you're also right that I should have been more honest with you. I just never thought I would meet a woman who got under my skin as you do. And by the time I realised that you had it was too late to explain it all.'

'It would never have been too late,' Effie choked out. 'If it had come from *you*. Not some stranger. Not someone who wanted to cut me down. I've had enough of that throughout my life. If you had really cared for me you would have protected me from it happening again.'

'I tried to warn you that I'm not a good man.'

She felt buffeted and fragile. Pushed and pulled between hating him and…and something else which she didn't care to acknowledge.

'That's bull. You *are* a good man, Tak.'

It felt as though the words were being torn from her mouth. She felt compelled to tell him the truth, yet simultaneously she didn't want to leave herself any more vulnerable and exposed than she already was.

'I should never have said what I did. It was a low blow, and whatever has happened you don't deserve that. You're an incredible doctor, you care about your patients, and you go above and beyond. Every time. You're an amazing brother—Hetti says so all the time. You practically raised your siblings without your mother. Sometimes *for* your mother. And you took care of her, too.'

He shook his head, and it was the terrible, tormented expression stalking the darkness of his eyes which really twisted inside her chest. Making her struggle for air.

'Tak…?'

'I wanted her dead,' he whispered at last. So quietly that for a moment she almost missed it.

When she heard him, she didn't answer. Her mind scrabbled around for something to say, the *right* thing to say, that might possibly ease some of that agony on his face.

But nothing came, and the more his eyes raked over her face, wretched, bloodless, the more her brain shut down, leaving her terrified that she might say the wrong thing and somehow make it worse.

In the end Effie did the only thing she could. She reached out and took his big hand in her two smaller ones, hating the way his body jerked as she did so. As if he didn't trust her, when all she wanted was to be there for him.

And then, finally, he started to speak again. 'That's why I let her push me all those years. Why I couldn't just tell her outright to stay out of my business and my life, to shove her idea of an arranged marriage. I hated her, and I wanted her dead, and I've felt guilty for it all this time.'

A gurgling, maniacal laugh bubbled in her throat and

it was all she could do to stuff it back down. This was all so horribly familiar.

'You think you're the only one who has wanted a parent dead?' she asked at length. 'Do you have *any* idea how many times I wished my mother would die? That she would drink herself into oblivion? Drown her failing liver until it finally gave out?'

'Well, I imagined mine might overdose on those pills of hers. Then maybe my father would come home, but I wasn't betting on it. At the very least I figured my siblings would be taken in by other members of the family. Even foster care would have been better.'

'I understand where you were coming from, but it wouldn't have been,' Effie blurted out before she could stop herself. 'You have no idea how bad it is. Plus, you'd have been split up. Your siblings ripped away from you.'

'I didn't realise that back then.' He hunched his shoulders. 'It's only since you came along and opened up to me that I've realised how good we really had it. How lucky we were not to have had *your* childhood.'

Effie shook her head. 'I'm not saying that. I would never say that. It's subjective. In some ways I only had myself to look out for. You had siblings to take care of. But then you were never alone and I was. It's different.'

'All I knew was that the more of a victim she was, the more stupid stunts she pulled to try to win him back. And the more of the monster it brought out in me.'

'You were a kid, Tak.'

'She was my *mother*.'

'She wasn't doing the job of a mother and you resented her for it. Of all people, I can understand that, Tak. Believe me. You were taking responsibility for your siblings when that wasn't supposed to be your job, and she left it to you.'

'But only because my father left *her* to do it. It should have been him I hated. Not her.'

Effie shook her head, her hollow laugh catching them both by surprise. 'It doesn't work that way. *She* was the one you trusted. The one you had expectations from. *He* wasn't. It was the same for me.'

He looked at her. Hard. As if he was trying to see right down to her very soul.

'Trust me, Tak,' she murmured softly. 'I understand where all that came from. And why.'

'Then you understand why I can't be with anyone, then. Why I would only end up hurting them, destroying them.' Bitterness leeched out of his voice, along with regret. 'Destroying *you*.'

'No. I don't see that at all.' She softened her words with a smile.

'Then you're a fool.'

'Possibly. But I think I just see the real you, whilst you're judging your childhood self on the standards of an adult. And I think you do too, or else why would you be here now?'

'I just came to apologise,' he repeated, but it lacked conviction even to his own ears.

The worst of it was that he wanted to believe her. He wanted to believe this version of himself which she claimed she knew. Of a man who might be worthy of her.

'I can't be with you.' He frowned. 'You have a daughter, responsibilities. I would only let you down and resent you for them.'

'Really? Are you sure? Only so far you haven't done either. When I needed somewhere to stay you stepped up. When I told you about Nell you asked me about her. When I confided about that shoplifting you gave me advice. It even worked—'

'You're not listening,' he broke in abruptly. But only because he'd realised he was beginning to listen to Effie and believe in her version of him.

'I *am* listening. I'm just pointing out all the ways I know you're wrong. Not to mention the peace treaty you negotiated between myself and my daughter, and the fact that you took her to that bowling alley party. You're a *good* man, Tak. You always have been.'

'I'm not,' he muttered, but it had lost more of its vehemence.

Slowly, gently, Effie bent her head forward until her forehead was pressed to his.

'Yes. You are. You fight for your family, and when you find the right woman you'll fight for her, too.'

And she said it with such certainty, such ferocity, that Tak felt all his walls beginning to tumble, stone block by stone block. As if her love was a wrecking ball which could topple even the best-built defences.

Love.

The word jolted him. Did she love him? Did he love her?

Possibly, he realised with a start. Perhaps he had even from that first night.

'I've already found her,' he heard himself say instead.

And then, because he didn't know what more to say, he did the only thing he could think of to do.

He snaked his hand up to the back of her neck, tilting her head until their mouths fitted together as though it had been inevitable from the very start of their conversation.

He poured everything he had into that single kiss. As if it would convey all the thoughts he couldn't articulate. As if it would make every word she was saying about him come true.

It was a kiss which went far deeper than anything he could have said, and it might have gone on for an entire eternity. Maybe two.

But it didn't. Ultimately it had to end.

'I didn't mean to do that.' He only half apologised as he lifted his mouth from hers. 'I tried to walk away, Effie.

But I couldn't. There's this dark…*thing* which twists and knots inside me. I don't expect anything from you. I came to tell you that I should have told you the truth from the start. And that I'm sorry I didn't.'

It hurt. So very badly.

'Yes.'

She sounded composed, but he could see the vein pulsing at her neck. A fraction too fast. Too fluttery.

'You *should* have told me that you were using me not simply as a buffer but to shock your family into leaving you alone. You should have been clear that you weren't inviting me to stay because you were worried about Nell and I not having a roof over our heads but because you wanted the dramatic vision of an unmarried single mother being your lover.'

'That's not entirely accurate. I invited you and Nell to stay because I couldn't stand by and watch you live in that flat,' he asserted. 'But once I realised the visual it was creating for the more traditionalist side of my family I admit I played up to it.'

'What about the dates? And taking Nell to that birthday party?'

'I took Nell because she needed the opportunity to go and meet new friends and you were working.'

'But the dating?'

'Yes…' He paused, not even sure himself. 'And no.'

'What about Paris?'

He exhaled heavily. 'I couldn't believe you'd never been out of the country before. I loved the idea of being the person to take you abroad for the first time. But I admit there was also a part of me that knew it would get back to my family and keep things stirred up.'

She nodded, as though she was grateful for his honesty. As though every single word he uttered wasn't rushing into her, pouring into her chest and stinging her heart and stopping it, the way a swarm of bees might kill an enemy one tiny sting at a time. Individually merely painful but combined ultimately fatal.

The way it felt for him.

'Why did you love the idea of taking me abroad?' she managed at last.

Tak fought to gather his thoughts. It wasn't an action he'd had to take before. 'I told you—you got under my skin in a way no one has ever done before. I didn't know what to do with it. It's how things became so confused.'

'I could have forgiven you all of that,' she whispered. 'If you hadn't been intimate with me.'

'Ah…' For the first time in a while that heady, intoxicating glint was reignited in his eyes. He could feel it. 'Now *that*, I can say with absolute honesty, was never part of the plan.'

She stared at him for a long, long moment, and time seemed to stand still. 'Never?'

That flash of hope in her eyes did things to him that he couldn't even understand, let alone explain.

'No, intimacy was never my intention,' he told her honestly. That was simply me finding myself unable to resist you.'

'You couldn't resist me?' Effie was trying to sound sceptical. Worldly.

Tak managed not to grin in triumph. 'How could I?' he murmured. 'Since I'd managed to fall for you.'

Her reaction was all he could have hoped for. From the shallow breathing to the shift in her body language, and from the quickened pulse to the way her all too expressive eyes betrayed her.

'You…you fell for me?'

'I'm in love with you, Effie.'

The words came out on their own. Yet they felt as right and as true as anything ever had.

'Surely you know that? Even if you don't trust me with your head, let your heart answer this one. I love you—and there's no game-play, no agenda. You're the one who broke through to me when I thought it was impossible for anyone to reach me. You're the one who made me finally see that, time and again, I was giving my mother the benefit of the doubt because of all that she'd been through with my father and with Saaj, but she was never going to be the woman or the mother I wanted her to be.'

He spoke as though it was a fact—like his lungs fuelling him with oxygen, or his heart pumping blood around his body. Not that either of them seemed to be functioning normally right now. They seemed to flip-flop between working too hard and forgetting to work at all.

Tak shook his head gently and lifted his palms to cup her face. 'You doubt it?'

She finally found her tongue, ready to counter him as she so often had. But this time her voice was full of awe, incredulity.

'How could I possibly have known? You never once even suggested it.'

'On the contrary…' He dragged his finger over her bottom lip, his eyes following the movement as if spellbound. 'I may not have said the words but I betrayed myself time and again every time I worshipped your body.'

'That was merely sex—'

Her voice was raspy, bumpy. But then, so was his.

'We both know that it was never *merely* sex.'

If only he'd allowed himself to admit that much, much earlier.

'Still, you can't just walk away from your family, Tak. I know how much your siblings mean to you.'

He had to concentrate. Answer her every question. But he was having a hard time not simply bending his head and claiming her again.

'Hetti is in despair,' he muttered, struggling to drag his gaze from those luscious lips of hers. 'She wants you to know how desperately sorry she is. She has no idea how my mother got hold of her key but she is adamant that she didn't give it to her. And Sasha has long since said she can do without the drama. She's trying to concentrate on her own family and she doesn't want them being dragged into that life. As for Rafi—he has loathed both our parents ever since he could talk. I don't think there's any chance of any of them being upset that I've finally decided to cut all ties.'

'It all sounds too perfect, too easy,' Effie vacillated. 'But I don't just have myself to think about. I have Nell. And, as ever, the idea of doing something which could end up harming my daughter in some way is something I refuse to even entertain.'

'I *know* how important Nell is,' he confirmed.

'I want to believe you,' Effie choked out. 'But love… it's a big deal.'

And then he gave up trying to fight his instincts any longer.

'I love you, Effie. And every time I tell you I only become more and more certain of that fact.'

'I want to believe you…'

'I know,' he murmured, lowering his mouth to hers again. 'I know that it's just been you and Nell for so long. I know that with everything you've been through in your life that you've never loved or trusted anyone else this way. But it's time to take that risk, Effie.'

'Tak…'

'Stop over-analysing,' he murmured softly. 'I love you, Effie. I'm *in* love with you. Let me prove it to you. Let me spend the rest of my life proving it to you.'

And then he claimed her mouth and set about honouring his word in the best way he knew how.

EPILOGUE

IT WAS ALMOST three years later to the day when Tak found himself staring at the 4D image of his new baby, who yawned widely before defiantly turning his back on them. It took everything Tak had to tear his gaze from the screen and down to his wife of eighteen months who, impossibly, appeared more beautiful to him with every passing day.

'It's incredible...' he breathed.

'Incredible,' Effie echoed, her hands instinctively reaching for his.

'Nell is going to be livid she missed this,' he smiled. 'Her new baby brother.'

'I promised her we'd watch the video with her as many times as she wants to as soon as she gets home from her exchange trip. Our family.'

Our family. Happiness spiralled through him. His baby, his wife and his stepdaughter—who, at sixteen, was beginning to exert her independence more and more.

Nell was going to be as stunning as her mother, and Tak could imagine the trail of broken-hearted young men she was going to leave in her wake. He might only just have become her stepfather, but he felt honoured that she had accepted him into her life as if he was the real father she'd never had. She had even tagged his name onto her own, just as Effie had.

'We have a new addition to our family, Mrs Robinson-Basu,' he whispered, awe flowing throughout his body.

'We do!' Her eyes shone brightly—too brightly.

'More tears of joy?' He laughed. 'You're turning into quite the mushy little thing, aren't you?'

'Shut up,' she chastised him with a laugh. 'And just be glad that I love you as much as I do, Tak Basu.'

'You do, huh?' he teased her, never tiring of hearing her say those words.

'I do,' she confirmed. 'I love you.'

'And I love you too.' He dropped a kiss on her lips, then on her stomach. 'And I love *you*, little one. With all my heart.'

* * * * *

FROM DOCTOR
TO DADDY

BECKY WICKS

MILLS & BOON

PROLOGUE

FRASER STOPPED TO rest his arms on the ledge at the top of Edinburgh Castle. Brick houses, trees, and in the distance sparkling water shone like a painting under a clear blue sky. He inhaled a lungful of fresh Scottish air. The city was so damn beautiful when the sun shone.

The surgery was crazy, as usual, and he'd taken a morning walk to prep himself, but someone needed him already. He could tell by the vibrations in his pocket.

He pulled out his phone, turning his face to the rare sun. 'Hi, Anton.'

'Fraser, good morning. I came across a file that might be of interest for the *Ocean Dream*, if you're still looking for a dialysis nurse.'

'I am.' Fraser smiled at two kids running around a cannon, pretending to shoot each other.

He couldn't really remember which positions had been filled and which hadn't—he'd been so busy. In truth, he hadn't had time to think much about working on the cruise ship at all this year. That was why he'd put Anton in charge of recruiting the medical team.

'I've found a great dialysis nurse in London who fits the bill. But—get this. She *also* has a five-year-old daughter who's on the kidney donor list. Rare blood type. The kid's never been on a ship before, so naturally I thought...'

'Sounds great.' Fraser held the phone closer as the kids ran shrieking around him. He really needed all this in an email, otherwise he'd forget, but he asked anyway. 'What's the nurse's name?' He started walking across the court towards the gate.

'Her name is Sara…'

Anton paused, obviously to look at something.

'Sara Cohen—and her kid's name is Esme.'

Fraser stopped abruptly and gripped the phone tight in his hand. A tourist almost walked into the back of him.

'Sara Cohen?' The name brought a thin sheen of sweat to his forehead. The cool breeze blew over it, giving him goose bumps. How long had it been since he'd heard that name? Six years? After a while he'd stopped counting.

He mouthed an apology to the lady he'd stopped in front of. Her eyes swept his tall frame, in jeans, a fitted shirt and blazer, and she blushed.

He stepped aside. 'Anton, when is the cruise, exactly—remind me?'

'A month from today,' Anton said. 'Her daughter is pretty pumped for it, as you can imagine. Sara's just waiting on the go-ahead from St Gilda's, where she works, but between you and me I think we've found our fit.'

Fraser's head was still reeling. *Sara Cohen had a five-year-old daughter?* Maybe it was a different Sara Cohen. 'What's her background?

He forced his legs to continue down the hill, through the crowds of tourists, past the bagpipe player in his kilt at the bottom.

Anton described the nurse's profile, some of which he knew, some of which he didn't. It was definitely the same Sara Cohen.

Six years had come between them. Six years of no contact… Aside from that one time he'd flown to London to talk to her and seen her with that other guy. The sight had made his insides burn. He'd regretted going there instantly, and hadn't attempted contact with her since. Not that she'd made any attempt with him either.

'What about the father?' he said now, trying not to sound as if he was fishing. 'Esme's father—Sara's husband?'

'It'll just be the two of them,' Anton said. 'She's single, as far as I know.'

In the car on his way to the surgery, Fraser's brain ran on overdrive. He could still see her face, standing in his bedroom, telling him they should go their separate ways. She'd never even let him have a say.

He could also vividly picture her standing with that guy, outside the restaurant at the end of her street. She'd been in a nurse's uniform. Had that been Esme's father? Why had he left them?

Think about this, he told himself sternly as he drove. He'd been about to cancel his work on the cruise—send someone else in his place. The Breckenridge Practice was busier than ever. Plus, living away from his mother in the new apartment still left him with enough of a twinge of guilt without him heading off to sea. His parents had run the practice from an extension of the huge family home for fifteen years. It still felt empty without his father.

But this was *Sara Cohen*. The woman he'd sworn six years ago he would one day make his wife.

Maybe he should rethink working on one more cruise.

CHAPTER ONE

No sooner had Sara heaved her suitcase onto her single bed and flung it open than a voice sounded out over the Tannoy, making her jump.

'Could all renal care specialists report on Deck One for orientation in five minutes' time? Thank you.'

She swept the back of her hand across her clammy brow and caught sight of herself in the tiny mirror, visible through the open bathroom door. Calling it a bathroom was a stretch, and already a source of amusement. She'd never been in a bathroom that looked this much like a cupboard before.

Running the tap and splashing cold water onto her face, she considered that she shouldn't have taken that call from her father back at the hotel, which in turn had caused them to board the *Ocean Dream* at the very last minute. Now she had barely any time to change before she was due upstairs to join Esme and her new on-board carers, plus all the other patients she'd be sailing through the Caribbean with.

'Anything can happen at sea. You'd better look after each other.'

She recalled the gentle warning in her father's words. She hoped he needed no real reassurance that Esme would be fine. She was in her care after all.

She also hoped Esme wasn't too scared, up on deck. This was a big deal for a five-year-old—let alone one like Esme. Not only was this the first time she'd been on a ship, or a boat of any kind, it was her first time away from the dialysis clinic.

She hurried to reapply her lipstick in the tiny mirror.

Esme was the lucky one here, really. She got to share a big cabin on another floor with several other kids—like a giant fun sleepover, complete with two carers on shift at all times. Sara was going to have to work night shifts, so sharing a cabin with her daughter just wouldn't have been an option.

Applying her mascara, she thought of her sister, and their conversation the night before they'd left London for Fort Lauderdale.

'I still can't believe you're working on a cruise. I thought you hated the ocean,' Megan had said.

'I don't *hate* the ocean. You *think* I hate the ocean because I didn't want to go snorkelling with you and your Latino lover. You were all over each other out there—I'm surprised the fish didn't throw up.'

They'd laughed, but they'd both known it was still a bit of a sore point that their last 'girls' holiday' together—almost a year ago now—had wound up with Megan frolicking in the waves for a week with a Mexican guy called Pedro, while Sara read the entire *Game of Thrones* series on her sun-lounger, feeling guilty about leaving Esme.

'It's not for pleasure this time anyway—it's for work.'

'I know...' Megan had sighed.

Megan knew all about the haemodialysis patients, of course, and how much Sara cared for every single one in her charge.

If it hadn't been for Esme's illness, Sara would probably never have thought about adding dialysis training to her medical repertoire, but she was thankful now, more than ever, that she had.

'Can you believe I get to introduce her to this new world,

Megan? I get to help *all* these people see places they never thought they'd see.'

'I think it's amazing, what you're doing,' her sister had told her sincerely. 'But just make sure you have some fun yourself this time, OK?'

'I know, I know.'

The dialysis care was just part of Sara's new position on the ship. She'd been hired as a member of the *Ocean Dream*'s wider medical team.

While she'd signed up for Esme's benefit, and for whomever else might need her expertise on-board, she knew that during their free periods the ship's staff were permitted to hang out on the main deck, where a lot of activities were set to take place.

They would be able to mingle with the guests and even go shore-side if the ship was in port. It was pretty much all-expenses-paid travel with a salary on top, and an opportunity she hadn't been able to refuse when that nice recruitment guy Anton had called.

Draping her ship ID on its lanyard around her neck, she hurried out of the cabin and made her way down the narrow corridor to the elevator, smoothing her blonde shoulder-length waves of hair as she went.

She observed again the opulence of the ship. Paintings depicting landscapes and seascapes hung on the walls of the dark wood-panelled corridors. The golden railings beneath them warned of potential bumpy waters. But she was more excited than nervous.

The *Ocean Dream*'s dialysis team involved a handful of dedicated professionals from the UK, who would be caring for individuals on dialysis. Most of their patients were travelling with their families from Port Everglades.

She'd been told some of the regular medical staff on board rotated around various ships throughout the season. It sounded like a fascinating lifestyle. But for her this was a one-off. She could never contemplate it long term while she had Esme's illness and her schooling to contend with.

'It's so fancy, isn't it?' An elderly lady giggled as she passed a painting of a golden-tailed mermaid.

'It's "a five-star hotel on the ocean",' Sara replied, quoting the website and hurrying on towards the upper deck, her green summer dress swishing at her ankles.

Passengers were still wheeling cases into staterooms on both sides of her and she felt another spike of exhilaration. The *Ocean Dream* was a luxurious beast, packed with almost five thousand regular customers, all paying top coin for, also quoting the website, *A unique combination of first-class accommodation, live entertainment, exceptional cuisine and a wide choice of restaurants, bars, lounges and clubs.*

Bermuda, Aruba and Antigua were all on the itinerary. And Sara was still grinning at the prospect of introducing Esme to the joys of sandcastle-building in the Caribbean when she reached the deck.

The harsh Florida sun launched at her head and shoulders, blinding her for a moment to the crowd gathered round a makeshift stage where Dr Renee Forster, the highly regarded leader of the dialysis team and one of the two practising nephrologists on board, was already speaking.

'Sorry I'm late,' she whispered to Esme's official carer, Jess.

Esme, standing at her knee height in denim shorts and a purple T-shirt, seemed concerned.

Sara took her little fingers. 'How are you doing, baby girl?'

Esme shrugged at the floor.

'We're so excited to have you all on board today!' Dr Forster, a tall African American woman with a hard New York accent, was beaming. 'As you can see, the weather is perfect, and our captain assures me that our departure and our days at sea en-route to Aruba will be plain sailing. Plenty of time for us all to get to know each other.'

Sara squeezed Esme's small hand reassuringly. She looked around her. It seemed her own daughter was set to be her youngest dialysis patient, which wasn't unusual.

Perspiring porters in white and blue uniforms were still loading crates and bags and boxes from ramps onto the ship. Palm trees were waving from the port like jealous passengers.

She noticed a kid in green board shorts far across the deck—not part of their group. He was whispering something to his mother, who looked away quickly when Sara met her eyes.

Instincts primed, she knew the young boy had been asking about the bandage over Esme's catheter, poking out above the neckline of her T-shirt. It was either that or the camcorder Esme wouldn't put down. It was practically glued to her hand these days.

'What a ship, huh?' she whispered, concerned that her sweet daughter might see the boy and feel embarrassed. Esme was already more than aware of how different she was from other children. 'Are you as excited as me right now?'

Esme just shrugged again. Something twisted in Sara's gut. It wasn't straightforward, bringing a kid on dialysis on holiday.

Dr Forster was still speaking. 'Remember, our nurses are experienced, licensed dialysis nurses, so you're in good hands. We're all here to ensure your exact dialysis prescriptions are met, and also that your special dietary needs are accommodated with the help of the ship's dining staff. That's them over there.'

Sara turned to where she was pointing. The line-up of catering staff raised their hands in greeting. They scanned the faces of the roughly twenty patients they'd be caring for, their eyes all lit up in excitement.

'I'd like to take this opportunity to introduce the wonderful Dr Fraser Breckenridge, our Chief Doctor and Head of the *Ocean Dream*'s Medical Department. He'll be overseeing all the medical issues aboard the ship, so chances are you'll see him around. Can you come up here for a second, Dr Breckenridge?'

Sara blinked. Maybe she'd misheard.

No, she hadn't misheard.

Time stopped and then started moving backwards.

Fraser Breckenridge, in all his gym-honed glory, was striding from her vivid memory bank, right into her present. She watched in shock as he took his place on the stage.

It can't be...

Dr Forster handed him a microphone. Sara scanned his muscled six-foot-three frame as his presence immediately dominated not just the stage, but the entire deck of the ship. It was really him. *Why?* And why did he have to look so good?

She couldn't help but stare. From where she was standing he looked exactly as he had the night she'd left him in his giant family home that doubled as the Breckenridge Practice in Edinburgh. She hadn't heard from him since—not that she blamed him for that entirely. She'd never thought she'd see him again.

She considered sneaking away from the orientation, but Esme still had hold of her hand. Besides, the second Fraser's thick, unmistakably Scottish accent filled the air with its sticky heat, her legs turned to jelly. God, she had loved this man. Just the sound of his voice brought it all rushing back.

'Thank you so much, ladies and gents,' he said with gravelly familiarity, towering over Dr Forster in spite of her own height, and sweeping a big hand through his mane of thick black hair.

Sara could picture his eyes too, up close, and the honest blue of them she'd been happy to swim in for hours. She swallowed as the deck seemed to close in on her.

'I'm privileged to be able to join you on this special adventure. I know that for some of you this is the first time you'll have been on a ship—am I right? Who's never been on a ship before?'

To Sara's surprise, Esme released her grip on her and raised her hand tentatively. Her throat dried up as Fraser's eyes travelled to her daughter and then landed right on *her*. A tiny trail of perspiration began its descent down her lower back. She raised her hand at him slowly, in greeting. He did the same—like a Martian making contact with another planet. A flicker of a smile crossed his lips.

'Well, it looks like we're going to have some fun on this cruise,' he said, after a pause.

Sara wasn't entirely sure if he was still talking to Esme, or to her. She was picturing his lips now, too. The way they'd used to seem to melt against hers.

She hadn't read the staff list. She kicked herself. She'd had every intention of running her eyes over it, along with the plethora of other information she'd been sent, but Esme had been in a panic over a missing shoe when it had arrived in her inbox and she'd been side-tracked.

'Let me tell you: this weather is a tad nicer than it is in Edinburgh right now. I hope you won't be too horrified if this pale white Scottish skin turns as red as a lobster's!'

Esme giggled at Fraser's words, as did most of the crowd. Sara just felt hot and bothered. She was back in that huge Scottish house now, standing stunned on the stairs, hearing his father tell Fraser what he really thought about their six-month relationship, hearing Fraser do *nothing* to defend it—or her. They hadn't known she'd been listening.

Fraser was still talking, introducing the other staff—

introducing *her*. 'Please also welcome Sara Cohen, one of our excellent dialysis nurses.'

She tried not to flinch as everyone turned to her and applauded, while Esme leaned into her shyly, clutching her camera. Annoyance was quickly overriding shock.

How dared he rock up here, on *her* adventure, six years after he'd let her go? OK, so she'd chosen to end their relationship herself that night, after overhearing their little family conversation. But if she hadn't done it Fraser would only have done it himself. She'd simply been saving him the bother and herself the heartbreak.

She hadn't needed any more heartbreak back then. Her mother had just died and her father had completely fallen apart. She'd been exhausted from taking care of him, all whilst dealing with her own grief. She'd been at Fraser's place for the weekend to cry in his arms, to let someone take care of *her* for a while. And then...

'Now, I'm sure you're all excited to get going and see what's planned for you. I'll hand you over to our events coordinator to tell you more.'

Fraser still had the audience enchanted.

'I'm looking forward to getting to know some of you over the next few weeks—although, let's be honest here, most people seem to have a better time on this ship if they never get to see me at all, if you know what I mean!'

Jess took Esme's other hand. 'Ready to meet the other kids?' she asked her daughter cheerily.

Sara dropped a kiss on Esme's cheek. Her heart was thudding as they walked away. A guy with a topknot called Tony was already on the stage, talking of tropical island walks and buffet lunches. And Fraser was heading straight through the crowd towards her.

She turned quickly towards the exit. She needed space to think. Maybe she and Esme could transfer ships. There was another one leaving in a few days' time; perhaps they could

switch and avoid this. It was the last thing she needed—
dredging up her painful past in the middle of the ocean,
with no escape.

'Sara Cohen! Come on—don't walk away from me, lass.'

Fraser's voice was a powerful lasso, stopping her in her
tracks. She closed her eyes as her hand found the smooth
cool steel of the door handle. *So surreal.*

'After all this time,' he said, putting a big hand to her
shoulder and causing goosebumps to flare on her hot skin.
'Weren't you even going to say hello?'

CHAPTER TWO

'WHAT ARE YOU doing here?'

'You didn't know I'd be on board?' He ran his eyes over her green dress, noting the way it nipped in at her slender waist. She'd barely put on a pound. In fact, maybe she'd even lost weight. Her bronzed cheekbones were sharper than he remembered. Perhaps her hair was shorter...

She bit her lip. He still remembered the feel of his tongue running along that lip.

'I can't do this,' she said. 'Please, Fraser, not here.'

She turned from him quickly again, pulled the door open and headed down the top floor corridor of the ship.

He followed her and caught her arm gently. 'Sara, come on.' He forced his voice to remain calm. 'Can we go somewhere and talk?'

A look of discomfort verging on pain flashed across her features before she pulled away from him. 'I don't know what's going on,' she said, standing against the wall in the corridor. 'But I'm here with my daughter and I'm here to work. This is just...' She folded her arms. Then she closed her eyes, appearing unnerved by his proximity. 'This is just not what I was expecting.'

'I'm sorry.' He stepped closer anyway, on the anchor-patterned carpet, till his feet were almost touching hers. 'I thought you knew I'd be here,' he said honestly. 'I assumed you'd have seen the list of medical staff and would have called me, or not taken the job if you had a real problem with it.'

He could smell her perfume—different from the one he remembered. It was like an extra layer to her he'd never known, and it served to widen the gap that had clearly grown between them over the years.

'How would I have called you?' she challenged him. 'I don't have your number any more.'

'I never changed it. You also know where I work. Remember? It's the house you walked out of with no credible explanation?'

Flecks of amber flickered around her pupils, launching him straight back to those nights when he'd spent for ever just lying in bed next to her, observing the colours in her eyes.

'Well, maybe I would have tried calling you if I'd known what was coming,' she said. 'But for now I suppose I should just try and transfer ships. If you'll excuse me?'

She continued towards the elevator at the end of the corridor. He followed her. He hadn't expected that. 'Cohen, we need to talk about this like adults.'

'Why?'

Her arms were still folded as she waited for the elevator. She scanned his tall frame as she dug her own nails into her flesh, exhaling a harried sigh.

'Fraser, seriously, what are you *doing* here? Aren't you supposed to be running the Breckenridge Practice in Edinburgh?'

'Things change.' He lowered his voice. This wasn't the place to explain about that.

A voice called out behind him. 'Watch out, mister!'

'Sorry, man!' Fraser had almost caused a deck hand to crash into them. The young lad was carrying a heavy crate of what looked like fruit towards them.

Pulling Sara against the wall with him, to make room, Fraser covered her hand with his against the smooth wooden wall and squeezed it tight.

'God, I've missed you,' he found himself saying. 'I like your hair like that.'

He swore he felt her shiver. For a second he saw a glimmer of the old her, the way she'd been before she'd taken it upon herself to end things just six months after they'd started something really good. The last time they'd exchanged any words at all she'd been just twenty-five, and he twenty-six.

'Let's go somewhere and clear the air,' he said, seizing his chance as the elevator doors opened. 'Sara, you never really let me have my say back then. I understand you were grieving for your mother, but a lot was going on and—'

'A lot is going on *now*,' she said.

Her walls were back up, clearly.

'Listen, I'm getting my stuff, then I'm going to see if Esme and I can be put on another cruise. This is beyond unprofessional Fraser. What makes you think you can trap me on a ship and tell me you've missed me, and expect me to just—'

'*Trap* you on a ship?' He smiled in spite of it all. The door shut behind them. The deckhand pressed the button reading 'Deck Four' with his elbow, still holding the crate. 'I would never trap you anywhere, Sara. I let you go six years ago, didn't I?'

She chewed on her cheek, looking at the floor. 'We let each other go, Fraser. The past is the past and it's where it should stay. I have Esme to think about now.'

'I never even knew you had a daughter.'

'She was a surprise for me, too.'

He frowned internally at this new information. 'I'm so sorry—about the dialysis, I mean.'

'We don't need your pity.'

'That's not what I…' He shut his mouth, seeing she was clearly uncomfortable. Almost as uncomfortable as the deck hand, now staring at his crate. What a tragedy for the family, though—as if Sara losing her mother hadn't been tragic enough.

Sara had been inconsolable after her mother had died. It had been extremely sudden. Cancer, stage three, terminal. After it had happened he'd flown to London to be with her. He'd skipped classes and his duties to stay beside her, then he'd invited her back to Scotland.

His father had been less than impressed.

He'd been under so much pressure back then, to help his parents secure the future of the practice. Remodelling had been needed, and new equipment, more staff. They'd needed money—*his* money, from the family trust fund.

He'd been juggling extra studies with extra work for his father, in order to qualify faster, when Sara had ended their relationship out of nowhere, citing the need to focus on her own family back in London. When she'd left him it had hit him like an avalanche.

The elevator doors were flung open. The deck hand shuffled off with his crate, without a word.

'Stop following me,' Sara huffed as he followed her down the corridor. She swiped her ID, which doubled as a key card, and went to shut the cabin door after herself.

He was ready for it. He wedged a foot in the door to stop it closing. 'Have you thought about Esme upstairs, all excited about this trip, while you're down here thinking about leaving? 'We have a job to do, here, Cohen.'

'Have I thought about Esme? She is *all* I think about!'

He regretted his words. 'I'm sorry. I just… God, woman, just let me in.'

She tutted loudly as she moved from blocking the door, and he squeezed into the cabin after her.

Looking around, he let out a small laugh that he stifled before she got even more annoyed. '*This* is where they put you?'

'Why? Where did they put *you*?' Sara looked confused now, forgetting her anger for a second.

He bit his tongue. It probably wasn't the best time to tell her that he'd been given a double suite all to himself. He had a leather couch, a balcony, a mini-bar and a TV, complete with a shelf full of DVDs. One of them was *Titanic*. He couldn't imagine anyone watching *Titanic* on a cruise ship...

Sara was gathering up items from the tiny bathroom to put in her suitcase. 'Wow... OK, Cohen, you're serious.'

'Stop calling me that.'

'I always call you that—it's your name, isn't it? Unless you're married.' He feigned indifference. Anton had told him she was single—as far as he knew, at least.

'I'm not married,' she confirmed quickly. 'I never was. Esme's father is long gone.'

He saw her cast a glance to his finger—checking for a ring, perhaps?

'I've been too busy to date much, never mind get married. The practice takes a lot of work,' he explained.

'I'm sure it does. It always did.'

Her dig stung.

'Don't you think it will look a wee bit strange to our patients if one of their trusted dialysis nurses disembarks before we've even gone anywhere?' he pointed out. 'You've come a long way for this, Sara. You both have.'

Sara ignored him, though she'd started packing more slowly already. She knew she had no intention of leaving—not really. She was just feeling put on the spot, out of her depth.

'So, how long has Esme been on dialysis?' He lowered himself onto the single bed and noticed two knitting needles and a ball of red wool sticking out of the case before she pulled a sweater on top of them.

'Too long. She was eight months old when she got E. coli. It got worse and turned into HUS.'

'Haemolytic uremic syndrome?' He was well aware of how such a disease could destroy the kidneys.

'She's on the transplant list but there's never been a match for her. I tell her it's because she's special—which she is. She's so special that none of her family can help her with a new kidney.'

The tone of her voice made him reach a hand to her arm again, briefly. 'That must be tough, Sara.'

She studied his long fingers. 'It's OK. We live with Dad and he helps out at home. We have things under control… most of the time. So where exactly is *your* cabin, hotshot?'

She clearly wanted to change the subject. 'Hotshot?' he said out loud. Sara was pretty hot too, from what he remembered.

They'd met in Edinburgh, where she'd been in training for an advanced nursing degree. At the time he'd been in and out of St Enid's hospital, in his last year of a three-year residency, and he'd noticed her at first because of her knitting. Sara Cohen had knitted whenever she'd had a spare moment. Baby clothes, she'd told him later, on their first date, for the kids on the children's ward.

He'd only *really* taken notice of her that time in the treatment room, when she'd done some tests on him ahead of a marathon he'd been about to run. He recalled it again now—that day the sparks had first flown—and couldn't help smiling ruefully.

'My cabin's up on the second deck,' he told her, picturing them both in his bed as he said it. He couldn't help it.

The Tannoy cut in.

'Ladies and gentlemen, we'll be leaving port in approximately fifteen minutes. Please do join us on the top deck for your welcome drink and to wave goodbye to land for a couple of days. We wish you all a safe and happy journey!'

'I have to go.' Sara dragged her suitcase off the bed, narrowly missing his foot with it.

Fraser took it from her hands with ease. 'Give me a break, Cohen. You know you don't really want to go.'

'I told you to stop calling me that.'

She flung the cabin door open and heaved the suitcase from his hands, hauling it out into the corridor. She made it to the elevator again, panting, and pressed the button.

Part of him was impressed. 'You're seriously going to get off this ship? In front of everyone up there?' he asked in the elevator. The mirrors reflected an infinite number of Saras. He didn't miss her looking at him, though.

'Yes, Fraser, that is exactly what I'm going to do.'

'I can't wait to see this.' He could tell she thought she'd gone too far with her dramatics to back down now. As stubborn as ever.

Back on deck, he held his hand up to stop a porter rushing to help her. Esme wandered over to them. She was holding a camcorder. He noticed her catheter now, the pink of her cheeks.

'Well, hello again, you.' He bent down to her height, held out his hand. 'We never officially met.'

The kid had Sara's eyes—almond-shaped pools filled with questions. What kind of father would abandon his kid? He didn't know the full story, of course, but he couldn't imagine it was a happy one.

'Are you having fun?' he asked her.

'Kind of. What's my mum doing?'

Sara was trying her hardest to stop three men from pulling in a walkway that led down to the pier. Someone blew a whistle. People were waving goodbye to others below.

'Your mum's just processing some new information. She'll be fine. I see we have the ship's film-maker on board already. Have you got any good stuff yet, Miss Spielberg?'

She giggled. 'Some.'

'Maybe we can take you behind the scenes sometime? Show you the kitchens and the bridge?'

Her eyes lit up. 'Yes, please! Can I get some film of *you*?'

'Only if you capture my good side. Which side do you think that is?' He turned his head from side to side, pulling different faces as he did so, and Esme giggled again, her whole face lighting up.

From the corner of his eye he saw Sara watching them. He stood straighter and took Esme's little hand as the ship juddered. It was too late for her to make her exit.

'No luck? You can always swim for it,' he teased as she approached them.

She rolled her eyes, but he didn't miss the slight smile on her lips. Esme skipped off to view the ship's departure through the railings.

'Thanks for that—she seems a bit happier now, at least,' Sara said with a sigh.

Her green dress blew against his legs. 'She's going to have a great time,' he assured her.

'She's bullied, you know. The kids call her names because of the central line in her neck. I got her the camera so she could make a video diary—show people she can live a normal life, doing stuff like this. I thought she could put it on her donor page.'

Sara swept her blonde hair behind her ears, following Esme with her eyes. Fraser thought again how messed up it was that they hadn't found a donor for her yet. 'That's a great idea.'

'I don't want anything to ruin this trip for Esme, Fraser.'

'Neither do I.'

'What's this doing here?' Dr Renee Forster had walked over and was pointing down at Sara's suitcase in the middle of the deck. 'Everything OK?'

'She spilled some water on it downstairs,' Fraser said quickly. 'She thought the sun would dry it off faster.'

Sara held up her hands. 'Silly me. But it worked; it's already dry.'

Renee raised her eyebrows. 'I see. Good to have you both on board. You know each other well, I take it?'

'We did a long time ago.'

Sara shifted uncomfortably on the spot and he tried not to smirk.

'We dated for six months, actually,' he said. 'We're in a kind of the-one-that-got-away situation.'

Sara turned to him in shock, but he shrugged his shoulders. Staff on these cruises had no secrets. And anything that needed to be addressed was bound to come out, one way or another.

As the ship finally pulled away to the cheers of the crowd, the thought made him anxious almost as much as it thrilled him.

CHAPTER THREE

'CAN I HAVE pizza tonight?' Esme asked. 'Because we're on holiday?'

Sara finished unhooking her daughter from the dialysis machine. 'Sorry, sweetie, but you already know that's not a good idea. Your diet should stay the same, so you're not poorly.'

Esme groaned and laid her head down heavily on the pillow.

'I know it's hard,' Sara sympathised. 'There's a lot of great food on this ship.'

That was an understatement. The food on the *Ocean Dream* was unlike anything she'd ever seen or tasted. Each buffet was like a dream, with everything from lobster sushi rolls to king crab soufflé, to marinated steaks and more cakes than she could count.

'If I can't have pizza, can I have ice-cream? Just a bit?'

Sara turned off the dialysis machine and readjusted the lines from Esme's catheter. 'We'll see. You *have* to stop pointing that thing at me!' She play-swiped at the camcorder lens that was pointed at her face.

'Dr Fraser doesn't mind being on camera.'

'Yes, well…'

Sara snapped off her gloves a little too loudly. She was burning to know more about Fraser—why he'd left the family practice, how often he did these cruises, whether he'd met anyone else since her. Especially that. But she didn't want to appear as if she was invested in anything Fraser Breckenridge had going on any more.

She'd meant what she said. Esme came first. She was all that mattered. Besides, they were professionals, and Renee was already looking between them like Cupid eyeing up the perfect target for an arrow.

Fraser had asked if they could talk privately once they reached Aruba and left the ship. She'd refused, maintaining she was there to concentrate on her work and Esme, not dwell on their past relationship. But a mish-mash of memories had kept her up the last two nights—things she hadn't thought about in years.

'Code Blue. Is anyone close to the casino? Can we get help in the casino, please?'

The Tannoy was practically screaming. Jess stood up from her chair in the corner. 'Code Blue in the casino? That's just next door!'

'Take Esme to the playroom, will you?' Sara unhooked another dialysis patient beside her and hurried outside.

The flashing lights and jingling slot machines in the ship's casino launched an attack on her senses. She gripped her *Ocean Dream* branded medical case harder as she started down an aisle, waiting for her eyes to adjust.

'Sara! Over here.'

People were being ushered away by a security guard wearing the ship's smart grey uniform. Fraser was crouched on his haunches over a large balding gentleman in his mid to late fifties.

'What happened?' She dropped to her knees beside him. It could have been the sight of him, knee-deep in an emergency, but her heart immediately upped its pounding.

'Cardiac arrest. Help me intubate him. I've already called for a stretcher.' He paused for a beat to meet her eyes. 'They said he won some pretty big money. He obviously got so excited he collapsed.'

Sara felt stabs of adrenaline, as if she was hot-wired to Fraser as he started CPR. Nosy onlookers in cruise ship attire and enough bling to sink the ship stood out against others who were happily still playing on the slot machines, only feet away.

She finished fixing the Ambu-bag and an oxygen cylinder, then quickly lifted out the nasal tubes. Fraser took over. His Adam's apple rose subtly above the collar of his white shirt and she followed it up to the dark line of stubble around his jaw as he pumped on the rich man's hairy, tanned chest. A Rolex watch caught her eye. A golden wedding band.

Fraser held the man's head back so she could help, and she lifted his puffy eyelids, noting the pale green irises. Behind her a slot machine dispensed more coins with a happy jingle. So bizarre.

She inserted the tube into the man's trachea slowly, while the efficient blur that was Fraser administered more CPR. His biceps flexed through his shirt. Sweat glistened on his neck. Someone was talking about a stretcher. It was close. But she could barely hear a thing against the pinging and spinning and chinking of the coins.

'Go again!'

Holding the man's head on her lap, she put two fingers to his neck as Fraser commenced with another set of compressions. His hair was falling almost into his steely blue eyes. He was completely focused.

She held her breath. Still no movement under her fingers. Fraser watched her shake her head and used the Ambu-bag for rescue breaths. Their shoulders were touching. A stretcher was being carried down the aisle.

'Everyone move aside, please. We have a medical emergency. Move aside, please.'

People responded quickly to Fraser, reading the waves of urgency in his words. Where was this man's wife? Sara wondered. Was she on board too? Maybe he'd come here without her? Lots of people came on cruises alone—some kind of escapism, she supposed, from whatever they hoped could be left on shore.

They lifted the man onto the stretcher together.

Was Fraser Breckenridge escaping something out here? He'd tried to call her after she'd left him six years ago, but she hadn't answered. When she'd fallen pregnant, after an out-of-character, grief-stricken, vodka-fuelled one-night stand, she'd seen it as one more sign that she and Fraser were truly over—especially when he'd stopped trying to contact her. Even if Fraser *had* wanted to be with her, there was no way she would have asked him to help raise another man's baby.

'Let's get him on life support,' Fraser said, jolting her back to the moment.

The medical centre, which was more like an infirmary, was located on the second deck. The smell of disinfectant was an extra punch to her swirling gut as they hurried in, and she clicked onto autopilot as they passed oxygen masks and pads and the IV.

Fraser arranged the patient on one of the few beds. It was just the two of them in the room. She started tugging the man's shirt open even further, noting the soft gleam on his bald forehead, the dents around his ears from his glasses. Where *were* his glasses?

She prepped him for the defibrillator, just as Fraser rushed to hook it up. She watched him administer the jolts at one-fifty, eyeing the defib screen for signs of life, and noticed, despite herself, the faint lines on Fraser's face that hadn't been there six years ago—extra layers of thought around his forehead.

There was still no pulse.

'Give me more,' he instructed.

She obeyed and prayed it would work. The room was

getting hotter. It felt as if hours had passed in the tiniest space she'd ever had to work in, packed with lab test equipment, immobilisation boards, X-ray and EKG machines and bottle after bottle of pills. Through the window land was now in sight, shimmering green under bright sunshine.

It was still a whole new world to her. It clearly wasn't to Fraser.

'We have a pulse!' she announced finally, and relief flooded her veins.

A knock on the door minutes later made her jump, and she found her hand on Fraser's arm. He steadied her, and at his touch she felt something inside her waking from a deep slumber.

'Is he alive? Oh, God, please don't tell me he's dead. He always said he wanted to die on a cruise ship… He blimmin' well said that before we left…'

A busty, tanned woman was talking at the speed of an auctioneer as she tottered over on high heels and placed two leathery brown hands on their patient's cheeks, peering with squinty eyes into his big round face.

'He's breathing,' she stated.

Sara couldn't tell specifically if the woman thought that was a good thing or a bad thing.

'You'll be happy to know he has more than a few years left in him yet,' Fraser told her.

Sara watched the woman pull something from her glossy designer handbag. 'I'm so sorry, Harry. I was in the wine club with the ladies.' She placed a pair of glasses on his face before dropping a tender kiss on his forehead.

Maybe she really did love poor old Harry, Sara thought, glancing at Fraser, who promptly shot her a wink. Love wasn't always black and white, after all. Perhaps she should give Fraser a chance to say his piece. What had happened between them hadn't all been his fault, after all; maybe they owed it to each other at least to get the past out, so that they could put it behind them and work together without it hanging over them.

Right?

No. Bad idea.

Hearing Fraser explain himself might mean she'd open a door that was better off closed. No matter the attraction that would never go away, everything was different now. Esme needed her mother's full attention. What if they couldn't find a donor for her?

Oh, God, she couldn't lose Esme.

CHAPTER FOUR

'WHAT'S THAT THING stuck to your body?' The kid in the bright green board shorts was pointing a finger at Esme's catheter. 'Are you an alien?'

Fraser's brow creased where he sat three feet away on a beach chair, but Esme dropped the spade she was carrying and turned on her camcorder.

'What do you know about kidneys? Three, two, one—go!' She was challenging the kid, with five years of confidence behind her words. 'I bet you don't know *anything*.'

The boy's face scrunched up. He put a hand over the lens as his mother called out from beneath a giant sun hat in the shallows. 'Marcus! What are you doing?'

'You're weird,' Marcus told Esme loudly, and ran off.

Sara was off her chair in a flash.

'It's OK, Mummy.' Esme sounded tired. 'I know he just doesn't understand.'

'No, he doesn't.'

Fraser watched Sara reapplying her daughter's sunscreen, listened to her chatter, trying to make her smile. She made a great mother. He'd always known she would make a good mother, and there had been a time when he'd actually thought they'd make a great team as parents some day—not that he'd ever told her that.

Sara had her work cut out for her, though. Esme was smart and resilient and beautiful, and who knew her fate, exactly? Some people on dialysis lived a long time. Others didn't.

He stood and got them both to pose with their backs to the ocean for a photo. Jess, the carer, took the camera and urged him into the shot.

'That's OK,' he told her, but Esme had other ideas.

'Dr Fraser, come and be in our photo!'

He waded into the shallows, eyes on Sara. Her expression gave nothing away. The hot sun was playing on her blue bikini top as Esme clung to their hands in the middle of them and demanded to be bounced up and down in the waves.

'Again!' she cried as they lifted her up and down.

'You're a bossy little Spielberg,' Fraser told her, picking her up and putting her on his shoulders in the surf. He pretended he was about to dunk her, lowering himself down into the water and then standing again quickly.

Esme screeched with laughter. When he caught her eye, Sara was laughing too.

'Where *is* this place?' Sara asked him later, taking his hand and letting him help her off the scooter he'd hired. He gestured widely in front of him, to the brownish-red boulders standing tall like fallen pieces of a distant planet in the middle of the desert.

'I thank you, fine lady, for accompanying me to the Casibari Rock Formations.'

He helped her unbuckle her helmet and held it as she shook out her hair. The sky was a deep blue, the scalding sun was trying its best to break through his sunscreen, and all around them cactuses sprang like gnarly hands from the dusty ground.

They'd left Esme playing on the beach with Jess and some other kids, and he'd seized his chance to get Sara alone—finally.

'They're so smooth and weird-looking,' she said about the rocks, stepping forward along the dusty path.

He couldn't help but see her bikini bottoms through her sarong; the curve of her ass. 'How did they get here?'

'No one really knows,' he said. Some people think aliens brought them here.'

She smiled. '"ET phone home"?' Her fuchsia sarong was billowing softly around her in the breeze. God, she was so beautiful. He could tell she didn't really know it. He wondered if there had been anyone serious in her life, since Esme's dad, and felt a sharp twinge of jealousy.

Sprinting onto a nearby rock ahead of her, he held a hand down. On the top of the huge, flat boulder, he watched Sara's face as she looked at Aruba, stretching out beneath their feet. They were about three kilometres from the capital, Oranjestad, where the ship was docked.

'On a clear day you can see Venezuela from here,' he told her, taking in the dusty browns, and then the emerald-greens and clear blues of the waters beyond. 'The first inhabitants from the Arawak tribe used to climb on these boulders and watch for storms on the eastern horizon.'

Sara lifted her sunglasses to her head and looked at him. 'You always did absorb this kind of stuff like a sponge. No wonder you took this job.'

He smiled, ran his eyes over her lips. 'How long did you say you've been doing these cruises?'

'This is only my second.'

He brushed a strand of hair from her face, gently. It coiled around his fingers. She didn't move, but she averted her gaze. Did he make her uncomfortable out here? Memories were funny things. He wanted to say he remembered the curves of her body, the way she'd used to moan when he pressed kisses on her ticklish tummy. But she'd made it quite clear that she wanted things to stay professional between them. He had to respect that.

'I know you love to see the world, but I still don't get why you're here—working, I mean.'

Sara lowered herself onto the rock and he did the same. She hugged her sarong-wrapped knees to her chest.

'You were pretty married to your family's practice, from what I recall.'

He was quiet for a moment and the birds sang in the silence.

'My father died two years ago,' he told her, watching a warbler flit from a tall bush. 'I put a locum in—just to get away for a while, you know? I did the cruise and really enjoyed it, and they asked me back for a second this year.'

'I'm so sorry.' Sara put a hand to his on top of his raised knee. Her voice was tight. 'About your dad. Fraser, I didn't know.'

'It was a heart attack.'

He missed his father, of course—he'd grown up worshipping the guy—but he'd never come to terms with the fact that his dad had resented his and Sara's relationship six years ago. Dr Philip Breckenridge had been an excellent doctor, but managing the finances of the practice had never been his strong point.

The money Fraser's late grandfather had left in trust for him was to have been released to him when Fraser qualified, on the proviso that he spent it to further his career. By pumping it back into the practice, Fraser would appease the practice trustees and save his parents from an uncertain retirement.

But when he'd gone to tell Sara he needed some time to concentrate on qualifying, so the money for the practice could be released, even knowing it wasn't great timing because her mother had just died, she'd already made her mind up.

'We should just call it a day, Fraser. It's too crazy right now; everything is changing.'

Her movement beside him startled him back to the present. Sara had turned to face him, cross-legged on the rock.

'I mean it, you know; I really *am* sorry about your dad, Fraser.'

'Thank you.'

'I know what it's like to lose a parent.' She curled her fingers around his, holding both his hands in the space between them.

His mind flashed back to them walking hand in hand around Edinburgh Castle, taking photos of each other on the cannons. She'd known grief herself then, of course, and he'd wanted to keep on helping her through it. He'd wanted her with or without all the problems surrounding them at the time.

But when he'd gone to London to see her, shortly afterwards, to tell her that he missed her and ask if they could figure things out somehow, he'd seen her with that…that guy.

'So, you live at home with your dad?' he asked her now. 'Because of Esme?'

He dropped her hands, took a bottle of water from his pack and took a swig, then splashed some against his face and chest.

'That's one of the reasons,' she said.

He noticed her eyes giving his abs an appreciative glance through his open shirt. He handed her the water.

'Haven't you ever moved in with a boyfriend, or…fiancé or anything? What about Esme's father? I saw you with him once, you know.'

Sara's eyes grew wide. She paused with her lips to the bottle and he realised he probably shouldn't have admitted it.

'You saw us?' she said. 'When?'

He shrugged. 'I'm assuming it was him. I came to see you in London a couple of weeks after you left. You'd already made it obvious you wanted to move on, but I guess I thought I could change your mind. I saw you with him outside that restaurant in your street…'

'You really did that? Came to London to see me?' She looked grief-stricken all over again for a moment. 'I can't believe you did that.'

He could see he'd upset her, but he had to ask. 'Would it have made a difference? If you'd seen me?'

She was quiet. 'I don't know. That was the one and only time we met, Fraser. We spent one night together and then he left the country for a job without ever knowing I got pregnant. It was a stupid thing to do, but I was still grieving for mum, and missing you, and for once in my life I'd had way too much to drink…'

'You don't have to explain.'

'So Esme wasn't exactly planned—not that I have any regrets.'

'Of course not. She's incredible, Sara.'

'She really is. I never knew I could love another human so much after…'

She trailed off, but he knew what she was going to say. After *him*. He'd never understood why she'd felt compelled to cut him out of her life so completely.

'Living with my dad seemed like the best way to care for him *and* Esme,' she continued. 'My grandparents lived in that house for over sixty years before they died. Did I ever tell you how the ceiling is peppered with marks from popped champagne corks? Over the years it's become a sort of map of my family's celebrations.'

'That's beautiful.'

He meant it. He'd been raised in a pristine house, where a champagne mark on a ceiling would have meant arguments, shouting, and a week of interior decorating right after.

Sara cast her eyes to the butterflies, swirling around another bush. 'I suppose I keep on hoping that one day soon we can pop another champagne cork to mark Esme's new kidney, and another for her sixteenth birthday, and one more for her wedding.' She let out a disgruntled sound. 'I just can't think of ever celebrating anything again until that first one happens. Sorry—I know that's weird.'

'It's not weird at all.'

Fraser kept his eyes on the ocean. To hell with the pain this woman was still going through, and the way it took the light from her eyes. It made her doubt herself and everything she did.

He took her face in his palms and she drew her hands over his impulsively. 'It *will* happen. We'll find a donor for Esme,' he told her resolutely.

'Help! Oh, my God, please help—is anyone there?'

The anguish in the voice caused them both to scramble up.

'Help!' The female voice came again. 'Over here!'

Springing into action, Fraser grabbed his bag and scrambled down the rocks with Sara, making sure she didn't slip. They raced further down the trail towards the sound until they found themselves face to face with a sight Fraser had never seen before.

Marcus, the kid in the green board shorts. who'd been mean to Esme on the beach, was lying on his stomach on the dusty ground. He was writhing around in pain with half a damn cactus sticking out of his backside.

Sara hurried to unfold a towel from their pack, so they could move him away from the dirt.

'He fell on it—he was running too fast!' his mother cried. Can you pull it out of him, Doctor? Should I?'

Fraser clasped her wrist. 'No, don't touch it!'

The woman in short blue dungarees and that giant sun

hat was crouching over her son on the ground now, trying to hold him steady. 'It's not poisonous, is it?'

'It's not poisonous,' Fraser told her, spotting some fabric from Marcus's board shorts impaled on the offending cactus, just metres from two abandoned bicycles. 'Just try not to move,' he told the lad. 'We don't want these little suckers going any deeper—and don't put your hands near your mouth if you've touched the cactus at all, OK?'

'OK…' Marcus was sobbing. 'It hurts!'

'I know it does.' Sara's voice was soothing as she took tweezers from a small case. 'Luckily it looks like the glochids are mostly in one area, so just keep still like Dr Fraser said.'

Fraser readied the gauze and antiseptic as Sara went to work on Marcus's poor inflamed skin. His backside was so swollen it resembled a bright red beach ball. It was very lucky they'd been so close.

Back on the *Ocean Dream*, they whisked a sore Marcus to the medical centre. He and his mother were both adamant that they didn't want to leave the cruise, and Fraser tried to make them laugh by telling them all the things Marcus could still do standing up—like fishing, or tennis, or painting standing at an easel.

'You can also help me make my video, if you like,' Esme interrupted from the doorway, just as Fraser was handing Marcus's mother a prescription for painkillers. The kid now had a significant amount of gauze taped to his behind.

Marcus's cheeks flamed almost as red as his backside when he saw her.

'Esme, why are you here?' Sara walked over to her quickly. 'Where's Jess?'

'In there,' Esme said, pointing to the coffee house next door. In her long denim shorts and star-patterned shirt she walked past Sara and pointed at Marcus. 'What happened to you?'

Marcus wrinkled his nose. 'I fell on a cactus.'

Esme's little brow furrowed as she took in all the gauze. For a second Fraser thought she might laugh, or say something mean. Marcus had been mean to *her*, after all.

'That must have hurt,' she said instead, her eyes narrowed in concern. 'Are you OK?'

'I'm OK.' Marcus sniffed. 'Sorry I called you an alien.'

Esme grinned. 'I suppose I *do* look a bit like an alien sometimes. Do you want me to show you my robo-kidney when you're better?'

Fraser stood next to Sara as Esme explained how she needed the dialysis machine for her kidney to function. He could practically feel Sara swelling with pride as Esme offered to play with Marcus, so he wouldn't feel like the only funny-looking one on the ship.

'She's as compassionate as someone else I know,' he whispered to her, nudging her arm. Sara looked up at him.

'If only that was enough to make us a match.'

He felt his chest tighten. 'I told you, Cohen,' he said firmly. 'It's going to happen.'

CHAPTER FIVE

SARA TAPPED HER toes to the music as she relaxed against her headboard, keeping one ear out for the radio. *Knit one, pearl one, knit one, pearl one*, she mouthed, feeling herself sink into her project as though it were some kind of meditation.

A meditation on Fraser.

She'd been thinking about one of their first encounters. She'd agreed to do some tests on him, prior to a marathon he was running for charity—not the sexiest introduction, by anyone's standards, but he'd made it so. Maybe they both had. She'd seen him around St Enid's but he'd never talked to her before…never looked at her like that before.

Three nights later they'd been laughing over hospital politics in a posh Italian restaurant and she'd never been so smitten in her life.

'Are you in here?'

The voice behind the door made her heart lurch. He had a knack of showing up whenever she was thinking about him…which probably wasn't surprising, considering he'd been on her mind since the second she'd seen him again.

She shoved her knitting under the pillow. She had a sneaking suspicion Fraser had thought she was a geek, always glued to her needles like some kind of grandma. Smoothing down her ankle-length baby blue dress, she opened the door.

'Hey,' she said. 'You found me.'

'Looks like I did.' His handsome face looked even more

tanned after their time outside at the beach. 'What are you doing?'

'Nothing.'

'Are you OK?'

'I'm OK.'

She was grateful for his attention, of course, though the slow burn of a fire that should have died a long time ago still made her weak and nervous. His blue eyes were searching. He'd sensed the thin ice she was standing on with Esme—the fear that came with never knowing when or if it would break—and his compassion was switching on that *thing* again inside her. He'd vowed to help, and he certainly knew a lot of important people. His family knew a lot of people. The more people on her team the better.

'I thought you'd be up on deck,' he said.

'Why?' She trailed her eyes along his triceps as he brought a hand up to rest it on the doorframe. His muscles flexed beneath his snug blue shirt. He was wearing khaki cargo shorts down to his knees, revealing toned and shapely calves.

'The tribute band?' he reminded her. 'They just did a pretty good job of Adele. I thought I'd come look for *"someone like you"*.'

She groaned at his pun, even before he started singing the song. He'd always sung in the shower. Sometimes she'd joined in.

'Come up and listen,' he cajoled. 'You've been working so much, and you shouldn't be cooped up in here alone.'

'I like the quiet,' she insisted, but his big hand on the doorway was moving towards her now, and seconds later he was pulling her out into the corridor, dancing with her down it towards the elevators as she laughed despite herself. Damn him.

The air up on deck was thick and muggy, hinting at a storm. It stuck to her skin like another layer of clothing as

Fraser pulled out a chair at a table near the band. He slid her chair back in after she sat and offered to get her a drink.

'Let me guess—vodka and cranberry, minus the vodka?' His eyes were twinkling in the soft lights around the deck.

She was impressed. 'You remember.'

'I remember lots of things about you, Cohen. Wait right here.'

She watched his firm ass in his shorts as he made his way over to the bar; observed the way he walked, the way he turned heads wherever he went. He'd always been handsome, but over the last six years he'd grown even more so.

She'd insisted on staying professional and she had to stick to her guns—though she really, really wanted to run her hands over *his* guns. She groaned at her own thoughts.

When she turned back to the table Dr Renee Forster was heading towards her. She took the seat next to Sara.

'How's it going?' Renee crossed her long legs. 'You seem to be doing a great job with the dialysis patients. Did I see Dr Breckenridge playing with your daughter on the beach before?'

Sara cast her eyes to Fraser. He was still at the bar. 'Yes, they seem to have formed quite a connection.' She cleared her throat as she realised it was true. It was rare that Esme took to men as she'd taken to Fraser. She couldn't stop filming his 'funny faces' with her camera either.

'He's a good man,' Renee said. She placed a slim, manicured hand on top of Sara's and smiled. 'I always wondered who it was that stole his heart.'

She excused herself and sidled off again, just as Fraser placed a drink down in front of her and resumed his position on the chair.

'What did Renee want?'

'She told me you're a good man.'

'Well, she's got that right.'

Sara took a sip of her drink. He'd ordered the same. Fraser, as far as she knew, had always been teetotal. And she hadn't had a real drink in years—although right now she was pretty tempted to order one. Renee's words were nice enough, but how much did she know about her and Fraser? How much did anyone on this ship know about their past?

She'd been thinking about their conversation on the rocks, when he'd told her he had come to London. What might have happened if she'd seen him there? She would have crumbled. But nothing would have changed in the end.

Then again, maybe *everything* would have changed.

'Nurse Cohen?' She turned in her seat to find Marcus standing there.

'How are you doing now, buddy?' Fraser asked. His arm was draped along the back of her chair.

'I'm feeling better,' Marcus said shyly. 'My mum said I should ask Nurse Cohen for a dance.'

He was looking at the floor now. Fraser's hand had found the back of her neck through her hair and she struggled to keep her face straight. She couldn't move—couldn't let her head sink back into the familiar comfort of his palm.

'I'd love to dance,' she said quickly, getting to her feet.

She put her hands on Marcus's shoulders. His head reached her belly button, half a metre away. He started shuffling his feet awkwardly on the deck and somewhere on the periphery of her vision she saw his mother take a photo on her phone.

Sara's eyes found Fraser, still at the table. He was sitting in shadow but his gaze was as piercing as if it was in full sunlight. If he'd come to see her in London he must have been more devastated over her leaving him than she'd assumed. Considering he'd been about to break up with her anyway, *why* had he done it?

When the song came to an end she was about to excuse herself from Marcus when Fraser strode over purposefully. His shadow seemed to fill the deck for a moment, his corded muscles even more defined in the low light and the fitted fabric of his blue shirt.

The lazy notes of a saxophone curled around the soft chatter as Marcus stepped aside.

'I was getting jealous over there,' he whispered into her ear, drawing her close.

She held her breath. The stars were twinkling above them. She'd never seen so many stars.

Her head came up to his chin, clean-shaven now. As he placed his hands on her waist she breathed in invisible clouds of his aftershave and that other scent, the one that was only Fraser... And with it came the memories—rolling in the bed, tumbling to the floor, laughing hysterically, then reconnecting, their backs being scratched by the carpet, the sheets over their heads.

He drew her close. 'I know how much you love this song,' he said, and she realised he was laughing softly.

They were playing *their* song—a slow, more provocative version of *Never Gonna Give You Up*.

She pressed her hands to his chest, laughing into his shirt. 'You asked them to play this?'

'Just for old times' sake. You smell incredible, by the way.' His fingers trailed slowly down the open back of her dress, leaving tingles in their wake.

'I was thinking the same about you.'

They started to dance. She pictured his shoes moving carefully around hers and wondered if they would ever find their feet together again. Her mind kept slipping from the strange here and now to his bedroom back then, at the start of it all.

The day they'd taken that undignified tumble from the bed to the carpet when they'd been listening to this song. They'd been cracking up at the fact that it had turned their sensual lovemaking into an instant eighties disco.

Her arms were circling his shoulders now. They were one night away from Grenada, and she couldn't wait to feel the sand there beneath her toes; beneath her back, as she made love to Fraser—maybe just once, *for old times' sake*.

She pulled away slightly. What was she *doing*?

'What were you knitting, back in your cabin?'

She could hear the smile lurking in his deep Scottish accent. His fingers had hardened at her retraction, refusing to let her get too far away.

'How do you know I was knitting?'

'I could hear the *click, click, click* through the door. I found it strangely arousing.'

Sara buried her face in his shoulder for a second as he repeated the clicking sound with his tongue.

'I used to imagine you sitting there knitting things for our kids. They'd either be too big or too small, and we'd have all these teddy bears and toys all over the house, all wearing your tiny knitted socks.'

'What would we do with the bigger ones?' she dared to ask him, though she wanted to ask when exactly he'd decided they'd have kids together one day.

'I'd save them for cold days…for protection,' he said into her ear.

'Is that right?'

His hair brushed her face softly as they danced, and she caught herself pressing closer against him, heart to heart, breathing in the steadying presence she'd missed and letting it claim her completely in the moment. God, they had been so good together—seriously good. They'd just…fitted.

She smiled against him as he moved with her to the music, but her thoughts refused to untangle.

She couldn't have Fraser *and* Esme. She had to focus on finding Esme a donor. Fraser was going home at some point anyway—back to Edinburgh, back to the life his father had planned for him from the start.

'She's no good for you, son. You're in danger of screwing it all up. What about your career? What about everything you've worked so hard for?'

His father's voice had been concerned, full of foreboding. It had made her shiver in her hidden place on the stairs. She'd saved Fraser the trouble of breaking it off—she'd barely waited till bedtime to get in there first. Pity the fool who came between members of the Breckenridge family, she'd thought.

It still stung that his father had been so unsympathetic, so cold as to try and drive them apart. It stung even more that Fraser had let her go without a fight. But what hurt the most now was knowing that he'd come to get her in London and she hadn't even known. Now their lives really were on different paths—more different than ever before.

Fraser's hands were on her waist still, controlling her closeness, even though the song had ended and the band were stepping off the stage. With every ounce of strength she possessed she forced herself to take a step back. The moon and the lights made a silhouette of his face. The spell was broken.

'What are we doing here, Fraser?'

He narrowed his eyes, but his reply was cut short by Harry, their cardiac patient, spinning through the crowd right up to their toes in his wheelchair.

'I've been looking for you!'

His bald head was gleaming pink under the disco ball, his puffy cheeks full of colour again. He'd made an excellent recovery. He motioned for Sara's hand and she watched in shock as he placed a giant wad of rolled-up bills into her palm and folded her fist over it.

'For you,' he said. 'My winnings from the casino that night.'

She shook her head quickly. 'I couldn't—'

'Plenty more where that came from. If it wasn't for you I wouldn't be here to spend it. So spend that, Nurse Cohen.' He released her and turned to Fraser. 'It's for both of you. Heaven-sent, both of you. And a match made *in* heaven, by the looks of it.'

CHAPTER SIX

'SHE'S FALLEN!'

Fraser heard the voice before he saw the elderly lady on the floor. She was sprawled in a pool of what looked like water, but might possibly be gin. He spotted a lime slice not too far away.

'Enid! Can you get up?'

A short man in a loud Hawaiian print shirt was fussing around her. Fraser moved him aside gently and reached for his radio. In what seemed like seconds his ears picked up the tapping of shoes on the deck.

'Stand back please,' came Sara's authoritative voice.

She appeared beside him with the stretcher as the crowds parted. He noticed several phones pointed at them.

'No filming, please,' she told them strictly, swiping a tendril of loose hair behind her ear. 'What happened?'

She was dressed in her white coat and fresh from the dialysis centre, he gathered. Her air of determination and swift efficiency, plus the lingering smell of her shampoo in the warm sea air, threw him right back to that summer with her in Scotland.

Enid was in her late seventies, maybe older. Her hair was pure white. 'She's having trouble moving,' he told Sara as she quickly handed him oxygen.

'Can you lift your leg, or turn it?'

Her voice was low, kind. He watched her hand move gently over Enid's hip and leg, inspecting for damage.

'Can you put any weight on this side?' Enid howled

again. Sara pulled a face and apologised. 'We have some swelling,' she announced.

He placed the oxygen mask over Enid's mouth.

'Looks like a break in the hip.'

She caught his eyes as she said it and he nodded, keeping his face expressionless so as not to panic Enid, or her Hawaiian-shirt-wearing husband. It was exactly as he'd feared.

'Will she be OK?' Mr Hawaiian Shirt looked panicked anyway. He sported one or two strands of white hair on an otherwise shiny head.

Fraser helped Sara lift Enid onto a stretcher. 'Are you her husband?'

'Yes, but we don't have insurance.' The man's face looked as white as his hair now.

'We'll do all we can. Come with us.'

'Should we call the Coast Guard?' Sara looked concerned. Enid was sucking in short, sharp breaths.

He shook his head. 'Not yet. I don't think we need to.'

She took the other end of the stretcher without so much as a flinch and together they lifted their patient and moved as one towards the top-deck entrance.

Now that they were inside, away from the eyes and phones and ears on deck, the old man asked him. 'How much will medevac cost?'

'Sir,' Fraser said, trying to keep his inner frown from showing in his face and voice. 'It's never good to travel without insurance. but that's not the main concern here. The main concern is your wife. We need a radiological diagnosis before—'

'What's that?' The guy looked flustered and confused. He started to sweat through his shirt as they headed for the elevator.

'X-rays,' Sara clarified, moving swiftly along.

Fraser was walking backwards now in the narrow walkway, and she was walking forward. He watched the sunlight from the porthole windows play in her hair the whole way.

'We'll take some X-rays and then we'll know more. Don't worry—we have it under control.'

She pushed the button for the elevator. Her hair was half pulled back in a bun and he noted her earrings suddenly— tiny little blue sapphire studs. She'd been driving him crazy all night, even after she'd gone to bed.

He'd thought about kissing her on the dance floor. God, he'd wanted to—or just nibble lightly on her ear for half a second. That had used to drive her wild. Holding her against him like that after all these years had made him think entirely unprofessional thoughts, but somehow he'd reined them in.

In the medical centre, they moved Enid off the stretcher and carefully onto a bed. Sara rolled the vitals machine over quickly while Fraser snipped with precision along the lady's floral skirt. He always felt bad cutting people's clothes.

The wheels of the X-ray machine screeched for a second on the shiny floor as Sara wheeled it over and plugged it in.

'Pulse is one hundred; blood pressure is eighty over fifty-five,' she told him.

Enid's husband loitered, watching, fanning himself with his own shirt. The room was hot, even under the whirring ceiling fans.

Fraser beckoned Sara to the corner of the room with him. 'We're almost at Grenada,' he said. The loose tendrils of her hair tickled his face under the fans as he leaned close. 'She's OK, but she'll be better off staying stable with us till we get to the island.'

'If you say so, Chief.'

He liked that word coming from her lips. 'I do.'

He cast an eye to Enid and her husband. He still couldn't believe some people travelled without insurance.

'Calling for medevac now will wind up costing them

more than waiting it out for an ambulance. And it won't make a difference to our Enid at this point. Get her some morphine.'

She turned to do exactly that. It still felt kind of mad that they were working together. He knew she was right to be wary—not just of him, now that he was practically a stranger again, but because so many staff relationships ended badly. Bad vibes between fighting colleagues made life awkward for everyone, and he knew Sara would never risk that around Esme.

'How long to Grenada?' she asked him.

'About one hour.'

Sara prepped the needle for the morphine—just a little…just enough to keep Enid out of pain. He watched her squeeze her hand reassuringly before administering it.

'We'll get her to a hospital on Grenada,' he said to Enid's husband. 'She'll be far more comfortable this way.'

The hour rolled by. Fraser made a call shore-side, transferred the X-rays, and had it confirmed by staff in Grenada that, yes, it was indeed a broken hip. Sara arranged for an ambulance at the port.

No one confirmed it had been spilt gin that had made Enid slip, but no one confirmed it had been water either.

'Is everything under control?'

Renee appeared after a brief knock at the door that gave them no time to move apart without her seeing them. He stepped away from Sara anyway. She did the same thing.

'Vitals are stable. The ambulance is headed for the port,' he told her, while Sara buried her head in her clipboard.

St George's Grenada was as busy as ever, but the crowds parted as he and Sara carried Enid off the ship and let the ambulance take her away.

'She'll be OK,' he said, watching it move along the road to the hospital, where he knew she'd be taken care of.

'She won't be getting back on the cruise, though, will

she?' Sara sighed beside him. 'Should we not go to the hospital too?'

'She'll be going straight in for surgery, and she's in good hands. Also, she was probably having the best time of her life right before this,' he told her.

He spotted Renee again, talking to another passenger wearing a giant sunhat. Also distracting him now was a youngish looking couple, possibly in their late twenties, deep in some kind of chilling disagreement. The guy, sporting a long black ponytail and a bare back full of tattoos, was yelling in what looked like a drunken rage at a woman in a leopard-print dress. In turn, she was simmering, arms folded. Her body language screamed discomfort.

Fraser had seen them around the ship. They were always either smooching in a corner or arguing. *Bad vibes.*

He was about to walk over himself when two security guards stepped in. He put his hand on Sara's. 'Let's go somewhere else,' he said quickly.

'What's going on with them?'

'I don't know, but they don't look happy.'

He started unbuttoning his white coat, zipped it into his bag, and motioned her to follow him fast, before Renee or anyone else saw.

'Come on, Esme's safe with Jess—aren't you hungry for a taste of Grenada? We won't be long.'

'I *am* pretty hungry, now that you mention it.'

Sara followed him, taking off her own white coat quickly. He folded it into the bag with his as they walked, grateful that he'd worn jeans and a loose white shirt underneath.

Before long they were seated at his favourite restaurant. The ocean glistened in the distance and Sara looked relaxed, finally. He watched her blue sapphire studs reflecting the sun as she studied the scenery.

'So, drama aside, what can you tell me about this place

that doesn't involve medical emergencies and ambulances, Mr Chief Tour Guide?' She picked up her cranberry juice.

He leaned back in his seat. 'Well, Grenada was founded by the French in the early eighteenth century. That's why it looks so...'

'French?' She smiled as he rocked for a moment on his chair legs.

'Exactly.'

Vibrant red roof tiles on a patchwork of pastel-coloured houses stretched before them, right up to the ocean. Fraser thought Sara had never looked as pretty as she did in a setting like this. Six years on and he swore she was even more beautiful. Her eyes were wiser, though, as if she'd seen too much—as if she was stuck inside her own head at times, maybe missing something wonderful while processing bigger things. She was used to putting Esme first, of course.

'I'm guessing you don't go on holiday much?' he said as two plates of jerk chicken were placed before them.

'It's just hard with Esme. And with the hospital. They're understaffed as it is.'

'Megan is happy to help, though, and your dad?' He remembered her younger sister, Megan.

She picked up a fork. 'Yes, but it's not fair to keep asking them, really, and I always panic if I leave her anyway. This is the first time we've been able to come away with dialysis care.' She paused. 'I did go to Mexico with my sister once. It was...interesting.'

'Oh, yes?'

'Long story—some guy called Pedro.'

He fought a stab of jealousy. 'You hooked up with a guy called *Pedro*?'

She laughed. 'No, not me—Megan. I read books. That's my idea of a good time these days, Fraser. Books and knitting.'

'And the butterfly collection?'

She smiled. She'd always collected things with butter-flies on them. He'd given her a butterfly-patterned lace bra once.

'You never felt the need to be the last to leave a party, but you could still start one whenever you wanted.' He lowered his voice, directed it across the table. 'Especially in the bedroom.' He couldn't resist. They both knew their sex-life had been incredible.

'Your father had so many plans for you,' she said after a moment, her lips still curved, smiling at the memories no doubt. 'He'd be proud of what you've done and what you're doing, Fraser.'

He reached across the table for her hand and she dropped her fork. 'I listened to him way too much.' He'd said it now.

'What do you mean?'

'He was always so set in his ways—you know that.'

His heart started to thrum. His father had been looming in the doorway after Sara had left in a taxi.

'She broke up with me. What did you say to her?'

'Nothing, son, I said nothing. But she's a smart girl—she knows she's bringing you down right now, Fraser. More to the point—wake up! There's more to life than women.'

'I know that.'

'Well, prove it, then. We need your help to keep this practice afloat. I know it's a lot to ask, son, but think of the future. Think of everything me and your mother have worked for. Now Sara's gone you'll have the space you need to get back on track!'

He'd had to bring Fraser's mother into it. God bless Aggie Breckenridge, who'd worked tirelessly her entire life to raise him, to keep the practice running, only to be told she might not be able to retire in the manner she deserved. They'd been ploughing every penny of their savings into modernising the practice and they'd still needed more.

He'd called and called Sara, determined to talk to her

and tell her what he hadn't found the courage to admit before—that his family were under significant financial strain and needed him. He'd been determined that in spite of her concerns they could make it work.

But when he'd flown to London and seen her with someone else he'd accepted that maybe his father had been right. He *had* been distracted from his studies. He'd had no other options then. He *couldn't* afford to let his family lose it all.

He'd kept his word, pulled himself up, got back on track. He'd qualified and then injected his trust fund money straight into the surgery, paying for new equipment, the latest treatments, three more highly qualified staff members. But he'd never forgotten Sara.

He stood and pulled her up from her seat, bringing both hands to her face.

'Fraser…'

His name was a breath as her hands came up again, over his. Their meals were forgotten.

'You and me, we had something really good,' he said, putting a hand to the back of her head and letting his fingers tangle in her soft hair as he touched his forehead to hers. 'We both know that.'

She closed her eyes.

'We were young,' he said. 'Maybe it just wasn't the right time for us back then.' He tilted her chin. 'When we get off the ship…'

'I don't know, Fraser.' She pulled away and her amber eyes seemed to rummage through his soul. 'Things are all so different. I can't do anything right now, with the way things are for Esme.'

'I know—and I know you're doing everything you can for Esme—but we're going to find her a donor.'

'You keep saying that…but how do you *know*?'

'I just do.'

He brought his nose to the tip of hers. He half expected

her to pull away, or push him off, but her hands came to his chest. She clutched at the front of his shirt and he kissed her—because he had to.

Sara moaned slightly against his lips as she kissed him back softly, just for a second or two, before she pulled away and dipped her head against his shoulder. His arms circled her impulsively and they stood there, her hair brushing his face in the breeze, the scrape of forks on plates a distant sound.

He wanted to lead her off the terrace and do more. He wanted to take her back to the ship and make love to her. But for the moment this would have to do. This and working on the plan he'd been hatching. It was now taking on whole new proportions in his head...

CHAPTER SEVEN

SARA WOKE WITH a jolt and almost hit her head on the ceiling. She'd slept in a fit of crazy dreams featuring tsunamis and Fraser…maybe even surfing a tsunami with Fraser.

Someone was banging on her door.

'Sara!' Jess burst into her cabin, waving her spare key card. 'Sorry.'

She sprang up in bed, throwing the sheets off. 'What's wrong?'

'Esme's missing.'

She clocked the time. One-thirty a.m. 'Have you looked for her?'

'Yes, of course!'

She pulled on jeans and a T-shirt, and was instantly thrown back on the bed. There was a storm raging outside and the boat was rocking. Panic was a fire flaming on her skin, and then came chills at the thought of her vulnerable daughter, missing.

Jess put a hand to the wall to stop herself from tripping. 'I'm so sorry… I came in for my shift and she wasn't there—there was maybe a three-minute crossover between staff. She must have slipped out then, and I can't find her anywhere!'

On wobbly feet they climbed the stairs up to the nursery floor. Taking the elevator didn't feel right with the ship this unsteady. Outside the night was black. No stars. They were by now, en-route for Florida once more, but from the views outside they could have been anywhere.

'She can't have gone far,' Sara said, though her heart was a sledgehammer. She felt more than queasy. The ground beneath her feet was unstable.

They checked the nursery again. She wasn't there.

'Where would she have gone?' Jess raked her hands through her hair. 'I'm so sorry, Sara. She knows she's not supposed to leave but she keeps on trying to do it.'

'You take the lower floors. I'll take the top. Tell Security on the way.'

Jess shot off in one direction and Sara took the stairs to the dining hall.

'Esme!' In the billiard hall she spun around. 'Esme!' The low lights were swaying on the ceiling, making shadows that slashed across the tables. She got down on her knees to check under the tables. 'Esme!'

Next came the aqua spa, then the hot tub room, where full-length windows revealed the ocean jumping above the covered well. No sign of Esme.

In an empty lounge with a shuttered bar she was starting to lose hope. She'd looked everywhere.

'Esme, where are you?'

The lights were off. An eerie chill cloaked her body.

'Sara? What are you doing out here?'

Turning around, she lost her balance and Fraser's hands shot to her forearms, holding her steady. He was clearly on duty and his white coat was open, revealing a red shirt.

'You're supposed to be in your cabin,' he said. His voice was gruff. 'It's too dangerous to be moving around in these conditions.'

'We've lost Esme.'

His eyebrows arched in concern. 'How long ago did she go missing?'

'About twenty minutes. We've looked everywhere. God, Fraser, what if she…?'

'She couldn't have got up on deck and fallen overboard.

It's all locked up. She's inside somewhere.' Fraser pulled out his radio, calling Security as he stepped with her into the hallway again. 'Was she alone?'

He took her hand in a firm grip that kept her steady in more than one way. She'd been about to break. 'We think so, but we don't know for sure.'

Their surroundings creaked and dipped as they made their way down the halls. She told herself he knew the ship much better than she did—every part of it. He would find her.

The light in the third deck kitchen was on. Fraser stopped abruptly and her hands landed on the solid wall of his back as she stopped herself from falling.

'There shouldn't be anyone on kitchen duty at this time,' he told her, swiping his key card and taking her hand again.

The sight when the door slid open made Sara gasp. Esme was sitting on the floor with Marcus, between two huge steel cabinets. The wooden spoon in a giant tub of ice-cream between them spoke of her sins…and of what Sara knew could potentially harm her.

'Esme—no!' She ran and ducked for the spoon, then threw it heavily into the sink as if it was made of hot tar. Tears burned her eyes. 'What are you doing, running away in the middle of the night? You could have been hurt!'

'I'm sorry.'

They reached for each other at the same time. Esme's frightened face melted her heart in a second. Fear became relief and more tears that Sara had to swipe away.

Esme started to cry herself. Huge wails in Sara's ear as she hugged her in her arms. Marcus stood up guiltily, his cactus-prickled backside clearly no longer an issue.

'How did you get in here?' Fraser scooped up the tub of ice-cream and put it on the counter. He didn't slam it down but she knew he was angry. He'd been worried for Esme, too.

'We found a key card.' Marcus held it out to him. 'Esme wanted ice-cream.'

'She's not supposed to have ice-cream.' Sara turned to her daughter's hot, wet face. 'Esme, you *know* you're not supposed to have ice-cream.'

Fraser was radioing someone—likely the kitchen staff. She felt his hand on her shoulder from behind, and exhaled deeply into Esme's hair.

'I only had two scoops.' She was sniffling now.

'It's OK.'

Fraser sent Marcus back to his cabin, being sure to take the key card from him first.

'We'll need to monitor her closely,' Sara told him, following him out into the corridor. Esme was a heavy weight in her tired arms.

'Let me take her,' he said, and he scooped her up as easily as he'd lifted the ice-cream.

She could see his concern for Esme etched on his face as deeply as hers as they made their way to the dialysis room—especially when Esme stopped him in the corridor.

'I feel sick,' she announced.

'I've got you, Spielberg.'

He started moving faster with her, running with one hand on the golden rail to keep them both steady as the ship rocked—less menacingly now, but still enough to topple him or upset Esme's stomach more. She could see her daughter's forehead was clammy. Esme *knew* she wasn't supposed to have ice-cream.

Fraser was trying to calm her. 'Wow, you've got heavier. Is that all the delicious dessert you just ate?'

Esme giggled in spite of her tears and again Sara felt so…grateful? In awe? Both. He was a natural with Esme.

In the dialysis room, she hurried for a bedpan as Fraser laid Esme down. She watched the way he acted, with such tenderness, and was thrown right back to their kiss on the terrace. It had shaken her. All the potential consequences and outcomes—those had been the tsunamis in her dreams.

'Do you still feel sick?' he was asking Esme now.

She nodded miserably.

'It's probably just seasickness and excitement,' Sara told him, stroking Esme's soft blonde hair. The little girl's eyes were red and swollen. 'She didn't eat that much. Two scoops, right, Esme?'

'Yes.'

Sara called Jess. Fraser prepared some insulin and shot her a look over the needle. He was asking if she was OK. She gave him a nod and his brow wrinkled under his hair.

'I'm OK.' Sara said it out loud. She was fine now, because Esme seemed fine, though she *knew* she shouldn't have eaten anything this late, or this near to her dialysis—least of all dairy.

Potassium levels increased whenever kidney function decreased, and things like ice-cream could cause all sorts of problems. She felt the guilt start to creep its way in. She shouldn't have brought her here, away from her usual daily routines, it was too risky.

Once Fraser had placed Esme carefully back in her bed in the nursery, he took Sara aside in the hallway. The last hour or so had passed in a blur and she was exhausted. She should probably go and sleep with Esme. But the way he was looking at her...

'You should stay with me,' he said.

She'd known he was going to say it.

'I'm just down the hall. It'll be even bumpier down on your level—you won't get any sleep.'

'I don't know if that's a good idea.'

Guilt was already making her want to run back to Esme, to cradle her in her arms, and now it was twice as strong because she also wanted to stay in Fraser's.

'I have a big enough space for two,' he said. He leaned

in even closer, till his lips were almost brushing hers. 'And I really need to kiss you again. It's been too long.'

'It's been two days.' The scent of him filled the air in his suite as she stepped inside it behind him.

'So this is where they put you,' she said as her hand found the wall. Her heart bounced in her chest as the door closed.

'It's better when it's not moving.'

Her eyes rested on the four-poster bed as he walked to a huge couch smothered in cushions. Maybe she shouldn't feel guilty for being here. Things happened, and Esme was having an adventure she'd remember for the rest of her life. Maybe *she* was, too. Besides, they didn't have to sleep together. That would complicate things and she'd regret it tomorrow—she knew it.

She observed the mahogany backdrop of cupboards, shelves and wardrobes while he poured her a glass of water.

'There's a big storm coming in the next few days or so,' he said, handing it to her and guiding her onto the couch.

'I thought this *was* a storm.'

Fraser took off his white coat, draped it on the back of a tall leather armchair, then sat down next to her. 'This is nothing—just a prelude to the main event. We try to be in port when bad weather like this is predicted. How are you feeling?'

He was so close she could practically feel the sparks flying. 'I'm fine, thank you, Fraser. Really. And I appreciate what you did tonight.'

His hand covered hers completely, where he held it on her knee. 'I did what anyone would have done. But are you sure you're fine? You've had a bit of a scare.'

'I'm processing it. I'm glad you're here.'

He brought her hand to his lips and let them linger there

a moment. She felt the familiar urge to be closer to him as tingles ran up her thighs.

'Esme's quite a handful, I can see,' he said, and she smiled, nodding.

He knew she'd been a mess, inside and out, probably, when Esme had gone missing. Did he also know the added torture of feeling so torn, like this? He was a total distraction from every moment she might have left with her daughter.

He took the empty glass from her. 'So...you can sleep in the bed and I'll take the couch.'

What? Sara blinked as he got to his feet. She hadn't been expecting that. She watched as he went about getting some blankets and a pillow from a cupboard above the bed and— forget the excuses—all she could think was, *No way...no way. How dare you do this to me now?*

So she said, 'Stop it, Fraser. You're not sleeping on the couch.'

She stood up, realising how forward she'd been but feigning confidence anyway. 'You've just worked a long shift. You should definitely have the bed.'

He dropped the spare blankets onto the quilt cover and raised his eyebrows. 'I am kind of tired. I guess if you insist...'

She watched him put his fingers to his shirt and pop the buttons one by one, slowly, on purpose, to make her smile. He unbuckled his jeans and she trailed her eyes over his lean, muscular thighs as he shook them aside. This was ridiculous.

'Having second thoughts?' he asked provocatively. 'You know it's much better when we stick together.'

He pulled the quilt aside, and when she reached him he pulled her close and kissed her in a way that made the bouncing in her chest turn to explosions. She raised her arms and he helped her off with her clothes, down to her underwear, stopping to admire her body just as he'd used to.

'I probably look different now,' she said, a little shy suddenly.

'Not so different,' he told her, stepping back to appraise her.

She saw the desire in his eyes and it boosted her, somehow. It had been a long time since anyone had seen her like this.

Still standing, Fraser swept her hair aside and kissed her neck, then her lips, and when the ship tilted they fell to the bed, still kissing. But when he pulled the sheets around them he spooned her from behind, holding her close.

'Much safer in here,' he whispered into the back of her neck. 'Remember the first time we slept together?'

He ran a hand along the length of her body, leaving flames in its wake. She wouldn't tell him she'd been thinking the same thing…or how much she was burning to have him touch more of her.

That first time they'd been in a bed smaller than anything on the cruise ship, in her student lodgings, drunk on each other…and she just a little on cheap Chardonnay.

'How could I forget?' she smiled. 'We broke a wine glass.'

'We're not doing that now, though,' he said, nuzzling her neck and lacing his fingers through hers.

'We don't have any wine glasses,' she whispered.

'That's not what I meant. We're not making love, because I know you'll wish you hadn't in the morning. Even though I want to do that with you all…night…long.'

She sucked in a breath. Her heart was a freight train. He knew her so well.

'Who says we would have slept together? The past is the past,' she said defensively.

But he chuckled and pulled her in tighter, and said nothing.

The rocking of the waves, now much gentler, lulled them to sleep eventually, and she dozed with her back to his chest and his arms locked around her. She had no dreams that she could remember; she just felt safe and content. But when sunrise crept through the windows she sat bolt upright.

The bed behind her was empty. Fraser was already gone.

CHAPTER EIGHT

THE SUN WAS hot on Fraser's shoulders as he swigged his coffee and crossed the street onto the Florida pavement. His mind was still racing over the details of last night, and the sight of Sara's head on his pillow after all this time.

It was a miracle they'd stopped at just kissing, but having her in his bed and in his arms again had filled him with fresh hope, and he was damned if he was going to ruin that by having her over-analyse any heat-of-the-moment sexual encounters—as he knew she would. Not unless the time was completely right.

She was worth waiting for.

The waiting room was empty when he walked in. He was more nervous than he'd anticipated he would be as he approached the young red-haired receptionist. The words *'Someone you know is hoping for someone like you,'* were framed on the wall behind her. He took it as a sign that he was doing the right thing.

'Fraser Breckenridge—good to see you again.' Boyd Phillips appeared from the hallway and offered his familiar firm handshake before motioning him through to a seat in a small quiet room.

'Thank you for seeing me at such short notice, buddy.' Fraser realised he was wringing his hands in his lap and moved them quickly to the arms of the chair.

Boyd noticed. 'Always happy to squeeze someone like you in. Everything OK? You look nervous.'

'I'm a little nervous,' he admitted, 'but only 'cause I might not be eligible.'

Boyd studied him over the rims of his glasses. 'Understandable. This is an admirable decision, and obviously an important one to you.'

A cactus sat between them, along with a photo of Boyd and his husband Bob, an addiction psychiatrist he'd met at a conference right here in Florida.

'I feel like it's the right decision,' he said.

'Aye, well, that feeling will help you a lot in the weeks to come. Hold on to that.'

'Yes, sir.'

Boyd gathered a set of forms that had to be filled out before proceeding with the tests. Fraser was grateful he actually knew this man, and could trust him. They'd known each other a long time, and Fraser knew Boyd probably wanted to ask him more than he was asking, but Boyd stuck to the essentials, as he'd hoped he would.

He knew the psychologist would be a different story.

Speaking to a psychologist was standard for non-directed kidney donors. And, in a green-carpeted room next to Boyd's, covered in posters much like the one in the waiting room, Fraser was made to talk about his reasons for wanting to donate.

The psychologist, a woman who looked considerably younger than Fraser's thirty-two years, was twizzling a pen in her manicured fingers, pursing her painted lips thoughtfully between questions.

'I used to be in a relationship with this little girl's mother.'

'Interesting… How long ago?'

'Six years, more or less. You could say life got in the way.'

'What do you mean?' She was drumming the pen on her knee now.

'Well, we were pretty young back then. I had to focus on my career and my family's practice in Edinburgh, while she moved back to London to help her family. Her mum died, and she had to... It's a long story. We just met up again.'

'How?'

'How did we meet up again?' He paused.

She was looking at him intently. He couldn't exactly tell her he'd done his best to ensure they were on the same cruise ship in spite of knowing Sara probably wouldn't have wanted to see him. He hoped things were different now.

'As I said before, we're both working on the *Ocean Dream*. I found out her daughter Esme is on dialysis. She's part of a new programme on the ship to care for the dialysis patients while they have a vacation. I suppose I saw things through both Esme's and her mother's eyes, and if I'm able to donate I want to.'

The psychologist chewed on her lip and scribbled on her clipboard, studying the forms Boyd had passed to her. She crossed one leg over the other and looked him in the eyes. 'Is it possible you're doing this just to get back into a relationship with this child's mother?'

Fraser sat back in his seat. He forced his gaze to stay directly on hers. The question shouldn't have surprised him at all. Obviously she wanted to know he was doing this for the right reasons. He couldn't deny it all came back to Sara. But, whatever happened between them in the future, this was still something he wanted to do. If Esme had been Sara's niece, or cousin, or even the daughter of a friend, having seen first-hand the struggle they were enduring, he'd have wanted to help if he could.

'I asked myself that at first,' he said, 'but, no. I'm a professional. I live to help those I can help—as do we all. I would do this for Esme whether Sara and I were together or not.'

'I see.'

He found himself smiling, picturing Esme's little face and enquiring eyes. 'You should see this kid—she's incredible. She has this camcorder that she takes everywhere. She's the brightest thing—always asking questions, making life out to be an adventure. I just want that to continue for her, you know?'

The woman started scribbling furiously, and although he was itching to find out what she was writing he shut his mouth. He had to let her make her assessment. He just prayed he'd said and done enough.

Next up was the urine test.

'This is the fun part,' Boyd said as his intern, a gangly guy with braces called Rishi, presented Fraser with a tube.

He was led down a sunlit corridor to the bathroom. Palm trees waved at him from outside through the windows. Sara would be awake now, probably wondering where he'd gone, and a twinge of guilt struck him. He hadn't told her his plan.

'As I'm sure you know, this test will throw into the light any sign of infection or other abnormalities,' Rishi told him. 'If we find any sort of blood, protein or glucose in your good stuff, Dr Breckenridge, you won't be able to donate. You've said you're not on any meds, any antibiotics…?'

'No, I'm not, that's correct,' he said.

'OK, then, we'll be right here when you're done.'

Fraser stepped into the bathroom. He knew he was fine already—he'd done his own tests prior to this. He'd been torturing himself by doing that, really, because whatever the tests told him didn't matter—the experts had to make their own minds up. It was Esme's health at stake… Esme's life.

He'd wanted to tell Sara what he was planning, of course, but at the same time knew it was probably too soon. He'd see if he was eligible to donate first, then he'd tell her. He'd asked Boyd about other options via email and on the phone, and he was on the case already, but what would be the point of getting her hopes up about *him* as a donor before he knew if he could help? They were there to enjoy Esme's first real holiday—not to wait on tenterhooks for something that might not happen.

Fraser's urine sample was placed into a container with some others as Boyd continued with his questions from behind his desk. He wondered exactly how many people were planning to donate right now, at this very minute. How many people had sat in this chair before him, willing to donate a part of themselves to help someone else?

'We'll be checking your blood for potentially harmful viruses. Things like hepatitis, HIV… Any nasty infection that could be passed to your intended donor will rule you out.'

Fraser didn't even flinch as the needle was inserted.

'We're also seeing how well your kidneys, liver and other organs are functioning… Your forms say you don't drink?'

'No, sir—I never have.'

'I remember that, actually.'

'I don't smoke, I don't drink—I also don't run marathons any more.'

Boyd flashed Fraser's pecs an appreciative smile. 'Doesn't look like you need to. The ship's gym seems to be doing you some favours.'

'Why, thank you.'

Boyd readied another needle. 'We're also making sure you have enough blood, and that your blood clots properly.'

'Understood.'

'This is just the start of quite a lengthy process, Fraser— I'm sure you know that.'

'I'm sure it'll be worth it.'

'I remember Sara,' Boyd responded, taking Fraser by surprise.

He was testing his glomerular filtration rate—GFR— which involved an injection of a chemical into a vein in his arm. Again, Fraser didn't flinch. The GFR test would measure his kidney's ability to clear the blood of the substance that had been injected.

'I remember you talking about her long after you broke things off.'

Fraser drummed his fingers on the chair's arm, watching the liquid empty from the syringe. Who had he been kidding, thinking Boyd wouldn't say something eventually?

Of *course* he'd talked about her—he'd loved her. He always had and everyone knew it. And to love Sara was to love everything about her—especially Esme.

CHAPTER NINE

'HER HEART-RATE SHOWS one hundred and three. It climbs when she moves so she's clearly still in pain, likely from the vomiting.' Fraser turned from Sara back to their sweaty young patient. 'Where does it still hurt?'

'Here,' the girl said, putting her hands to her stomach. 'I think I'm going to throw up again.'

Sara helped the teenage girl out of her vomit-covered T-shirt and into a clean white one. The teen appeared to have contracted some kind of respiratory infection, and Fraser had his suspicions as to what it was.

'Lucky you came to us when you did,' Sara said kindly. She was fetching another bedpan now, just in case. She didn't look up at him as she worked. She hadn't done all afternoon. He knew he was still in the doghouse.

'Take care of this please, Chief?' she said to him, again without making eye contact.

She handed him the dirty T-shirt. He took it, glad of his rubber gloves. Sara could have just thrown it into the laundry bin herself, but he said nothing. She was still mad at him for disappearing on her. She had every right to be; he'd left her lying alone in his bed, after all.

But she'd looked so peaceful there. And, God, he'd missed the sight of that face, still and silent, her hair splayed on his pillowcase.

'Were there any other women after me?' she'd asked him before they'd drifted off.

'A couple,' he'd admitted. 'But none that made me feel like this.'

'Like what?'

'Like we could all go down on this ship and I wouldn't care as long as I was holding you like this.'

The second he'd said it he'd regretted it, because Sara wouldn't think of him if that happened—she'd think of Esme. Esme would always come first... And if he'd tried to explain then where he was going at such an early hour she'd have wanted to come too.

Either that or she'd have stopped him going. He wasn't sure which.

The phone rang. Sara beat him to it. He watched her movements in her long white coat and too-white sneakers as she held the receiver to her ear. She was tanned already...she was glowing.

'We have the results,' she told him a few minutes later.

He walked closer, out of earshot of their patient. 'The urine antigen?'

'It's not Legionnaires'—it's Pontiac fever.' She finally met his eyes.

They could be at odds with each other as much as Sara Cohen wanted, he thought. It didn't change what had happened, or the fact that their closeness had dredged up some long-suppressed feelings. Sure, they'd just about managed to keep it platonic, but he knew they'd *both* been fighting doing more in his bed.

Fraser cleared his throat. 'OK,' he said, 'Pontiac we can deal with.'

Better than Legionnaires'.

He didn't say it out loud. He didn't need to. They were both thinking it. During his last cruise they'd had a case of that, and the ship had been forced to cordon off the hot tubs. It was rare in people under fifty, but not unheard of.

'Have you been in the hot tub or the swimming pool in

the last few days?' he asked the teen. Her long red hair was stringy with sweat.

'No. Can I go now?'

'No.'

She started coughing again wildly, into her hand. Her forehead was glistening with sweat.

'You're not going anywhere,' Sara told her pointedly. Fraser watched her put a hand to her back and pat her gently. 'Sorry to say, but it looks like you have something called Pontiac fever.'

'What's that?' She looked horrified, her red hair sticking to her pallid face.

Fraser let Sara explain while he fixed an IV and its tubes.

'It's a milder form of Legionnaire's Disease…'

'A *disease*?' She looked even more horrified now.

'It's not transmitted from person to person, but it *is* contracted by inhaling bad bacteria from water. Did you sit under any kind of water jet or spray anywhere? Go anywhere with strange air-conditioning?'

The girl wrinkled her nose. 'No, I don't think so.'

'Think,' Fraser told her. 'It's important.'

'She *is* thinking, Fr… Doctor.' Sara paused. 'She's battling a fever. It's OK if you can't remember, honey.'

That had told *him*. He frowned in her direction and she pretended not to see. She'd said it in such a way that only he would know how annoyed she was—at *him*, obviously, not at the girl for her understandably cloudy memory.

He let it go. She was stressed about a Legionnaires' outbreak. She was thinking of Esme and the other dialysis patients. Those with weak immune systems were more likely to contract the condition, which put the dialysis patients at high risk should there be an issue with the ship.

He adjusted the IV as the teen swiped at her clammy face with a cool towel. 'Actually, there were ventilators pointed at us in that seafood restaurant.'

'Which restaurant?' Sara's voice was calm but anxiety was practically a cloud around her.

'Back in Florida. I knew that place was dodgy. Mum said it had the best prawns, but she really meant the cheapest. We won this cruise in a competition, you know?'

'Where's your mother now?' he asked.

'I don't know. She doesn't know I'm here.'

Fraser looked at Sara. They spoke without words. They had to find this girl's mother as soon as possible for tests. Even if she wasn't showing any symptoms it was better to be safe than sorry. Both Legionnaires' and Pontiac could take a couple of weeks to manifest at times, though it was deeply unlucky to contract either.

Sara ushered him aside while the teen hacked some more behind them.

'I'll call Miami. Tell them to report this—see if it links to any other clusters of Pontiac. There haven't been any other cases on the *Ocean Dream*?'

'Not yet on this trip. Never on any trip before, and not on this ship. It's practically brand-new.'

'Are you sure?'

She searched his eyes. He wanted to touch her.

'I'm sure. Cohen, I know what you're thinking, but it's probably a one-off. It's not contagious.'

'I know, but what if something has been overlooked?'

'Highly unlikely—they've triple-tested everything on here.' He couldn't help it. He placed his hands firmly on her shoulders. 'Sara, they wouldn't have allowed dialysis patients on board at all if there was any doubt that it was safe. You *know* this.'

She bit her lip. He'd never seen her so riled up in a medical setting. Keeping her status as a mother separate from that of a nurse must be tough in times like this. He pictured Boyd back at the clinic, running the tests, concluding… hopefully any day now…that he could be a donor for Esme.

'You're probably right,' she said, drumming her fingers on her leg.

Her hair brushed his fingers.

'I know you're right. It was the restaurant.'

'I'm sure it was the restaurant. We'll call them right now.'

CHAPTER TEN

SARA TRIED TO ignore the way her knee kept nudging Fraser's unbidden in the back of the buggy.

'This is one of my favourite islands,' he said as they started the bumpy, winding journey away from the bustling port where they'd docked in the Bahamas.

Esme looked wonderstruck, sitting on his knee, taking it all in. She had wanted Fraser to come with them to the pineapple plantation, the same way she'd wanted him at the beach in Aruba that time, and most evenings at their dinner table.

Sara's brow creased involuntarily under her sun hat as she fanned herself with a map. She couldn't exactly have argued with her daughter. They had been instructed to leave the ship anyway.

Renee had promised to call as soon as she'd heard from the seafood restaurant and had the ship's engineers check everything out again, just to be sure the problem didn't lie there.

She wasn't proud of the way she'd cracked over the Pontiac fever case. The times when Esme's health might be further at risk were the only times that it interfered with her job. The thought of what might happen to Esme or any of the other dialysis patients should there be any trace of Pontiac on the ship was not even worth contemplating. At least Fraser understood that.

He was filming Esme now. She listened as the little girl

gave him a running commentary on the types of trees they were passing. She was making up names for them all.

'Mummy, Mummy, look—that's the Sara tree, and that's the Dr Fraser tree!'

'That's great,' she replied as Fraser cheered. She was trying and probably failing to sound upbeat. Esme always knew when she was down. She was usually the one to bring her up.

Esme looked enchanted now, though. Fraser seemed to love telling her stories about the time he went travelling. Before they'd met, and before his medical studies began, he'd spent six months seeing South America—the Galapagos, Ecuador, Chile and Peru. He was feeding Esme's imagination at every opportunity, answering her endless questions, and it unsettled Sara more than she could say, because she knew Esme dreamed of having a father figure in her life although Sara had always told herself they didn't need one.

'This is a very important part of the Bahamas, Esme,' Fraser was saying now in his best tour guide voice. 'The British settled here in the seventeen-hundreds—you can see it in the architecture. Looks a bit like home, don't you think?'

Esme wrinkled her nose.

'It doesn't look anything like the Britain *I* know,' Sara told him, smiling in spite of herself. It really didn't. It was a lot hotter, too. Her map was falling apart.

'You OK?' Fraser asked her, putting a hand to her knee suddenly. 'You're very quiet. I'm sure we'll hear something soon.'

'I hope so.' He squeezed her knee and she resisted the urge to touch him back. She was still annoyed with him for slipping out the other morning without waking her. He was hiding something—she could feel it.

When they reached the pineapple plantation she lingered behind, gathering her thoughts.

'They look like pine cones, Mummy!' Esme cried, pointing at the baby pineapples poking from their spiky green leaves on the ground.

She was filming everything, as usual. There were rows and rows and rows of them, stretching into the distance under the grey sky.

'Come on, Cohen, you're falling behind! You don't want to miss out on planting your own pineapple, do you? We'll name it after you.'

Fraser stopped on the trail between the rows of plants. His black curls were sticking out around his red baseball cap. His eyes narrowed when she caught up to him.

'You're not still angry at me, are you? I told you—I had to go and see some people and it was too early to wake you up.'

'I'm not angry.'

'So you've been avoiding looking me in the eye for no reason, have you?'

Sara stopped in her tracks. She crossed her arms automatically, cutting him off like a roadblock. The slight breeze was picking up the bottom of her turquoise dress and trying to ruffle it against his khaki shorts, as if even their clothing couldn't keep away from each other.

'Fraser. I know you. I know you're keeping things from me.'

He stepped closer and stared into her sunglasses.

'I can't have men around who lie to me,' she continued, lifting the glasses up to her head so she could look him straight in the eye. 'Not with Esme. She's been through enough. *I've* been through enough.'

'I understand. It's nothing for you to worry about, I promise you.'

'Is it someone else?' She felt embarrassed the second he frowned.

'Is that what you really think? Cohen, I can barely even keep up with *you*.'

He looked genuinely offended at her words. She kicked herself internally as he looked away and out at the pine-apples.

'I'm sorry,' she said, ramming a hand through her hair. 'It's just everything's getting a little overwhelming, you know? I told you we should focus on our work, I told you this couldn't happen, but I did it anyway.'

She went to walk past him but he caught her arm, drew her back. His eyes drilled into hers. She pulled her glasses back down to protect her thoughts.

'OK, so you're angry at yourself—I get it. But don't take it out on me and don't beat yourself up over some-thing so stupid.' He lowered his voice. 'We didn't even *do* anything, Sara...'

'I should have been with Esme.'

'You were where you wanted to be,' he said. 'You were where *I* wanted you to be. And I'll tell you where I was the other morning, but not yet. Sara, you know me. You'll just have to trust me.'

A young girl no older than seventeen, in a flower-patterned headscarf, was explaining the pineapple industry in Eleuthera with pride, but all Sara could think about as she went along with the tour was Fraser, always two steps behind her, his eyes burning into her back like the sun.

She was being too hard on him.

It was easier being hard on him.

Their guide started leading them down another path to-wards an open patch of land. Three people were on their hands and knees in the dirt, planting baby plants and sow-ing seeds. Sara watched as Esme was led over to them and handed a seedling.

'Will you film me, Dr Fraser?'

'You bet I will.' He took the camera. 'Tell me what you're doing—don't miss anything out.'

Esme launched into a comical explanation as she went along, talking straight into the lens.

'He's so good with her,' the guide whispered at her side.

'He is—very good with her,' she agreed, noting how Fraser treated Esme like an equal, rather than a broken little kid. Esme adored him for it already.

'Cover it up with more dirt!'

Esme had buried the baby plant and was patting the dark soil firmly all around it to keep it in place. Everyone clapped and she beamed as if she'd just performed the greatest task on Earth.

'You should plant one too,' she announced. She picked up another seedling and held it out to Sara. 'Plant it with Dr Fraser, Mummy. You have to share it.'

Sara got on her knees beside him and he handed her a tiny shovel. Her fingers brushed his as she took it and she felt those sparks again, the need to hold her breath. She'd wanted nothing more than to make love with him, to reconnect the real way, but he'd been adamant they keep things PG-rated. Was it because he'd known he was about to get up early and leave, and not tell her where he was going?

'Is here OK?' Fraser asked Esme. 'You getting a good shot, Spielberg?'

'Here is perfect—plant it next to mine!'

Sara dug with the tiny shovel, trying not to over-analyse everything that was going on with Fraser. Instead she found herself studying Esme in the sunlight. The way her little nose and eyes crinkled as she concentrated was adorable. She'd long thought these quirks and expressions reminded her of something and had always assumed it was home. If home could be a person, not a place.

Their guide crouched down, smiling with kind eyes.

'You know, in two years' time you can come back and pick your fruit to eat.'

'I might not have two years,' Esme said bluntly, pointing to the line poking out above her clothing. 'See this catheter? It means I have a robo-kidney. They're really smart, but they don't keep you alive for ever.'

'Baby, don't say things like that!' Sara was horrified.

The poor guide looked frazzled.

'It's true, though, Mummy. Isn't it, Dr Fraser?'

Sara felt sick. She tried to stand but she felt Fraser taking her elbow, keeping her in place.

He turned to Esme. 'Of course you have two years—and much more than that, lass. You've got a whole lot of exciting stuff still to do.'

'But I don't have a donor.'

Esme sounded matter-of-fact, as if she'd thought about this endlessly and had come to terms with it. It made everything so much worse.

Sara let Fraser hold her down, trying to soak up his strength. He was right. She had to act normal. But this kind of thing *was* normal for her. Maybe it always would be.

CHAPTER ELEVEN

'ARE YOU READY to watch your mum do something really cool?'

Esme jumped up and down with glee as Fraser led them all to where an instructor was pulling lifejackets out of a plastic container on the shoreline, three feet away. Fraser took a small one and carefully buckled Esme into it. Sunbeams were glinting off his sun-kissed skin. He stepped closer to help Sara fasten the straps of her own lifejacket.

'No need to worry,' he told her, inches from her face. 'This guy knows what he's doing with newbies.'

The way he tugged on the straps was possessive, purposeful, pulling Sara closer to him with each tug.

'I trust him,' she said. She looked Fraser in the eyes. 'I trust *you*.'

He smiled, but cocked an eyebrow. 'Do you?'

'I want to.'

'I'll take that for now.'

He winked at her and she knew their earlier confrontation was forgotten. Of course she didn't think there was anyone else. He was hiding *something*, but he'd told her he would tell her eventually—which probably meant it was a surprise or something. She wouldn't put it past him; he'd always been a huge romantic.

At any rate, they had bigger concerns.

'Any word from Renee about the ship yet?' she asked him. Already she was hot in the lifejacket. The water was a pale inviting blue on the white sand.

He pulled out his phone for the hundredth time in the last hour and checked it. 'Nothing. I'm sure everything is under control. No news is good news, right?'

Sara frowned as he dropped it into a waterproof bag. That wasn't always the case. They'd had no news about a donor for Esme, *ever*.

She found herself resisting the urge to let her fingers rub a smear of sunscreen into his shoulder as he turned to their instructor, Ruben. How she'd let him talk her into going out on water skis she had no clue, but this was *her* holiday, too. She had to find something to tell her sister about—something exciting that she'd never done before.

'OK, you're looking good,' Fraser said, and she watched his gaze sweep her breasts in her bikini, and then her legs as he stepped back on the sand. 'You're looking *really* good. But I've told you that before.'

'Have you been water skiing before, either of you?' Ruben asked them. He was short and bald, in a black T-shirt and board shorts.

Sara shook her head, no, as Fraser said yes. She couldn't help her eyes lingering on the grooves of his six-pack as he pulled on his own lifejacket, recalling how she'd run her hands over him, her lips glued to his, almost desperate for more after so long apart.

She tried to focus as Ruben demonstrated how to make the most of her time on the water. 'Now, the important thing to remember is that if you fall, don't resist—just let go.'

'Don't resist—just let go. OK.'

They covered how she should assume the proper cannonball position, how she should keep her knees together, and how to let the boat do all the work—and the whole time Fraser nodded and murmured in agreement, as though he'd done it a thousand times and couldn't wait to get in the water.

She wondered whether anything ever scared Fraser

Breckenridge, because if it did she'd never seen it. Except his father, she thought suddenly, surprising herself. And the thought of losing his mother. Fraser had always put his family first.

In the tender boat, Fraser made sure she and Esme were seated properly before he took his place beside her. Esme was beside herself with excitement. Sara watched her film Fraser putting a medi-bag into a waterproof bag.

'You're not about to miss a second, are you Spielberg?' Fraser laughed. 'How long is this movie going to be when you're done?'

'Long enough for two sequels,' Sara told him, shaking her head.

Before long they were chugging out into the turquoise water. Every now and then she caught the reflection of another boat or a snorkeler in Fraser's sunglasses as the scenery swept past.

'Do you want to go first, or should I?' he asked, breaking into her thoughts.

She turned to him. The wind was tugging his hair in all directions. She noticed a few flecks of grey in his stubble she'd never seen before.

'I think you should go first,' she said.

'That could be a bad idea.'

'Why?'

'What if you're so intimidated by how awesome I am that you don't even want to take your turn?'

She laughed. 'If anything, I'll be better than you. I don't weigh as much.'

He made a *pffft* sound. 'I don't think weight has anything to do with it.'

Their instructor turned around. 'Actually, the skis are made for different weight ranges, so it is quite important to use a pair that suits your size.'

Sara smirked. 'Better stick to medicine, Chief.'

'Fine, I'll go first. Show you how the pros do it.'

Ruben glided the boat to a stop and turned off the engine. Fraser stood up, puffing out his chest in the lifejacket, making Esme giggle.

The boat was bobbing now that they were on relatively open water. A jet ski was already cutting through the waves nearby. The couple on the back were passengers on the *Ocean Dream*—the pair who were always arguing, Sara realised now, noting the guy's long ponytail and his back patterned with tattoos.

She turned to Fraser, now sliding his feet into the bindings.

'Ready!' he called, assuming the starting position.

The muscles rippled in his arms as he gripped the handle. He looked like some kind of James Bond extra, wearing black gloves and red shorts. He gave the camera a salute before Ruben drove on a little faster, then faster, till Fraser rose on the skis, standing up straight, skidding along behind them.

Sara watched in awe as his body twisted and weaved in the waves. The wind seemed to soften, allowing him to be at one with the water…right before he hit a rogue wave and toppled over.

Sara's breath caught. Fraser disappeared, but in seconds he was popping up again, straight back onto the skis, skidding on the surface as before. Esme was squealing in delight. The spray showered up around him in all directions. James Bond had nothing on Fraser.

Something else caught her eye. She froze. There in the surf to the right of Fraser, shining and glittering and leaping, was a dolphin.

'Esme, look!' she cried.

Esme's eyes grew round. Fraser had seen it too. He steadied himself expertly as the dolphin continued to swim alongside him. Mesmerised, Sara watched its long, silvery body gleaming in the light before it reached the boat and appeared to circle around them.

'Wow!'

The dolphin darted and zipped underneath the boat, and then swam alongside, leaping and bounding in their spray. She turned to look for Fraser again, but what met her eyes was a scene of horror.

The couple on the jet-ski were heading straight for him.

'Fraser!'

In a blink it was over. The rope was flailing on the water but Fraser had disappeared.?

'Fraser!' Hot tears flooded her eyes as she scrambled to try and see him. 'Where is he?' She turned to Ruben. 'He's gone!'

Esme was crying.

'It's OK, baby,' she soothed her.

Ruben cut the engine. The girl on the jet-ski was screaming hysterically. Mr Ponytail looked panicked. In a second Sara was in the water, swimming as fast as she could towards the spot where they'd collided. But swimming was not her strong point. A million scenarios screamed through her head, even as her professional voice was telling her to stay calm, to conserve her energy.

He still hadn't surfaced. Then there was a movement in the water below her. A hand on her leg. She drew in a sharp breath, spinning around. Fraser was coming up right in front of her, blinking. She reached for him, holding on to his lifejacket, letting them float along together while she caught her breath. Tears were still stinging her eyes with the salt water.

'I'm OK.'

She saw the panic in his eyes. His wet, handsome face was dripping an inch from hers.

'I'm OK. But the coral got me.'

She released him. 'What?' He was wincing now. Then she noticed the blood. It was turning the water red around them.

'I'm shark bait.'

'Not funny.' She spun her head in all directions. Ruben was already driving the boat to their side. Mr Ponytail and his girlfriend were hovering on the jet-ski, yelling at each other.

'You could've *killed* him, Trevor!' the girl was screaming.

For one sickening moment Trevor looked as if he was going to hit her.

'Hey, it's OK,' Sara called out, aware of Esme watching it all.

Trevor reined back his hand, as though reconsidering his violent outburst. The dolphin was nowhere to be seen.

Ruben helped Fraser onto the boat and Sara hauled herself up after him. Blood was spilling down Fraser's right thigh and calf to the floor. She hurried to grab some towels, and when she turned back she saw he was lowering himself to the floor, leaning against the side of the boat. The bulk of him was heavy as he rested on her shoulder for a moment.

Esme got to her knees, concern written all over her face. 'What's happening?'

'We have to get the coral out of me before I turn into a reef,' he told her, bringing his leg up and holding it around the calf. Esme looked stunned, but the blood didn't faze her.

'Esme, go and sit with Ruben,' Sara said, pulling the waterproof bag towards her and unscrewing a bottle of water.

Fraser winced as she dabbed at the cut. Blood was gushing from the wound, soaking the towels.

'You're cut up pretty badly—you might need stitches. Ruben, take us back to the shore as quickly as you can.'

'I'll be OK,' Fraser insisted. 'We'll just clean it and bandage it for now. You need to take your turn.'

Was he serious? 'Are you *insane*? Fraser, we need to get you back...'

'Sara, I'm fine.'

'You could have *died*!' She was pouring alcohol onto a cloth from the medical kit but the words made her choke. She paused with the cloth in her hand. 'I could swear I saw him hit you.'

He caught her wrist, right before she could apply the alcohol. 'You're shaking,' he whispered, so Esme couldn't hear them. 'Sara, the jet ski hit the rope, not me. It didn't touch me. I saw it coming and I got out of the way. I just went too deep onto the coral. I'm OK.'

She snatched her hand away. 'You almost weren't.'

She pressed the cloth to his wound, catching the blood as it continued to trickle down his calf. He sucked in a breath. He was right. She *was* shaking.

The phone rang and Fraser pounced on it. She listened as he said, 'OK, thanks...' in a way that didn't even hint at what had just happened to him. Her heart kept on thudding erratically.

'The restaurant's reported a couple of complaints this week,' he said. 'They're shutting down while they fix their air-con.'

'Oh, that's not good.'

'Well, at least no one else on the ship ate there; they've accounted for everyone and no one is showing any symptoms. The good news is that it's not the *Ocean Dream*, so we're in the clear.'

'Can we do anything?'

At the question Sara turned to see Mr Ponytail, still bobbing at the side of the boat. His girlfriend was quiet now, but she had a face like thunder. Had they been arguing before this accident had happened? Was that why this guy had been distracted?

'You can be more careful next time,' she told him, pulling hydrogen peroxide from the bag. 'Go back to the ship—we're fine here.' She mixed it with fresh water and started flushing the wound. 'And I suggest you stop these public displays of…whatever it is…on the ship. You don't know who's watching.'

'Pot, kettle, black,' Trevor replied quickly, looking between them.

Fraser scowled as Sara's cheeks flamed and the couple sped off.

There was still no sign of the dolphin.

CHAPTER TWELVE

FRASER STUDIED SARA'S suturing handiwork on his tanned leg. The stitches looked a bit like a constellation, he mused, observing the shape and doing his best not to bunch up his face in discomfort.

'Looking good, thank you,' he told her as she placed the gauze and needle beside the bed and pulled off her gloves. 'What would I have done without you?'

'You'd probably have a coral reef starting to grow in your leg. Esme believes you about that, you know.'

He swung his body from the bed, sitting on the edge of it. His limbs were achy and tired. He knew he'd be bruised tomorrow from the force of the blow.

'You'd look quite cute with a little Nemo swimming around you,' she said, packing up the medical kit. 'Still, you were lucky it wasn't worse.'

'I know.'

'I don't know what I was thinking.' Sara paused and looked at the carpet. 'I shouldn't have even been out there, Fraser. What if something worse had happened to me? What would Esme have done?'

'You can't put your entire life on hold because of what might or might not happen, Cohen. You were having a good time out there before the accident, weren't you? We all were.'

She dropped the bag on the bed beside him. 'Yes, but that doesn't mean I can run off and be irresponsible whenever I choose.'

'You weren't being irresponsible. That stuff is called living your life.'

She was quiet, contemplating the notion.

He reached for her hand, moved the bag and sat her down next to him on the bed. 'All this to see a dolphin.'

'What is up with that couple anyway?' she asked. 'Do you think there's something dark going on there? Whenever I see them they're arguing.'

'I know,' he said. 'If not loudly then really, really quietly in a corner somewhere, which is worse.'

'Much worse,' she agreed. Then she looked at him. 'We don't do that, do we?'

He grinned, and she clearly couldn't hide her smile either. 'I should probably go,' she said, a little reluctantly.

'Maybe you should.' He kept his hand over hers on the bed, then turned her head towards him. He could barely conceal what she was doing to him, being so close right now on the bed.

He shifted, turning his body towards her, ignoring the pain as it ripped through his leg. He hadn't wanted Renee to walk into the medical centre and see him like this, so they'd come straight here, and now he was finding it impossible not to touch her.

'Don't move just yet,' Sara admonished, standing up.

He saw her eyes drift over his bare torso, felt the energy course between them as she wrestled visibly with her own desires.

It had started to rain outside. He could hear it pattering on the circular windows. The ship was swaying, even though they were still in port. They weren't leaving for another day, when they'd be cruising on to Antigua, but in bad weather a lot of people tended to stay on the ship, where they knew food and shelter were guaranteed.

'I have a job to do.' She still wasn't moving.

'You're not on duty for another hour.'

'This just…isn't a good idea.'

'I happen to think it's a very, *very* good idea. See how stressed you are? We can easily fix that.'

Sara bit back another laugh as he urged her to stand between his legs. 'You're making it way too easy to be distracted,' she said.

'I was hoping you'd say that.'

He put his hands to her waist and pulled her even closer. Hang doing nothing more than kissing—they wanted each other, didn't they? He'd wanted her since the second Anton had phoned him and recommended her for the job on the dialysis team. They didn't have to sleep together just yet. But he didn't mind if they upped things from PG a little.

Sara narrowed her eyes in front of him. 'I'm supposed to be keeping away from you…this…'

'Who says so?'

She was silent, then she rolled her eyes. 'Me, I suppose. And Renee. She knows something's up between us and she doesn't need any more encouragement.'

'Something's definitely *up*,' he said, casting his eyes for the briefest of moments down to the red shorts he was still wearing.

She laughed, and groaned again, but didn't exactly object when he put both hands beneath her ass and pulled her swiftly onto his lap. In fact her legs wrapped around him instantly, as did her arms. For a second he forgot the stinging pain still shooting around his stitches.

Her palms came up against his cheeks before moving to his hair. She gripped it in bunches and let out a deep sigh as she pressed her head to his. 'What am I doing?'

'Anything you want to.'

He ran his hand through her damp hair as her knees sank into the bed either side of him. He wanted her so badly. He'd seen genuine fear in her eyes when she'd faced him in the water after his accident. She'd been trying not to show it, taking control and switching to nurse mode almost instantly, but he could read her changing moods like chapters. They'd never stop caring for each other, no matter what happened or didn't. The love they'd felt clearly hadn't gone away—it had simply been locked up for a while.

Her knees gripped his middle, straddling him on the bed, and it was she who kissed him first.

They'd used to kiss like this for hours, but they didn't have hours right now. In minutes their clothes were on the floor. They were still kissing wildly, running their hands all over each other on the bed, when a flash of pain made him wince and crumble.

Sara scrambled off him quickly. 'Oh, God, your stitches—are you OK?' She looked traumatised. 'I'm so sorry.'

'I'm good,' he managed, even as he throbbed all over... and not just from the stitches.

She was laughing now a little—embarrassed, maybe— standing on the floor in just her blue bikini bottoms. 'You need to start the antibiotics,' she told him, leaning over him again on the bed and putting a hand to his chest.

Her cheeks were red and flushed. They'd been about to make love; he'd been about to get a condom. He brought his hand to her face, urging her back down on the bed, but pain flashed through his leg again and he grimaced.

'Fraser, I'm telling you—at least take an ibuprofen.' Sara stood back, started pulling on her clothes. 'I'm going to get more bandages—I have to re-dress that.'

'No, you don't.' He breathed through the pain as it stabbed like knives.

'You're so stubborn.' She buttoned up her dress, shooting him a wary look. 'Anyway, I know we do this to each other, but it's not a good idea, Fraser—you know that.'

'No, I *don't* know that.'

'God, I don't even know what I'm *doing* after all this time. I keep making this mistake…'

'This is not a mistake, Cohen,' he told her resolutely. His leg was throbbing. If only she would stop with this nonsense. 'Don't tell yourself these things are *mistakes*. You're allowed to have some fun, aren't you?'

She froze.

'That's not what I meant,' he added quickly. 'I mean, yes, we have fun, but…'

'It doesn't matter.'

She wriggled her flip-flops onto her feet and swept her hair up onto the top of her head in a messy bun. She looked and sounded tired, more than angry.

'Call this fun, if you want, Fraser. Call it whatever you want. It doesn't matter anyway, does it? Once we leave this ship we're never going to see each other again.'

Fraser stood. He was naked now, right in front of her, and he didn't miss her eyes sweeping his entire body before she closed them and appeared to restrain herself.

'Start the antibiotics,' she ordered, turning for the door. 'Or that's going to get worse.'

He strode ahead of her quickly, through a surge of pain, and put a hand to the door, keeping it shut. 'You really think I'd be doing this with you if I never wanted to see you again?'

She looked away, gnawing on her lip now, at his shoulder height.

'Sara, please talk to me.'

'I don't see how we even *could*, Fraser. Our lives are completely different now. You're going back to your surgery in Edinburgh; I'm taking Esme back to London…'

'Why do you always have to make excuses?'

'What do you mean, *always*?' She blinked at him. 'It's not an excuse. It's the truth. I have a sick daughter who needs me every hour of every day that I'm not working,

and sometimes even when I am. I can't just gallivant around
the world when I get home, doing what I like, where I like,
with *you*. I need a plan.'

Guilt raged through him as she moved his hand from
the door. He opened his mouth to tell her about the plan—
the plan he'd set in motion. The plan that might not make
it to fruition, which would then make her feel even worse.
He shut his mouth again.

'I'll see you later,' she said, kissing his cheek, then fling-
ing open the door and leaving him standing there, naked.

He hopped back behind it, wary of unsuspecting eyes.
She was driving him crazy.

He crossed to the coffee table, where his laptop was
open, pulling on his shirt and boxers as he went, being careful not to aggravate his stitches. Dropping to the couch, he
dialled into the ship's private Internet connection. Only a
few people had access and he was one of them. Maybe it
would be here now—the good news he'd been praying for.

He pressed 'inbox', and when the messages had downloaded—surely slower than when the Internet had first been
invented—there it was, finally.

It was not good news.

The transfer centre needed something else from him.
Luckily he could sort it out once they reached Antigua,
but it meant he couldn't take antibiotics. He couldn't have
them in his system if he had to do more tests.

Frowning to himself, he pulled on clean shorts, wincing
at the pain. This was the toughest job he'd ever had to do.

CHAPTER THIRTEEN

'SO, I'M GOING to tell you about my robo-kidney,' Esme explained.

Marcus was enthralled. He'd been waiting patiently for the chance to see what made Esme so special since the start of the cruise. It had been tough finding the time and space to entertain him in the dialysis unit, but Sara had promised Esme.

'First I weigh myself. Today's weight is sixteen point five. Then I take my temperature. Ninety-eight point four, which is good.'

Sara smiled to herself. Esme was enlightening Marcus as best as she could about all the wires and tubes and beeps. Her daughter knew the procedure by heart, of course—something that impressed Sara and pained her all at once. Would there ever be a day when they wouldn't have to go through this?

'Then they take my blood pressure, and a little bit of blood from my lines. They hook me up to the dialysis machine.' Esme patted it with one little hand. 'Which is what they call my robo-kidney. See these two tubes?' She pointed at them, one by one. 'The red one takes the blood and the machine cleans it, and the blue tube puts the blood back in.'

'So why can't you eat ice-cream?' Marcus asked. His brow was furrowed as he stood there studying the dialysis machine with interest, looking at all its buttons and tubes.

Sara masked a small laugh, putting a hand to his soft brown hair. After all this technology and machinery; and after seeing Esme's catheter and lines every day, still all the kid really cared about was why she couldn't eat ice-cream.

'No one should eat ice-cream in the middle of the night—especially when they're supposed to be in their beds.'

'Dr Fraser!' Esme trilled in delight as he appeared in the doorway.

Sara had her back to him, but at the sound of his voice, all the hairs stood up on the back of her neck.

'Hey,' she said, turning around. He stepped into the dialysis room, holding up a hand. The sight of his tall, broad frame made her heart start to beat a little faster under the harsh lights.

'What's going on in here, Spielberg? Where's your camera?'

'Mummy says I can't bring it into the dialysis room any more.'

Fraser's blue eyes fell on Sara as he stepped towards them. 'Mummy is probably right—a lot of private things occur in rooms like these.'

Sara swallowed involuntarily. She couldn't help remembering what was underneath his clothes...the way she'd left him standing naked as she'd flung open the door.

She hadn't really seen him much since she'd left his cabin the other day. The medical centre had been ridiculously busy and she'd been roped into attending a parent/child picnic and sleepover in her time off. But of course Fraser had been on her mind constantly.

She'd been ready to make love to him. She'd been caught in the moment, relieved that Trevor's damn jet-ski hadn't sliced off his beautiful head. But him being in pain had made it *not* the right time and she was glad now, because she was already getting too close to him. So was Esme.

'What's happening?' she asked him, busying herself with tidying away some equipment.

'How is your leg?' Esme asked him before *she* could.

'I had to pull three fish out of it this morning,' Fraser told her, pulling a face.

Both she and Marcus giggled. The sound made Sara smile.

Esme motioned for Fraser to move to a chair and made a thing of examining his chest with a broken stethoscope Sara had given her earlier.

Fraser looked as handsome as ever in his white coat—a look completed by his trademark sneakers, ideal, like her own, for gripping a swaying deck. His hair was less dishevelled than she'd seen it last, when she'd rammed her hands through it while kissing him passionately. There was no other word for it than passion. They'd always had that in spades.

The thought made her hot again. Damn him.

'Your heartbeat is strong,' Esme was telling him now.

'Good to hear it.' Fraser put his hand to his heart. 'Can you hear any more fish swimming around in there?'

Esme pressed the stethoscope to his belly button. 'I can hear a jellyfish!'

Fraser pretended to look horrified. 'Oh, no! What about sharks?'

Marcus clapped his hands. 'He's full of sharks!'

Sara leaned on an empty bed, watching them. 'How are the stitches really?' she asked now, stepping towards him on the chair.

'Totally fine,' Fraser said, too quickly. 'Healing nicely already. I was actually wondering if we could just…'

'Let's have a look?' Sara noted how Esme shuffled up closer to get a better look.

'I've looked plenty of times myself, Nurse,' Fraser said, clearing his throat somewhat anxiously. 'How about we check for more sharks inside me, huh?'

He went to take the stethoscope from Esme, but Sara

took it herself and put it behind him on the counter. He sounded as if he really didn't want her looking at his leg. His tone had put her on guard immediately.

'Esme, go and play with Marcus—his mum is waiting outside.'

'Do I have to?'

Sara raised her eyebrows. She was surprised that Esme even wanted to see anything like this without her camera to record it. She'd told her not to film so much. She was only going to go home and make her watch all this footage of her and Fraser over and over, torturing both of them.

'Show me,' she commanded him now, getting down on her haunches in front of Fraser as the kids ran from the room.

'If you insist.'

He started rolling up his jeans. Her fingers brushed lightly through the hair on his lower calf, his warmth making her heart increase its pounding. She looked into his eyes, but he wouldn't look at her now.

Something was definitely up. She knew him too well. But she knew not to push him, too. She re-dressed the wound in silence, before the Tannoy summoned them both back to work.

'How long have you been having these headaches?'

Sara fixed the bed around the young Irishman. His fiancée had sent him in a panic after he'd blacked out on a sun lounger, and she was more than concerned for his wellbeing already.

'On and off for about a year. I thought they were just stress headaches, because of my wedding.'

The guy was in his late twenties. His name was Conor, and he looked guilty the second he said it.

Sara put a hand to his forehead. 'What do these headaches usually feel like?'

'Like someone's stabbing me in the frickin' eyeballs.' Conor grimaced in pain. His voice was breathy, faint. 'I haven't had one in a while, so I thought the cruise would be OK. But the casino just now…all the lights and the noise. I had to lie down. Can you give me some painkillers? I'm sure it's nothing worth wasting your time over.'

'The lights and noise made it worse?' Fraser was listening to their conversation in obvious concern and Sara met his eyes. They both knew this wasn't good.

'Sometimes I see flashes behind my eyes too.' Conor was still holding his head.

'How long have you had these flashes?' Sara asked him.

'They started a few months after the headaches did, I think.'

'Have you been to your doctor at home about this?'

'No. Like I said, with the wedding plans, and then this cruise to celebrate my mam's sixtieth, there's been a lot going on.'

'Your health should come first,' Sara told him. 'Do you drink?'

'No. I used to.'

'Why did you stop?' Fraser asked, stopping his notes. 'Did it make your headaches worse? And the flashes?'

Conor looked at him in surprise. 'How did you know?'

'Lucky guess.'

Sara watched as Fraser reached for the ophthalmoscope, stood beside the bed and shone the light into Conor's eyes one by one. When he examined his left eye, Conor cried out in pain.

'Oh, Jeez, that's worse. Can you please just give me something.'

'Worse when you look to the left?'

'Yes. Much worse.'

Fraser put the ophthalmoscope down while Sara attached the blood pressure cuff around Conor's arm. 'Have you had any other problems lately? Any pains? Any blood in your urine? Anything like that?'

The colour had drained from Conor's face now. 'Yes, a little… I thought it was because I ate too much steak.'

'Blood pressure is normal. Is it just your head that hurts right now?'

'Yes.'

'How long ago did you last see blood in your urine?' Fraser asked.

Sara instructed Conor to turn and applied pressure slowly down his left side. When she pressed lightly on his kidneys, Conor winced.

'Yeeow, that hurts! The last time I saw blood? I don't know—a couple of days ago, I think. I forgot about it.'

'I don't want to panic you,' Fraser said, keeping his voice low. He glanced at Sara again. 'But we need to run some tests. You're showing signs of polycystic kidney disease, and with your headaches combined you'll need to be checked for brain aneurysms.'

'What?' Conor looked distraught.

Sara felt her mouth turn dry. A cruise ship was no place for this poor man. Over fifty per cent of people with aneurysms died when they ruptured, and even without the test Conor, with his wedding on the cards, was showing all the signs of having one.

'What's an aneurysm?' he was asking Fraser now. 'I mean, you can treat that, can't you?'

Fraser shook his head. 'I'm not going to lie to you, pal, we can't. It's deadly serious.'

'Deadly?'

'It's a weakness in the wall of one of your brain's blood vessels,' Sara explained, putting a steady hand on his arm. 'When the blood runs through your brain, the weak spot pushes that thin wall outwards, which forms a bulge—a bit like a balloon with too much air inside it.'

Conor's eyes were round as she continued.

'If it ruptures, the blood can leak out into your brain tissue—which is not good at all. We need to get you to the hospital as soon as possible; we can't help you here.'

'Oh, Jeez, my mam will have a fit,' he moaned, seeming to forget his own pain for a moment.

It never failed to upset Sara that so many people experienced disturbing symptoms like blood in their urine and blinding headaches and still couldn't find the time to seek medical advice.

They were almost at Antigua now, and thankfully another storm had passed them by with nothing but a bit of heavy rain, enabling smooth sailing. Still, there was the rest of the day to go, and the open water wasn't an ideal location to be dealing with a suspected advanced aneurysm.

'We'll need to monitor you here until we get to Antigua,' Fraser explained as Sara went for an IV. 'You'll need to see a neurologist there for an MRI scan. You have insurance?'

'Of course.'

Sara breathed a sigh of relief. That was one good thing, at least. They'd managed to save poor Enid and her husband a health insurance nightmare by not calling for medevac, but if a situation was a matter of life or death, as this one was, they'd have no choice.

'We'll give you something for the pain, for now, but you should probably think about cancelling any flights you have booked for the meantime...'

'I can't do that. I've so much to do back home. Are you saying I might get stuck on the next island? Ouch.' Conor clutched at his skull again.

'That depends on what the neurologist there has to say,' Fraser told him, moving the IV closer for Sara. 'But you can't fly like this. You're lucky nothing happened on your flight out to the US—it might have exacerbated the situation.'

'This is a nightmare.' Conor gripped both sides of the bed as Sara hooked him up to the IV.

'We'll need to check his neurological function every few hours, and we'll arrange for an ambulance at Mount St John's,' he told her moments later, when he'd taken her aside. 'The Medical Centre on Antigua is one of the best in the Caribbean—he chose a good time to come to us... if you know what I mean.'

Sara nodded, trying not to notice again how sexy he looked, trying not to recall the way her body had almost glued itself to him.

'I'll call St John's,' Fraser said, but as he went to the telephone he stumbled slightly.

'Fraser? You OK?'

'I'm fine.'

She frowned. It looked as if it was taking every ounce of his strength not to make a sound in front of their new patient, and she could see he was in a lot of pain. 'Is it your leg?'

He straightened, held his hands up as if to stop her coming any closer. 'It's fine,' he said.

She stepped towards him anyway. 'Why are you still in pain?'

He lowered his voice. 'I told you. I'm all right, Cohen, I'm handling this.'

His guarded tone took her aback. She glanced at Conor, but he had his eyes closed, oblivious, thankfully. 'You did start the antibiotics, didn't you?' she asked. She'd held her tongue before, but this was something that could affect his work, and she couldn't let that happen here.

Fraser busied himself getting Conor's meds together. She could tell he was avoiding her. Come to think of it, he had been avoiding her ever since it had happened.

'Fraser, you know as well as I do that that was a deep

wound. Just because you didn't get wiped out by that jet ski, you're not invincible, you know. What's going on?'

'Nothing.'

'That's not true. I know you, don't forget.'

He stood in front of her, closer, blocking her from Conor's eyes—not that the lad could hear from where he was. 'The meds make me feel queasy,' he explained. 'I don't need that on a ship that could be caught in another storm any second.'

She frowned, putting her hands on her hips, then quickly folded them when she realised she sounded and probably looked like his mother. This man was driving her crazy.

CHAPTER FOURTEEN

FRASER LOCKED HIMSELF into his cabin and sat at the laptop. He had to be quick. Sara was monitoring Conor, who was worrying both of them—not that they were telling the guy's fiancée that.

Jude was such a sweet girl, with her wild red curls and freckled nose. They were very young to be getting married, he thought to himself, grimacing again with the pain he'd been trying and failing to hide all day. Then again, if you loved someone, why waste precious time? He'd wasted enough of that himself, living without Sara.

She could call their encounters 'mistakes' all she wanted, but he was damned if he was letting her go again at the end of this cruise without a fight.

The glare of the computer's light filled the cabin. He found himself holding his breath as the emails downloaded, as slowly as ever. He hated hiding this from her, lying to her. He'd never been seasick, ever. He just had to wait a little bit longer.

Boyd had explained in a previous email how his intern had somehow misplaced his original urine test. Fraser had been too agitated to read or remember the finer details, but thankfully this email confirmed that he now had an appointment scheduled in Antigua for another one.

He let out a sigh of relief as he closed the email. 'How can you lose a urine sample?' he muttered to himself for the thousandth time. But he remained grateful that, wherever he was in the world, people could help him.

Another email drew his attention. This one too was from Boyd, fresh in his inbox.

Fraser, I wanted to send you a personal note about this.

I have a couple of things to attend to at the hospital in Antigua this week. I'd like to meet you there and talk to you about something else while you're there. There have been some interesting results concerning your blood tests that I feel we should discuss before going any further.

No need to panic, but I think we need to sit down in person.

See you soon,
Boyd

Fraser read the email again, anxiety making him restless. What did he mean 'interesting results' concerning his blood test? Fraser had performed his own blood tests; he knew he was clean. Whether or not he'd be a match for Esme was a different story. What if this delayed things even more?

He tried not to feel disappointed. Of course these things took time—that much had been explained to him numerous times. He sat back on the couch, running his hands through his thick hair.

He wanted to tell Sara everything about his plan, right now, but if he did her mind would be elsewhere while she was working, and that wouldn't be fair on her, or Conor, or on any of their other patients. He didn't doubt her ability to focus in an emergency, of course—he'd seen that side of her countless times—but he didn't want to rock the boat, so to speak.

What if he wasn't eligible at all?

What if all this was for nothing?

It was all making him feel far more queasy than the ocean did.

'Fraser, are you there? We need you back here, ASAP.'

Sara's voice on the airwaves sounded worried. Standing up, and ignoring the shooting pain in his leg, he grabbed the radio.

'Conor's getting worse,' she told him, the second he stepped back into the medical centre. 'He kept saying it was the worst headache yet, then he described the sensation of having a flush of water over his head. Eyelids drooping. Double vision.'

Conor's fiancée Jude stepped aside to let Fraser through. She was panicked to say the least. Her cheeks were as red as her head of flaming red curls. 'What's going on? Why is this happening?'

'Wait outside, please,' Fraser told her quickly, taking her elbow and ushering her to the door.

'Please, let me stay,' she begged. Her big green eyes were pooling with tears.

'It'll help us do our jobs better if you wait outside.'

'We'll let you know what's happening when we have some news,' Sara told her.

Jude left reluctantly. He could see her shadow outside as he went back in and picked up the phone.

He watched Sara work as he started to co-ordinate with the Coast Guard's flight surgeon. If Conor had experienced any bleeding into the space between his brain and surrounding tissue it was bad news. There was nothing they could do on the ship about a subarachnoid haemorrhage, if that was what he was experiencing. It was likely he'd need a lumbar puncture.

'This is serious, and we're still fourteen miles from land,' he said into the phone. 'Yes. There *is* a risk to life, limb and eyesight. He's breathing, but his blood pressure is rising.'

He caught Sara's questioning glance. His words must be worrying her and he knew it.

'It's OK,' Sara whispered to Conor at his bedside, though

Fraser was pretty sure that at this point Conor couldn't hear her. 'Help is coming.'

He was put on hold. He caught Jude peeking through the glass of the door and his heart went out to her as Sara applied the pressure cuff again. Ruptured brain aneurysms were fatal in roughly forty per cent of cases like Conor's, and even if a patient survived, over sixty per cent experienced some sort of permanent neurological deficit.

No one could deny that waiting till the ship reached land would at this point be putting Conor's life even further in danger, but Fraser knew full well that there was a certain hierarchy involved when it came to a Coast Guard deciding to perform a medevac.

He glanced to the window. The sky was getting darker as the world outside inched into twilight, and the wind was picking up again.

'They won't send help?' Sara asked him as he stood there, still on hold. She walked over to him. Concern was written all over her face. 'We really need them here *now*.'

'I know.' He held a hand over the receiver. 'But sending a helicopter medevac is viewed as being a last resort,' he whispered. Her perfume smelled like lilies. 'The Coast Guard knows we're pulling the ship into port soon; also that we have competent medical staff on board.'

'But there's only so much we can do in this case.' She was clearly trying to keep the horror she was experiencing from her voice.

He held a finger up to his mouth. Someone was back on the line.

'Yes, yes…' He paused, looking to Sara. 'Yes, we can provide a professional.' He paused again as Sara's eyebrows shot to her hairline.

She motioned to herself with a pointed finger. 'Me?'

Fraser nodded his affirmation and watched her let out

a deep breath, obviously trying to compose herself as he carried on making the arrangements.

'They're on their way,' he said when he hung up. This time he placed a hand at the small of her back and led her to the side of the room. 'Are you OK to go with him? They need a nurse from the ship.'

'Yes, of course,' she told him, flustered.

Conor was out cold.

'Are you sure? The helicopter medevac team are only equipped with the basics. If he needs more, which he likely will, we have to sacrifice a member of the ship's staff.'

'Of course—of course I'll go. But what about…?'

'Esme will be fine. Don't you worry. Jess is here, and Marcus, and me.' Fraser put a firm hand to her shoulder, forcing her eyes to meet his. 'I'll prepare Conor for evacuation. He'll need extra blankets—it could be a cold and bumpy ride. Go and get your things together—warm clothes for you too. I'll get a message to Jess and tell her to meet us on deck.'

'Do you think he'll make it?' Her fear was evident.

'I don't know,' he said honestly.

Sara pulled on jeans and a red cardigan, the warmest things she had with her for a Caribbean cruise. She packed an *Ocean Dream* backpack with clothing for the night and made her way to the deck. The beating of her heart was the loudest thing in her head, but she heard Fraser before she saw him.

'Out of the way please!'

He was making his way over to her quickly. His broad shoulders were highlighted by the ship's lights, which were also shining on Conor, lighting the scene of the emergency for the helicopter. It was controlled chaos.

The bright yellow bulk of the medevac was a whizzing beacon in the sky. It couldn't have been too far away when they called, thank goodness. Sara felt angsty for a million reasons. And she couldn't see Esme yet.

'You all set?' Fraser stopped in front of her, his sneakers almost touching her black flats. 'Are you OK with this?' His hair was wilder than ever in the wind. His white coat was thrashing about his frame. He leaned in closer, speaking over the noise. 'This is about as exciting as these cruises get, Cohen.'

'You're telling me.'

'You'll be fine.'

His fingers were twitching at his sides, as if he too was finding it hard to resist reaching out to her before she was hoisted into the sky.

'I'll meet you at the hospital as soon as I can.'

'I'll take care of things,' she said, pulling her cardigan round her tighter as the helicopter inched ever closer overhead. 'Where's Esme?'

Fraser was being called on the radio. From the corner of her eye she registered the arguing couple again. The black-haired girl was shoving Mr Ponytail's chest with her palms, angry at him about something as usual.

She should probably talk to that girl at some point, she decided. But she couldn't think about that now.

'Mummy!' Esme was rushing at her from Jess's side, running across the deck in her pink pyjamas. 'Mummy are you really going up in the 'copter?'

Sara reached for her, scooped her up into her arms, breathed in the scent of her warm hair. 'Someone is very sick,' she said. 'I have to go with him to the hospital. I need you to be brave and do what Jess tells you, OK?'

'Can I come?' Esme asked in a small voice as she put her down.

Fraser crouched down to Esme as the wind whipped at their clothes. 'This is something Mummy has to do for work. She has to go and be a superhero—is that all right with you?'

Esme studied him. 'Yes…' she said cautiously, after a moment.

Renee was with Conor, talking over what was happening and what was about to happen with his family as the staff prepared a special stretcher for the airlift.

Sara would have to be raised along with him; there was no way the helicopter was landing on the deck. So surreal.

Fraser caught her bag as it threatened to blow from her shoulder. The rotor blades were drowning their voices already. Esme watched the helicopter with fascination, one hand locked in Fraser's, her camcorder focused on the scene. Sara didn't have the heart to tell her to turn it off. She'd probably never seen anything so exciting in her life.

She kept her head down the whole way over to the stretcher. They'd loaded Conor up and were making space for her beside him. Time was ticking. In reality it had only been a few minutes, maybe seven or eight, since they'd made the call to the Coast Guard, but under such pressure it felt like an eternity.

She said a silent prayer as Jess came for Esme and Fraser took control of the situation. She followed his every command as she was buckled and strapped.

'Make sure Conor's head is supported…make sure his tubes are wired and not about to blow away…make sure he's covered in yet another *Ocean Dream* blanket.'

He was already covered in at least six.

She looked up at the paramedic, readying himself to be lowered onto the deck, and tried not to think what might happen if the winch broke.

'Stand back, please!'

Security were in action around the deck, stopping those passengers who were moving about the scene with their cell phones.

Her breath caught in her throat as the paramedic started lowering himself on the line towards them. He was swaying in the wind, his bright orange jumpsuit turning him into some kind of exotic emergency bird.

'Please help him…we're getting married,' Jude sobbed. Her bright red curls were being flung in all directions by the wind and the helicopter blades.

Sara felt for a moment as though she were floating above the scene, rather than a part of it.

In seconds she was lifted into the dark sky. She caught her breath as the wind threatened to steal it. Fraser's eyes were on her. She could still see him from above, on the deck with his hand above his eyes, shielding his face from the bright lights.

She was a professional—she could deal with this. But as the ship became a strip light in the distance, and the endless sky stretched before her, just the thought of him and Esme *both* being so far away was terrifying.

CHAPTER FIFTEEN

CONOR HAD NEEDED seven and a half hours of surgery to clip the aneurysm in his brain.

'He opened his eyes and asked if we'd started the surgery yet,' the surgeon said.

Fraser watched as Sara lowered her head beside him. She was exhausted—that much he could tell. Her eyes held shadows he hadn't seen before.

'They can't let him die. Please, we're getting married,' Jude had whimpered on their way over to the hospital from the port.

He could see her now, through the glass, sitting at Conor's bedside. She looked calmer, but her desperation born of fear had snapped off another piece of Fraser's heart that was always reserved for his patients.

He couldn't help wondering what Boyd was about to tell him regarding his blood test. His concern had escalated, and all the drama combined had meant he hadn't slept a wink either.

'The fact that he came to us when he did, and that he was in your care when it ruptured, saved his life,' the surgeon said now to Sara. He was twiddling his long grey beard with two fingers. 'It didn't cause any irreversible neurological injury.'

Sara looked relieved. 'Thank goodness for that.'

She was still in her clothes from last night, which were crumpled at best. Her long cardigan looked cosy, like something he wanted to snuggle against with Sara still inside it.

'It was a blessing that the Coast Guard was so close,' Fraser said. 'Any further away and they might have written off our case. Conor certainly wouldn't have survived if they'd waited for the ship to reach Antigua.' He looked to Sara. 'Not a bad result for your first medevac.'

She threw him a weary glance. 'Thanks to *you*, Fraser.'

'Take a compliment. We make a pretty good team.'

He noticed her smile, albeit a little tightly, no doubt thanks to her tiredness.

Conor was blinking groggily. Jude was clutching at one of his hands. His mother, nearly forty years wiser, was clutching the other one even harder.

'You should go and get some sleep,' he told Sara, thinking of his own mother for a moment.

He still felt guilty every time he left her, even after two whole years without his father being around, though she insisted she was fine in that big old house all alone.

'I can keep an eye on things here for the next couple hours, sort the records.'

'Are you sure?' Sara swiped a hand over her eyes and forehead.

'Of course I'm sure. There's some other stuff I have to do here anyway,' he told her, stepping aside with her. 'I'll meet you back at the ship?'

He hoped she'd agree. His appointment with Boyd was set to commence on another level of the hospital any minute now. He would have had to come here anyway, of course. He just hadn't planned on Sara being there, too.

'I've spent enough time on that ship,' she told him, taking him by surprise. 'Esme's going on a trip on a glass-bottomed boat. Isn't there something fun *we* can do, Mr Tour Guide?'

She crossed her arms and looked up at him expectantly. Conflict took him hostage. He wanted nothing more than to spend some down-time with Sara, but this was a strange day in general.

'You don't want to sleep?'

'I'll do that later.'

In her eyes Fraser saw a glimpse of the playful girl he'd fallen for back in Edinburgh. 'Not if I can help it,' he said softly, before he could stop himself.

A laugh escaped Sara's mouth. She reined it back in behind her hair and turned it into a yawn as the surgeon turned to them questioningly.

'OK,' Fraser said. 'If you want to do something fun, meet me at the beach I told you about the other day? You remember the one?'

She raised her eyebrows. 'I remember. Two hours, OK?'

'That should be long enough. Bring Esme, if she's back from her trip.'

'What do you have to do here anyway?' she asked him. Her face held a sombre expression now. 'Did you bring someone else from the ship?'

'No, it's just admin. See you soon—I might even buy you an ice-cream.'

Fraser took the stairs two at a time, stopping to help an elderly lady into a wheelchair on his way.

'Such a handsome darling,' she said, and grinned at him through gappy teeth.

Fraser saluted her as he hurried on his way.

Passing the dialysis clinic, he recalled the brand-new idea that had sprung into his brain and refused to go away over the last few days. He'd been pondering over opening a dialysis unit at the Breckenridge Practice. Maybe Sara would help him run it. It was just the kind of business decision his father would have approved of—a way to grow the practice into something more, with far-reaching potential.

He couldn't wait to be able to talk about it all with her. Hopefully after this second test, and whatever it was concerning Boyd about his blood tests, their prospects would at least be a little clearer and he could maybe even reach the beach this afternoon with good news.

'Dr Fraser Breckenridge?'

The Caribbean woman who opened the door to him was probably eighty-five. Her white coat came down to her feet, which were in rather scuffed trainers.

'That's me,' he said, amused. 'I'm looking for Dr Boyd Phillips.'

'He'll be back soon. He's asked me to take another urine test first.'

'Fair enough.'

She opened the door to let him inside the tiny, somewhat stuffy room. He couldn't help remembering, in the face of this elderly nurse, the time a younger Sara had called him for tests before his marathon—the playful Sara, who was slowly but surely coming back to him in spite of her reservations...

'Fraser Breckenridge?' Sara had looked up as he'd closed the door to the white and too-bright room. 'Here for your tests?'

He'd stepped inside and noticed her hair: long, blonde, but not the tacky kind of blonde, the kind that was natural and always looked good messy.

'Yes, that's me,' he'd said, shutting the door behind him. 'Thanks for doing this. I know you probably have something more interesting to do.'

'I can't think of anything more interesting than this.'

Sara Cohen had almost perfectly symmetrical eyebrows that were real, not drawn on with pencil, and her words had held no trace of sarcasm. She'd scanned some papers. Her nails were pale purple.

'So you're running a marathon, huh?'

'Indeed I am. As long as I'm innocent on the inside.'

He had smiled serenely with what he'd hoped was suspicious purity. He hadn't known why yet, but he'd wanted her to wonder about him.

Sara had raised her perfect eyebrows. 'You don't strike me as the innocent type.'

She was teasing him. His interest in this woman was mounting. Sure, he'd seen her about the hospital. She was pretty, friendly—nothing to write home about…or so he'd thought. She was great with the kids. All the kids at the hospital loved her—almost as much as they loved him.

She'd leaned against a cabinet with one hip and eyed him in a way that had made something stir in his jeans. Her tight fitted white coat ended just above her knees and her shoes were dark blue velvet flats, as if she was planning to ballet dance away from her nursing duties. She was graceful.

He had wondered what she looked like naked.

'Well, there's a lot you don't know about me,' he'd told her.

'Apparently so.'

'I know about you, though. I've seen you knitting.'

It had come out before he could think. He was usually able to play it cooler than this.

She'd lifted her eyes from his running shoes up to his face. 'What does that tell you about me?'

'It tells me you're either pregnant with triplets or you just really like knitting… OK I don't know about you. I think I want to find out, though.'

He'd rested his backside on the back of a chair. Had seen a battered copy of *Lord of the Flies* sticking out of a satchel on the floor by her chair. He'd seen her reading too, in the canteen. Big novels like this. He'd never told her, but he'd read every single one of the books he'd seen her reading long before.

He liked this little game they were playing, and he liked Sara too, with her butterfly earrings and her fondness for literature, and shoes he could picture her dancing in...naked.

But he couldn't get distracted. He really needed this drugs test.

'Listen, I need these results back pretty quickly, if that's OK?' He'd stood, looked up around him for the container. Surely she would have it ready.

Sara had opened the drawer by her hip and pulled out a container with a small white lid. 'We're all set.'

'Sperm sample?'

She'd held the container out to him carefully between two fingers, slightly away from her body. 'You know very well we need a urine sample,' she'd said. 'For now.'

The more he'd grinned, the more her own lips had twitched at the corners. He'd seen the laughter fizzing in the colour of her irises. The way she'd said 'for now' had been unmistakably flirtatious.

'Do you need a drink of water first?'

'I'm good—thanks for caring.' He'd stepped a little closer, pressed his hands into his denim pockets so as not to touch her.

'In that case,' she'd said, lowering her voice in mock seduction, 'the bathroom's through there, Fraser Breckenridge.'

They'd been inches apart.

'Maybe when I'm done we can go get some lunch?' he'd ventured.

'That depends on how innocent you are.'

Fraser had held her gaze, more than slightly aroused ahead of his bathroom visit. So *this* was Sara Cohen. If this *had* been a sperm test, he'd probably have no problem right about now...

CHAPTER SIXTEEN

'ALL DONE?' BOYD motioned Fraser through into another room and into a chair on wheels by a desk.

'Let's hope it's second time lucky.' Fraser took his seat in the stark white room, trying not to show how the anticipation was messing with his head.

'Apologies for the mix-up with the urine sample,' Boyd said. 'I hope it wasn't too much of an inconvenience.'

'Not at all,' he replied, just because it was polite. 'So, what is it you want to discuss in person?'

Boyd sucked in a breath and let it out slowly. He took off his big round glasses and dangled them from his fingers over the desk, all of which put Fraser's nerves even more on edge.

'Boyd, what have you found?'

'It's interesting,' he replied, sitting back in his chair, studying him. 'Fraser, how long have you known Esme, exactly?'

'Since the start of the cruise we're on,' he said. 'Why?'

Boyd slid a piece of paper across the desk to him. 'Fraser, I don't want to alarm you, but did you ever think there might be something that her mother isn't telling you?'

'What do you mean?' Fraser took the paper in his hands. 'What am I looking at, Boyd?'

'The blood tests show you're a perfect biological match to Esme. Fraser, this kind of blood type is so rare you're possibly the only person who *could* be her donor.'

Boyd tapped his finger on the piece of paper. The letters

and numbers blurred before Fraser's eyes. He could hardly believe what he was hearing.

'I don't understand…' He did, but it didn't seem possible.

'Fraser, Esme appears to be your daughter.'

The world seemed to skid to a stop. All he could hear was his heart pounding in his ears. When he looked up Boyd was still studying his face in concern.

'This can't be true.'

'I'm afraid it is.' Boyd rested his arms on the desk, still holding his glasses. 'I hate to be the one to break this to you, Fraser, but either Sara doesn't know herself or she's been keeping it from you. I think you need to have a talk with her before we go any further. No matter what the new urine tests show…'

'This is crazy, Boyd.'

He stood up, strode to the window, raking his hands through his thick hair. Palm trees waved at him from under a blue sky, but all he could see was Esme's face, and Sara's too.

'It can't be.'

'I understand this completely changes things. It must be quite a shock.'

'That's an understatement.'

Fraser turned around again and paced the small room, drumming his fingers against his thighs as the world shifted around him. Anger. Denial. Shock. Some strange new hope. It was all bubbling inside him now.

He sank back into the seat heavily, took the piece of paper again. He blinked as unexpected tears pooled in his eyes, and embarrassment made him slam the paper down again hard.

'How could I not have known this, Boyd? All this time.'

'You say you've been apart for five or six years, right? With no contact? Did you ever try to make contact?'

'Only once, about two weeks after we broke up.'

He stared unseeingly at the desk, remembering Sara standing there with her one-night stand. Whatever had happened, she clearly hadn't wanted a man around to help her with a baby, and from what she'd said to him so far, the way she'd been pushing him away, she was wary of having one around now...

This was more than he'd bargained for. He was a *father*? He had a *daughter*? A sick daughter he'd missed out on knowing all this time.

He took the paper and got to his feet again.

'Fraser, take some time to think about this,' Boyd said calmly.

But Fraser was already striding for the door.

CHAPTER SEVENTEEN

'HONEY, WHAT ARE you doing?' Sara rushed across the sand to Esme. 'You can't do things like that. What's the problem?'

The little girl whose sandcastle had just been unceremoniously bulldozed by Esme was screaming the beach down, pulling a total tantrum in her pink two-piece swimsuit.

Sara took Esme's wrist and led her aside gently. She was always gentle, no matter what. 'Baby, tell me—why did you do that?'

'She told me I was going to die!'

White heat, all over her.

Words like this tore her to pieces. She composed herself as Jess appeared in her giant yellow hat. They'd been having such a nice time until now.

She crouched down and put her hands on Esme's little waist over her cotton sundress. 'Esme, you're not going to die.'

The kid's mother was walking over now, wearing sunglasses far too big for her face. 'What happened?'

'I'm so sorry about that,' Sara told her.

She was starting to wish she'd gone back to bed, like Fraser had suggested; she was far too tired for all this. Come to think of it, where was he? He was supposed to have been here twenty minutes ago.

The woman spoke loudly, haughtily, over her screaming daughter. 'I don't know what kind of parent lets their child—'

'Excuse me?' Sara stood rigid.

The woman shut her mouth. She was looking at Esme's catheter. Her face had turned slightly pale, like everyone's did when they started viewing Esme less as a child and more as some precious flawed person who might keel over and expire at any moment. Her illness brought out the best and the worst in people all at once at times. Other mothers with healthy children suddenly felt guilty, or woke up to the fact that they were blessed.

This woman seemed particularly ashamed. 'I'm so sorry. I didn't see…'

'That doesn't excuse her from being naughty,' said Sara.

'She told me I was going to die!' Esme cried again.

'If you cross over the *bridge*!' the kid in pink insisted, pointing to the smashed elements of her creation. 'I told you—you only die if you cross over the bridge! You smashed my bridge!'

'It's only a game,' Sara told Esme. 'She was including you in her game. You're not going to die. She didn't mean it like that.'

'Where is Dr Fraser, Mummy?'

She looked at her helplessly. 'I don't know, sweetie. He's supposed to be here…'

'What *is* that…thing?' The screaming child had stopped her tantrum and stepped up close to Esme, inspecting the lines running up from the neck of her white dress.

Here we go again.

Esme swiped at her eyes. 'It's my catheter. I'm on dialysis. I have a robo-kidney, and you're right. I might die.'

Sara wrestled with the need to flop down onto the sand and close her eyes. She took a deep breath and let Jess lead Esme away from the drama towards the shoreline.

'You are *not* going to die,' she whispered after her anyway, and the horrible woman, now sufficiently apologetic if only with her eyes, slunk away, back to her sun chair.

Another half an hour passed. Esme was happily building

sandcastles again, but still there was no sign of Fraser. She watched the waves lap the shore, seeing his eyes and the way he'd looked at her that time when she'd asked where he'd been in Florida. He wanted to tell her, he'd said, but he couldn't yet.

She'd made peace with that, and even grown to believe he was planning some kind of nice surprise for her. But he'd skipped out on her again now, when he knew she'd be with Esme. When he knew Esme would be disappointed if he didn't show up.

Annoyance bubbled into anger. She was back on that staircase, feeling what she'd felt the first time her thoughts about Fraser Breckenridge had weighed her down rather than lifted her up.

She'd flown back to Edinburgh six months after they'd started dating and three weeks after her mother's death. Just to be near him. She'd felt bad for leaving her father, but her sister had been with him and both of them had told her that she should go and do something nice for herself.

They'd eaten dinner an hour after she'd arrived—Sara, Fraser and his parents. All the way through their perfectly *al dente* pasta his father had looked between them, as if he was dying to get something out in the open. It had been after dinner, on her way back from the bathroom, that she'd heard them talking.

'She's no good for you, son. You're in danger of screwing it all up. What about your career? What about everything you've worked so hard for?'

His voice had made her shiver. And what had been worse was the fact that Fraser hadn't defended her or their relationship. That fact was the knife that kept on stabbing her in the heart, every time she thought about that night.

The rest of the evening had been awkward. She'd made her excuses, gone upstairs to his bedroom. Fraser had come in when she'd been sitting on the bed, staring at the floor, knowing her heart was about to be torn into even more pieces.

'What are you doing up here?'

'Just thinking.'

He sat down on the bed beside her. 'OK… Well, I'm glad I've got you alone. Listen, I was hoping we could talk.'

She had struggled to breathe as his hands had left dents on the bed either side of him. She'd already known what was coming. He was going to end their relationship.

'You know I need to qualify this year, Sara. You know the practice needs me. So…'

'You don't need to explain, Fraser—honestly. I've been thinking I should talk to you, too.'

She'd stood up then, paced the room while the lump in her throat had caused her physical pain. 'This is just such a bad time. My dad really needs me… I shouldn't even be here.'

'Sara…'

'We should call it a day, Fraser. It's just too crazy right now…everything is changing. Under the circumstances I think it's best. I'm so sorry. I shouldn't have come here.'

Her taxi had sounded its horn outside and Fraser had stood up in surprise, yanked the curtain aside. 'What the hell—?'

'That's my cab to the airport.' She'd reached for her bag.

Fraser had walked up to her purposefully, making her gasp as he snatched the bag back and held her by the shoulders. 'Sara, what's happened? Why are you saying this? Talk to me.'

But she'd pulled away, reached for the bag she had already packed. 'Fraser, we've just been delaying what you know needs to happen. I don't belong here. I need to be with my dad and my sister in London. And you need to be here.'

His mouth had been a thin line. His fists had curled to his sides. She'd been convincing enough.

'It's what I need right now,' she'd continued, though her tears had been coming thick and fast. 'I should go.'

She hadn't been able to keep on talking. Her heart had been hurting too much. But she hadn't been able to stick around for him to break up with her either.

Whether he did it now, or next week, or next month, he was going to do it eventually. His family and career meant too much to him for her even to try to keep a place in it right now. She'd leave quickly, like ripping a sticking plaster off, before the real pain of a deeper wound could kill her.

She had cried the entire way home...

Sara blinked at the beach scene in front of her. They were building more drama around themselves now; she could feel the weight of it, making her sink again. And when it came to Esme she couldn't allow herself to sink, or even to float passively along. She couldn't wait around for anyone to prove themselves to her—not him, not anyone.

Gathering up her stuff, she called to her daughter and headed to a small boat bobbing on the waves. A skinny guy with dreadlocks was arranging water skis on the back of it, checking the fuel tank. As she bartered for a deal she forced herself to feel excited, to focus on Esme and to give her a memory she'd remember for ever—however long that was.

'Where's Dr Fraser?' Esme asked again as they zoomed out onto the ocean, just the two of them.

'He's busy.'

'Doing what?'

'It doesn't matter.'

'Is Dr Fraser a daddy?'

Sara's heart lurched beneath her lifejacket. 'Why do you ask that?'

Esme just shrugged, staring out at the waves.

'If you want to come back, remember to pat your head. If you want me to cut the motor, act like you're slashing your neck with your hand.'

They were bobbing now and adrenaline was making her knees knock as the driver got everything into place.

She glanced around for jet-skis. There weren't any in the immediate vicinity. Her mind flashed to Trevor and his girlfriend. She would find them and talk to them as soon as they got back to the ship. Again she'd let Fraser distract her from what she needed to be doing; something wasn't right with them.

The driver started up the boat. Esme started her camera rolling. And Sara had no choice but to do what she'd been adamant she would do...with or without Fraser.

She moved slowly at first, till she caught her balance... then faster, till she felt as if she was flying.

It was a rush, a total thrill when she managed to stand, and when the boat and the driver and Esme were so far ahead that she couldn't make out their expressions any more.

Her knees were bent, her arms were straight and her head was up, facing forward, with her hair flying out behind her.

'Whoo-hoo!' Esme hollered from the boat.

Sara could see her now. 'Whoo-hoo!' she hollered back. 'I'm doing it!'

For the next half-hour or so Sara fell, got up and went again, over and over and over again, until she was buzzing from head to toe. She was a strong, capable woman, able to do things by herself. Fun things.

How many more experiences like this could she squeeze into this trip before she'd have to go back home...? Home to where Esme would be stuck again, waiting...waiting for what?

Was she really going to die?

Her thoughts began to whirl with the wind, like tsunamis rushing past her ears. Fear, loss, guilt. Annoyance that she still couldn't get Fraser and his deeply upsetting absence out of her head.

She fell—hard.

She crashed into the water like a bomb, face-first, in a move so undignified that she was quite shocked. Her life jacket kept her afloat as soon as she slowed, and she was on her back, blinking her salty lashes at the sky.

It was only then that she realised her face felt as if someone had punched her.

CHAPTER EIGHTEEN

SARA WAS STANDING by a bed when Fraser arrived, tending to a woman called Jasmine who appeared to have broken her foot or her ankle. The young girl with black bobbed hair, in too-short denim shorts, was sucking in breaths as if it really, really hurt. She had a very large bruise surrounding her right eye, but he recognised her instantly.

She was the girlfriend of Mr Ponytail—one half of the couple who seemed to be permanently at each other's throats. Trevor…that was his name. Did he even remember the way he'd almost killed Fraser with a jet-ski?

'She told me she slipped on the bathroom floor,' Sara said, but the look in her eyes told him something else was going on—just as they'd suspected from the start.

His jaw pulsed as she stepped up close to him and pulled him aside. Speaking of bruises, at least Sara's face was looking better than before.

He'd been pleased she'd gone water skiing on her own, but he'd told her right there and then, after she'd tracked him down to ask why he hadn't come to the beach, that something had happened. He'd told her that they needed to talk—but not till they'd left the ship for good.

Then he'd shut the door in her face and reminded himself that they didn't have long till they left the ship, so he'd do as she had first requested and stay professional, while he processed this life-changing news and while Sara went back to ensuring his daughter was having the time of her life.

'She's not saying much,' Sara whispered. 'I went to talk

to her last night. I told her she had to get away from any situation that was causing her distress. Trevor came back to the lounge and heard me.'

'This isn't your fault.'

'He probably got angry at her...'

'This is *not* your fault.'

He turned away from her before he touched her, or pulled her out of the room and asked her how the hell he had a daughter after all this time. Those big eyes could always make him crumble. So could Esme's. And now he knew why.

He had a daughter. It was killing him, keeping it inside. But it was for Esme's sake that he had to for now.

Sara was talking quietly to Jasmine. Trevor was staring at him from the plastic seat in the corner, nervously wringing his hands on his lap. His trademark ponytail was dangling limply down his back like the tail of a dead cat.

Fraser held out his hand to him. 'Dr Fraser Breckenridge—I believe we've met already.'

'Yes, hi...' He sounded awkward. 'I'm...'

'Trevor. I know. What happened? You say she slipped?'

Jasmine was doing her best to straighten herself on the bed without adding any pressure to her leg or ankle. Sara hurried to stop her.

'Yes, I slipped.' Jasmine said it with a clenched jaw and a quick glance at Trevor which told Fraser pretty much all he needed to know. She was covering for him.

'Any more pain?' In his peripheral vision, he saw Sara going for the X-ray machine.

'No, not really. Just the entire leg now.'

'We're going to help you—don't worry,' Sara said, wheeling it over.

He helped her prep it and adjust Jasmine, and as they took the X-rays he wished to hell that he could see inside Sara's head, too.

Of course he wanted to talk now, but waiting for the right place and time was vital. It was better than raising their voices in an emotional confrontation, if it came to that, or having to spend the rest of their time here working together when…when she might have been lying to him for years.

He literally couldn't stand the thought.

'Nothing else hurts,' Jasmine said now as he continued checking her over.

'What about that mark on your face?'

She looked away. 'It's…it's nothing. That's an old bruise.'

'It doesn't look old,' Sara said.

'Well, it is.'

'Well…as far as your foot goes it looks like a sprained ankle, but we have to be sure it's not a fracture.'

Jasmine's ankle was swollen to about three times its regular size, and was already turning a nasty shade of grey, ringed by an angry purple.

Fraser took over while Sara helped her to get more comfortable, stabilising the suspected fracture site with a pillow splint. Trevor still looked anxious. He kept standing up and then sitting down again on the hard plastic chair in the corner, twiddling his ponytail and his fingers.

'Do you want to wait outside?' Fraser asked him.

'No. I want to be here with Jasmine.'

'Just go, Trevor,' Jasmine's voice was weary as Sara adjusted a pillow under her head.

'Wait outside, please,' Fraser said sharply.

'Why?'

'Just go. I'll be out in a second.'

They all flinched when Trevor slammed the door behind him.

'What were you doing when you slipped?' Fraser asked Jasmine quietly.

'I told Nurse Cohen here—there was water on the bathroom floor. The pain shot up my leg…sharp, it was, like someone with a chainsaw was inside it… Then it all went numb. He had to carry me here.'

'We'll give you something for the pain,' Sara said, 'but, Jasmine, you have to tell us the truth about what happened. Covering for him won't solve anything.'

Jasmine bit her lip, but refused to say anything more.

'You have a lateral malleolus fracture—that's a fracture at the end of the fibula, right here,' Fraser informed her minutes later, once he'd looked at the X-rays. 'Luckily your tibia is OK. Nurse Cohen, would you prepare a cast?'

'Of course.'

'We'll have to get you crutches, I'm afraid, Jasmine, and put you on some painkillers. They'll make you more comfortable. I'll be right back.'

Outside, he folded his arms in front of Trevor. 'I've heard you and Jasmine arguing before now. And I have to ask: does this injury have anything to do with an argument?'

Trevor stiffened and mirrored his stance with his own arms. His biceps were covered in black and white tattoos.

'What are you implying? She slipped in the bathroom—she already said that.'

'What happened to her face? It's not an old bruise. I know what a fresh bruise looks like.'

Trevor looked directly into Fraser's eyes with his small beady blue ones, then appeared to bloat with pure, unadulterated anger. 'Why are you asking me all this anyway?' he yelled, waving his arms in the air. 'Your job is to fix her foot and nothing else. What gives you the right to ask about my personal life?'

Fraser didn't budge an inch. 'Please don't raise your voice to me. With all due respect, this is part of my job.'

The door opened and Sara stepped outside. 'Dr Breckenridge?'

'Everything's OK,' he told her.

'Jasmine seems pretty shaken up over something,' she said, looking at Trevor now. 'More than just her ankle, maybe.'

'You're *still* going on about this? Seriously?'

Trevor seemed outraged at her presence, and made to step towards her. Instinctively Fraser put an arm between him and Sara, and held his hand up to stop him.

'Is this because of the jet ski thing?' Trevor seethed. 'It was Jazz's fault anyway—she was telling me to go towards the dolphin!'

'Would you please lower your voice?' Sara said.

Fraser stepped slightly in front of Sara. 'Trevor, tell me, is there anything else you want to tell us about what happened to Jasmine today?'

Trevor made an obnoxious snarling noise and then stormed off away from them.

'He shouldn't be left alone,' Sara told him.

'I'll keep an eye on him.'

Fraser headed for the elevator, frowning. He knew Jasmine hadn't simply fallen in a wet bathroom, so why on earth was she defending Trevor? He couldn't get his head around it. But he was no psychologist, and who knew how hard the heart fought the head in those situations? How many couples put up with months, even years of arguing and abuse out of fear or out of love?

He couldn't even imagine getting so sick of someone that it got to the point of physical abuse; he'd never been in a relationship like that in his life. He would only ever love Sara Cohen—and, more than that, their daughter.

CHAPTER NINETEEN

'SO, WHAT'S HAPPENING with you and that sexy Dr Brecken-ridge?' Jasmine asked as Sara prepared her cast. Her voice was the kind of faux chirpy that spoke volumes about her pain.

Sara pulled on latex gloves, resting a bowl of cold water on the table by the bed. 'We just work together,' she said. She steadied Jasmine's raised ankle and separated a pile of fibreglass strips. 'I'm more interested in what's happening with you and Trevor.'

'Nothing's happening. Like I told you before, Trevor is just a bit crazy sometimes. You've seen it yourself—he almost killed your boyfriend. He blames me for everything.'

'With his voice, or with something else?'

Jasmine looked away.

'It's OK to tell me. It will go no further than you want it to,' Sara said.

She picked up one of the strips and dipped it in water. The water started to swish a little.

'He *is* your boyfriend, isn't he? Dr Breckenridge? We had a bet, me and Trevor.'

'How long have you two been together?' Sara kept her voice low and calm, applying the strip over the padding. Jasmine was not going to quit.

'Me and Trevor met at college—it's been five years too long now. You didn't answer my question.' She was drumming her nails on the bed now, doing everything she could to distract Sara from the issue at hand. She seemed to harbour some deep-rooted fear of getting Trevor into trouble.

'Nothing is happening with me and Dr Breckenridge.'

'Nothing?'

Sara sighed as she worked. She wished she *could* talk about it to someone. There had been something serious and unrecognisable in Fraser's tone, and in his eyes too, when she'd found him that night…when he'd told her they had to talk but only once they'd left the ship for good.

It had chilled her to the bone. But she respected that whatever he had going on, if it was that serious, it made sense for them to talk later. They were working together, after all.

She considered that maybe someone on the ship had spoken to him about them and he didn't want to embarrass her. Or maybe he'd finally woken up and realised that Esme was getting too close to him, that she herself was carrying too much baggage. She was afraid now even to approach him about that. She knew she wouldn't actually be able to stand to hear him say that and then have to work beside him without being able to get away. He was right—maybe they did need some space.

Jasmine had been watching her laying the strips. But now she said, 'I don't believe there's nothing. I can practically feel the flames coming off the both of you. I've seen him playing with your daughter, too. I thought she was his for a bit.'

'No, she's not his,' she replied, laying another strip across Jasmine's calf.

Jasmine lay back down again. 'We saw you all together on that boat. Is that stuff allowed when you're working on these cruises? Don't they get all funny about staff hooking up unless they're married?'

'I don't know.'

Sara's brow was perspiring slightly under the fan. The

gentle pattering sound at the windows had turned to heavier rain. The ship was moving with what felt like a lot more purpose too—up and down, up and down. She could feel it in her stomach again, like the night they'd lost Esme.

Jasmine was looking at her expectantly.

'It's…complicated,' she told her. 'Keep still, please.' She moved the swishing bowl of water closer, worried that it might tip over.

Jasmine groaned. '*All* relationships are complicated.'

Sara considered her words. 'Is yours? Tell me how you really got that bruise.'

'I told you.'

'Tell me the truth.'

'There's nothing to say.'

Sara's reply was cut short by a huge crash of thunder. It ripped through the room, through the walls, and made Jasmine almost jump off the bed. She yelped as her ankle slipped from its support and the bowl of water went flying.

Sara hurried to reposition her. 'Sorry—try to stay as still as you can. Can you believe this weather?'

'They said it would rain, but this is actually a bit scary. I *knew* we should have paid for the good season cruise.'

Jasmine clutched at the sides of the bed as Sara retrieved the bowl and ran fresh water. She carried on with the cast as quickly as she could, while the rain lashed even harder at the circular windows. She caught sight of the sky through the glass for the first time in hours. It was a deep, dark grey, verging on black.

'You'll have to stay here for now,' she told Jasmine when she was done. She snapped off her gloves, moved the bowl of pasty white water to the sink. 'Dr Forster will be in soon to monitor you. If you touch it, please just use the palms of your hands—we don't want you denting it, OK? That could irritate the skin under the dressing and you don't want to be left with sores and scars.'

She crossed to the cupboard and took out some crutches. 'Usually we'd wait forty-eight hours or so to move you, but with weather like this we'll leave these here just in case.'

Another strike of lightning lit the sky outside.

'Will I be able to fly home when we get to Florida?'

Sara paused with the crutches. 'With Trevor?'

Jasmine shrugged.

'Jasmine, I would advise against going anywhere with him after this.' She gestured to her cast. 'You're not fooling anyone—or yourself, I'd imagine. Do you really want to spend your life with someone who treats you like this? What if you say nothing and he does it to someone else?'

Jasmine closed her eyes, balled her fists.

'You should be able to fly just fine if you can get an upgrade that allows for more leg room,' Sara said, her tone softer this time. 'But we're stopping in Puerto Rico first—how would you like to say goodbye to him there?'

'That wouldn't be a good idea.'

'Why?'

Jasmine was still clenching her fists. 'He hits me.'

She said it through gritted teeth, as if even getting the words out finally was painful.

Sara laid her hand on her arm. Thank God she'd admitted it. Tears were glistening in Jasmine's eyes now; she was clearly terrified.

'He won't hit you any more,' she said resolutely, 'whether he stays on the ship or not. We can help you out of this.'

'Don't tell him I told you anything. Please, don't tell anyone—not on the cruise.'

Sara's heart was breaking for her. 'Why? What do you think he would do?'

The thunder crashed outside again. Jasmine clammed up and refused to say anything else.

It worried her, and so did this storm.

CHAPTER TWENTY

ON THE TOP deck, Sara found a few merry passengers vacating the outer decks, carrying plates of food inside. She assumed the others were already far too seasick. There was no escaping the rain either—not even under the deck's huge umbrellas. Through the windows in the corridor she saw a giant potted plant slide right across the deck in the lingering twilight.

Where was Fraser? She had to tell him what Jasmine had said so they could figure out what to do together. She'd said nothing to Renee when she'd arrived, reading the pleading look in Jasmine's eyes, but she couldn't risk another act of violence on Trevor's part.

Renee had slipped Sara an all-access key card before she left. Everyone knew anyway.

They had to alert someone. Fraser had gone to find Trevor, so maybe they were in Trevor and Jasmine's cabin. What was it Jasmine had told her for the charts? Cabin 202.

Knocking on the door, she had trouble standing up. 'Fraser, are you in there?'

She clutched at the doorframe, hoping Esme was still OK downstairs, watching cartoons with Marcus and his mum.

'Fraser? Trevor?'

There was no answer. She swiped the key card, but the room was empty. Curiosity got the better of her and she stepped into the bathroom. It was clean, with no sign of blood. But that didn't mean anything.

She headed for Fraser's suite. Security had ordered everyone to stay in their cabins, so she couldn't imagine where else he would have gone. Besides, Fraser's cabin was big, and he likely had Security in there with him, figuring out what to do with Trevor in private. With Jasmine's confession they could get the law involved more easily.

She let herself in, feeling strange as she did so. 'Are you in here?'

His cologne lingered in the air. A pang of longing struck her core as she saw the bed. There was no one here.

She stumbled to the bathroom just as another lightning bolt struck the ocean outside the circular windows. 'Fraser?'

Maybe he'd come back alone.

No, he definitely hadn't.

On the way out she saw it—something she hadn't noticed before on the table by his laptop. She crossed to the couch and picked up the pile of photos.

The sight of Fraser's mother in one picture took her by surprise. She looked older than Sara remembered, by more than six years. Grief would do that to you, she thought sadly. Dropping to the couch at another lurch of the ship, she flicked quickly through the rest.

She knew what she was looking for even before she found it.

Holding up the photo of her and Fraser, she couldn't help smiling at the memory. They'd been at a gala ball, a month after they'd started dating. She was wearing the butterfly necklace he'd given her. He'd always said this was his favourite photo of her. It was slightly ruffled round the edges now.

He probably missed that old Sara, who'd had nothing to worry about but books and stupid butterflies.

Something else caught her eye. An official-looking document, sticking out from beneath the laptop. The heading was in big black and red type: *Florida Transplant Institute.*

Her pulse quickened as she gripped the table-top. What the hell was she doing? This was Fraser's private stuff and she had no business going through it—and besides she had to find him.

On second thoughts…a transplant institute?

Pulling the paper from beneath the laptop, she realised she was shaking. Something deep in her bones was telling her this concerned her and Esme, so much so that she could barely read beyond the address of the institute…

Beep-beep.

The door to the room sprang open. Sara's heart almost crashed through her ribcage. She leapt up from the couch, holding the piece of paper behind her back quickly, feeling it flapping against her under the ceiling fan.

'What are you doing in here?' Fraser stood stock still in surprise in the doorway. His broad frame almost filled the corridor.

'Looking for you.' Her voice was strangled as he moved towards her, his eyes narrowed now. He'd seen the photos, no doubt laid in a different place than he'd left them.

Sara moved away from the coffee table. 'Jasmine told me,' she managed. 'She just told me. Trevor hits her.'

Fraser was still looking at the photos. 'I thought as much. Trevor needs to get off this ship ASAP. He's downstairs with Security. Jasmine's safe with Renee now, right?'

'Yes.'

'Good…good job.' He crossed to the fridge, grabbing a can of Coke.

Her fingers trembled around the document. She knew beyond all shadow of a doubt that whatever she was holding behind her back was what Fraser had been hiding, and what he had shut her out from. She gripped the arm of the couch with her other hand and sat down again. It was hard to stand upright.

'They're probably going to be ready for him in Puerto Rico, as soon as this storm's over.'

She swallowed. 'To do what?'

He held out the Coke. 'To arrest him, Sara—what do you think? What's wrong?'

He stepped closer to her, suspicion written all over his face now. She was acting weird, and she knew it. She stood and made to step away, around the table, but a jolt from the ship made her stumble against him.

The piece of paper drifted to the patterned carpet and Fraser's eyes followed it.

'I didn't mean to see it,' she said quickly as he slammed down the can and picked it up. 'I didn't read it—just the header. But, Fraser, why do you have a letter from the Florida Transplant Institute?'

The rain was pounding at the window. He held the paper in his hands and seemed to look straight through it to the floor. His voice was strained when he spoke.

'I wanted to wait till we were off the job to talk about this,' he said, dropping it to his side. 'I told you that. I wasn't planning to hide anything from you.'

'Wait for what? Fraser, is this about Esme? Did you find a donor?' She couldn't disguise the hope from her voice. Her heart was thrumming.

Outside, the wind was howling.

'Maybe.'

'Maybe?'

'I just thought that there might be few things you need to tell me first.'

His voice was different now—not angry, just loaded, filling her with fear at the fact that she couldn't quite read him.

He put the paper back down on the table. She racked her brains. 'I don't know what you mean, honestly. What do I need to tell you?'

'You honestly can't think of anything?'

'No, Fraser—stop being so cryptic and just tell me!'

Pain flashed in his eyes as he looked at her, and it made her feel ill.

'I went to the Florida Transplant Institute to see about donating a kidney myself,' he said.

Her hand flew over her mouth.

'I didn't want to tell you unless I knew I could do it, Cohen. I know you said Esme has a rare blood type, for a start, and that the chances are slim. I wanted to be sure I was eligible before giving you anything else to worry about.'

She was silent as his words sank in. The swaying of the ship and his news were both making her queasy now.

'Esme is my daughter, Fraser—did you not think I had a right to know?'

'Of course I think you have a right to know. I just didn't want to put any more pressure on you while you were working. I wanted Esme to have a good time while you were here...'

'Esme? Fraser, I asked you where you were that morning.' She felt light-headed. 'You should have just told me then.'

'I know, and I'm sorry.' He sat down next to her. 'This hasn't been easy. I was trying to do the right thing, believe me. But, like I said, if there's anything you need to tell me, please just do it now.'

She shook her head at him. The Coke can slid across the table. There was only one thing she could possibly need to tell him, and she couldn't think how he'd found out. Why did it even matter now, anyway?

He was looking at her imploringly.

'OK,' she said. 'OK, Fraser—yes, I broke up with you because I overheard what your dad said to you, and I *had* to do it first. You didn't even defend me, or us, and I didn't want you to hurt me any more than I was already hurting over Mum.'

'What are you talking about?' He got down on his haunches in front of her, put a hand to her knee. His hair was falling into his eyes.

'I broke up with you because I *knew* you were about to do the same thing to me. Fraser, you have to admit you would have done it eventually. Is that why you didn't try and talk to me when you saw me with someone else in London? You knew I was better off without you while you worked to get your career on track?'

Fraser dragged his hands through his hair, shaking his head. He looked genuinely perplexed.

'I heard your dad say I was no good for you,' she continued, more warily now. 'He said you were in danger of screwing everything up, everything you'd worked so hard for before I came along.'

'You overheard my father talking to me?' Fraser's eyes were incredulous spheres.

'Yes, after that dinner. And I heard you say absolutely nothing in my defence.'

'Sara, you only heard half of it!' He stood up and the ship swayed, making him crouch back down and grip the table. 'They wanted me to finish my studies with no distractions, so I could release the money my grandfather left for me in the family trust fund as quickly as possible and pump it all into the surgery. They were going broke!'

'Broke?' She didn't understand. The Breckenridge family had always seemed extraordinarily wealthy.

'I was completely backed into a corner. I had to do what they asked. I was too ashamed to tell you what the situation was really like… I was young and too proud maybe. I don't know.'

'Too proud? To tell me your family were in financial trouble?'

'Yes, and to tell you *I* was in trouble with my studies. I was juggling it all fine for a while. Until I wasn't. I would have told you—maybe even that night. I tried to talk to you, remember?'

'I only remember being confused...'

'We should have talked to each other. I wanted to work something out, so I could be there for you, *and* get back on track, *and* fix the family mess too. But you broke things off before I had the chance. And then you slept with *him*, Sara.'

Sara just stared at him, speechless. All this time and she'd never known. She could feel a headache coming on. It was both their faults, then, their break-up: the doomed result of a series of grief-related bad decisions and general miscommunication. They'd been so young, and so much had been going on all at once.

'Cohen,' he said now. 'Whatever you heard, whatever was said, none of it meant you had to hide Esme from me.'

She blinked at him, her mind a carousel. What on earth did Esme have to do with anything that had happened back then?

'You had no reason to get involved with Esme,' she managed. 'Fraser, I appreciate what you've done, trying to help me, but you don't need to be getting involved with Esme's battles—at least not without talking to me first. Esme is my number one priority—you know that. She's *my* daughter, after all.'

She saw his jaw twitching, as if he wanted to say so much more than he was saying. Then the thunder cracked again and he got to his feet.

'Listen,' he said. 'Go to your cabin, please, where it's safe. When the storm passes I'll come and get you.'

She panicked, sensing a gap wider than ever opening up between them. If it wasn't this that he thought she needed to tell him, what was it?

'You need to talk to me *now*.'

'We'll talk later. I need to go downstairs and tell them what Jasmine has said.'

'I'll come with you.'

'No, I don't want you around Trevor.'

'I can handle myself.'

'Please,' he said, softer now. 'Sara, I'm saying this because, despite everything, I still love you.'

He was already reaching for his jacket.

His words had stunned her. *Despite everything?*

'Go and find Esme,' he said. 'Stay with her.'

'She's with Marcus and his mum...she's safe,' she heard herself say. Her ears were roaring at his words—all of them. 'Wait, Fraser, I don't want you to think I'm not grateful for what you're trying to do.'

'We don't know for sure yet if I'm eligible. I'm just waiting on one more test result that's got delayed.'

'I can't believe you're doing this. *Why?*'

'If you don't already know,' he said, pulling on his jacket, 'now is really not the time for me to tell you—trust me.'

The Coke can rolled completely off the table.

Fraser paused in his exit, seeming to compose himself. He strode back over, leaned down with his arms either side of her on the couch's back, and kissed her.

'You're scaring me now,' she said, bringing her palms to his cheeks.

'I love you,' he said again. 'You know I do.'

He pulled away, then headed for the door.

'We'll talk later, I promise. Just stay where it's safe.'

CHAPTER TWENTY-ONE

'WHAT'S HAPPENING?' FRASER walked into the medical room to find several items on the floor. Renee looked flustered and Jasmine was in tears.

His head was reeling the more he ran over everything, and he didn't have it in him to think straight, let alone get into the issue of Esme being his biological child with Sara.

Another fact was slowly sinking in: the fact that she had broken up with him in Edinburgh as a result of overhearing half of a stupid conversation. If she hadn't… If she'd only spoken to him, and he to her… They'd both messed things up.

But he couldn't think about it now. The ship was bucking wildly.

'Grab that!'

Renee called to him to catch the X-ray machine as it slid quickly in his direction. He stepped over a rolling pill bottle and fixed the machine back in place behind a steel counter.

Renee walked to him unsteadily even on flat shoes. 'Fraser, there's a situation on deck.'

'What kind of situation?'

She lowered her voice as he stood on a rolling plastic cup. It crunched under his foot before he picked it up.

'Someone's up on deck in the storm and they're refusing to come inside. Security are on to it.' She flicked her eyes to Jasmine and back. 'I'm not sure, but I think…'

'Trevor.' He cursed under his breath. He'd left him with Security, while he'd rushed to attend to a kid who'd been struck by his overzealous brother wielding a tennis racket. The boy had needed nothing more than an ice-pack, but everyone was going nuts, cooped up inside.

'When was the last time you saw Trevor?' Renee asked.

'Ten minutes ago. He was with Security. They're meant to be watching him till we get to port, but he kept on saying he needed to do something, and we don't technically have any right to keep him in one room.'

'What did you say to him?'

'I told him Jasmine had confirmed he'd been hitting her.'

Fraser's jaw was clenched. He'd also told the staff not to let him out of their sight, so Trevor must have used some grand excuse. Or demanded to use the bathroom and slipped off somehow.

There was a loud crash, just outside the room. Jasmine shrieked. Fraser yanked the door open to find a painting from the wall face-down on the floor. An ashen-looking woman in a purple robe was staggering down the hallway towards him.

'Come in here,' he said, hurrying towards her, gripping the railing as he went.

The woman was moaning and tripping over her robe, clearly in agony. Sara appeared just as he was helping her.

'I told you to stay in your cabin,' he said. 'I said I would come and get you later.'

'Don't tell me what to do—I want to help,' Sara said, bristling.

'Get her a bedpan,' he told her, too busy to argue.

He swiped the rolling pill bottle from the floor and Sara took the woman from him and led her to a bed—just as she threw up on the floor.

'Stay in here,' he said now, to everyone in the room. 'Don't come out until you hear it's safe. I'm serious, all of you.'

'Where are you going?' Sara looked up, her eyes narrowed as she held the woman's hair back.

Their new patient's purple robe was trailing in vomit. Jasmine was still crying.

'To the deck,' he said. He didn't wait for any protests. He didn't have time, and he wouldn't have listened anyway.

'Dr Breckenridge—you can't go out there!'

A security guy tried to stop him on the top deck. He recognised him from before.

'I'm medical staff and this is an emergency—I need to go out there. You weren't supposed to let him go.'

A crowd of people were gathered around the windows with cameras, ignoring the command to stay in their cabins. Did *anyone* follow orders on this ship?

'The ship was tipping. I only took my eye off him for a moment and he made a run for it,' the security guard explained.

'Let me go out there.'

'It's not safe...'

Fraser thrust open the door. He was faced with the swirling ocean, a blackened sky. A blast of wind shot inside the ship and tugged at his jeans and white coat. He shut the door behind him, leaving the security guy struggling to stop a man following him out with a camera.

The sea spray lashed at his face, but across the deck he could see shadows in the rain. They were bulky, broad-shouldered. Some of the security team had followed Trevor at least.

He made to move towards them, but each motion was like wading through a swamp. Every time he tried to move the wind would blow him backwards and pain shot through his leg. He pushed it away as best he could; he still hadn't taken the damn antibiotics.

Then he saw what the security men were looking it.

Trevor's long wet ponytail was swaying like a rope in the wind. His tattoos were disappearing along with his neck, head and shoulders as he took small steps backwards into the darkness.

'Don't do this!'

A member of Security was holding his hands up. Another shone a flashlight into Trevor's face. His T-shirt was a flapping flag as Fraser forced his legs to move forward.

'Trevor, let's go back inside.'

The howling wind took his breath. Trevor didn't move. He clearly had something terrible planned.

'I have to do something.' Trevor was as white as the moon.

'Not this. Listen to me. You don't need to do anything drastic.'

'Yes, I do.'

Fraser saw his eyes flit to the edge of the deck and the heavy lounge chair standing strong against the gales. The perfect ladder.

'I promise you, you don't,' he called.

'My dad used to hit me, you know.' The flashlight on his face showed his beady eyes filled with despair. The fury was gone.

A call for help.

Fraser had seen it before from people like this with secrets to hide. Secrets that were hurting them and others.

'Let's go back in and talk about things.' He inched closer to Trevor in the seconds when the wind died down. At the same time Trevor leapt onto the lounge chair and stepped up to the edge.

Security men rushed forward, but Trevor lunged for a rope and pulled himself up high, away from their arms' reach. He was teetering on the edge now, holding on tight to the swaying rope over the pounding ocean.

'Fraser!'

Fraser spun round. Sara's white coat was a billowing sail. She had one arm around Jasmine, who was staggering towards him on crutches.

He caught her before she toppled. 'Her plaster isn't even set properly!' he yelled.

Jasmine held a hand up at him. 'Don't blame Sara—I begged her to bring me!' She clocked Trevor, who was still clutching the rope. 'Trevor, please, get down from there!'

The wind and rain was whipping round them now.

'There's something bad inside me, Jazz…it's in my blood.'

Trevor was clearly distraught. Fraser forced himself to say nothing that might push the guy literally over the edge, but he reached for his radio—slowly.

'No!' Trevor saw him. 'Don't you dare!'

'Fraser, stop!' Sara looked appalled. 'He's going to jump.'

Jasmine was whimpering between them.

'OK… OK…' Fraser shoved the radio back. 'Trevor, why don't you just let me help you get down from there?'

He forced himself one step forward.

Trevor stepped over the side.

'No!'

Fraser got to the edge first. In a heartbeat he'd caught Trevor's arm, snatching his wrist, slippery with rain. Salt water stung his eyes, and he could barely see, but he clamped down with an iron grip and somehow Trevor swayed like a pendulum but didn't fall.

Sara was next to him now. He tried to pull Trevor higher, so she could reach him too, but Trevor's hand slipped and he had to use every ounce of his might to stay holding on.

'Please, don't drop me!'

So now he wanted to live.

Without hesitation Sara reached down over the edge,

while a security man reached for her. She clamped a hand over Trevor's arm. Then she grabbed him by his shirt.

'Now!' she yelled.

The wind whipped her hair into Fraser's face as together they dragged him inch by inch, writhing and groaning, back from the edge. They all toppled backwards as he tumbled onto the deck, and Fraser crawled to Sara while Security took over. They were wrestling to hold Trevor down; he was panicked now—not wanting to die, but not wanting to be there in their control, at their mercy.

Jasmine seemed to fall to the deck and they hurried to help her up, one on each side, acting as the crutches that had rolled away. They were all soaked through.

A crowd of stubborn passengers surrounded them as they finally stepped inside.

Jasmine was concerned for Trevor as they dripped their way back to the med room. 'What will happen to him?'

'Security will take care of things,' said Fraser. 'Does your leg hurt even more now?'

'No, it's fine—I told you.' She was limping, but luckily it didn't look as if she was in any more pain than before. 'Will they have him arrested now?'

'They won't let him go this time.'

He avoided Sara's eyes the whole way to the med room. He wouldn't say it. He wouldn't say that he'd warned her not to go up there. Sara knew she should have listened.

Pain shot through Fraser's own leg. It almost made him stagger on the threshold of the medical room.

Sara spotted it instantly. 'Fraser?'

'I'm OK. Are you?'

'Yes. But your leg…'

'I said I'm fine.'

Renee hurried over to help. She'd clearly been tending to more seasick patients: the evidence was on the bed sheets.

She'd told them she could handle things, but Fraser knew she couldn't—not on her own.

'What happened? she asked them, taking in their wet clothes and hair.

'What happened was that Trevor *did* try to take the easy route out, but changed his mind.' He winced as he moved.

'Let me check your leg,' Sara said, swiping her wet hair back. 'And don't say you're OK—I can see you're not.' She sat him in a plastic chair and crouched in front of him while he rolled up his jeans. 'You didn't take those antibiotics, did you?'

She frowned as her fingers traced the skin at the edge of his coral reef wound. It was still purple, and part of the cut was bleeding again.

'You told me it was because they made you queasy,' she whispered, 'but it was because of the tests for Esme, wasn't it? You didn't want them in your system.'

He leaned towards her in the chair. 'Yes—the other test I told you about...the one I'm still waiting for...'

'You should be putting yourself first—'

'Esme comes first,' he said, watching as she dabbed antiseptic on his wound—not that he hadn't done that already, earlier in his room.

'Go and lie down. I'll take care of things here,' she said when she was done.

'You both need to go—to change your clothes at least,' Renee instructed.

Fraser looked to Sara. They needed to talk.

'Stay with me,' Jasmine said to Sara suddenly, reaching for her hand. 'Please don't leave me, Nurse Cohen.'

Jasmine's eyes were red and swollen. She clutched Sara's hand and Fraser could see in Sara's face that she was torn. Jasmine was really scared of Trevor now—scared to be around him and scared not to be.

'There are some spare clothes in the cupboard. I'll be

fine,' Sara said, just as Fraser had known she would. 'I'll stay here. Go rest your leg.'

He lingered a moment longer, but other people were listening. He knew there would be no talking tonight—not while so much else was going on.

CHAPTER TWENTY-TWO

THE POLICE OFFICERS were carrying guns, as was the way in Puerto Rico—and probably most of the rest of the world now, Sara mused. She was standing in line for snacks and drinks, with her mind still running over all that had happened.

Trevor hadn't taken too kindly to being arrested and dragged off the ship by two burly police offers in black, but thankfully the situation had been handled properly and poor Jasmine was out of danger now.

She and Renee had tended to ashen patients most of the night, and she had barely slept as the ship had continued to rock back and forth. She still didn't know how she'd summoned such supernatural strength when it had come to heaving Trevor back onto the deck. But the way Fraser had looked at her…it made her smile a little.

They hadn't found time alone to talk properly yet. She knew that whatever it was he had to tell her was serious, but the knowledge that he might be close to being able to help Esme filled her with fresh hope that overrode any fears, somehow. It was the first time she'd allowed herself to feel this much hope. She had to keep it alive.

She looked at him now. He was seating Esme in the front row for the sea lion show. Jess and some of the other kids from the ship weren't far away.

'Don't forget the apple juice!' he called to her across the rows of happy people.

He was dressed in a green shirt and the same khaki

shorts he'd danced in with her on deck. The aquarium was packed. She was really too tired for the mayhem of it all, but she'd been planning to show this place to Esme ever since she'd agreed to work on the *Ocean Dream*.

Fraser's hand brushed hers as he took his apple juice and she sat with Esme between them.

'Chilled—just the way I like it.'

He shot her a smile that sent the feel of his kisses straight back to her. A cheer from the crowd made Esme shriek in excitement and her cup of apple slices almost went flying.

'Be careful, Esme,' she told her.

Esme rolled her eyes.

Her catheter was a reminder of what her future would still entail if Fraser *couldn't* help. Sara scolded herself. No, she had to keep that hope alive.

'Have you heard anything yet?' she whispered to Fraser. 'About the other test?'

He lifted his sunglasses to look at her. 'Not yet,' he told her. 'Please don't worry. I know it's hard not to think about it, but this is why—'

'Why you didn't tell me. I understand.'

'We'll see each other later—alone. I've made a reservation.'

'A surprise?' she asked, raising her eyebrows.

He dropped his eyes from hers. 'You could say that.'

'Mummy, look!'

Esme was jabbing the air emphatically in the direction of the sea lions now plodding onto the wet deck. Their huge brown bodies reminded Sara of heavy sacks of potatoes.

'I see them—wait till you see what they can do.'

The swimming pool was gleaming—like Esme. She noticed how Fraser's eyes lingered on her daughter adoringly as she focused in on the action with her camera.

'How much footage have you racked up now, Spielberg?' he asked Esme. 'You must have enough to make three movies?'

'A lot,' she replied, turning to him with the lens pointed at his face. 'Say something about the sea lions!'

Sara hid a smile behind her hair as he made something up about sea lions. The two of them had been chattering happily the whole way here, picking each other's brains, making each other laugh... All they did was laugh.

'Will I still see you when we go home?' Esme asked Fraser suddenly, putting her camera down. 'The cruise is nearly over.' She pulled a sad face at him.

'I hope so,' Fraser said, casting a quick glance at Sara that made adrenaline spike in her veins.

They could tell her now, if they wanted. They could tell Esme that Fraser's spare kidney might potentially be hers, that her years of dialysis, of running back and forth to hospitals and avoiding delicious things like ice-cream might soon be over.

But the words wouldn't even form properly in her mind. As much as she wanted to, she almost couldn't fathom saying them out loud to Esme after all this time. Especially as a result of Fraser's sacrifice. A flush of love for him took her by surprise and she squeezed his hand. His tanned fingers were laced through hers on her lap.

'You can come and visit me and Mummy,' Esme continued cheerily. 'I'll take you to the dialysis centre!'

'I'm sure you'd make the second-best tour guide in the world after me,' Fraser said jokingly. But he didn't make any promises.

Sara bit her lip. They'd tell her together, if the results of this final test meant he could go ahead with the transplant. Maybe he *would* come and visit them from time to time—when he wasn't stuck in Edinburgh, working flat out at the surgery.

She studied his hand in hers. She didn't want to get her

hopes up regarding a new relationship, even though his declaration of love had struck her deep to her core, unleashing butterflies every time she thought of it. They both knew Esme came first. Everything depended on her getting better. Sara would have nothing to give Fraser if Esme didn't get better. She would only be half of herself.

A pair of volunteers had found their way to the pool deck. Two giant sea lions were now performing tricks, batting a beach ball between their snouts, each perched on a wooden podium. A tall, lean man and a young girl—father and daughter, perhaps?—were being zipped into wetsuits and handed some fish.

'Why can't *we* do that?' Esme asked Fraser.

'I'd be too scared,' Fraser told her, pulling a face.

'*I'd* look after you.'

'I know you would.'

It was a strange bond that he and Esme had formed so quickly. And she couldn't deny she felt bonded to Fraser too—even more so, knowing what he was trying to do for her daughter. Not for the first time she wondered whether *they* would have had a daughter together some day, if things hadn't got so messed up.

A shriek from the poolside made Esme swing her camera round. Both Sara and Fraser stood up in their seats at the same time.

'Mummy, what's happened?'

'I don't know, baby, don't panic.'

She strained her eyes to see what was wrong. She couldn't see the man any more—just the little girl he'd gone up there with. There was motion in the water. And only one of the two sea lions was still on a podium.

'Oh, God—you don't think that he was attacked?' she said apprehensively.

Fraser grabbed the medical bag he'd brought from under

the bench. The crowd was going wild now, panicking, rushing to the front to see better.

'Is anyone here a doctor?' a voice on a megaphone was booming.

'They're supposed to be friendly, aren't they?' said Fraser. 'Maybe he fell in or something.'

They looked at each other in horror. In seconds Fraser was squeezing out of their row with the medical bag, hurrying to the front.

'Where is he going?'

'To see what's wrong.'

Sara clung to Esme as she watched the green of his shirt find its way to the scene. Then she came to her senses. She motioned to Jess, who took Esme under her wing, and then followed in Fraser's path as fast as she could.

There was still movement in the swimming pool when she got to the front. Flashing her ship ID, she tore up the steps beyond the security barrier, just in time to see Fraser drop his shirt on the poolside and dive straight into the swimming pool.

The sight made her freeze in her tracks.

The lifebuoy he'd taken with him appeared suddenly in the deep blue water, which was swishing so hard all she could see was a blur beneath the surface. Her heart stood still as she forced her feet to move towards the little girl. She was no older than Esme.

'You're OK.' Sara dropped to her knees next to her, feeling water soak through the fabric of her dress instantly.

'My daddy got pulled in by…by Sammy the sea lion!'

The little girl was sobbing in heaving bursts, trying to make her way to the edge of the pool. Sara held her back. The staff were a blur now too, fetching nets and poles. The other sea lion was honking. It almost sounded like laughter, she thought with a chill.

'He'll be OK,' she said, hoping to God it was true. 'What's your daddy's name?'

'Simon.'

A woman in the blue and yellow aquarium uniform was trying her best to keep some other sea lions happy further up the deck, throwing them fish from a bucket to distract them.

'They *never* do this,' someone was saying behind her, aghast. 'What did he think was wrong with that guy?'

A hand broke the surface of the pool. Fraser emerged, clutching the kid's dad. A male staff member was at his other side and together they swam with him back to the deck. Simon was aged around thirty-five. The sea lion was still circling as they swam. It looked playful to Sara, under the blazing Puerto Rican sun, not at all threatening—but who knew what these things were capable of?

'Daddy!'

The kid was distraught now. Sara kept on holding her back. Two other staff members were running towards him with a stretcher now. Simon was motionless, pale and limp. He had a nasty gash on his inner thigh, where the sea lion had clearly made a grab for him and dragged him off the deck by its teeth.

'Help me get him up—he's not breathing.'

Fraser's commands were intended for the aquarium staff so Sara did the best thing in that moment—she stayed with the little girl. All around them people were staring, recording on their phones, just like always. She tried to block it out. A woman was calling from beyond the security barrier now, waving through.

'Hey! Baby—come here! Excuse me!'

'Mummy!'

Sara released the girl and she ran towards her mother.

'They won't let me up!' the woman said, reaching for the child. 'He's my husband. Is he OK?'

'It's safer there,' Sara told her, turning to Fraser.

His shorts and hair were dripping—not that he seemed to notice. She got on her knees. Simon was laid down flat on the stretcher. She checked his unblinking eyes, his breathing and pulse. Someone was radioing the hospital.

'I didn't think sea lions could do this,' she breathed, reaching for the Ambu bag beside him.

'They're wild animals—they can do what the hell they like,' said Fraser, unzipping the front of the wetsuit to Simon's waist. He placed one hand over the other and started rapid compressions on his hairy chest.

Sara placed the Ambu bag over his face. Her heart was skidding. The sea lion was still swimming circles in the water, and the crowd were snapping photos so fast the flashes were almost blinding her.

Fraser's chest was rising and falling next to hers as he breathed heavily in blatant exhaustion. She could hardly believe what was happening—they weren't even on duty. But they were never off duty, she realised. It was one thing after another, twenty-four-seven.

So much for this being a working holiday... She'd had her work cut out for her right from the start.

She held Simon's head, still gently squeezing and releasing the bag. Simon wasn't responding.

'More compressions,' she said, but Fraser was already on it.

She could see in his face how focused he was, how he too was trying his best to ignore the crowds and their camera flashes. Sara resumed her prayers as she counted the compressions. Simon's wife and daughter were watching and the kid's face was streaked with tears.

'We'll need to shock him,' Fraser said now.

One of the aquarium's assistants had already called for the defibrillator to be readied in the emergency room.

Sara noticed that Fraser was limping slightly, trying to

ignore his obvious discomfort as they hurried to get Simon inside on the stretcher, away from public attention. They rushed down the steps, pushing through the crowds until they reached the aquarium's ER. It was even more basic than the one on the ship.

'The ambulance is on its way,' someone said.

Sara inspected Simon's wounds. The wetsuit was totally torn around his thigh and groin. She didn't like to think what being bitten by a sea lion must feel like. She could tell it was a pretty bad wound, but it was the water that had harmed him more than anything.

'The sea lion held him down like he was some kind of toy,' Fraser told her incredulously as they moved him from the stretcher to a clean white bed. 'No one knows why. Was he carrying tuna snacks in his pockets or something?'

Sara readied the machine. Simon's wet hair and wetsuit were soaking the bed now, and Fraser was leaving puddles on the floor as he worked. He dashed his hand through his wet hair. His muscled torso was on full display and she didn't miss a female staff member eyeing him up and down as he worked.

'Charging...*clear*!' he said, putting the paddles on his chest.

Simon's muscles contracted and his limp body gave a jerk at the current charging through it.

The clock seemed to stop.

Again and again they tried.

'We have a sinus rhythm—he's back,' she announced moments later, as the machine showed a blip she'd honestly thought she'd never see.

Simon started coughing wildly. Behind her the ER room door was flung open and two paramedics rushed in with a blast of warm Puerto Rican air. Someone had also let Simon's wife and daughter into the room.

'Is he going to be OK?' the little girl asked. Her face was flushed—like her mother's.

'I think he is now,' Fraser said.

Relief was written all over his face. He seemed to remember he was shirtless suddenly, and looked around for his clothes.

The female aquarium staff member was still looking at him appreciatively. She stepped forward quickly and handed him his green shirt, gushing her praise and thanks in quick Spanish.

Sara was frazzled, hot, grateful and still slightly shocked as she filled the paramedics in on the situation en route to the ambulance, where the pair of them were thanked over and over for being so quick off the mark.

'This has never happened before,' the goatee-bearded aquarium manager reiterated outside the ambulance. 'We think Sammy was just playing.'

'It's no one's fault,' Sara said, though some people were leaving the park, clearly afraid of the animals. This would *not* be good for business. She spotted Esme and Jess close by, waiting for them.

'Lucky we were here,' Fraser told the manager, and she registered a small flutter of disappointment as Fraser put his shirt back on.

The manager turned to them as the ambulance drove away. She was about to leave, to get Esme and go and do something slightly less exciting, but the manager reached for her arm.

'Can we do something for you?' he said. 'To say thank you before you go?'

CHAPTER TWENTY-THREE

FRASER COULDN'T BELIEVE that Sara had almost refused the aquarium manager's kind offer. Looking at Esme now, reaching her tiny hands towards the dolphin's smooth face in the water, he swore he'd never seen a kid look so happy.

'Thank you for this, Fraser—this means the world to her.'

Sara was sitting on the edge of the pool next to him. The sun was twinkling in her hair and in her eyes and he couldn't help thinking she was the most beautiful woman he'd ever seen, even after all this time. Beautiful inside and out.

He swished his feet next to hers in the blue water, touching her toes with his for a second. Being in an almost empty aquarium had its benefits—though he did feel bad for the guy who'd just borne the brunt of a curious sea lion's teeth.

'I didn't think she'd ever get to swim with dolphins,' Sara told him.

'I didn't think *I* would ever get to swim with dolphins,' he said, and grinned.

He had managed to score free dolphin encounters for them, and for all the kids in Jess's care. It was going to be the talk of the cruise ship. Esme was being buoyed up by her lifejacket, as well as being held by one of the female aquarium employees. Marcus was floating nearby, waiting for his turn.

'You definitely know how to turn on the charm—you've got fans for life here.'

Sara cast her eyes to the woman who hadn't stopped eyeing him up and down since she'd handed him his shirt and Fraser nudged her.

'I prefer British nurses,' he told her, smiling as her cheeks flushed a little more.

'You think the wetsuit's doing its job OK?' Sara looked concerned again. This was the reason she'd refused the offer for Esme to swim with the dolphins at first.

'It's fine. The catheter's protected—don't worry. Look at her…she's loving it.' He picked up Esme's camera as Esme was instructed to place a hand on the dolphin's dorsal fin. 'Give us a wave, Esme!'

She did so, beaming at him with so much happiness that he couldn't help melting just a little.

'She's going to want to do this every week now,' Sara said.

'Who wouldn't?' He zoomed in close as the creature started gliding slowly around the pool, smooth and controlled as it had been trained to be, pulling Esme along.

In his bag, his phone started to buzz. He reached for it and moved away, leaving Sara on the poolside.

'Boyd?'

'Hey, Fraser, how's it going?'

'I'm just at an aquarium with Sara and Esme.' Sara was looking at him. His heart had started to hammer. 'Do you have news?'

'I do,' Boyd said. 'Thought I should tell you myself: your tests are all clear. You can proceed with the final tests alongside Esme when you get back to Florida—just let me know and I can arrange it. I assume you'll want the surgery at home, in London or in Edinburgh? It's up to you.'

Fraser took a deep breath, composing himself. Behind him, Esme was squealing in delight at the dolphin swim and Sara was clapping her hands. Their excitement only enhanced his own.

'This is great, Boyd, thank you.'

'Congratulations,' Boyd said. 'Did you talk to Sara?' There was concern in his voice now. 'About Esme being yours?'

'I haven't had time yet, Boyd. I didn't want to discuss it on the ship at first, but… Long story. I'll tell her everything tonight. This is great news, though. I can't thank you enough.'

Back at the pool, Sara turned to him expectantly. She was biting her nails. He looked at her face and took her hand. 'That was the transplant institute. I got the all-clear,' he said.

Sara's eyes flooded instantly with tears. 'You mean…?'

'I can help her.'

She stared at him, blinking back tears, till he put his arms around her and pulled her in close. 'We'll talk about it later—all of it, everything—just you and me,' he said, kissing the top of her head, hot with sunshine.

'Fraser, I can't believe this. Her whole life will change.' She pulled away and met his eyes. 'Because of *you*.'

He felt a rush of pride and joy and pure, pure love for both of them, but he knew he had a big conversation ahead.

He couldn't help studying Esme's features through the viewfinder when he picked the camera up again. He'd been finding himself doing this ever since he'd found out—studying her nose, her lips, comparing them to his. She was *his* daughter.

The knowledge was still baffling. She looked like Sara—that much was certain—but the more he looked at her, and the more he spoke to her, the more he saw pieces of himself in her and he loved it. He loved everything about this situation—except the fact that he'd been without her so long. Maybe now he could make up for lost time, if that was what Sara wanted after the surgery.

He was still finding it tough to imagine telling Sara that

he was Esme's father. He was almost certain, judging by their last conversation, that she didn't know. They'd always been so careful with contraception, after all. It made sense that she'd have thought Esme was the result of her one-night stand, and never considered anything else.

He had no idea how she would react tonight. Would she be upset, or angry, or in denial once she knew? And how would Esme take it?

'It's your turn!'

Esme called him into the water as both she and Marcus and the other kids had taken their turns. The dolphin was almost smiling, as if it was waiting for this swim specifically.

He and Sara both zipped into their wetsuits. Fraser slid into the water and held out his hand. Sara's blue bikini straps were visible at the back of her neck and he tucked them into her wetsuit as she placed her hands on his shoulders. They floated together for a second, and Esme paddled over, but just as she reached them, and Fraser took her little hands in his, the dolphin leapt from the water, arched over them and dived in, nose-first, with barely a splash.

'Whoa!'

Esme's arms came up around his and Sara's shoulders as she floated between them. The trainer told them that the leap meant the dolphin liked them. It felt good, he thought. He liked it—the three of them together like this.

He tried to fight the nerves that kept striking while they swam and had their photos taken, and while Marcus filmed them on Esme's camera. Would all this still stay the same once Sara knew?

They were two days away from Florida. He wanted more of Sara's kisses. He wanted openness, and honesty, and to see the look on Esme's face when she discovered she was finally getting a new kidney—from her *real* father.

CHAPTER TWENTY-FOUR

'ARE YOU READY?'

'I still don't know where we're going.' Sara picked up her bag and slipped her ship ID into it, smiling up at him with glossed lips.

'That's because it's a surprise,' he said.

'You're very good at those,' she quipped, which made the ball of knots in his stomach tighten.

He wouldn't let it show.

He led them off the ship. The night was balmy and the port held a lingering smell of fruit and fried food as they made their way beyond the docks to the motorbike he'd hired. It had been the longest afternoon, knowing what he knew, but also knowing he had to wait for this moment.

'Another one of these?'

Sara frowned at the bike as he handed her a helmet. Her lilac dress fluttered around her wedge shoes. He was dressed in full-length khaki pants and a white shirt, slightly undone at the neck. They were both tanned now—another sign that their time on the ship was coming to an end.

'You'll be OK,' he said. 'You've swum with a dolphin, you've been water skiing alone, you've been up in a helicopter and you've saved a man from falling overboard…'

'I think you'll find *you* played a part in most of that.' Sara was smiling as he stepped towards her on the gravel path and helped her fasten the helmet. Palm trees swayed overhead.

'What I'm saying is, you've done a lot that you should be proud of, Cohen,' he told her.

'And so have you. Especially the Trevor thing. I'm glad Jasmine booked a flight home without him. We probably helped to change her life, you know. Hopefully for the better.'

'He told me that his father used to hit him,' he said now, studying her eyes under the night sky.

'So…like father like son?' she said with a sigh.

'Our fathers make us who we are, I suppose. For better or for worse.'

She seemed to contemplate his words, just as he was. He registered a flash of anger towards his own father, but he harnessed it to the breeze and sent it away. It wasn't the time for blame or comparisons; it never should be. He had Sara back now. And he had Esme too.

Guilt blew through him over blaming his father; for not being man enough himself to talk about his problems with Sara sooner.

She gripped his middle from behind as he drove them along the coast to the private beach of an expensive hotel, where they dined at a table so close to the sea that the waves almost lapped at their feet while they ate.

Lobster, prawns and rice served in scooped-out pineapple halves. Virgin mojitos and memories of their time together back in Edinburgh. They feasted on it all.

They talked about telling Esme about her upcoming surgery, and all the ways her life would change, but the waiting staff kept coming down to the beach to check on them, and it wasn't till their plates were cleared and the bill was paid that he could lead her across the sand to a quiet *cabana* and sit her down for their private conversation.

Sara's face in the moonlight showed blissed-out perfection as she nestled into the thick white cushions on a day bed surrounded on three sides by white linen curtains.

She was leaning back on both elbows, legs stretched out

in front of her, eyes closed. The waves on the sand were a lullaby, even as nerves rattled him.

There was no more postponing the inevitable.

He turned her face to his. 'Do you even know how beautiful you are?' he said, and kissed her softly.

He slid his fingers around hers and trailed one thumb over her ring finger. When he pulled away she was still looking at their hands.

'Can you believe we're here now?' she said. 'I really thought you were going to break things off with me all those years ago, Fraser. I was so scared of being hurt by you that I hurt myself instead.'

He found himself swallowing back a lump in his throat. He put an arm around her on the cushions and breathed in the scent of her hair.

'I should have spoken to you about the stuff that was going on at the practice. And I *knew* my studies were suffering, and that I probably wouldn't pass the exams if I didn't get my head on straight, but I wanted to be there for you too.'

'*I* knew that I was holding you back; your dad was right about that even if it was brutal for me to hear it.'

He nodded sagely. 'And you wanted to be there for your family after your mum died. But I still think we both would have come to our senses and figured something out, Sara, if I hadn't come to London and seen you with *him*.'

She let out a sigh that he felt on his chest through his open shirt. 'Fraser, I can't believe you didn't say anything to me when you were there.'

He watched a crab scuttle along the sand. 'You'd made your decision—that's all I really saw,' he said. 'Then I just got on with things, Cohen—made my family happy. But if I'd known about Esme...' He paused.

Sara was facing him now. She reached a hand to his face. 'You couldn't have known I'd get pregnant with another man's baby,' she said. Her eyes were ringed with sorrow as she looked at him. 'Fraser, if you'd talked to me that day I might not have got pregnant by him at all.'

'Sara, listen…' He put a hand over hers, facing her on the cushions. This was the last time she'd look at him without knowing. He composed himself mentally, swept a clump of hair away from her eyes in the breeze. 'Sara, you *didn't* get pregnant with another man's baby.'

She was quiet. Her hand heated up under his and her cheeks began to flush. 'What are you talking about?' she said eventually.

'That's what this note says.' He pulled it out from his pocket—the one she'd picked up in his cabin. Her fingers were trembling as she took it. 'Esme and I have the same rare blood type,' he told her, watching her face. 'We're a perfect biological match.'

Sara shook her head. Her cheeks were redder than ever when he lifted her chin towards him.

'Sara, *we* are Esme's parents.'

'It can't be right.'

'The proof's right here.' He tapped the paper with his finger while she studied it in disbelief. Tears were glistening in the corners of her eyes. 'At first I thought you knew! I thought you were hiding it from me because you didn't want me as Esme's father, or didn't want *anyone* as her father. I'm sorry I hid it when I found out—but, honestly, I was in shock. It also was not the right time to have that conversation. I was going to wait until we got back to Florida, but…'

'This is crazy.'

He put a hand to the back of her hot neck, into her hair. 'It's good news if you want it to be,' he said.

'I didn't know,' she whispered, still shaking her head. 'You and I were always so careful with protection. I promise

I wasn't keeping anything from you, Fraser—why would I do that?'

He moved the paper away and took her hands in his. 'I know. I believe you.'

'I thought she was *his*. Fraser, I *swear* it.'

'I said I believe you.'

She looking into his eyes through a wall of tears, the shock of discovery sinking in hard. He wrapped his arms around her shoulders, holding her small shaking frame tightly.

'You're really her father…' she breathed, sinking into him as they rested against the cushions. 'How could I not have known this?'

'How *could* you have known this?'

He held her tighter, allowing the weight of the truth to drift slowly from his shoulders. She hadn't got up. She wasn't angry. She was just shell-shocked—as he had been.

'I know you'll think there's a lot attached to this transplant now, with me being Esme's father,' he said, realising he had to reassure her. 'But I wanted to do this for Esme *before* I knew—it's how I found out. It's all I want if it's all *you* want. I won't come between you, or get in the way—'

'I'm so glad it's you, Fraser,' she said, cutting him off. Her fingers were latched in his hair. Her eyes were pooling. 'I mean, I'm thinking a thousand things, but the only one that matters is that I'm so glad *you're* her father. No matter what happens now, I mean that.'

'I'm glad it's me, too,' he told her.

And he was shocked at the water he felt in his eyes the moment the words left his lips.

CHAPTER TWENTY-FIVE

IT HAD BEEN inevitable that they'd made love that night, Sara mused, scooping a croissant from the buffet platter and putting it on her plate.

The final breakfast. The very last morning of the cruise. She'd come so far in so many ways it was almost unfathomable.

She'd been running over it for the past two days, while tending to her patients—re-dressing wounds, checking the eyes of a gentleman who'd smashed his glasses... The way she and Fraser had stayed glued to each other in that *cabana* for hours.

They'd been kissing to the sound of the rush of the Puerto Rican ocean—and talking, of course. Going over all the similarities between him and Esme, all the little things about her that now made sense, and all the things about her life and situation that hadn't...

'Mummy!'

Esme was calling to her from her seat next to Fraser. Sara watched the sunlight on his hair, saw how it fell on Esme's too, and lit her up even more. Father and daughter. It was still so overwhelming. She'd had no idea. No idea whatsoever in all this time.

Or had she?

She carried her plate across the deck towards them, contemplating all the times she'd been moved by something in Esme that had seemed familiar. So strangely familiar and yet she'd never quite been able to place it.

How quickly everything could change.

'How are you feeling?' he asked her now, pulling out her chair. He was wearing jeans and sneakers, like she was, ready to depart the ship.

'I'm OK,' she replied, but butterflies were swirling so hard inside her that she didn't even want her croissant.

They'd spent a night together in Fraser's cabin, unable to resist each other, but no one else was supposed to know that.

She was feeling the perfect mix of excitement, bewilderment, nervousness, anticipation and exhilaration all in one. She had an inkling that Esme would feel the same very soon.

They'd decided on the beach that night in Puerto Rico that they'd tell her Fraser was to be her donor when they got to Florida. Florida was now in sight.

'Esme, you know the cruise is almost over...' She picked up the croissant she knew she didn't want. 'Have you had a good time?'

Esme was beaming. 'Yes, Mummy, I've had the *best* time.'

Fraser folded his arms and turned to her in his chair. 'So have I. And you know what? Your mum and I have a surprise for you.'

Sara caught his glance and felt her heart somersault. Esme was pressing her hands together. Her eyes were like saucers.

The port was ahead, busy and green and surrounded by boats under blue skies. They'd have several hours once they docked to get their things off the ship, to say their good-byes. She could tell that Esme would be sad to leave Jess and Marcus, but hopefully what they were about to tell her would make her feel better.

'Esme...' She lowered her voice and shuffled her chair closer. From the corner of her eye she saw Renee at the breakfast buffet, but in this moment she really didn't care *who* saw them.

'I know you like Dr Fraser,' she said, as her emotions bubbled up again, 'and it turns out he can do something incredibly special for you.'

Esme looked between them, intrigued. Fraser's support- ive hand was warm over Sara's now, and under the table his foot nudged hers. She took another nervous breath.

'Baby, it turns out that Fraser can be your donor. He can help you, Esme. He's a match! We found out on this trip.'

When the words were out, she realised how crazy they sounded, but Esme's big eyes had widened even further over her breakfast plate. She started jumping up and down in her seat with excitement.

'Really?' She was looking at Fraser in awe. Then look- ing back to Sara.

'I *can* help and I will,' Fraser told her. 'We just have to do some tests together—if you're OK with that?'

'I'm fine with that.'

The way she said it sounded so grown up for a five-year- old. She'd been through more in her five years than a lot of kids would go through in their entire lifetime. Sara put a hand to her soft hair as Esme climbed onto Fraser's lap and hugged him. It was a bear hug, and it made her heart soar when he returned it. *Now* she understood the bond between them. Had they felt it, the two of them, without even knowing why?

'Do you know *why* Dr Fraser is such a good match for you?' she ventured now, as Esme settled on his lap and picked up some pineapple—her new favourite fruit.

'Because he likes making movies with me?'

Sara smiled. 'No, baby.'

'I'm a match because I'm your daddy,' Fraser said qui- etly, taking his cue. 'Is that a good enough surprise for you, Spielberg?'

Esme paused with her pineapple. A huge blast from the ship's horn shook Sara to the core. Florida had crept up on them even sooner than she'd anticipated it would.

'You're my daddy? My *real* daddy?' Esme looked delighted.

'Yes!' Fraser and Sara said at the same time.

Esme blinked a few times, wonderstruck. 'Why have I only just met you?'

Sara took her little hand. She'd been expecting this. 'It's complicated, and we'll tell you the whole story very soon. But for now you have to get ready to have some tests done in Florida.'

'Now? Today?'

'No time like the present,' Fraser said. 'We have to get my kidney over to you before the coral reef takes over.'

'Can we film it?' Esme asked, leaning back against his chest and nibbling her fruit, as if the news of her brand-new parent was old already.

'I don't know...'

'It would make the perfect ending to my film,' Esme coaxed, turning to him.

'You're going to make a great director one day,' he told her, putting his arms around her.

And there it was. Right there in their identical expressions when they grinned at each other. That strange feeling Sara had always felt was 'home' when she looked at Esme was all because of Fraser, and it had never even crossed her mind.

She shook her head, smiling ruefully.

'You look like a happy bunch,' Renee said, walking over and putting her hands on the back of Sara's chair. 'I'd like to thank you both personally for everything you've done on this trip. Did you have a good cruise, Esme?'

'The best—because I'm getting a new kidney *and* a new daddy,' she said bluntly, from Fraser's lap.

Sara felt her cheeks flaming once again. This was why they hadn't told Esme sooner; the whole ship would have known.

Renee's eyes said it all, though. She had known all along that something bigger was going on between them than general squabbles between exes, and she hadn't once pressured them. Sara was grateful. All the drama they'd been part of with Trevor and Jasmine had only served to highlight how special *their* relationship had always been, and she knew Renee could see that, too.

'I see. Well, that's great news,' Renee replied. There was genuine warmth in her eyes when she looked at Sara. 'I guess this is the start of a whole new journey, then. Will we see you all back next year?'

Fraser shrugged. So did Sara. She wasn't about to decide on that for definite yet, but in all honesty, after everything they had gone through on this cruise, she far preferred performing her medical duties on land.

Esme looked overjoyed as they ate and talked and said their goodbyes to everyone who came over to wish them well.

Sara couldn't stop looking at Fraser. For the last two nights she hadn't been able to get enough of him. His mouth and his tongue, his closeness, her legs wrapped around his middle. Their lovemaking was even more passionate than she remembered.

When they'd finally fallen into bed that night in Puerto Rico, after talking on the beach for hours, it had felt only right that they make love. And she had told him herself, when he'd been moving deep inside her, 'I always knew it felt right with you...'

They had no set plans beyond the transplant operation—not yet. But for the first time in a long time she didn't feel the need to make any. Somehow she knew in her heart that things would be OK.

CHAPTER TWENTY-SIX

'THIS IS QUITE a thing you've done—you should be proud of yourself.'

The kindly nurse was bustling about the room, and Fraser watched her place a vase of flowers by the bed and smiled at the familiar Scottish accent.

'Congratulations,' she said.

'Thanks, but it was really a no-brainer,' he said. 'I don't need two kidneys.'

He tried to sit up against the pillows, but the grey-haired nurse stopped him with a firm hand to his shoulder.

'Not yet.' She turned to rearrange the flowers and place the card he'd received from Boyd back upright. 'You might be sore for a couple of days, but I'm sure whatever discomfort you experience is for the greater good.'

'It definitely is.'

'Your daughter is the one you donated to?' She was smiling with her eyes. 'She's a lucky girl. You know what? My youngest nephew needed a kidney. He was water skiing on a family holiday just six weeks later. So a strong man like you should have no problem getting back to regular life—maybe even sooner than that.'

'Water skiing, huh?'

Fraser couldn't help feeling amused, even though he'd been slightly uncomfortable from the moment he'd arrived at the hospital. Not because of the surgery. That part didn't faze him. He'd have done anything to save his daughter's life, and the thought of having done so made his heart swell. He just wasn't used to being the patient.

'How's Esme doing?' He was anxious to see her—and Sara, of course.

'She's doing tremendously. Do you want me to take you to her?'

'I would love that.' He reached for the iPad on the bedside table, and the other items he'd brought along for this moment.

Fraser tried not to fidget with the IV and gauze as the nurse helped him into a wheelchair. The sight of himself in a blue gown was amusing, to say the least, as he was wheeled past the reflective windows in the hospital.

The surgery had gone to plan—as he had known it would in the hands of trusted friends and colleagues like Boyd—but there was one more somewhat elaborate plan he still had to put into action.

'What's on the iPad?' the nurse asked.

He smiled. 'Kind of a documentary,' he replied, sliding it against him down the side of the wheelchair.

It had all been go, go, go since they'd departed the *Ocean Dream* in Florida, and after the tests he and Esme had completed there had all verified that he was the perfect match for her, in every way, they'd opted to have the surgery performed in Scotland.

He'd had time to think since leaving the ship, about how back then, if he'd known Sara was pregnant with his child, he would have gone to the trustees and asked them outright to release the money. There would have been exceptional circumstances, after all. All their problems would have been fixed a lot sooner if his stupid pride hadn't been bruised by seeing her with another man.

He'd been alone for a few weeks with his thoughts while Sara had been preparing Esme for the operation back in London.

His mother had loved his plan to open a dialysis unit on the Breckenridge Practice premises. It had been hatching for a while in his head, and now she seemed to have found a new lease of life in planning a children's play area, and a special safe place for weary parents to gather and exchange tips on caring for kids on dialysis. It would bring more people to the surgery, and more expertise, more experience. Even more so if Sara and Esme joined him.

His stomach jumped inside. He could hear Sara's voice now.

She turned from Esme's bedside when the nurse swung the door open to her room. 'Fraser!'

Esme's small frame looked fragile in the bed. She smiled when she saw him. She was wearing pink pyjamas with a unicorn on the front.

Sara hurried to him and thanked the nurse, wheeling his chair to Esme's side. 'You're awake. How are you feeling?'

She leant in, dropping a light kiss on his lips, which he returned. Her eyes were shining. She looked well, as if years of worry had floated away, leaving her refreshed, reborn. Her hair brushed his face as she studied him up close.

'You look good to me,' she said, and smiled. 'Very good.'

'I feel good,' he said. 'I could murder a cheeseburger, though. How about you, Esme?'

'Am I allowed to eat those now?'

Sara sat on the side of the bed, ran a hand gently up Esme's small arm. 'I don't see why not—in a few days.'

'I'll have five—and some ice-cream,' Esme replied, matter-of-factly. 'I can eat what I want now I won't have to do dialysis, can't I?'

Fraser wanted to say something along the lines of *like father, like daughter*, but he didn't. He just reached for the iPad and pulled it out.

Sara looked suspicious, but she was almost smiling. 'What's that?'

'You haven't seen an iPad before?'

'Very funny.'

Sara looked tired, but beautiful as ever in a warm blue woollen jumper, skinny jeans and black heeled boots. This was definitely not the Caribbean any more. She watched, intrigued, as he swiped the iPad and brought up a video.

'I hope you don't mind, but I have another surprise for you both,' he said.

He handed it to her and she held it between them so Esme could see. A lump formed in his throat as she pressed play. Seconds later she gasped, and Esme squealed in delight from the bed.

'You made another movie!'

'Your footage was just *so* good,' he replied, winking at her.

He studied their faces as they both took it in, and the words *my family* took root in his head.

Sara's hand kept flying over her mouth, as if she couldn't believe it. But it was all in there: a documentary, of sorts, of their time on the cruise. Stolen moments that Esme and Marcus had captured. A friend of Boyd's had helped him edit it, so the nights he'd had to spend without them hadn't seemed so long.

'Fraser, this is amazing!' Sara gushed, as Esme fought to hold the iPad in her hands.

There they were, he and Sara, swinging Esme between them on the deck of the ship. There they were again, dancing, looking into each other's eyes and laughing at something. There they were in the little boat with the water skis, and again on deck the night of the medevac. And with the dolphin at the aquarium.

Esme had captured it all—their togetherness—and he'd had it edited in the way he wanted Sara to remember it: the two of them falling slowly back together in spite of everything that had threatened to keep them apart.

He cleared his throat as another shot came up. Him, on the final day of the cruise, in his cabin. The sheets behind him were messed up, and only Sara would know why. He'd filmed this part himself.

'Sara, this has been one hell of a trip. And I want you to know that, whatever happens, I am and always will be madly in love with you—and with Esme too.'

His on-screen self was nervous. Fraser could hear it in his own voice.

'Now, please look at the real me, in front of you. I *hope* that's where I am!'

Sara looked up from the iPad as the picture of his on-screen self cut out. There in the hospital room Fraser pulled the tiny blue box from his pocket.

'I can't get down on one knee,' he said, holding out his hand to her from the wheelchair. 'But I can still say the words.'

She was shaking her head in disbelief.

'Sara Cohen,' he said, 'will you do me the utmost honour of marrying me?'

She sprang from the bed and dropped to her knees in front of the wheelchair. 'Oh, my...'

She trailed off as Fraser took her hand in his and held up the ring box, now open. Her eyes scanned the sparkling silver band and her mouth fell open at the practically blinking white diamond commanding attention at its centre.

'Yes!' she said, laughing through her tears, and Esme echoed her answer.

'Yes, yes, *yes*!' Esme squealed. 'Mummy, show me!'

Sara watched him slide the ring of her dreams onto her finger and took his face in her hands. 'I love you,' she whispered, up close. 'You have no idea how much.'

'Mummy, *show* me!'

Esme was adamant. Laughing, Sara stood up, but she

kept one hand in Fraser's as she showed off her brand-new jewellery.

'It's so sparkly!' Esme was delighted.

Fraser's mother had helped him pick it, in the end. She was over the moon that they'd got back together—especially after hearing about everything that had happened—and was even more excited about having a granddaughter than he'd anticipated. She'd actually said she had never been so proud of him, and that, had he been there, his father would have been proud too.

'So, are you going to come to England and live with us?' Esme was looking at him now as if she had the whole thing planned out in her head already. 'Or are we going to live with you in Scotland?'

'I don't know what will happen yet,' he said honestly. 'Your mum and I still have to talk about some things. But…'

Sara was still staring at her ring. He hoped the giant diamond was everything she'd ever envisaged in an engagement ring. It was definitely what she deserved. And by the look on her face she was pleased.

'I'm setting up a dialysis centre on the Breckenridge Practice premises,' he said.

Sara's eyes sprang to his. She shook her head, as though everything was still sinking in.

'I want to create a safe place where kids can feel special, no matter what battles they're facing. And I want you to help me. And you too, Esme—you're my expert on this matter.'

'I get to help kids like me?'

Esme looked fascinated, and excited, just as he'd hoped. He envisaged a great life for them all in Edinburgh. There was plenty of room at the house, and in his central apartment—room for Sara's father too if he wanted to visit, or to stay.

Sara was looking at him in wonder, biting her bottom lip. 'You're amazing…' she said.

'It'll be a team effort,' he replied. 'But a fun one and a rewarding one, I hope. I couldn't sit back and not do everything in my power to help people like Esme. And Boyd's looking into funding…'

'It's a great idea,' she said. There was pure love and admiration in her eyes.

Esme was looking at him thoughtfully. 'Now that I have your kidney, you're a part of me.'

'That you are,' he told her fondly.

'And you *are* my daddy, so maybe I should call you Daddy.'

He couldn't help the smile that spread across his face. He wished he could stand up from the wheelchair, but he'd been instructed not to. 'What do you think, wife-to-be?' he asked Sara.

Her eyes told him she'd never thought she'd be sitting there, knowing Esme was safe and healthy at last, with a working kidney *and* a father.

'I think that would be fine by me,' she said after a moment. And when she kissed him again he didn't need words to know that she'd be moving to Edinburgh, and that their family would never be separated again.

'In that case, there's one more thing,' he said.

He reached behind him in the wheelchair and pulled out a bottle of champagne. Sara's eyes grew wide and flitted to Esme.

'Not for now.' He laughed, holding it out to her. 'Save it. It's for popping in your house—to mark this occasion. I figured you could finally make that extra cork mark on the ceiling.'

EPILOGUE

One year later

'THIS IS WHAT I used to call my robo-kidney!'

Esme was pointing the arm of her new toy stethoscope at one of the dialysis machines and Sara hurried over, unable to wipe the smile off her face. The centre had only been open a few months, but already Esme thought she ran the place. To be fair, she probably did.

'I see you're getting the full tour,' she said to the young boy in a bluc tracksuit. He was hiding shyly behind his father.

'So this is the famous Esme,' the man said, shaking Sara's hand just as she registered the now all too familiar twinge of nausea starting to curl about her intestines and beyond.

She struggled not to let it show, casting her eyes to Fraser across the room.

'You used to be on dialysis?' the kid whispered, peeking out slightly, intrigued now.

This was the effect that Esme seemed to have on people. He was just seven, this boy who held the same look of uncertainty that Esme had used to hold in her eyes. It was his first time at the centre.

'I was, but my daddy gave me one of his kidneys,' Esme said proudly. Her chest seemed to swell in pride as she motioned to Fraser, who turned at the sound of the word 'daddy'. 'That's my daddy over there. He's the biggest hero for saving my life. Maybe we can find someone to give you a kidney too? But for now the robo-kidney will do the job for you. And I can tell you everything you need to know.'

Fraser smiled from across the room. He excused himself from the parents he was talking to by the weighing scales and made his way over. Sara's hand went automatically to her belly, as if the tiny seed inside her had registered his presence. She took a deep breath, willing the sick feeling to pass.

'Welcome,' Fraser said, shaking the man's hand.

His fingers brushed Sara's lower back through her jacket and Esme curled her arms around Fraser's waist. She looked up at him adoringly from between them.

'Thanks for coming,' Fraser went on. 'I see you've met our top kidney specialist.'

He lifted Esme easily into his arms and Sara's heart swelled at the sight of their faces pressed together for a second.

'She's six going on sixty,' he said, and Esme giggled.

Sara felted uncomfortable, and she looked at some charts, embarrassed. Fraser noticed.

'Are you OK,' he asked her as he put Esme down.

She nodded and moved her hand from her belly, aware of their patients again and of how ridiculously busy they were. He didn't know about the baby inside her yet—no one did.

Being pregnant now was probably bad timing. When they'd agreed to start trying for a baby shortly after the wedding she hadn't actually expected it to happen so soon. They had only been married six months. She hadn't even allowed herself to get excited yet.

They continued the tour together, Fraser and Esme, while Sara administered dialysis to an Iranian man who'd moved from Glasgow to a village nearby, just to come here. Pride flowed through her as she took in the magnitude of all that they'd achieved in such a short amount of time.

They were well on track to becoming the second largest kidney care provider in the UK, with more machines than anywhere else in Scotland. A growing number of patients of all ages and backgrounds were signing up, having heard about the experienced husband-and-wife team, plus their adorable daughter, who were running it.

They could accommodate up to three shifts of patients a day now, and had patients visiting three times a week for four hours or more. Most people knew Esme by now, and if she wasn't there they'd ask for her—especially the kids.

It had been Esme's idea to bring a 'wall of fame' to Edinburgh, too. It was where each kid shared a little information about their lives outside of dialysis.

'We used to have one of these in London, where I got my dialysis treatments,' she was saying now, pointing at the photos of kids' faces, each one in the centre of a colourful paper flower.

Without the dialysis herself, Esme was even more vibrant and playful—and perpetually excited about new adventures and ice-cream.

Sara wondered yet again how she'd feel about her latest news.

She glanced at Fraser as another twinge of nausea struck. She gripped the desk quickly, and one of the biomedical technicians—a lady called Liz—put a hand on her arm to steady her.

'Mrs Breckenridge? Are you OK?'

'I'm OK, thank you,' she said, but she knew her face was probably too pale.

Liz frowned and lowered her voice. 'Let me take over. Maybe you should go and lie down? Someone in your condition shouldn't be on her feet so much.'

Sara gaped at her in surprise. Liz pulled an imaginary zip over her lips, and winked at her before taking over her duties.

Unable to stop the nausea now, Sara stepped aside quickly, into the water treatment room. Taking long, deep breaths, she leaned against the huge cool tank, waiting for it to pass.

'Sara?'

When she opened her eyes Fraser was closing the door to the room and stepping towards her under the glaring sterile lights.

'I saw you come in here—what's the matter?'

She swallowed, aware that she probably looked terrible.

'You look green,' he confirmed, putting a big hand to her forehead. 'Here, sit down.'

He pulled a chair away from the wall and motioned for her to sit, but she stayed pressed against the cool tank. It was making her feel better.

She closed her eyes, still sucking in breaths as Esme's high-pitched voice carried in from the treatment room.

'Fraser, I'm pregnant,' she said, putting a hand to her belly again.

His eyes widened in front of her. He stared at her in total shock for a moment.

'I know there's a lot going on,' she continued, 'with this place and with Esme, but...'

'Why didn't you tell me?' Fraser's look of shock was transformed into one of pure exhilaration. 'Sara, this is... This is really good news. I think... Don't you?' He put his hands to her shoulders and stared deep into her eyes. 'You *are* excited, aren't you?'

'I am,' she told him. 'I *am*. I just know how busy we are...'

'Family comes first,' he said firmly. 'You know that.'

'I do,' she said, feeling silly now.

She'd known he'd be excited. Slowly but surely, she allowed herself to feel excited too. The look on his face meant everything to her.

He ran his hands through his hair. 'Wow… I'm going to be a dad again—really?'

He pulled her close and she sighed with relief into the skin of his warm neck. Her nausea was fading, thankfully, and in its place was a new set of butterflies. He'd *always* given her butterflies.

'How long have you known?' he asked.

'A couple of weeks,' she said. 'I wanted to be absolutely sure before I told you. Are we ready for this?'

'Of course we're ready for this. 'You know, I *should* have known,' he told her now, stepping back and smiling at her mischievously.

'Because of all the hot sex we've been having?' she whispered, raising an eyebrow.

He grinned. 'No! Well, yes, but mostly because of *this*.'

Fraser reached into the pocket of her white coat and swiftly pulled out her knitting needles, still laced into a ball of pale blue wool.

'Click, click, click,' he teased, smiling as he held them out.

She snatched them back, laughing. 'One pink mitten, one blue mitten—just in case,' she told him, shoving her work in progress back into her pocket. 'Seriously, Fraser, are you ready for this?'

She scanned his blue eyes, looking for any trace of doubt. She saw none.

'We have help,' he said. 'We have money, we have time, and we have this house. We have Esme. Sara, we are *all* ready.'

He brought her fingers to her lips before he kissed her up against the water tank. She prayed no one would open the door.

'I think we need to get some more champagne,' he said after a moment against her lips, 'and some ice-cream.'

'Ice-cream?'

'Isn't that how Esme celebrates all her good news now? I happen to think she's going to be crazy for a new brother or sister.'

'As crazy as I am about you?'

Sara wrapped her arms around her husband. Seven years and a daughter had brought them to this point, and in a few more months they'd be a family of four.

She had no idea what lay ahead, but she'd try to stay true to the promise she'd made herself and Fraser…that every day would be an adventure that they'd cherish, no matter how stormy the ride.

* * * * *

MILLS & BOON

Coming next month

MENDING THE SINGLE DAD'S HEART
Susanne Hampton

Harrison's head was telling him to pull back but his heart was saying something very different.

They were two professional people who had spent time getting to know each other outside of work and he had allowed it to go too far. Now he needed to take her cue and set boundaries. Jessica had been upfront about her intentions. Stay six weeks and leave town. There had been no deceit, no false promises. He had to try and colleague zone Jessica immediately and put some distance between them. He had no choice, for his own sake. But he doubted how successful it would be after the kiss they'd shared.

'I can assist with that...'

'You've done enough.' Enough to unsettle him. Enough to even at that moment make him want to pull her close again. Enough to make him kiss her again. He was so confused, and she had made him think clearly when he'd felt her pull away. Now he had to do it too. 'I'll email hospital admin when I get home and let them know to roster cover for you until eleven. It's not the entire day off, but it's a few extra hours' sleep. I arranged the same for the other staff before I left. And the neurosurgeon is flying in from Sydney mid-morning, to consult on the two suspected spinal cord injury patients.'

'You certainly have everything under control.'

'It's best for everyone that way.' Though Harrison knew he was losing control with Jessica. And that was not the best option for a man who had finally gained control of his life.

His tone had changed and he could see it hadn't gone unnoticed by Jessica. Torn best described how he felt. He didn't understand what he had seen in her eyes only moments before. It confused him. Her gorgeously messy blonde hair fell around her beautiful face and she looked less like an accomplished temporary Paediatric Consultant from a large city hospital and more like a fresh-faced country girl. She was so close he could reach out and cup her beautiful face in his hands and kiss her again.

He had to leave before he went mad with the gamut of emotions he was feeling.

Opening the door, he walked into the icy night air without stopping to put on his jacket.

Or say goodnight.

Continue reading
MENDING THE SINGLE DAD'S HEART
Susanne Hampton

Available next month
www.millsandboon.co.uk